"Written by a politically savvy Washingtonian, *Eleanor vs. Ike* is a fascinating combination of truth and fantasy, about a gallant woman leader whose great potential—in real life—was never fully realized but is now presented to us by Robin Gerber in a brilliant fictional re-creation of the leader she might have been."
—James MacGregor Burns,
Pulitzer Prize-winning author of *Roosevelt: The Lion and the Fox*

★

"Lively and entirely plausible. *Eleanor vs. Ike* is a bold and imaginative extension of Robin Gerber's work. She is a writer ahead of her time and has written a crackerjack novel that is both politically and historically astute."
—James Reston, Jr., author of *The Conviction of Richard Nixon*

★

"This timely book, coming in our current era of political dynasties, creates a fantastic historical 'What if?' I'm a huge admirer of Eleanor Roosevelt, and this book had me rooting for her through every plot-twisting, page-turning minute."
—Kitty Kelley

★

"Beltway insider Robin Gerber knows what goes on behind the scenes in a presidential campaign and how to merge the might-have-beens with the what-really-weres of history. . . . I cast my vote for *Eleanor vs. Ike*." —Ellen Feldman, author of *Lucy*

★

"A great read, full of drama and intrigue. Even more fascinating, as Gerber tells the story, is that it very well could have taken place."
—Norman Adler, political consultant

★

"A terrific political yarn, full of intrigue, excitement and suspense. . . . The very plausibility of [Eleanor Roosevelt's] candidacy is what kept me turning the pages to see if she would beat Eisenhower!"
—House Majority Leader Steny Hoyer of Maryland

★

"Gerber's fascinating and inspiring Eleanor Roosevelt is a presidential candidate with a complicated love life. I could hardly put the book down as Eleanor's 'What if?' political campaign raced toward election day."
—Dee Dee Myers, former White House Press Secretary

Also by Robin Gerber

LEADERSHIP THE ELEANOR ROOSEVELT WAY:
TIMELESS STRATEGIES FROM THE FIRST LADY OF COURAGE

KATHARINE GRAHAM:
THE LEADERSHIP JOURNEY OF AN AMERICAN ICON

ELEANOR VS. IKE

Robin Gerber

AVON

An Imprint of HarperCollins*Publishers*

HarperCollins books may be purchased for educational, business, or sales promo-
tional use. For information please write: Special Markets Department, HarperCollins
Publishers, 10 East 53rd Street, New York, NY 10022.

FIRST EDITION

Designed by Diahann Sturge

Library of Congress Cataloging-in-Publication Data
Gerber, Robin.
    Eleanor vs. Ike / Robin Gerber. — 1st ed.
        p. cm.
ISBN-13: 978-0-06-137321-3
1. Roosevelt, Eleanor, 1884–1962 — Fiction.   2. Eisenhower, Dwight D. (Dwight
David), 1890–1969 — Fiction.   3. Presidents — United States — Election — 1952 —
Fiction.   4. Political fiction.   I. Title.

PS3607.E7296E44   2008
813'.6 — dc22   2007034937

08 09 10 11 12 ov/RRD   10 9 8 7 6 5 4 3 2 1

For Ariel and Sam,
who will see a woman president of the United States.

Acknowledgments

This book would not exist but for Stefanie Tade, my savvy, brilliant, and indefatigable agent, who believed in me and this idea. Her efforts, coupled with the vision and marvelous direction of my editor, Sarah Durand, allowed this first-time novelist to find her writing heart. Thank you.

Thanks also to my amazing friends, and Eleanor-connected acquaintances, who read, encouraged, listened, and offered their wisdom: Ilana Bar-Din, Carol Beach, Arlene Begelman, Susan Curnan, Lisa Dobbs, Peggy Engel, Starr Ezra, Sandy Foote, Peter Franchot, Robin Gradison, Cindy Hallberlin, Susan Hengel, Marylu Jordan, Linda Karson, Kitty Kelly, Sheila King, Susan Land, Richard Lehfeldt, Laura Liswood, Nance Lucas, Anne Maher, Peggy McCormick, Sarah Priestman, Jim Ramey, Mary Saily, Cynthia Schneider, Rose Schwartz, Lisa Stevenson, Bradley Swann, Pamela Toutant, Mary Von Drehle, Stefanie Weiss, Linda, Dena, Caroline, Nancy, Lynn, Sherry, Charlie, and the women of Tuesday morning.

Thanks to my sister, Dee Francken, an early and perceptive

reader who helped me with the daunting transition to fiction; to my brother, Steve Gerber, for unwavering support; and to my enthusiastic cousin, Liz Siegel, and my nephew, James Francken, whose wise literary counsel gave me heart.

Special thanks to Celinda Lake, the best pollster in America, who didn't hesitate for a second when I asked if she would create a "real" poll for the book. Her amazing team of Karen Emmerson, Cate Gormley, Caitlin Murphy, Matt Price, Anita Sharma, Rebecca Sizelove, and Tresa Undem brought their brilliance and energy to my fantasy. The results are stunning and terrific fun.

Special thanks also to reader and friend Norman Adler, who taught me everything I know about politics. And to Larry O'Brien III, for sharing wonderful memories of his father with me, as well as the Kennedy Campaign Manual from 1960.

Thanks to the great William Morrow team: Liate Stehlik, Adrienne Di Pietro, Pam Spengler-Jaffe, Kristine Macrides, Donna Lee Lurker, and super-assistant Emily Krump.

Finally, thanks to my daughter, Ariel, who, from the first now-long-deleted sentence, generously turned her literary sensibility and knowledge, sense of plot, and ear for dialogue to the task of helping her mother. Her advice was invaluable, and our friendship unmatched. Her brother, Sam, still at home, never tired of prodding me forward, and brought his trademark equanimity to my writerly moments. They are the blessings of my life, as is my husband, Tony Records, the most Eleanorean man I know.

PART I

CHAPTER 1

Eleanor's Choice

Paris, France, January 1952

Lucy was dead. Eleanor Roosevelt sat alone in her suite at the Hôtel de Crillon and looked at the obituary a friend had mailed to her the week before. It was from the newspaper in Aiken, South Carolina, dated January 7, 1952: "Lucy Page Mercer Rutherford, fifty-seven years old, died from complications of kidney disease. Widow of Lord Edward Rutherford."

Eleanor took care to place the clipping inside her diary, tight against the binding. She smoothed the cover, pressing down on it gently, and then she pushed the book a few inches closer to the vase of white long-stem roses that sat in the middle of the side table. Looking up, she stared toward the grand French doors that led to a balcony overlooking the Place de la Concorde and the prized view of Paris that always captivated her. But in her mind's eye she had gone back thirty-four years, to the dressing room in her mother-in-law's house in Manhattan on September 19, 1918.

Every second of that afternoon was seared in her mind. She had just struggled to open Franklin's dome-shaped trunk, its heavy lid straining against the hinges as it fell back. She smiled at its disorder, thinking that her husband must have done his own packing before he left France. She was still wearing her Red Cross dress, having rushed from the army canteen to the dock when she heard about Franklin's condition. Pulling up the simple midcalf skirt, she knelt to reach under and lift a pile of clothes. Franklin's phlegmy cough came from the next room and pricked the worry in her mind. He'd been carried off the *Leviathan* with double pneumonia according to the doctors, but a terrible influenza had also coursed through the ship. She'd heard some people had died of it during the crossing. What if Franklin had been exposed?

As Eleanor stood, clothes filling her arms, something fell from the pile back into the trunk. She looked down and saw letters addressed in a familiar hand, tied with a white silk ribbon. She knelt again, gently laying the clothes on the floor next to the trunk. Her hand trembled as if she were afraid the packet would explode when she touched it.

The ribbon gave way with a small tug and she pulled the letter from the top envelope, unfolding the stationery with rising dread. She thought she could smell a sweetish scent coming off the tissue-thin paper. "Franklin, dearest . . ." Eleanor's eyes burned suddenly, then blurred with tears. She wiped them quickly with the back of one shaking hand. "Being separated from you is unbearable. I dream of you as I go to sleep and see you in my mind the moment I awaken. Do you remember our last drive in the Shenandoah? That lovely cottage where we were alone for hours in each other's arms?"

Eleanor's stomach turned, vomit rising in her throat. She was certain of the letter's author, yet she couldn't bring herself to look at the signature. Minutes seemed to pass before she lowered her head and saw what she knew would be there, "You have all my love, dearest, as I know I have yours. I only await your safe return, Lucy." The "L" was larger than the other letters and had a flourish, the kind of boldness that Eleanor knew Lucy possessed.

Eleanor's legs had started to shake, and she fell back to sit on the floor. Her feelings were terrifying and familiar. She had lived through the life and death that was love and lies before. She had lived through it over and over again. When she was small, her father, her beloved father, would hold her on his knee, call her "Little Nell," promise to take her away from her scolding mother, promise to take her to the Taj Mahal, promise, promise, promise, and then he would ride away, and she would sit in the window seat and wait for what seemed to a child like all the days that had ever passed. And when her mother yelled at her for believing him, for loving him, for being a foolish, ugly child, she could feel her small sturdy heart twist into a knot that grew tighter and tighter with each betrayal.

Then Franklin, so handsome, so confident, chose her. He told her he loved her and promised himself to her, promised he would love her forever. Only after that did the knot begin to loosen, only then and slowly, as their years together grew.

Suddenly, Eleanor tore the small white Red Cross cap off her head, the hairpins flying in all directions. She pulled frantically at her bun, her chestnut hair falling loose below her shoulders in thick cascades. She drew her knees up to her chest and, as she had done when she sat waiting for her father and couldn't bear her sadness, she pulled the tresses across her face with both hands and wept into their dark and fragrant comfort.

"Eleanor?" Franklin's voice was weak, and the effort to speak brought on a resonant fit of coughing. "Is something wrong?" he managed to croak. She gathered the letters in her hand and rose carefully, not sure that she could stand, and walked with stiff legs into the bedroom. Even in his sickness-induced stupor, Franklin knew that he had never seen such rage and misery on his wife's face.

"Here!" Eleanor swayed and grabbed the bedpost as she threw the letters at his chest. "If you don't want me, Franklin, you don't have to have me. Leave me. Go with her. Go this minute." Her voice rose to a shout, fractured by intermittent sobbing. "You . . . you never loved me, did you? All lies. All these years. How could you do this? How? What of the children? Don't you care about them?"

"What is going on here?" Sara Delano Roosevelt's sharp voice cut through the room as she stood in the doorway behind Eleanor, bewilderment and anger coursing over her features. "Eleanor, whatever is wrong? Franklin must rest, he . . ."

"Mother," Eleanor fell against her mother-in-law, wrapping her arms around her neck and heaving with uncontrollable weeping. "Help me, Mother, please."

Franklin hadn't moved. He lay weighted down by the heavy smell of camphor rubbed on his body and the wool blankets tucked tight up to his chin. Next to the bed, the stern portrait of his father, James, seemed to him like a physical presence in the room. Franklin looked toward his mother with the face of an errant child who knew his punishment couldn't be escaped. Sara moved Eleanor to a chair and gently lowered her, then walked to the bed and gathered up the letters. A quick glance told her all she needed to know.

"That girl was too pretty, too clever, too coquettish. I always thought so. She was a foolish choice for your social secretary, Eleanor." Sara sighed. "But you didn't know any better. And you were down in Washington where I couldn't help you. Well, Franklin? You must say something."

"He can have a divorce, Mother." Eleanor's voice was flat. "You can divorce me Franklin, you can leave me. I shall not protest."

Eleanor sat very straight on the edge of the chair, her face stiff and streaked, her hands folded in her lap.

"I won't hear of such a thing," Sara turned on Eleanor in a fury. "I will not tolerate it. You have five children. You do not get divorced with five children. You do not . . . *we* do not get divorced in this family."

"Mother," Franklin's words were soft with weakness, "Mother, please listen. I love Lucy. God knows I'm sorry, Mother. Eleanor, I'm so sorry I . . ."

Eleanor sat like a piece of fine and delicate porcelain that would shatter at the slightest movement.

"You may love her, son, but you will not be divorced from Eleanor." Sara had drawn herself up like a general, and she spoke with the icy calm of a woman who made no idle threats. "You will not get a divorce because if you do, if you even try to do so, you will not get another penny from this estate." She looked up at the painting of her husband. "And I am quite sure your father would agree. I don't think you, or your errant young consort, want to live in penury."

As Eleanor sat in her Paris hotel remembering Sara's grand harangue, she felt a wry smile turn her lips. "Penury." Yes, that was the word Sara used. Eleanor would never forget it. "Penury." That did it, of course. Franklin loved the grand life into which he'd been born—sailing at Campobello, parties at the Chevy Chase Club, weekends in the countryside, tickets for all the best shows. More than anything else, he loved his dream of following Uncle Teddy to the White House. That would take money, too.

Oh, yes, Eleanor thought, Franklin loved his very good life and his ambitions more than he loved Lucy, or her, or anyone for that matter. So he chose. Eleanor remembered his exact words. "I'll never see Lucy again, Eleanor. I swear that to you." And she, desperate to feel wanted again, had believed him.

Franklin had traded love for ambition and money. Did he make a good bargain, Eleanor wondered, as she pressed her handkerchief against her eyes? Did she?

A sharp knock on the suite door brought Eleanor back to the present. Her secretary, Maureen Corr, had pushed open the massive double door without waiting for her boss's response. "There's a phone call for you from the White House, Mrs. R. I'll put it through."

CHAPTER 2

A Hole As Big As God

Across the Atlantic, President Harry S. Truman watched the gray morning sky turn steel blue as he waited in the Oval Office to be connected to Eleanor in Paris. Rising over the Atlantic's Delaware shore, the sun threw an orange glow across the Chesapeake Bay, streamed past East Capitol Street's row houses, and bathed the Capitol's east front in a regal cloak. But only early rising workers were rewarded with a sight that caused the most jaded to slow their pace in the January cold.

For a few minutes of flaming glory, the Corinthian columns that ringed the East Portico were lit as if for a great ceremony, but that hour was not yet at hand. A year stood between the empty stage and the day when the next president of the United States would be sworn into office. High atop the Capitol's massive dome, sturdy in the sharp wind, stood the bronze Statue of Freedom, graced by sword and shield, ready to bear witness.

But for the moment, the political future was uncertain and unknowable. For the Democrats, Truman was toying with various schemes, which was why he wanted to catch Eleanor before she left the United Nations' meeting in Paris.

"Hello, Eleanor. Glad I caught up with you. Are you in the middle of packing?" Truman began.

"Not at the moment," came the curt reply. Eleanor was still shaking off the painful memories that Lucy's obituary had raised.

"Now, now, Eleanor. I think I know why you're annoyed. You saw the picture, didn't you?"

She paused, unsure for a moment what he was talking about. Of course, now she remembered. No wonder Harry was calling.

"Yes, Mr. President, I did see the picture."

"And you think I set that up."

"Well, yes, actually I do." Truman had jerked her thoughts back to the present and she tried to sound firm. "I am not interested."

Earlier that morning, Maureen had bounded into her suite as she was having breakfast. Her youthful exuberance seemed to set the room in motion.

"Good morning, Mrs. R.," Maureen spoke in her lilting brogue, a triumphant smile on her heart-shaped face as she handed Eleanor the *International Herald Tribune*.

Eleanor's eyes narrowed and she pursed her lips as she read the caption under the front-page photo. The former First Lady remembered the picture being shot. She was sitting next to President Truman discussing her upcoming trip to Paris. The photographer had asked the president to look toward Eleanor, point at some papers, and smile. The photo made her and Truman look like happy conspirators. The caption read, "Mrs. Roosevelt on the Democratic ticket?" Eleanor had suspected that Harry was behind the gambit. His call made her certain.

"Eleanor, it would be historic and exhilarating. Taft is a relic, the Old Guard Republican. Together, we could beat them again," Truman said.

"Taft doesn't have it all sewn up. General Eisenhower might get in, I hear. Seems he's a Republican, after all, despite our hoping otherwise. But that doesn't matter. I am not interested."

"Eleanor, think about it. No woman has ever been vice president."

"Or president, either. And that's because the country is not ready."

"You may be right, but they would be ready for you. Even Bess thinks so, and that's saying something."

"Give Bess my regards, Mr. President," Eleanor said, as if she were saying good-bye.

"All right, all right. But I would like you to give this some thought."

"Here are my thoughts at the moment, and frankly, they are much more serious than a vice presidential bid. You must send Frank Graham as a roving ambassador to the Near East and Asia. We really do not understand them too well. They have a profound distrust of white people. The only ones they have known were either colonizing them, or in our case, our businessmen."

"I'm not sure Graham's right for that job," Truman replied.

"Well, it must be someone conciliatory, as I've tried to be, and reasonable. They do have some points, for instance, on race. They believe the Soviet attitude is better than ours. Mr. Bokhari of India came up to me very angrily and said, 'You do not care what happens to the children of Asia; they are colored, not white like the children of Europe.'"

"Now, that's not fair," Truman cut in.

"Fair or not, they see us giving more aid to Europe than Asia or Latin America. It pushes them toward Soviet economic policy, as well."

Truman had gone silent at the other end of the line, and Eleanor could almost see his mind working.

"How about this?" he finally said. "You're the best person to be a roving ambassador, Eleanor, not Graham or anyone else. After all, in places where they hate us, they love you."

"I'm not sure you're right about that. If they love me, it's because of Franklin."

"No Eleanor. They loved Franklin *and* they love you. He's been gone seven years. All your work at the UN, the Declaration of Human Rights, that's all you. Don't sell yourself short, now. It's a wonderful idea, and while you're traveling, you can consider my other offer. The New Hampshire primary's not until March 11. I'm not going to announce anything before then, so you have some time."

"My mind is made up as to that, Mr. President, but I will consider the trip east. If we don't understand these people, we'll never be able to help them grow into strong democracies."

An hour later, when Maureen came in to see how the packing was going, Eleanor's mood had lightened. She could never have told Harry, but with her term as a UN delegate ending, Eleanor viewed the future with dread. Hadn't she told that reporter that one of the basic requirements for happiness was "feeling that you are in some way useful"? She was sixty-seven years old. How would she continue to be useful? Certainly not as a mother; her children were grown and only brought guilt and trouble.

Just before she'd left for the UN meeting, David Gurewitsch had been at her house in Val-Kill for dinner along with her sons, John and Elliott. She couldn't fathom their resentments—of her, of each other, and especially of David. Wasn't she entitled to her own happiness—to her own personal relationships?

David was about to turn fifty, trim and elegant in a three-piece suit and taller than Eleanor by several inches. While practicing medicine in New York in 1944, he had made a house call and met the president's wife when she answered the door. Because of a shortage of civilian nurses, she had been ministering to her friend, Trude Lash, one of David's first patients. As Eleanor watched, David gave Trude an intense and thorough examination. He spoke gently and deliberately, and Eleanor soon asked him to become her doctor.

Three years later, after Franklin's death, Eleanor was scheduled to fly to Switzerland. She discovered that no flight was available to take David, who had tuberculosis, to Davos for treatment, so the former First Lady arranged for him to accompany her.

The twenty-four-hour trip turned into four days because of bad weather and mechanical problems. Held over in Shannon, Ireland, David was moved to barracks a mile from the airport, which could only be reached on foot. Eleanor walked up and back every day, bringing David food, drink, and books from which she read to him. She refused to leave his side, and they gradually began sharing their life stories.

"My father drowned in a Swiss lake just before I was born," David told Eleanor as she sat on the side of his bed. "My mother never recovered. I once wrote her a note on the thirty-fifth anniversary of my father's death. Do you know what she wrote back?" Eleanor's eyes were glassy with tears as she shook her head. "She said, 'Don't you know that for me every day is the seventh of July?' I felt like I had one parent I never met and one I never knew."

"I had my father until I was ten," Eleanor said quietly. "My little brother died the year before my father, and my mother the year before that. I don't know how a child bears such loss. My soul had no time to heal." She saw her tears mirrored by those in David's eyes, and words she had never spoken rushed from her mouth. "I loved my father so much. He was the only one, the only one who seemed to love me." Her shoulders shook as she tried not to sob. "But he drank, David. He drank horribly and my mother and Uncle Theodore made him leave us. Leave our home. But I was a child. I knew something was wrong, but no one explained. I couldn't believe anything could be wrong with my father. To me, he was the world." Eleanor couldn't go on.

David's arms reached around her for the first time, and he pulled her close. She couldn't deny her attraction to him. He was tall like Franklin, with a similarly long face and strong chin. But he had told her he was at the tail end of his marriage, separated from his wife and seeking a divorce. Eleanor had already been named in the divorce papers that the wife of her bodyguard, Earl Miller, had filed against him in the 1920s. She didn't want to be in that situation again. And she found it hard to believe that this handsome man would be attracted to a woman eighteen years his senior. She lay folded in his arms for long silent minutes, deep in a canyon of confused emotions.

Once David recovered from his illness, he asked Eleanor to dinner when they were both in New York. Soon his picture appeared on her bedside table, for the nights when he didn't stay with her. She brought him to Val-Kill as well, but once the children realized that David was sharing her room, they became belligerent toward her. David soon found himself in the role of Eleanor's protector.

During the dinner in Val-Kill, when Eleanor's sons, John and Elliott, began arguing, David put his fork down with calm deliberation, watchful of a coming storm. Sure enough, the young men began talking louder, and then jumped up from the table, their arms locking as they tried to land blows. Eleanor sprang from her chair, trying to grab one, then the other. "Stop this, stop this. You two are like children. What is wrong with you?" she cried out in frustration.

"What's wrong? What's wrong, Mother?" Elliott asked in a mocking tone. "How about this, you were never there for us, unless it was just to push, push, push. We could never be successful enough," he yelled.

"You and Father never understood," John's bitter voice pitched in. "Total strangers were more important to you than us. They still are," he finished, throwing a furious look at David and pushing Elliott roughly aside as he stomped out.

David put his arm around Eleanor and eased her out of the room. They walked out the back door toward the garden, the tang of its winter decay caught in pockets of air as they drew near. "They're right, David," Eleanor talked as she wiped tears away with the back of her hand. "Of course, they're right. My children would be much better off if I were not alive. I'm overshadowing them. It's terribly unfair."

"You must be who you are," David said, stopping and holding her close. "They will find their way, and they'll learn that you're not the cause of their troubles."

Eleanor knew he was right. What good or bad she had done as a mother was past. That role held little for her now. Before Truman's call, she had felt fretful. She was not needed as a mother, no longer a First Lady, done as a UN delegate, and not interested in a political campaign running second to Harry.

What would be her purpose in the world? She dreaded the hole in herself that grew as her responsibilities shrank. The hole that she feared would fill with depression. The hole that would send her into what she called her "Griselda" moods, where she locked herself away from everyone. The hole as big as God. Harry's suggestion that she go east had a halo of salvation that only she could see.

"Maureen, there's a change of plans," Eleanor said, as the young woman came into the suite with a copy of *Paris Match* in her hand. "We're going home . . . but we're going the other way."

CHAPTER 3

The Country's Not Ready

"Are you keeping a journal?" David asked as they neared the airfield and Eleanor scrawled faster in a small notebook. They had flown together from Israel where David had joined her after she toured the Arab countries.

"I would like to write a book about this trip. What do you think of this?" Eleanor said, raising her pen and reading from her notes, "'The Soviet Union has made a religion out of a political creed—communism—but the followers of Islam have made their religion the controlling part of their politics. They seem to be united not only against Israel, but also against all non-Muslims. Their sense of religious community governs their every act, even against their self-interest. Yet Israel must find a way to peace.'"

"Too true," David said. "But it's going to be hard to get Americans to care about the Middle East as long as this mess in Korea is going on."

"Well, I have to try, but I agree with you. I wanted to go to Korea on this trip, but Harry forbade it. If he hadn't overstepped the Congress two years ago and committed our troops as he did, we wouldn't be in this position. He knew he should have . . ." The noise of the plane engines grew louder as they neared the runway, and Eleanor raised her voice so David could hear her.

Suddenly, David interrupted her, pointing out the window in excitement. "Look at that crowd. Just look at that! Do you see, Eleanor? They've come to welcome you."

A sea of women had gathered at the airport, along with thousands of schoolchildren dressed in bright uniforms and waving the Pakistani flag, its crescent and star set off on a deep green background.

"David, that's not for me," Eleanor said, "that's for someone of importance who's arriving."

David gave a knowing smile and turned to Maureen, who was sitting across the aisle.

"How many times have we heard that?" he said, and Maureen chuckled.

"You know," Maureen said, "she really believes it."

"Oh yes, I know," David said, and he leaned back in his seat, taking hold of Eleanor's hand, its visible veins and folds contrasting with David's smooth skin.

David stood behind Eleanor as she stepped off the plane. Women dressed in the uniforms of the various military groups of the All Pakistan Women's Association lined up to welcome her. They placed wreaths of flowers and a golden garland around her neck. The elaborate decoration reached below her waist, its two chains of interwoven gold tinsel holding an intricate heart-shaped pendant at their end that was as big as a dinner plate. Some of the women knelt as Eleanor walked to the waiting car.

Maureen had already found a copy of the *International Herald Tribune,* and handed it to her boss. The primaries for both parties were in full swing in the United States, and with just four months before the conventions, neither party's nomination was assured. No one knew if President Truman would run for reelection. Besides speculating on who Truman would run with, if he ran, the press had reported that the president was looking at possible replacements if he decided not to run. The brilliant, liberal governor of Illinois, Adlai Stevenson, was high on the list, although Stevenson had reportedly told Truman he wouldn't run. On the Republican side, the front-runner and son of the former president, Robert Taft of Ohio, was nervously watching General Eisenhower. The man who had led the invasion of Europe, and shared the glory of winning World War II with General MacArthur seemed to be edging toward the race.

"There's a small story inside the second section, Mrs. R.," said Maureen, "but I knew you'd be interested. The Lisbon meeting of NATO ministers ended, and it looks like the Republicans are pushing Ike to give up his military command and come home to run in earnest. Some of them have already put his name in for the New Hampshire primary."

"I'm not surprised at that," Eleanor replied. "If Eisenhower wins in New Hampshire, I'm guessing he'll get into the race in earnest. And if he wins the nomination, it will be a tough fight for Harry."

"*If* the President runs again . . . You know there are rumors he'll drop out, and . . . maybe you should look at these." Maureen handed Eleanor a newspaper clipping. "These came in the mail just before we left Paris."

Eleanor looked at the article headlined "Woman President" from the *Washington Post*'s letters to the editor: "It occurs to me that Eleanor Roosevelt would be an excellent candidate for the presidency. She has the experience in both domestic and foreign affairs that we need in these critical times. Lillian H. Kanegis, Washington, D.C."

"Well . . ." Eleanor glanced at Maureen, and the younger woman thought she caught a hint of interest. She'd seen enough to know that the big shots had limited influence on her boss, but when it came to ordinary folks, the kind who wrote Eleanor hundreds of letters every day, the former First Lady was more receptive.

"The other one's even better," her secretary spoke up quickly, pressing a second clipping into Eleanor's hand.

"Mrs. Roosevelt in '52" read the headline.

The person I have in mind for president has all the qualifications needed at a time like this: extensive political knowledge and experience in both foreign and domestic issues; is above political ambition, highly intelligent, and diplomatic; and has a thorough, almost intimate understanding of what the office requires. This person further has a wide acquaintance with many efficient and honorable public servants and we could be assured of an excellent cabinet. There is only one barrier: our candidate is a woman—Eleanor Roosevelt. It might be fun to have Dr. Gallup run down a survey on how the people feel about it. Violet Clark, Alexandria, Virginia.

Eleanor handed the clipping back. Maureen could tell by her expression that her boss was going to put on her patient but firm voice.

"Mrs. Clark put it quite well, Maureen. The country is not ready for a woman president. We don't need George Gallup to answer that question. And I'm not going to test that idea. It wouldn't be good for the party. It would stir the Republicans up even more than they are right now. Besides, I have absolutely no interest in running for president."

Eleanor looked away from Maureen's imploring face. Was she telling Maureen the truth? She didn't want to run for vice president, but *president*? Had there been moments in those twelve years as Franklin's closest adviser that she had wished for his power?

That she would have made different decisions? She couldn't deny it. But after the war, women had been pigeonholed as caretakers, homemakers, mothers, and helpmates. A woman in the Oval Office after American men had saved the world from fascism? A woman as commander in chief of the armed forces? No, that would be impossible, Eleanor thought. But how unfair! She knew women who had given everything to the war effort.

She thought about the firestorm of letters she'd received after her *Reader's Digest* piece in January 1944. She had argued that women were critical to the war effort, and should be given more responsibility. Some people accused her of wanting to see mothers slaughtered, of being a home wrecker, and endangering male soldiers by forcing them to serve with the weaker sex. But thousands of letters poured in from women, and even some men, who agreed with her.

"So far, the WACs have been the only ones allowed overseas," Eleanor had written. "This seems ridiculous to me. The restriction on the activities of our other women's military services is not due to any feeling of Congress or the military authorities that women cannot do the job. It is due, rather, to a false chivalry, which insists that women be protected from war hazards and hardships, even against their own wishes. Some women accept this point of view, but I believe most of us would rather share more fully in the experiences of our men."

As she thought about Maureen pushing her toward the presidency, Eleanor remembered those last words. She had fought every step of the way to share the experiences of men. Going back to the 1920s, she had battled her own party to give women equal power. Three decades later, was it time to fight for the experience that no woman had ever been able to claim? She knew she hadn't been completely honest with Maureen. She did have an interest in running for president. But what of it? A few women wanted her to run, but that wouldn't win her the nomination. She understood her party better than that.

But Maureen wasn't giving up. She decided to try another tack. "James is leaning toward Senator Kefauver's nomination," she began, referring to Eleanor's eldest son, "but he said he'd love it if you would . . ."

Eleanor hesitated, and David, who had been listening, couldn't restrain himself.

"Maureen, I don't think you should keep pushing this. It's a terrible idea for many reasons. Mrs. Roosevelt is already the target of crackpots threatening to kill her. Running for president?" His voice had risen with skepticism. "Why don't we just paint a target on her back? And she would never have a chance to rest. She's not a young woman like you. She needs her time to . . ."

"David, you really don't have to say anything." Eleanor's voice held the slightest hint of irritation. "Maureen, my son James doesn't know this country the way I do. The American people simply aren't ready for a woman president. We have many fine men in our party, and one of them will be chosen and will be an excellent nominee, I'm sure." Eleanor hoped she had shut down the conversation.

"Fine men, exactly, Mrs. R. Fine men. But look at you. You could prove that there are fine, capable women," Maureen shot back. "None of the men running hold a candle to you. You know the American people better than any of them. You know foreign policy, you know every leader." Maureen's voice turned sharp, and her eyes, black as her hair, had a bright excitement, even as she worried that she'd gone too far.

Maureen had meant only to raise the subject of the presidential primaries, but her boss's resistance frustrated her. She had never met anyone like Eleanor. "Her energy is astonishing," Maureen had written to her mother. "She's thirty years older than me, but wears me out. And she's always kind and generous, not just to me, but to every poor homeless soul we might pass, and every person who writes for her help with everything from Social Security payments gone astray to legislation to get more aid for poor women and children. She's endlessly curious about people, and in some ways, hopelessly hopeful." But not hopeful enough to run for president, Maureen thought impatiently.

"I appreciate your loyalty, dear," Eleanor said, "but my life is quite full as it is, I think you'll agree. I had my years in the White House, after all. That part of my story is over. It's out of the question for me to go back."

Eleanor caught the echo in her words. She had been standing on the steps of her apartment building in New York City in 1945, shortly after Franklin died, when a reporter approached her. "Mrs. Roosevelt," he had asked, "what's next?" She hadn't expected the question, and hesitated for a moment. "The story is over," she told him, and she turned quickly and went into the building. But the story hadn't been over at all. Truman had called. She had taken the UN assignment and more. Was she wrong again? Why had every step forward in her life caused so much fear and resistance? Eleanor impatiently pushed the thoughts from her head.

"Let's get back to work, Maureen," Eleanor said.

"Yes." David had grown too impatient to stay silent. "We have a tight schedule here, after all. When is that meeting with those girls in Lahore?" he asked, taking Eleanor's arm and beginning to walk more quickly toward the waiting car.

From Lahore, Eleanor had flown to Bombay, met with Prime Minister Nehru, and agreed to a final speech before the Indian parliament. She was looking forward to the end of her whirlwind tour, and to getting back home to Val-Kill. As she sat on the stage of the Indian parliament, she began to regret that she had agreed to appear.

When Eleanor rose to speak, the male ministers barely hid their contempt. They had expected a formal address read at a podium from a thick book filled with notes and statistics to guide the speaker. Instead, Eleanor walked to a standing microphone holding a small purse at her side, and spoke as if she were having a chat with them over tea.

"My friends," Eleanor began quietly, knowing her tendency to be shrill when she felt tense. "I understand your aloofness. You've shaken off the domination of one foreign power, and you're wary of others. But, after all, who could understand better than Americans? We were once in your position. We had been a young country, and we had to get rid of the British too. Your problems are more difficult, but you are meeting them in the way our people met theirs." Straightening her shoulders and catching the friendly smile of one of the few women ministers, Eleanor praised Indian neutrality in the struggle between the United States and the Soviet Union.

"I know that you are mistrustful of the Russians *and* of America. And I know that Russia does not want you to accept the American foreign aid that we are offering. But most of your people have been hungry all their lives; they have been hungry for generations. We want to help relieve their hunger."

Some shouts of approval and scattered applause could be heard.

Eleanor's voice rose. "Communism doesn't offer freedom . . . just the opposite. But we believe that the Soviets can be fought with bread as well as guns. That is also why we want to help India." Eleanor smiled warmly and leaned toward the microphone. "I look forward to continuing the free and open discussions that I have had throughout your country since arriving here. The Indian people I have met possess all the vigor and resilience your young country needs. I have no doubt, no doubt at all, that yours is a bright future. Thank you."

Eleanor could see that many ministers were rising to applaud, but the American attaché had taken her arm and was ushering her quickly off the stage to a side room where a group of international journalists waited with questions.

"What's this?" Eleanor asked in a whisper. "You didn't tell me ..."

The reporters were already moving closer and throwing out questions.

"Mrs. Roosevelt, are you worried that India could become a Soviet satellite. Is that what you and Prime Minister Nehru talked about?"

"Prime Minister Nehru is committed to democracy. Firmly committed. And we shall help him in every way to achieve his dream."

"Mrs. Roosevelt," Carl Stoddard of Colonel McCormick's *Chicago Tribune* jumped in, shouting over his colleagues. "You mentioned the Soviets in your speech, but nothing about Korea. Why are you avoiding talking about that situation?"

"This was a speech about the economic and cultural relations between India and the United States," Eleanor replied, surprised at the aggressive political tone of the questions.

"But Mrs. Roosevelt," Stoddard pressed on, "wouldn't your time be better spent pressing the president to get out of the war in Korea that he jumped into without congressional approval?"

"Your paper supported that action, as I recall, Carl," Eleanor said sharply.

This time, Jon Funderman from the Hearst Syndicate pressed the issue. "More than twenty thousand boys have died, Mrs. Roosevelt. Shouldn't the president have supported MacArthur and let him go into China?"

"I believe the Soviets were behind this conflict. Expanding our attack into China would have been a mistake and a dangerous expansion of the fighting. The president was right."

"Was he right to fire MacArthur too?" came the next question in swift response. Truman's already dismal popularity had plummeted to 23 percent when, only ten months earlier, he had fired General Douglas MacArthur, who was commanding UN forces in Korea. Immediately, the White House was deluged with twenty thousand angry telegrams a day, some cursing the president for firing the man many saw as the country's greatest war hero.

"I have said this before," Eleanor replied. "General MacArthur's public comments criticizing the president's policies in Korea were intolerable. I believe we have our best chance for a broader peace now that he is gone. Now, if you'll excuse me."

As Eleanor turned to leave, she pretended not to hear the final question that was shouted at her back, "Is there any truth to the rumor, Mrs. Roosevelt, that you may join President Truman as his running mate?"

CHAPTER 4

The Next Lincoln

Outside Paris, France, February 1952

General Dwight David Eisenhower had finished blending the flour and pepper into the pan of melted butter. His short, thick fingers were wrapped around his favorite slim-handled wooden spoon, and he stirred the mixture with slow, even strokes. His free hand clutched a handkerchief, and he blew his nose in loud blasts that echoed through the lofty ceilings of the old chateau. His normally ruddy face looked chalky, and what hair he had left to comb splayed in all directions behind the high reaches of his forehead. As he tried to concentrate on his task, the thin line of his lips slumped with frustration. Every time he sneezed, in multiple spasms that weren't more than five minutes apart, his wife, Mamie, took the sudden explosion like a body blow.

"Good heavens, Ike, do you have a cold again?" Mamie had tried to read the morning paper, but the sneezing and blowing and the clatter of cooking had set her nerves on edge. She stood in the kitchen doorway seeming more diminutive than usual in her flat house-slippers. Her imp-shaped face was puffy from lack of sleep, and the creases between her eyes had deepened with annoyance.

"It's not my fault, you know," Ike said with stuffy irritation.

"And chipped beef again?" Mamie asked.

"I like chipped beef. It makes me feel better."

"Well, I'm sick of it," Mamie answered, as she made a show of retying her dressing gown a bit tighter. She had bought it the day before at Alice Cadolle's little lingerie boutique in the rue Cambon. She suddenly felt foolish for thinking that Ike would notice its rich flowered silk and flowing lines. "And you know," Mamie said without trying to hide her irritation, "Marie can cook that for you. You should be sitting down, sipping tea."

"I can't stand tea and I can't stand the way Marie cooks my chipped beef. I like the way *I* cook my chipped beef." Ike didn't look up from the bubbling pan.

"All right. Have it your way, like you always do. I'll be upstairs getting dressed," Mamie said. "You do remember that the Cochran woman is coming in an hour, don't you?"

"Yes, that's why I dressed *before* I came downstairs," Ike said, giving her a disapproving look. Mamie turned without a word and walked toward the stairs.

"You're not having breakfast?" Ike called out, but there was no reply.

An hour later, when the doorbell rang, Mamie hadn't come back downstairs.

Ike buttoned his sweater, waving off the housemaid as he went to open the door himself. "Hello Jacquelin. Step right in. I'm trying to keep the cold out," Ike said, as he opened one side of the heavy mahogany doors just enough to let his guest in.

"Someone told me you flew yourself here," Ike said, shaking

his guest's hand and waiting while she took off her coat. "Is that true?"

"Not this time, General. But if the supreme commander of NATO needs a lift . . ." Cochran laughed, smoothing back her blond hair that curled into an exaggerated flip at her neck. She had the creamy skin of a starlet, but she'd made her money selling cosmetics. She'd dubbed the line "Wings," and flew solo around the country to promote it. Ike gave her a wan smile.

"I'm afraid I'm not up to any traveling right now," he said.

"Well, we'll just have to get you in shape," Cochran said with brisk cheer. "My, what a beautiful place this is." She had walked into the grand hall to look at the statuary and views beyond the dormant winter gardens.

"You must come back when we're in bloom," Mamie said, as she came down the winding staircase, the full skirt of her shirtwaist bouncing with every step. "We have a golf course, a pond stocked with trout, and my husband has the best vegetable garden," she said, as the two women shook hands.

"Yes, it's true. We've had sweet corn, two kinds of beans, peas, radishes, tomatoes, turnips . . . great bushels of 'em," Ike said, lighting a cigarette as they walked into the formal parlor. He let out a sharp cough, and Mamie shot him a look of annoyance.

"Well, it's a very grand house, Mamie!" Jacquelin said, looking up at the antique crystal chandelier hanging in the center of the room.

Mamie looked embarrassed. "I'm afraid it's too grand and too French for me, and the plumbing and electricity always need repair. I can't wait to get back to the Gettysburg farm."

"Same for me," said Ike, "my painting's better there, too." He tried a small laugh, but coughed instead. "Well, someone told me it was, but I know I don't have a bit of talent."

"I can't comment on that, General, but you have something else . . ." and Jacquelin held up a movie reel. "A whole lot of people who want you to be our candidate for president. Wait until you see this."

As she spoke, Jacquelin noticed that Mamie seemed to start at her words, and the look of vague annoyance on her face turned to fear. But for the first time since her arrival, Ike seemed to perk up and even smile a little.

"What did you do, interview my military staff? They're hardly objective," Ike said.

"Jacquelin." Mamie had stepped between her guest and her husband. "We don't want to be rude. Before we do any movie viewing, we need to get your bags inside and show you to your room. Then I have a nice luncheon planned. I've invited one of my French friends who is anxious to hear about your flying adventures." She turned to her husband.

"And, I'm afraid the general is a bit under the weather. He'll be wanting a nap. Why don't we plan on the movie after dinner? Now let me have Henri get your luggage," and she bustled out of the hallway before Ike could object.

"She's something of a general herself, I'm afraid," he said, with the uncomfortable feeling of a child who had been scolded. "Let's sit in here for a minute."

Ike led Jacquelin to a stiff-backed Louis IV couch, its snowdrop upholstery framed by delicate carved wood. He sat opposite on its twin, instinctively trying to swing his arm over the back of the couch, but his torso was too short. He flailed for a moment, grabbing at the wood, then gave up and slapped his hand on the seat next to him.

"This furniture wasn't made for people. I don't know who it was made for, but not for real people. Now on the farm in Gettysburg . . ."

"You should start thinking about Washington, not Gettysburg. Truman is on his way out," Jacquelin said.

"Fine by me. The mess in Washington stinks to high heaven. It's no wonder. Do you know how far Abilene, Kansas, is from Kansas City, Missouri?"

Jacquelin shook her head.

"One hundred . . . one hundre . . ." Ike pulled out his handkerchief just in time to catch a tremendous sneeze. "Oh, I'm sorry, Jacquelin. One hundred and fifty miles, that's how far. I grew up in Abilene hearing about the Pendergast brothers in Kansas City. They're the ones who brought Truman up in politics. Their bread and butter was gambling, prostitution, and bootlegging, and don't think it didn't spill over to Abilene. Made my parents furious. Patronage was the name of Truman's game from the beginning. Why do you think they called him the 'senator from Pendergast' when he came to Congress?"

"I'd never heard that," Jacquelin said with a laugh. "You know his line, don't you? Our president likes to say, 'my house is always clean.'"

"Bull sh . . . sorry." Ike coughed and turned red. "He's got five-percenters right on his payroll. You want a government contract, just pay that five percent to a Truman crony. Hell, that Vaughan character whose been hanging around his campaigns for the last ten years has gotten more deep freezers than he could handle. He must have a whole lot of steaks he wants to keep frozen."

"Yes, and Bess got one, and Justice Vinson, too."

"Oh yeah, that's right. Truman said Bess just got that for the lunchroom at the White House." Ike and Jacquelin shared a laugh.

"How could he think anyone would believe that?" Jacquelin said. "He's completely out of touch, and he needs to be out of office."

"What are you two finding so amusing?" Mamie came in with a drink in her hand, looking a bit calmer. "Would you like a drink, Jacquelin?"

"Not yet, no thank you. We were just talking about our president's way of getting little favors, like deep freezers."

"Oh." Mamie smiled. "Well, that whole Refinance or Re-something Corporation thing was so complicated, but I know this, that Lauretta Young, the White House stenographer? She got the most gorgeous natural royal pastel mink coat! I heard it was worth more than nine thousand dollars. And all because her husband was Truman's friend and steered some loan money to some business or other. It was so complicated, that whole story. But I loved that coat." Mamie's blue eyes sparkled. She spread her skirt and sat down, looking satisfied.

"Oh, oh, wait, remember? There was that other thing in '46 or '47, I think," Mamie piped up again. "That tax thing. Remember? All those IRS employees were fired for fixing taxes or something."

Ike was staring at his wife like she was a stranger. He could never understand how she went from one emotional extreme to another so quickly. When he was around her, he felt like he was on a frozen pond, taking each step with exaggerated care, his heart pounding when he heard a crack and a vast sense of relief sweeping through him when the ice felt firm and thick.

"You have a good memory, Mame," he said, managing a small smile. "There was that tax collector in Brooklyn, Marcelle or Markel or some such. I was president of Columbia at the time, and it was all over the news in New York. This character says with a straight face, 'I did make more than $190,000 in outside work in addition to my $10,500-a-year salary for the IRS, but that was legal.' That's what he said! 'That was *legal*,' and he smiles like the cat that swallowed the canary. Turns out, he'd only reported about $65,000 in income." Ike shook his head and pulled out his handkerchief.

"I remember," Jacquelin said, "and Truman's answer was something like, 'there's always going to be crooks.' I heard the president's own staff couldn't keep up with all the corruption charges in the administration."

"Well, that's what happens when a party's been in power too long," Ike said.

"Exactly why I'm here, General. I can't wait until after dinner. You're in for quite a show."

That evening, Jacquelin loaded up her film in the projection room normally used for military affairs. She, Mamie, and Ike sat down to watch the documentary of an Eisenhower rally in Madison Square Garden.

"This film produced by *Citizens for Eisenhower,*" read the opening credits.

"I had nothing to do with that group, you know," Ike said to Jacquelin.

She just smiled and fidgeted with the sound control.

"When was this filmed?" Ike asked, as the reel began.

"At midnight just outside the Garden, after a boxing match three days ago. That's fifteen thousand people you're looking at, and it was televised and carried on the radio," Cochran said with satisfaction. "And, you know New York. It's controlled by Democrats. They did everything but turn the fire hoses on us to stop this from happening. Look at this!" she said, leaning forward and clapping her hands together.

The crowd was chanting in unison, "We want Ike! We want Ike!" Banners were held high over people's heads, and placards were waving in antic arcs before the cameras. For nearly two hours, they sat watching the cheering and the speeches by politicians and Hollywood stars. When the film ended, Ike sat in stunned silence.

"We did this on three days' notice. If you had been there, General, the streets wouldn't have been able to hold the crowd," Cochran said.

Ike didn't reply. He got up and poured drinks for the three of them. When he carried the tray back to the couch, Jacquelin jumped up and pulled on Mamie's arm to get her to stand. Taking her drink, Jacquelin raised her glass and tipped it with a loud clink first against Mamie's, then against Ike's. Looking into Ike's eyes, she spoke as if she were at a state dinner in the White House, "To the president."

Eisenhower froze. He put his drink down, as if it were too heavy for his arm. Then his eyes filled, and tears overflowed and ran down his cheeks. Roughly wiping at his face with his handkerchief, he sat down heavily. Mamie didn't move until he motioned for her to sit down. The only sound was the soft whir of the movie projector's motor. Jacquelin was full of expectations, but she had never expected to see General Eisenhower in tears. She didn't know what to do other than wait. Finally, Ike broke the silence.

"My mother was the finest person I've ever known." His eyes filled up again, and he pressed the handkerchief against them impatiently. "If I do this . . . if I do this . . . I will do it in her spirit." Again, he had to stop, his voice choking. "I got angry once when I was a boy, so angry at her and my father that I went outside and pounded the trunk of our apple tree with my bare hands. I couldn't stop crying, cried into my pillow for an hour after they sent me to bed. Then my mother came in with bandages for my hands." Ike's tears came faster as he went on, "She said to me, 'He that conquereth his own soul is greater than he who taketh a city.' That was one of the most valuable moments of my life." Mamie and Jacquelin listened quietly as Ike talked for nearly an hour. Finally, lighting another cigarette off his last, he got up to fill his glass. Turning to Jacquelin he said, "You can go back and tell Bill Robinson that I'm going to run."

Jacquelin sat for a moment, overwhelmed by her emotions. She wanted to hug him, but she knew that wouldn't sit well with Mamie. Instead, she stood up and gave a mock salute, smiled broadly, and snapped to attention.

"Thank you, General. I am convinced that if you take this nomination, you will be our next Lincoln. Now, I'm thinking it's time I got to bed. I want to be off early tomorrow." Mamie hadn't moved or said a word. Cochran sensed they needed to be alone. Taking her drink, she kissed Mamie lightly on the cheek and shook Ike's hand before going upstairs.

After she left, Ike suggested to Mamie that they go into the library. His wife followed in silence. Ike took his time starting a fire, and they sat in their favorite chairs facing the hearth.

"Would you like another?" Ike pointed to her glass. Mamie held it up, and he walked over and took it from her. He mixed the scotch and soda without really seeing it, handed it to her, and sat down with a deep sigh.

"I know this is asking a lot of you," he began, watching her carefully.

Staring at the fire, Mamie replied, "I was looking forward to being together. To being in Gettysburg. To having some kind of normal life for once." She straightened her back and folded her hands in her lap.

"We *will* be together," Ike said quickly. "I want you with me, I *need* you with me when I'm campaigning, Mamie."

"I don't really think so."

"You're wrong. You're my secret weapon," he tried to sound lighthearted.

"Are you sure you won't just need a driver?" she replied, the bitterness edging her voice.

"I'm not . . . I'm not sure what you mean." Ike's voice weakened, as if he'd been kicked in the stomach.

"Oh, I think you know just what I mean." Mamie turned toward him, lifting her chin and glaring at her husband.

"Mamie, Mamie, please. I've told you so many times. Kay was a friend. That's all. A friend and my driver."

"Oh yes, of course, your *driver*. I wrote you every day that you were overseas, every single day, and all you sent me were lies, cheery little lies. Do you think I didn't know?"

"Mamie, you don't choose to believe anything I say, then or now. We were in the middle of the war. She was a young girl, like a daughter. . . ."

"A daughter? A daughter?" Mamie's voice was rising. "She hardly looked like a daughter to you in those pictures that were in the paper every other day. Having drinks on the beach? Riding your horses together?" Mamie's words pierced Eisenhower like a thrusting bayonet.

He thought about the picture of Kay he carried with him under the extra flap in his leather card case. She was holding Telek, the little Scotty they'd bought together, and standing next to the boxwood hedge just outside the cottage door. He knew keeping the photo was risky, but sometimes—looking at the warm smile that swept across Kay's face, remembering her trim body so smart in the uniform he'd had made for her, the way her eyes opened wide and lit up when she saw him, the silky perfume of her hair, so thick his fingers would tangle in it—sometimes he just needed to look at her. Once, when he'd been at Columbia, he thought he'd seen her in the audience during a convocation ceremony, but the woman he thought was Kay seemed to disappear, and he decided his eyes were deceived.

The last time they had been together was so difficult. He had failed her again, and then made a promise and failed at that, too. He couldn't imagine that Kay would ever want to see him again.

That last night in London, Kay had driven him up the winding driveway to Telegraph Cottage. When she jumped out to swing the white pole aside, he watched her calves tense with the effort. As they drove on, he could see the smoke rising from the chimney of the mock-Tudor house. Lights shone on both floors, setting the gabled roofline in contrast to the ten acres of dark woods that stretched behind it. How he loved to ride with Kay through those woods in the early morning! He felt a twinge of regret driving past the big garden where he'd managed to tend some vegetables in the summer. There wouldn't be another summer, another garden at the cottage—their cottage. It was October 1945. The war was won, and he would be called home soon.

He sensed Kay's sadness. She knew too, of course. He had promised to bring her to Washington. He wanted to. He meant to.

They were in the cozy parlor, in a corner of the house that offered some privacy, sitting on the davenport with its deep cushions. He had gotten up to close the door and then turned and said to Kay, "Come here." He could see her flying up from the sofa and into his arms. Then he showed her the papers he'd gotten so that she could get American citizenship. She had been so happy. She had held him so close. Their kisses grew more urgent, and then she was undressing in front of the fire and helping him do the same. He wanted her so much. So very much. Her skin was smooth and hot and she was ready, so ready for him. But he failed her again, failed her utterly. He remembered her speaking with soft kindness, "It will be all right. Next time." But he knew better. He was fifty-five years too old, and it had been too long.

The next day he left for the states, but he never sent for her as he said he would. Oh, she got her citizenship, and then married that Morgan fellow in New York. He never saw her again and he never stopped thinking of seeing her. He didn't wonder that Mamie sensed it, but he had no idea how to change anything. He wasn't sure that he wanted to.

"I don't know what else to say, Mamie." Ike's shoulders slumped, and he dropped his head. "I want you with me," he said after several minutes ticked by. "That's it. You'll have to decide." He left the room with slow, deliberate steps. As he climbed the stairs, he kept his head down, willing himself not to look at the oil he had painted of Telegraph Cottage at dawn that hung on the landing.

Mamie watched him go, her anger seeping out as he disappeared. She could feel the tears burning her eyes, but she fought to hold them back. Then the nausea came, and she struggled against it. She had been ill so many times over the last ten years. Her weight had finally gotten up to 118 pounds, although just last year after a bout of pneumonia, she'd been down to 102 again. Food didn't interest her, and when she did eat, she often couldn't keep it down.

The idea of campaigning with Ike made her feel sick. She hated public appearances. She detested traveling. But if she didn't go . . . She thought of Kay Summersby, so vigorous, so young. She was somewhere in the States, and Ike would be doing so much traveling. Mamie pushed herself up from the brocaded chair and went to the sideboard. Switching to vodka, she felt a moment of satisfaction when she saw that Marie had remembered to refill the decanter that morning as she had requested. She poured the clear liquid into a stout glass, and grabbing a magazine to hold in front of it, hurried to her bedroom.

CHAPTER 5

Duty

Hyde Park, New York, March 1952

Eleanor sat finishing her morning coffee at the long, rough-pine table that was one of her favorite spots in Val-Kill cottage. The morning papers, some letters, and a pile of notes were scattered around her. She had just fed a few pieces of wood into the small but satisfying fire in the brick fireplace that covered a wall of the kitchen. The March wind stirred enough of a back draft to give the air a smoky flavor. Eleanor heard a light tap, and the florist from town poked his head in the back door.

"I have your three dozen glads, Mrs. Roosevelt." Eleanor motioned for him to come in and got up to find her purse.

"You're our best winter customer," the deliveryman told her with a welcome-back smile.

"A home must have flowers, and much as I like yours, I must admit, I'm anxious to test the ground in the garden to see if I can get in my first bulbs."

"Don't forget the mothballs."

"I won't." She laughed. "That was a good suggestion. My squirrels have enough to gorge on without eating my bulbs."

After he'd left, Eleanor took care as she rinsed her china cup and saucer, small treasures from the Revolutionary War–era service of her great-great-grandmother. Then she moved quickly to perform her secret ritual on the flowers before her guest, Queen Juliana of the Netherlands, came downstairs.

Minutes later, her young friend, the author Gore Vidal, walked in the back door unannounced. Eleanor was on her knees, her backside sticking out of the tiny downstairs bathroom as she fussed with the huge bunch of gladiolas, which she had placed in the toilet.

"Eleanor, is that you? I'm afraid I've never been treated to this particular point of view, shall we say."

"Gore, oh my goodness. You've found out my secret," Eleanor said, laughing as she backed out on her knees, then accepted Vidal's hand to get up.

"Has Elliott sold off all the flower vases, then?" Vidal said archly. Like many neighbors in the Hudson Valley towns around Hyde Park, he had been furious to hear that Eleanor was letting her son, Elliott, sell off large parcels of the Roosevelt property. Springwood, the house where Franklin had been raised and where he and Eleanor had lived, had been turned into a national historic site. The locals feared that Elliott's real estate wheeling and dealing would lead to fast food restaurants and tourist traps popping up to accommodate the visitors pouring into the little town.

"Don't be mean, Gore. I only keep the glads here until I can arrange them. I have a theory that the leachy old porcelain and well water make them quite happy. And Elliott has plans. You'll see. People never give him enough credit."

"Perhaps you need to listen to someone other than Elliott when it comes to Elliott. I'm picking up some rumors about his business dealings that are not altogether savory."

"Gore! You shouldn't listen to such nonsense. Elliott is nothing if not honest and aboveboard. I appreciate your concern, but it's misplaced and it is, frankly, irritating. I know my own son. Now, come in. I have some coffee left." Vidal gave an exaggerated shrug and began to unbutton his coat.

"What do you think about our esteemed president's decision?" Vidal asked, as Eleanor gave a last pat to the flowers.

"I think I'm rather happy I wasn't in the midst of six thousand Democrats at the D.C. Armory who paid a thousand dollars a plate for dinner and ice cream shaped like a donkey," Eleanor laughed.

"Donkey ice cream?" Vidal made a face.

"Don't you read the news, Gore?" Eleanor had taken the paper off the table.

"I must have missed the important parts," Vidal replied, as Eleanor arched an eyebrow.

"Perhaps you'll consider this of more interest," she said as she began reading, "'President Truman had just finished telling the crowd, "We can win the sixth presidential election in a row for Democrats."'" Eleanor affected a strong midwestern twang as she imitated Truman. "'This Missouri farm boy is here to tell you that the Republicans have a dinosaur strategy that will only get the dinosaur vote—and there aren't too many of them. They'll try to make the people believe that everything the government has done for the country is social-ism . . . here you are, with your new car, and your home, and better opportunities for the kids, and a television set—just surrounded by socialism.' A pretty good speech so far, wouldn't you say?"

"Indeed."

"Then, just as he had the crowd completely behind him, our

president says, 'I shall not be a candidate for reelection.' I suppose he should get credit for keeping a secret."

"Why do you think he did it?" Vidal asked.

"He said he wanted a quieter life, but he can't shake the taint of these scandals. They just seem to have piled up. It's probably the reason he lost the New Hampshire primary to Kefauver . . . and then there's McCarthy." Eleanor's voice rose with anger. "It infuriates me to say the man's name."

Two years before, in Wheeling, West Virginia, the pompous, ambitious Republican senator from Wisconsin had figured out what it took to capture the national stage. He had been speaking at a Lincoln's birthday event for the Women's Republican Club.

"The great difference between our Western Christian world and the atheistic Communist world," McCarthy told the crowd, "is not political, it is moral. Karl Marx dismissed God as a hoax, and now, his followers are in our midst. Our great democracy will be destroyed not by enemies from without, but rather because of enemies from within." Pulling a paper from inside his suit jacket, McCarthy raised his voice. "The bright young men who are born with silver spoons in their mouths are the ones who have been most traitorous," and he waved the paper, saying, "I have here in my hand a list of 205 people . . . a list of names that were made known to the secretary of state as being members of the Communist Party and who nevertheless are still working and shaping policy in the State Department."

With that speech, McCarthy became the nation's Communist hunter-in-chief.

"I agree with you that he's a greater threat to democracy than those he's chasing," Vidal said, "but, let us remember, our president has not managed an approval rating over 32 percent in the past two years." Vidal walked into the living room as he talked. "We have to add that fact to the toll being taken by McCarthy and his ilk. You like Adlai, don't you?"

"I do. He worked with me in the UN. He's brilliant and committed to the right causes."

"There's a story going around about him, but I'm afraid it is rather uninspiring, to say the least."

Eleanor looked quizzical, so Vidal went on.

"He was telling a friend about his meeting with Truman in January. Adlai said Truman wants him to run for president so he can save the world from Dwight Eisenhower, and the way I heard it, he didn't sound like he thought he was up to the job."

Eleanor replied defensively, "He feels an obligation to the people of Illinois. He already pledged to run again as governor. And his ex-wife has become quite the socialite, flitting all over. He told me he wants to be around for his boys. They asked him not to run. Those reasons make sense, don't you think?" but Eleanor herself didn't sound convinced.

"Adlai's a gifted man, but a president has to be able to make up—or at least appear to know—his own mind, especially about the far-from-trivial matter of assuming the presidency," Vidal said sharply.

Stevenson was fifty-two years old, a brainy, well-mannered aristocrat, divorcé, and Princeton grad. He was known by the public for his extemporaneous wit and often-stirring words, and by his friends for his expertise at letting others pick up a check. Stevenson had won the governor's race handily, although it was his first run for office. He'd earned a reputation as a crime fighter and reformer. But he was an oddly reluctant politician.

"Adlai would probably make one of the best presidents we have ever had," Eleanor replied, "but if Ike gets the nomination, I think the hero worship around him will make it an impossible race for the Democrats."

"Come, come, Eleanor, let's not ignore Adlai's other problem," and Vidal gave Eleanor a sardonic smile.

"Please, Gore, I don't like gossip."

"Hoover saying he's a homosexual is gossip, and malicious at that," Vidal agreed, referring to the FBI director, who was trying to discredit Stevenson because he believed the governor was a Communist.

"But I'm talking about Alicia Patterson *Guggenheim*, the very married newspaper publisher, who like the very married, fabulously wealthy Marietta Tree is apparently sharing Adlai's bed, along with . . ."

"Gore, I won't listen to this."

"The Republicans are listening, Eleanor. Adlai is open to a loud whispering campaign. I hear he keeps his love letters or 'tender bits' as he calls them, by his bed just to make Marietta jealous." Vidal laughed at Eleanor's shocked expression. He wondered what Eleanor would say if she heard the lines from a juicy letter that had been shared with him. After Alicia's paper, *Newsday,* passed the 100,000 circulation mark, Adlai had written her, "So you've made it—you indomitable little tiger. I could just bite your ears with savage joy."

"Gore, how on earth do you know these things?" Eleanor said, sensing he knew more than he was saying.

"It doesn't matter."

"Eleanor?" a voice called from the back door, and in a moment, Eleanor's friend, Esther Lape, walked in.

"Well! We have a party," Eleanor said with a welcoming smile. "Come in, Esther, you're just in time for politics and coffee."

Esther and Eleanor had been friends since the 1920s, working together on feminist and political issues. When she was First Lady, Eleanor had rented an apartment in Greenwich Village from Esther and her lifetime partner, Elizabeth Read, and often stayed with them at their country house in Connecticut.

"Hello, Esther, we were just assessing the presidential race," Vidal said, as they walked into the living room. "I don't see Ike riding into the nomination on a giant wave, do you? The Taft forces are strong. Republicans have a fight on their hands," Vidal said, as he settled into one of the cozy, flower-brocade armchairs.

Much of the furniture in the rambling twenty-room house came from a workshop Eleanor had started with two other women in the 1930s as a way to help employ workers in the Hudson Valley during the Depression. The living room, like other rooms in the house, was cluttered with small tables, sideboards, chairs, and lamps, all surrounded by rich red knotty-pine walls. Photos of Franklin, the family, friends, and scenes from Eleanor's travels were hung all around and also sat on the lace-covered console table that divided the sitting area from a small book-lined alcove.

"Like your perspicacious son, James, I am leaning toward Kefauver," Vidal went on. "He's the only one who had both the guts and good sense to get in against Truman."

"But Kefauver's put himself at odds with the party by sweeping Democrats up in his criminal hearings in the Senate," Eleanor said, as she walked to the kitchen to get Esther coffee.

"Marquis Childs in the *Post* called Kefauver 'Sir Galahad in a coonskin cap,'" Vidal said. "Rest assured, it is going to be a crowd. Bob Kerr from Oklahoma has jumped in. There is noise about Averell Harriman, Jim Farley, Speaker Rayburn, Soapy Williams . . ."

Esther laughed. "Where did the governor of Michigan get the idea . . . ?"

"I know, I know, but that is why this is going to be quite a brawl," Vidal said. "It's wide open. In 1924, our irresolute Democratic forebears went for 103 ballots in Madison Square Garden. We might beat that this time. And, Mrs. First Lady of the World," Vidal said in a teasing voice, "after your triumphant grand world tour, some people are even talking about you getting into the race."

Eleanor had just walked back into the room, as Esther spoke up. "You would advance the cause of women's rights if you did run, Eleanor, whatever the outcome. Maybe you're right when you say the country's not ready for a woman president, but you can help make it ready. Sometimes, and I hate to say this, but sometimes I think you just don't want to get into the rough-and-tumble of a campaign . . ."

"Esther, how can you say that to me?" Eleanor's words came fast and angry. "That would be rank self-indulgence. I would be the last one to allow myself to decline to run for public office because of any such reason. You know I've urged other women to be less sensitive when it comes to politics and to learn the same kind of give-and-take as men."

"Of course, I know that," Esther said, returning Eleanor's fire. "And I also know that the title of your first book was *It's Up to the Women*. Doesn't that include you?" Vidal was nodding, and they watched Eleanor as she placed the coffee with exaggerated care next to Esther, then walked over to the French doors and looked out over the pond.

"Are you saying I owe something more, Esther? That I haven't given enough?" Eleanor's voice was quiet. She turned toward her friends, her face a mixture of doubt and anger. "Is there some duty that I have not yet fulfilled?"

The next day, Eleanor took the train to Washington, and by midmorning she was sitting in her third meeting of the day. She had gone to New York senator Herbert Lehman's apartment for early coffee and an informal discussion about her world travels with some of his Senate colleagues. Then, Franklin Jr. had arranged for her to meet with Republicans and Democrats on the House Foreign Affairs Committee. Walking to the other side of the Capitol, she had stopped by House Speaker Sam Rayburn's office. As she walked down Independence Avenue to meet Secretary of Defense Robert Lovett for lunch, Maureen handed her the April 7, 1952 issue of *Time* magazine, which had just hit the stands.

"Great picture, don't you think?" Maureen said, as Eleanor looked at the cover. *Time*'s illustrator had portrayed Eleanor from the shoulders up. Her image covered the center of a large clock, its Roman numerals arrayed like a crown around her head. She seemed to be speaking, the furrows in her forehead making her look serious, but the creases around her eyes as they looked toward a distant crowd showed warmth and humor. Her thick, wavy, salt-and-pepper hair cut sensibly short, she wore her signature three-strand pearl necklace, a black top, and no earrings. The caption read, "Eleanor Roosevelt: The jet plane with a fringe on top."

"It's all about your trip. There are lots of great pictures inside, and you have to admit, Mrs. R., you do look presidential."

Eleanor let out a short laugh. "Maureen, you simply won't give up."

"You're the ambassador extraordinaire according to this. And there's also a story about who might take the president's place on the ticket," Maureen said.

"Let me see," Eleanor said with a mocking look of disapproval. "Well, Ike is picking up steam against Taft according to this, especially after winning the New Hampshire primary," she said as she scanned the pages. "And, in case you didn't notice ... my name is *not* listed among the Democratic hopefuls, Maureen," and she handed the magazine back.

"Eleanor!" A man's voice called from behind her on the crowded sidewalk, and she turned to see Adlai Stevenson and an aide hurrying to catch up.

"How good to see you, Adlai," Eleanor said as he kissed her on both cheeks. "What are you doing here?"

"Meeting with the Illinois delegation, that sort of thing," he waved his hand as if swatting a fly. "It looks like we're going the same way. Would you mind terribly if I spoke to you privately for a minute? Will you excuse us, please?" Adlai said to his aide and Maureen. He led Eleanor to a secluded bench on the 2nd Street side of the Library of Congress where they sat under the gnarly branches of a cork tree.

"I've wanted to speak to you, Eleanor, about this running for president business. I just . . . I just feel so torn, so absolutely at sea," Adlai said, giving her a plaintive look.

"I've heard your reasons, Adlai. You've told me, as have others. I must tell you this; Franklin was terribly ill when he ran for his fourth term. Although he never spoke of it, I'm quite sure he knew that the war might be the end of him, and it was, but he ran anyway because the country needed him. I believe the country needs you, Adlai. Are any of your objections more important than that?"

Adlai bent his head to take off his eyeglasses and Eleanor noticed the brass safety pin that held together one side. But she was more surprised to see tears in Adlai's eyes when he looked up. He took her hand and she could feel that his was moist and soft.

"The presidency feels like a dreaded responsibility, but I don't want to shrink in fear, or self-interest, or false humility." He hesitated as if struggling to go on. "The words from Matthew keep running through my head, 'If this cup may not pass from me, except I drink it, Thy will be done.' Does that seem like sacrilege, Eleanor?" His long face looked more drawn than Eleanor had remembered it.

"No, Adlai, not to me. It's right to draw on the wisdom and power of the Lord," she said gently. "But you must decide without reservation. It is far too important for anything less." She patted his hand. "I'm sorry, I must go or I'll be late. Do take care."

"That looked serious," Maureen said as Eleanor rejoined her.

"Yes, Adlai is a serious man. Come, we don't have much time, and I need you to go over the other items."

Maureen began talking as they walked. "On politics, an International Association of Machinists poll gave Stevenson 53 percent, Kefauver 37 percent, and the rest were in single digits. And on *Meet the Press* last night, McKinney made a big deal about saying that anyone who wants the nomination has to work for it." Frank Mc-Kinney was chairman of the Democratic Party.

"He obviously meant Adlai."

"I guess so," Maureen said. "Governor Stevenson's attractive, don't you think?" Maureen asked, giggling and glancing back over her shoulder. "I mean in a bald-headed, intellectual divorcé kind of way. With a bow tie."

Eleanor smiled indulgently. Over the years, Maureen had been too busy working her way up the career ladder to find a husband. She had come to America from Ireland ten years before as an un-educated, unstoppable twenty-year-old. Seven years later, Tommy, who had been Eleanor's assistant as long as anyone could remem-ber, had plucked Maureen from an employment agency. Eleanor valued Maureen's loyalty as much as her ability. No one knew bet-ter than Tommy how much Eleanor needed a trusted gatekeeper.

For nearly twenty-five years, Tommy had been Eleanor's friend, sharing private agonies and public triumphs, as well as fulfilling her role as assistant. But Tommy was ill. Now Maureen, with gay shirtwaists that showed off a trim figure and a three-strand pearl choker that mirrored Eleanor's longer one, brought the youth and vitality Tommy knew were needed. She saw the grooming of her successor as her last gift to Eleanor.

"The League of Women Voters is having its national meeting on May 1." Maureen was trying not to drop her notes as she shuffled through them while pushing her purse strap back up on her shoul-der. "It's going to be a preview of issues and candidates in both parties. They want you to speak.... Sorry, need to catch my breath. I need longer legs to keep up with you, Mrs. R. Um, let's see, you know, the polls are showing that women are going to play a bigger part in this election than ever before."

"Tell the league I'll do it. And find the polls. I'll use them for my speech."

"You also received the formal request from Brandeis University to be the speaker at their first commencement."

"That's fine."

"There's also this really disturbing letter from the FBI." Maureen was holding the letter out to Eleanor.

"Just tell me what it says," Eleanor said.

"Mrs. R., it says . . ." Maureen hesitated, "it says that you shouldn't take any trips into the South because they have information that the Ku Klux Klan is offering $25,000 to anyone who can kill you," Maureen gulped hard, "and they say they can't guarantee your protection."

Eleanor laughed. "Maureen, don't sound so worried. I never asked for the FBI's protection, and I wouldn't trust J. Edgar Hoover to protect me anyway. Really, dear, don't be worried. I have that trip to the Highlander school planned, and I'll be fine. I'm certainly not changing it."

"Well, all right, but I mean, they're probably not making it up."

Eleanor stopped and turned to her assistant. "Don't be so sure. This is Hoover, my dear. And even if they're not making it up, that wouldn't stop me. Courage is more exhilarating than fear, Maureen. And in the long run, it's easier. Now, what else?"

Maureen looked skeptical. "You got a request to speak at the Democratic Convention."

"I wasn't planning to attend the convention. You know that," Eleanor said.

"Well, the president wants you to talk about your trip and the importance of the United Nations. He's sending a letter."

Eleanor sighed. She had hoped for a quiet summer in Val-Kill and a chance to finish the book about her recent travels. She didn't relish the thought of being drawn into the intrigues of a contentious convention, and her little talk with Adlai didn't make her feel any better. But she knew Harry wouldn't take "no" for an answer.

"I suppose I'll have to go," Eleanor told Maureen. "But let's make it a quick trip, in and out."

"All right, Mrs. R. But I'm sure that the president and Speaker Rayburn and the others will really want you to stay," Maureen said, never imagining how prophetic her words would become.

CHAPTER 6

Fair Play

Chicago, July 11, 1952

Robert A. Taft, presidential scion, Harvard/Yale man, and Ohio boy with roots so deep in his native soil he could have sprouted buckeyes, was wearing his Cheshire grin. Keeping a keen eye on the camera, he adjusted the vest on his best gray suit, its muted pinstripes underscoring a sophisticated taste. Taft brought a studied determination to the task of looking confident, calm, and presidential.

"One minute," the producer called, shooting his index finger into the air.

Taft took his handkerchief out and patted the naked and powdered reach of his head, hoping not to shine like a Westinghouse bulb.

"Five, four, three, two, one . . . you're on."

Dan Seymour looked straight into the camera, "Good evening, ladies and gentlemen, and welcome to the CBS television show *We the People.* Tonight, on the eve of the Republican Convention, presidential candidate Senator Robert A. Taft of Ohio is joining us. Welcome, Senator Taft."

Taft gave a short nod, his smile never changing, his hands still on his lap.

"Senator Taft, I understand you're very confident of the outcome of the nomination."

"Yes, Dan." Taft reached inside his suit coat without taking his eyes off the host, and pulled out the squat square urine-colored paper that viewers could easily recognize as a wad of Western Union telegrams. "There are a lot more telegrams back in my suite, Dan. I have more than 607 votes promised to me. That's three more than I need to win."

"But people do seem to like Ike, as all those buttons say." Seymour sounded genial, but for a brief second Taft looked grim. He'd been denied the nomination in 1948. That wasn't going to happen again.

"Have you seen our buttons, Dan?" Taft reached in his pocket and held up a small pin. "'But What Does Ike Like?'" Taft read, pointing to the words. "You see?" The smile snapped back into place. "General Eisenhower must take some stands on issues, Dan," Taft said in his most reasonable voice. "He must stand for something after all, not just be a symbol without substance. Our delegates are very smart people, Dan. They see through the platitudes spoken without purpose. Yes, I'm confident that I'll win this week, and I'll go on to the White House."

"But aren't the Eisenhower people challenging the seating of your delegates from Texas, Louisiana, and Georgia? They claim you're running the convention and only allowing delegates who are loyal to you to be seated. They say you're keeping out other delegate slates from those three states that would support Ike." Seymour smiled as he finished, as if he'd just asked Taft to talk about his grandchildren.

"I'll have two hundred more votes than General Eisenhower on the first ballot, Dan. The whole delegate thing, that's about Eisenhower's people wanting to let Democrats come into our Republican primaries back in Texas. I guess the general's just not experienced enough to know that in America politics doesn't work like that." Taft's smile got lost in the struggle to control his temper. As he fought to reclaim it, he looked as if he was grimacing.

The next morning, a crowd of reporters stood outside the International Amphitheatre in Chicago waiting for Ike's man to appear. Rodeos and livestock shows had filled the amphitheater's twelve thousand seats before it became a convention hall. Even with the brand new air-conditioning system that had been installed that year, there were back rooms and hallways where the smell of manure stamped into sawdust still lingered. Outside, the stink of the nearby stockyards coated the hot July air.

As they jostled toward the entrance, delegates sporting "Taft's Our Man" straw hats and "I Like Ike" sandwich signs bumped up against each other and traded barbs. The smells of boiling coffee, hot dogs, and pretzels from the jumble of street vendors mixed in an unappetizing stench. The rising chorus of delegates trying to talk over the crowd and hail seldom-seen political friends competed with the street sellers' shouts: "Get your Polish sausage here," "Buttons, buttons, every button and pin on sale," "Hot coffee, hot, hot coffee," "Pop for sale, get your Squirt here." Only the slightest breeze worked its way in from the lake, but it wasn't enough to flutter the army of pint-sized American flags that every delegate seemed to be carrying into the vast convention hall.

Tom Dewey pushed his way through the carnival-like scene. The failed Republican presidential nominee, and Taft nemesis from 1948, had turned political mastermind for Ike. He was armed with an answer for Taft's glib defense of the delegate fight. With the pugnacious swagger of the mob prosecutor he'd once been, Dewey asked, "Why is Senator Taft trying to bolt the doors to our party to keep out disillusioned Democrats who we have converted to Ike supporters? We Republicans need a political revival that will result in a lot of Democratic conversions. The Texas slate Taft wants to exclude does represent Democratic converts, and thousands of Republicans, too!"

Several journalists shouted at once, "What does the general think, Tom? Where is he?"

"He'll be right here tomorrow, ready to answer your questions."

Ike was in Denver. He had been waiting out the brawl, thinking it looked unseemly to comment. Then Dewey called and told him he might as well get out of the race if he didn't get himself to Chicago, pronto. As Ike boarded the plane for Chicago, he felt bullied and unsure. What did he know about slates and delegates and convention rules? He wished he had one person he really trusted on his campaign crew. He missed being the unquestioned commander in charge of the troops.

Ike got to the Blackstone Hotel by early evening. The Beaux-Arts masterpiece on Lake Shore Drive sat next door to Conrad Hilton's massive hotel, which served as convention central, pulsing with campaign staff, television crews, and delegates.

Ike had just lit a cigarette and was looking out from his suite at the great, placid expanse of Lake Michigan when Henry Cabot Lodge arrived. The Massachusetts senator was Ike's official convention manager. He came into the suite looking a lot more chipper than his candidate.

"You know why this is a famous place, Ike?" Lodge asked, trying to create a lighter mood.

"Not really," Ike replied, pacing to the window.

"In 1920, a reporter wrote that the compromise that gave our party Warren G. Harding happened in a smoke-filled room of the Blackstone."

"So that's where the expression comes from, 'smoke-filled room'?"

"Yep, so keep that cigarette burning," Lodge said as he lit a cigar, "because we're going to make history again, right here."

Ike didn't look impressed as Dewey walked in waving some newspapers.

"Look at these stories. Taft's people made a major misstep yesterday by not letting the TV crews into the Credentials Committee meeting. It made them look like they're hiding something."

"Aren't they?" asked Ike. "Isn't that our argument? That they're being unfair?"

"Look," Dewey said, "Southern Republicans have been choosing their slates the same way for eighty-four years. That's what Taft's claiming, and he's right. Our delegations from those states aren't any more legitimate than theirs, but you know what, General? It doesn't matter."

Ike looked perplexed, so Dewey went on. "When the hero of the free world," he pointed at Ike, "calls for fair play, the other side looks like cheaters, whether they are or not."

"I'm not sure I'm comfortable with that," Ike said, stubbing his cigarette hard into an ashtray.

"Look Ike, we tried to run slates of legal delegates in these states," Lodge said. "Taft's people refused to let us in the room. All we're saying here is, don't let a Credentials Rules Committee controlled by the opposition decide who gets to cast a vote for the Republican nominee. Let's make a motion that none of the contested delegates from either slate be seated until their qualifications are approved by a majority of all the delegates."

"Okay . . ." Ike hesitated. "That seems fair," but he couldn't shake a nagging sense of doubt.

"All right then," Dewey said, brushing quick fingers over his thick black mustache and looking thoughtful. "I've got the line. You said it, Ike: 'fair play,' that's it. We're demanding 'fair play.' Got it, General?"

The next day, as Dewey had promised, Ike stood in front of the convention hall and spoke to reporters.

"General, do you believe that Taft's people are unfairly blocking your delegates from being seated?"

"I do believe that," Ike replied. "In fact, I'm shocked by the smoke-filled rooms and Star Chamber methods of Taft's people. I demand fair play."

The next day, the *Chicago Tribune* headline screamed, "Eisenhower Calls for Fair Play," and Dewey made sure a flyer echoing the front page was on every delegate's chair.

Like mosquitoes hatching on a fetid pond, Taft watched "Fair Play" placards multiply and fly into the hall as the proceedings began. Tempers rose and fistfights broke out on the convention floor between Taft and Eisenhower supporters. Shouts echoed from far corners of the room and were taken up like a chorus: "Taft's a thief," "We demand fair play," "Eisenhower's a liar."

Walking outside to meet his wife, Taft saw the actor John Wayne launch himself from a cab as if he was going to attack an Eisenhower sound truck. "Why don't you get a red Commie flag?" Wayne was shaking his fist and shouting. Meanwhile, inside the hall, John Roosevelt, Eleanor's youngest son, had just stood to second the nomination of General Eisenhower.

Away from the convention floor, in the Boulevard Room at the Hilton, the Rules Committee was meeting behind locked doors to determine which delegates, Ike's or Taft's, would be seated from the states of Texas, Georgia, and Louisiana. Outside, the television news cameras and reporters were desperate to find out what was being said.

Suddenly, Ted Church from CBS grabbed his colleague, Bill Downs, by the arm.

"I've got it. Come on." He pulled Downs out of the crowded hallway and raced for an elevator.

"Where are we going?" Downs said. "I heard NBC may have sneaked a mike in that room. Maybe we should wait and see if they get anything."

"Forget that. They got caught by Hilton security. But I just realized that CBS has a radio wire in that room to broadcast dance band concerts. We just have to get it turned on."

Ten minutes later, CBS and the nation were listening to the screaming match going on in the Republican Rules Committee meeting.

"When did you start to believe in majority rule?" came the sonorous voice of Ike's man from Texas, Roger Peterson, speaking with calm authority.

"All my life," Henry Zweifel, a Taft man and national committeeman from Texas responded with some heat.

"You mean when you came to this convention, and not a single moment before," Peterson replied sharply. He had been at the nominating caucus in Zweifel's garden in Texas when Zweifel had forced a hundred Ike delegates to leave because they outnumbered the Taft delegates.

"The Ike delegates at the caucuses and state convention in Texas were a bunch of stragglers," Zweifel spit back.

"Mr. Zweifel is absolutely not telling the facts," Peterson announced to the committee. "There wasn't a straggler in our state convention. Every single man was certified by the secretary of state." Peterson's voice began to rise. "Every single man was certified by a county convention, by a county in Texas. There was not a straggler there. Not one." He began shouting, "And when you say there were, Mr. Zweifel, you and the other Taft men are not telling the facts. *General Eisenhower demands fair play!*" Peterson screamed the last words.

From a suite at the Hilton on the fifth day of the convention,

Herb Brownell was orchestrating the floor action for Ike. He was a master strategist and vote counter. A shy man with a swaybacked walk, he gravitated to back rooms and backhanded plays. As he had done for several days, he slipped out of his suite on the eleventh floor and took the elevator to another man's room on the fourth floor. Then, when he was sure no reporters were hanging around, he took the stairs to Ike's suite.

Ike was watching the proceedings on television. He couldn't hear the maneuvering on the convention floor, but Brownell brought news.

"Taft had it in his hands and threw it away with his secret meetings and compromises that smelled like deals. We still need to shoot low, Ike, but I think it's moving our way. We're hearing about Taft delegates finding our floor managers and pledging their support on the q.t."

"We'll see," Ike said, as he reached for Mamie's hand.

At that moment, National Chairman Guy Gabrielson stood in front of the twelve-foot-high Civil War portrait of Lincoln that hung above the speakers' platform, craning his neck over his potbelly and shouting into the microphone as he hammered the gavel.

"Quiet please, quiet. We have the results of the first ballot. . . . Quiet in the hall."

Ike, watching on television, turned a Salvation Army coin over and over in his fingers and held a Boy Scout souvenir in his other hand for luck.

"The official ballot count is . . ." the chairman paused, as if he'd lost his place, "five hundred and ninety-five votes cast for General Dwight David Eisenhower." Cheers and screams erupted with such force that the chairman was drowned out. He went on gamely, moving his mouth closer to the microphone. "And five hundred votes for Senator Robert A. Taft." At that moment, Senator Edward J. Thye of Minnesota began screaming for the chairman's attention as he waved the standard for the state of Minnesota. "Minnesota wishes to change its vote to Eisenhower," he repeated, as others in the delegation took up the cry. Once Minnesota threw itself into Ike's corner, Taft's support collapsed. On the second vote, Ike swept the delegates and the nomination was his.

Ike turned to Mamie, his eyes filled with tears. She reached up and gently wiped his cheek, and he hugged her, unable to speak. Amid the toasts and congratulations, a jubilant Dewey threw his arm around Ike.

"These delegates believe you're a winner, Ike. And they're right. You are going all the way to the White House!"

"I think I should go see Taft," Ike said. "Don't you?"

"Yes, yes, of course. Good idea. We'll need to keep that isolationist crowd in the fold of the big Republican tent you're going to build, General."

Lodge had walked up while Dewey was talking. "After you pay your visit to Taft, we have another matter to discuss. I'm afraid you don't get a break here, General. You have to announce your running mate."

"I didn't realize that was up to me."

"Yes, it is up to you, although Tom and I have some ideas. I've asked the senior team to come up in an hour to discuss it with you."

In the chaos of Ike's upset victory, it took several hours before Tom Dewey, Herb Brownell, Henry Cabot Lodge, and Sherman Adams rejoined the nominee in his suite.

"Someone told me I need a vice president," Ike said, smiling as he interrupted the excited conversations between the men. "I want a man with special talent. And I want a man who's good at flushing out subversive influences."

"What about Taft?" Brownell offered, although he knew who Dewey had in mind. Brownell had run Dewey's campaign in 1948.

Experience told him that it was better to give Ike some names to reject, so he could feel better about the name Brownell already knew would be chosen.

Dewey gave a sardonic smile. "He'll need some time to get over himself."

"I had a good talk with him," Ike said, proud that it had been his idea to go see Taft. "He was very cordial. I think he'll be supportive. I really do."

"Don't bet on it," Dewey replied quickly. "But we need to pick someone who is acceptable to him and the rest of the old guard."

"Anyway, Taft's too old, and we need a westerner," added Lodge.

"Well, Earl Warren's a westerner, but he's sixty-one," said Brownell, referring to the popular governor of California who had made a long-shot bid for the nomination.

"Right," said Lodge, "that's only a year younger than Ike. We have to do better than that. Bringing a youthful look to the campaign is important."

"Nixon's only thirty-nine, conservatives love him, and he campaigns hard."

"Right," Lodge said, "and no one ever accused him of being a security risk. He's Mister Protect-America-from-Communism, right behind his pal McCarthy."

"Fine, gentlemen, but you know he's got a difficult personality. He's actually antisocial, I'd say. Very brooding and inflexible." Sherman Adams offered his first comment. The taciturn governor of New Hampshire had agreed to be Ike's official campaign manager.

"That's all right. Ike's the extrovert and the compromiser. Nixon can be tough and nasty—won't matter. We need Ike to appeal to independent voters. Nixon will be sure we don't lose Republicans along the way," Dewey replied. "By the way, Ike. Henry and I felt him out, and he's hungry for it."

Ike looked surprised, wondering why he hadn't been told before. Lodge jumped in. "Nixon will collect a lot of money in California. He's the first native son to run for national office since Hoover."

"Let's just be sure he *raises* the money without raising any bets," Dewey said, as he and the others shared a laugh.

"Is that story true?" Ike asked. "Did he bankroll his first race off poker winnings from his gambling when he was overseas?"

"That's the story. He played every night and made about six thousand bucks. Hey, he was a reserve officer. He handled cargo. I guess he had time on his hands."

Ike laughed. "That could be. Kind of strange to be a Quaker and a gambler, isn't it?"

"I've thought of him as a Quaker with a mean streak ever since he won his first congressional race by accusing his opponent, Voorhis, of taking contributions from Communist-controlled labor unions. That got him on the House Un-American Activities Committee and into that whole Hiss affair," Lodge said.

"That caused some ripples at Columbia," Ike said. "You know, Whittaker Chambers was a Columbia dropout."

"The Hiss case made Nixon. We wouldn't even be talking about him if it weren't for that. He'd be just another senator," Brownell added.

Ike had watched the televised hearings and remembered the case well. It began when Whittaker Chambers testified before HUAC that Alger Hiss was a Communist and spy for the USSR. Hiss, a Harvard-trained lawyer with square-jawed good looks, had clerked for Oliver Wendell Holmes, run the State Department policy office, and traveled to Yalta with FDR. By the time Chambers accused him, Hiss was a respected, retired statesman running the Carnegie Endowment. Chambers was short, pudgy, and pasty looking. He had fled a family with little means and many problems. He confessed to being a Communist and he insisted that Hiss was a traitor.

Alger Hiss had a simple response. He told the committee with perfect poise, "I am not and never have been a member of the Communist Party." He claimed that he "never laid eyes on" Chambers.

It was hard to forget the way Nixon stared at Hiss. Unlike his colleagues, Nixon didn't buy the story that Hiss didn't know Chambers.

"Didn't the end come for Hiss because of some strange bird?" Dewey asked.

"Right," Ike smiled. "It was the prothonotary warbler. It's got this little sharp beak and bright yellow head. Chambers told the committee that Hiss and his wife were amateur ornithologists and had seen a prothonotary warbler near Glen Echo, Maryland. Then, when Hiss testified, Nixon asked very innocently, 'What hobby do you have, Mr. Hiss?' When Hiss said 'ornithology,' this other congressman sort of gulps and says, 'Have you seen a prothonotary warbler?'" Ike laughed like he was about to deliver a punch line.

"And guess what Hiss says? 'I have!' he says, 'I have!' Nixon got him dead to rights, all right."

"That was a hell of a way for a fresh-faced congressman to bust into the national press," Dewey said with admiration.

"I guess he's a pretty good choice," Ike said, as Mamie walked into the room.

Adams looked at her. "You two couples will look good together," he said. "He's painted himself as the hardworking family man, and Pat's the perfect political wife, just like Mamie." He smiled at her.

"What are you talking about?" Mamie asked.

"What do you think of Dick Nixon for my running mate?" Ike replied.

"Well, I'm not sure . . ." Mamie hesitated, surprised that Ike had asked her opinion. "Maybe I shouldn't say this."

"I wouldn't have asked if I didn't want to hear what you have to say," Ike said irritably. He had his doubts about Nixon, but he didn't want to seem indecisive in front of his advisers.

"All right, Ike. I just don't like the man. There's something dishonest about him, I think. I just had the feeling, watching him talk about Hiss, that he would do anything to get ahead. He's not like you. Are you sure you can trust him?"

Ike turned away, as if he hadn't heard her, and Dewey tried to clear the air.

"Well, you remember what Cactus Jack Garner said about being veep: 'it's not worth a bucket of warm spit.' Uh, sorry, Mamie. Nixon can definitely help, and I don't see where he can do much harm."

"I trust your judgment, Tom," Ike said. "And, you're right, I'm the one who's supposed to be in charge. Can't see where he'll be much of a problem. But tell him to be sure to keep his nose clean."

"Right, we'll have a chat with him, then send him up here," Lodge said.

A short while later, Nixon was ushered into the suite. Ike stood ramrod straight waiting for him, his face a serious mask. Nixon had been working to calm the tremors that had seized him ever since Dewey gave him the news that the general wanted to see him. He understood what was about to happen. He rushed toward Eisenhower too eagerly, embarrassed by his own lack of decorum.

Ike offered his hand at the end of a straight arm, keeping Nixon at a distance as he approached. In a formal voice, he said, "Dick, I expect this campaign to be a crusade for what Republicans believe in. I am in it for the rights and values that America stands for. Will you join me in such a campaign?"

Nixon looked startled. He had expected the offer, but not the pretension.

"I would be proud and happy to," he said, feeling like he had stammered, even as his mind raced: *Is he rebuking me for some reason? He's taking me, but he doesn't really want me,* Nixon fretted to himself, as his cheeks flared with the force of his smile. *They just need California and a young face. He thinks he's better than me, damned puffed-out pigeon-faced old man.* Nixon's mind careened on into the potholes of his insecurities, even as he squeezed Eisenhower's hand and shook it with vigor.

"I'm glad you are going to be on the team, Dick. I think we can win, and I know that we can do the right things for the country," Eisenhower finished stiffly. He had been trying to take the measure of the man, but looking straight into Nixon's eyes, Ike's mind was filled with the echo of Mamie's words, "are you sure you can trust him?"

CHAPTER 7

Hogs on Ice

Val-Kill Cottage, Hyde Park, July 12, 1952

Maureen came into Eleanor's bedroom and saw that her boss had her small leather suitcase sitting open on the untouched bed. She realized that Eleanor must have slept out on the screened second-floor porch to catch what cool breeze might come along. That porch, overlooking the pond and woods beyond, was a favorite spot. Maureen knew Eleanor hated to leave it.

"Maureen? Maureen? Is that you?" Eleanor's voice came from the bathroom, and Maureen walked toward it. Eleanor was taking some powder and cream out of the medicine cabinet. Maureen found the room amusing. The cabinet and mirror, shelves, towel rack, and sink had all been raised to accommodate Eleanor's height, so that the whole room seemed off-kilter. Eleanor turned, an angry look on her face, and shook the compact in her hand at Maureen's face.

"Did you see the paper this morning? Did you? Good heavens, I have lost my respect for General Eisenhower. How could he pick that man?"

"You mean Senator Nixon," Maureen said. "I knew you would be upset."

"It's unspeakable. He could have chosen Earl Warren, or the other senator from California, Knowland. But Nixon? The man smeared his way into Congress. Does Ike think he won't do the same now? The general is proving more of a fool in politics than I guessed he would be. He's heading for the gutter with McCarthy by this route, mark my words."

"I'm sure Mrs. Douglas isn't happy," Maureen said.

"Well, she's gone back to acting, so losing the senate race to Nixon two years ago might not have been the worst thing. I did so want her to beat him after the way he went after her. I was out there, do you remember?"

"Oh yes, Mrs. R., I do remember. You sent me one of those 'Pink Sheets' they put out, all but calling her a Communist, and you had Katherine Hepburn sign it for me. She wrote, 'Dear Maureen, Nixon's a coward right down to his pink underwear.' And she underlined the word pink." Maureen laughed.

"I can't believe you remember what she wrote," Eleanor said. "Nixon had said Helen was 'pink right down to her pink underwear,' so that's why Kate wrote that."

"Oh, gosh. I never knew that. I just wish I could have met her. I saw *The African Queen* three times. She was so straitlaced, but then she was so *brave*. Hepburn takes the best roles."

Eleanor had walked back into the bedroom and put her little cosmetic bag in the suitcase.

"I agree, and she's been a great friend. Nixon was using every dirty trick in the book against Helen, and made up some new ones. He had his campaign workers walking up to perfect strangers and saying Helen was a Communist. Kate and I saw one young man with a Nixon button pigeonholing people, and you should have seen her swoop down on him with that furious face she can put on. But it didn't do any good. The night before the election they phoned thousands of homes just to say, 'Remember, Gahagan Douglas is a Communist.'" Eleanor paused and smiled at Maureen. "But Helen got the last laugh in a way. You know, she called him 'Tricky Dick' in one marvelous speech she made, and that name seems to have stuck." Eleanor closed her suitcase with a loud snap. "All right then, I'm ready to go."

"You haven't packed very much for two weeks," Maureen said, looking doubtful.

"Oh, I'm only going to Washington for a few days to speak with the president about the Universal Declaration of Human Rights. Then I'll be back here for little Eleanor's birthday party. So I'll have a chance to repack for my trip to Chicago. Oh, don't forget to arrange for the ponies and for Mr. Harrison to come as the clown."

"Already done, Mrs. R. Oh, but I forgot to tell you. Ruby Black called to say her daughter, Joan, is going to be covering the convention for the Associated Press."

"Like mother, like daughter," Eleanor smiled.

"Ruby covered you?"

"Oh yes. She was part of the original group of women who came to my press conferences, where I only allowed *women*."

"That seems brave."

"It was Lorena's idea. It was quite effective, and I made wonderful friends. Have Tommy tell you about it while I'm gone. She'd enjoy that. And put a note on my schedule to look out for Joan Black. If she's anything like Ruby, she'll be extraordinary."

* * *

Chicago, Illinois, July 21, 1952

A little more than a week later, as delegates gathered for the beginning of the Democratic Convention, the young woman Eleanor planned to meet was feeling anything but extraordinary. Joan Black sat in an overstuffed chair in the lobby of the Conrad Hilton Hotel. Every president since 1927 had strode through the Hilton's grand stair hall, under its heaven-is-in-reach pastiche of billowy clouds and rosy color that decorated the vaulted ceiling. All the Democratic bigwigs in town would be milling around, which was why Joan had chosen that spot.

The twenty-five-year-old reporter for the Associated Press alternately nursed a paper cup of coffee and an Old Gold cigarette as she looked over the scene. Straightening the razor pleats on her new tan skirt, she took a deep drag and tried to push the events of the previous night out of her head.

Once again, that smarmy Martin Cannady from the *Post-Dispatch* had too much whiskey and got obnoxious. Why couldn't she hang out with the other reporters at the bar in the Blackstone without being treated like a hooker? She had a policy of never dating any of them. It was hard enough to get any respect. But Cannady didn't want a date, anyway. She knew that. Once he had a few drinks, he just started waving around his room key and throwing his arm around her, trying to press his mouth to her ear. Joan's face burned as she thought about how she finally managed to push him off, and how, as she walked out, he called after her, "See you upstairs, honey?" The other men had laughed.

Joan's hand shook with anger, and she put the coffee cup down so hard that some of the bitter black liquid jumped over the side. "Oh, shit," she blurted out, as she grabbed the *Daily News* to blot the spill. As she pressed the newspaper on the table, her eyes fell on the front-page photo. A smiling General Eisenhower stood by a rushing river, a fly-fishing pole in his hand, and next to him, a tall, strikingly good-looking young man smiled for the camera as well. "The Republican nominee takes a break in Colorado" read the caption.

"Why don't I ever meet someone like that?" Joan said under her breath, looking at the young man next to Ike and tapping a long, newly manicured red fingernail on the picture. "I wouldn't even care if he was a Republican." She laughed to herself, wondering for a split second if what she'd said was true, then she ran both hands through her curly auburn hair in a way that made its red highlights stand out. "I need to either get to work, or go buy that pair of peekaboo pumps with the ankle straps that I saw in the window at Marshall Field's yesterday," she announced to the near-empty lobby.

What would be the best strategy, Joan wondered, for getting an exclusive interview, or at least the first shot at one of the candidates? Joan was only five feet tall. Even the highest heels couldn't make her tall enough to pop off a few questions before her mostly male competition could beat her to it. That's why she'd learned to stay ahead of the game.

Joan had begged her editor to let her cover the convention, hoping to push her way into political reporting, a spot usually reserved for the men. She wanted to do it on her own terms, not telling anyone at the paper of her background. She focused on Governor Stevenson, knowing his supporters were hoping for a draft of their man, and that he was giving the opening speech.

The previous evening, she had been at Stevenson's press conference. "I'm not qualified or equipped to be president," Stevenson had said.

"Who is?" Joan called out.

"Nobody but God is really equipped to be president," Stevenson replied.

"That's not what your supporters believe," Joan shot back. "They have a 'Stevenson for President Committee' set up on the fifteenth floor."

"I have not associated myself with that," Stevenson replied, looking uncomfortable.

But Joan knew Stevenson had talked to the group. She had gotten on hands and knees the night before, pressing her ear to the opening between the door and the floor of the Stevenson Committee suite when she saw the noncandidate go into the room.

"I do not dream myself fit for the job . . ." Joan had heard him say as she scribbled on the notepad she had set on the floor. "Please abide by my wishes not to nominate me, nor to vote for me should I be nominated," Stevenson had demurred.

Joan thought about General Sherman's line, "If nominated I will not run, if elected I will not serve." Stevenson hadn't quite said that. Was he being Shermanesque or just coy? Joan still wasn't sure, but she wasn't done trying to find out.

Looking around the lobby, Joan eyed the elevator in anticipation. Maybe a spot right next to those shiny brass doors was the best place to launch her attack. She walked over near one of the elevator girls, thinking that her uniform—black jacket, white shirt, knotted tie, shoulder epaulets, gray skirt, and black heels—made her look like a candidate for West Point. The girl looked at Joan expectantly, "What floor would you like, Miss?"

"Oh no, that's all right," Joan said as sweetly as she could muster so early in the morning. "I hope you don't mind me just waiting around here."

Joan's ploy worked. Just moments later, Stevenson came out of an elevator with several aides in tow. "Governor, Governor." Joan approached quickly and touched his arm. She could see the recognition in his eyes when he looked at her.

"Have you changed your mind, Governor? Will you accept a draft?" Joan pressed.

"Didn't I speak to you last night?" Adlai answered in a teasing tone, shaking his finger at her. Joan smiled.

"What's your name, young lady?"

"Joan Black with the AP."

"Black, Black. You wouldn't be related to Ruby Black would you?"

"Yes, I'm her daughter."

Adlai gave her a broad smile. "Well, I've had dinner with your mother at Mrs. Roosevelt's house. I'm not surprised to see she has such an intrepid and," Adlai winked, "attractive daughter. You have a bright future, Joan Black."

"Thank you, Governor, but about *your* future, now that the Republicans have nominated Eisenhower and Nixon, wouldn't you want to be the one to answer their charges that Democrats are corrupt and soft on communism?"

"I have been thinking that Democrats should make a proposition with our Republican friends . . . that if they will stop telling lies about the Democrats, we will stop telling the truth about them." Joan, and some other reporters who had gathered around, laughed as they took down Stevenson's words.

"That sounds like a candidate talking," Joan said smiling.

"Right now, I am going to give a welcome speech to the delegates of this great party of ours, that's all. You can quote me on that, Miss Black, and I do hope to see you again." Adlai held out his hand with formal courtliness, then walked out quickly to a waiting car.

Joan smiled to herself. She knew her editor would be pleased. A good day's work already and it wasn't even nine o'clock. She didn't even feel bothered when four of the seasoned pros from the dailies walked right by her and went into the Hilton's Lakeside Green cocktail lounge. She knew they saw her, but they never invited her to join them unless it was after hours when they had other things on their minds. She thought about crashing their little party, but decided she didn't need any more of last night's treatment so early in the morning. Why ruin what was starting out to be a good day?

The cocktail lounge had the stale smell of cigarette and cigar smoke that had nested for years in the flocked wallpaper, velvet upholstery, and oriental carpeting. The curtains were drawn and the lights dim. Other than the splinters of light that stole in at the sides of the windows, it could have been midnight rather than morning. The newsmen nursed cups of coffee, getting frequent refills and passing around a pack of Chesterfields. Edward Folliard of the *Washington Post* sipped his first scotch of the day.

"Shall we handicap the field, gentlemen?" James Reston of the *New York Times* asked.

"Well, Kefauver has to be the odds-on favorite. He won most of the primaries. But Truman's behind Averell Harriman," Folliard said, drumming his fingers on the table with nervous energy. "He's from New York and he was ambassador to Russia and Great Britain. He's got a government résumé as long as my arm, but, let's face it, he's never campaigned for anything."

"Yeah, then there's Bob Kerr," said Marquis Childs, Folliard's colleague at the *Washington Post*. "He's an effective senator, but a little too effective for the oil and gas interests in Oklahoma. He's in their pocket, and he doesn't even try to hide it."

"Dick Russell's got a good reputation—honest, fair, knows farm policy inside out . . ." Childs went on.

"But he's a segregationist," Reston cut in impatiently. "Since that mass lynching in Georgia in '46 and Truman's push for civil rights reform, things have gotten far too polarized for someone like him."

"What about Barkley?" Childs said. "He's a pretty popular vice president. If he weren't seventy-five, I think he'd be the favorite."

"Maybe," said Folliard talking fast, "but I hear labor thinks he's too old and that's the kiss of death, so to speak. Let's face it boys, the party may not like Kefauver, but the public likes his anticorruption theme."

"Are we so sure Stevenson won't jump in?" Reston said.

The others just shook their heads or threw up their hands with a chorus of "it's anybody's guess."

"Oh, hey, nobody's mentioned Mrs. Roosevelt," Folliard said, laughing, as he finished his drink and held his glass up for the waitress to see. "The *Post* ran a couple of letters encouraging her to get in the race. I think there could be a movement afoot."

"Even if that were half of a credible idea, she's not interested," Reston said.

"What makes you so sure, Scotty?" Childs asked.

"I know her. She was condemned during the war for serving in the Civil Defense Department with LaGuardia. Don't you remember how the Republicans went after her for cronyism? She doesn't have the stomach for playing politics like FDR did. She wants to keep saving the world . . ."

"And God bless her," Childs broke in.

"Doesn't matter anyway. This country would never elect a woman as president. Not a chance, even if that woman is Eleanor Roosevelt," Reston continued.

"True, true, but then again," Folliard said with a lascivious tone, "maybe some people wouldn't exactly see her as a woman, in *that* sense, if you know what I mean."

"Stop it, Ed. You really can be disgusting," said Childs. "Anyway, what about Rayburn? He may be Speaker of the House, but I think he's had this on his mind for a while. He sees a deadlock on the horizon, maybe a chance to jump into the gap."

"Mr. Sam," as Rayburn was often called, had turned seventy years old in January. He carried a lifetime of political battles in his head along with a bipartisan reputation for honesty, fair dealing, and taciturn toughness. He liked to tell young aides, "Son, always tell the truth. Then you'll never have to remember what you said the last time." He lived that advice, and became the most powerful Speaker of the House in history. Short, plain looking, and plain speaking, he came from the poor dirt of Bonham, Texas, but he'd sat with Franklin Roosevelt and helped save a country during the Depression and the Second World War.

"Well, the *Wall Street Journal*'s on it," said Reston, as he held up the paper and read, "'Speaker Sam is one of the better bets to cop the Democratic nomination.' So says Allen S. Otten."

"Well, here's to Speaker Sam," Folliard said, holding up his glass. "The Democrats could do worse, that's for sure."

The men who were toasting his chances of getting a presidential nomination had missed seeing the Speaker of the House that morning. Sam Rayburn had gotten up at 5:00 a.m. He wanted to arrive early at the International Amphitheatre at Halsted and Forty-third streets, where the convention would be held. As he stood in front of the full-length mirror smoothing his vest and carefully attaching his gold watch chain in the predawn hour, the Hilton was coming to life.

Taking up a city block across from Grant Park and Lake Michigan, the biggest hotel in the world had been refurbished in time to host the Republican Convention two weeks before. Chicago, Carl Sandburg's "hog butcher for the world," was also the "City of the Big Shoulders" for politics.

The Republicans had spared no expense when they commanded the Hilton. Chairman Guy Gabrielson had led his troops from the Royal Skyway Suite, the most expensive in the hotel at $110 a night. But Sam Rayburn didn't care for such pretensions. His suite was on the 13th floor, down the hall from the Democratic headquarters, and close to the three floors reserved for television and radio studios. He wanted easy access to the people who would be organizing the first nationally televised conventions.

Two thousand staff members were taking their posts in the early morning hours. Maids tied their aprons as they prepared to make up 3,500 beds; cooks' assistants lugged crates from the massive refrigerators, preparing to squeeze 7,500 oranges for fresh juice before the day was out; smartly uniformed elevator girls checked their stockings before taking the controls of the hotel's fourteen elevators to transport more than 100,000 people; and deep in the hotel's bowels where pipes hung hissing from the ceiling, squads of launderers sorted mountains of sheets, towels, and tablecloths for washing, drying, ironing, folding, and shipping throughout the Hilton's 79,000 square feet.

By the time Sam Rayburn walked through the grand lobby, the hotel was fully prepared for the demands of delegates, politicians, and dignitaries. The doorman greeted the Speaker by name as he held open the heavily paneled front door. Sam was surprised to see Strom Thurmond on the sidewalk, already waiting for his car.

"Good morning, Strom." Sam's hand was lost in the South Carolina governor's big grasp.

"We're the early risers," Thurmond drawled, deep vertical lines creasing his face as he gave Sam a big smile. "I suppose you have to be sure this convention goes just as easy as sliding off a greasy log backward, since you're in charge again."

Thurmond knew Sam would catch his irony. At the convention in 1948, Thurmond led a walkout of southern delegates in protest over the adoption of a civil rights plank. They started the States' Rights Democratic Party, the Dixiecrats, and held a separate convention that nominated Thurmond for president. "I wanna tell you, ladies and gentlemen," he had railed at the States' Rights delegates, "there are not enough troops in the army to force the southern people to admit the nigger race into our theaters, into our swimming pools, into our homes, and into our churches." His defection had almost cost Truman the election.

"I'm going to do my best Strom, but you know delegates can be as independent as a bunch of hogs on ice."

Thurmond chuckled without much humor. As Sam got into his car, he knew he had good reason to think that he had seen everything in politics, but he had a vague intuition that the next five days would surprise even him.

CHAPTER 8

The Hamlet of Politics

Karen Emmerson and Cate Gormley had grabbed seats at one of the front tables for the Women's Solidarity breakfast. They had arrived in town the night before, driving the three hundred plus miles from Traverse City, Michigan, in Karen's old panel-sided Chevy station wagon. They sang oldies from their high school days as they coasted down one side of Lake Michigan and around its tip through Gary, Indiana, where the rotten-egg smell of industrial waste chased them up to Chi-town. They headed straight to the Gayety Café where they were greeted by a banner across the front of the building that read "Playground for Conventioneers," in red, white, and blue. They found some of the other Michigan delegates at the back of the smoky, steamy bar watching a performer named Atlantis shed her clothes as she swam in a glass-fronted, water-filled tank. Over the jazz music of the live band, Karen eagerly joined in the debate that swerved from guessing Atlantis's next trick to debating the various candidates' chances to capture the nomination.

Karen had just turned thirty. Married for eight years, she had three children and a love of politics that came from her parents. Her dad was a union electrician, and her best memories with him were going to political rallies and stuffing envelopes at the union hall while the men argued over endorsements and which politician was the best friend of labor. She married Jim when he was home on leave in 1944. He'd been through the apprentice program and started working alongside her dad when he got back from the war. "Electricians are never out of work," her dad told her. Jim liked her to keep her hair bleached blond and long enough for a ponytail. He didn't like her leaving him with the kids, but her mom was pitching in, and she'd promised to call every night. She'd already broken that promise, but the convention was proving so much fun, she brushed any worries about Jim's annoyance from her mind.

Chicago still had the wide-open, anything-goes quality of the city that had been gateway to the West, and an amusement park for crime bosses. It was a place where a full-blooded, headdressed American Indian served coffee at the Porterhouse Room and a uniformed Nubian with a three-foot plume in his hat did the same at the Pump Room, a place where Miss Polly Shaw used parrots to pluck off her bra during the strip show at the Silver Frolics, and where delegates could pay fifty cents apiece to see the spot where John Dillinger was shot thanks to his betrayal by the "Lady in Red."

Delegates danced the night away to the music of Lawrence Welk's orchestra, and the most well-heeled ate at Henrici's, where the wooden racks were draped with fedoras. Perle Mesta, ambassador to Luxembourg was known as the "hostess with the mostess." Her party for the Rhode Island delegation was the most sought after ticket in town.

"Last night was the latest I've stayed out in about five years, and about the most I've had to drink in a really long time," Karen said, laughing and tipping her paper coffee cup against Cate's as they waited for the 7:00 a.m. meeting to get started.

"It sounded like complete chaos at my house when I called this morning," Cate said, looking worried. "Chuck couldn't get Judy to put her clothes on, and George was screaming, 'I hate first grade' at the top of his lungs. I'm sure Chuck was late getting Judy to day care, so he probably got to work late. I hope I didn't make a mistake coming with you."

"Don't worry. They'll survive. Of course, who knows what our houses will look like when we get back. Oh, look, that's India Edwards. I saw her on television last week. This is so exciting! We probably wouldn't be delegates at all if it weren't for her."

"Well, you're the delegate. I'm an alternate," Cate said, pointing to the spot on her badge just under the crossed American flags and white star where the word "alternate" had been stamped.

"Same difference," Karen waved her hand like she was clearing the air. "Delegate, alternate. We're here, right? The Democrats have six hundred women. The Republicans only had about three hundred fifty. That tells you something doesn't it?"

"Oh, look," Karen pointed at the stage and put her coffee cup down too hard as she stood up and started clapping.

"Good morning, ladies!" India Edwards's eyes were alight, and the tight curls on her head bounced as she seemed to dance toward the microphone, waving to friends, bending forward to talk to someone at the stage edge, and shaking hands with the other women dignitaries who were taking their seats behind her.

"I'm India Edwards, vice chairman of the Democratic National Committee and chairwoman of the Women's Committee, and I'm here to tell you to get set for the greatest woman act in political convention history!"

Women had started to stand as soon as she began speaking. Now the windowless room exploded with cheers and clapping. Three hundred metal folding chairs had been set around the round, cloth-covered tables, but women were already standing along the bunting-draped walls for lack of seats. Many women waved signs reading, "India for vice president."

India's smile broadened, "We have six women making major talks at this convention, including Mrs. Eleanor Roosevelt."

Still standing, the crowd went wild. Suddenly, a chant overtook the room: "Eleanor for president, Eleanor for president."

"We have women on every committee, and a woman is cochairing every committee," India continued. "Now, you may have heard that two weeks ago, there were only men on the Credentials Committee." Boos came from around the room.

"But not anymore. There are now *three* women on that committee. Ladies, we are not asleep at the switch. We have women everywhere so that we can be heard on every issue! We want the women of America to know that Democrats care about them and their concerns. The *Republicans* don't seem to care, of course," India affected a tone of outrage, "they only had four women speakers at their convention. They made a serious blunder when they failed to add any women when they increased the members of their National Committee. But are we surprised? "

"Noooo!"

India turned her palms up and lifted her arms up and down, encouraging the crowd's shouts.

"Now, some of you may remember that at the last convention there were beefsteaks and market baskets floating from balloons around the room, just to remind the men what we women have to deal with." Many of the women laughed and nodded their heads.

"Well, wait until you see what we have planned this time around! We're speaking to America's women, and we know they're listening. Our interviews and polls tell us to expect a *huge* turnout of women in this election, and we want them to vote *Democratic*!"

"Isn't she amazing?" Karen shouted to Cate over the din. "She's been talked about for vice president, you know."

"She is, she really is, but I just can't wait to hear Mrs. Roosevelt!"

Two hours later, the two women followed the horde of other delegates filing past the doorkeepers into the massive hall. Loudspeakers alternated patriotic music with the upbeat tunes of the times. Hank Williams's voice cut through the delegates chatter with "Hey, Good Lookin'," followed by a brass band version of the "Stars and Stripes Forever," followed by the silky voice of Patti Page delighting the Tennessee delegation with her version of the "Tennessee Waltz."

Karen and Cate had just found the long rectangular Michigan banner bobbing above the seats of their delegation, when Chicago's Mayor Kennelly walked to the bank of missile-shaped microphones pointed toward his head. He looked like a man who had been dragged into duty, and he quickly turned the podium over to Adlai Stevenson to give the official welcome.

The governor, dressed in a pinstriped suit and a blue silk tie adorned with white Democratic donkeys, walked down the stage that jutted into the audience like the prow of a cruise ship. It had been designed to allow television cameramen to pivot their equipment and catch every angle. Banks of white-hot glaring lights shone down from above the balconies, adding their heat to that of the crowded delegates. The air-conditioning system couldn't keep up. Men began shedding their suit jackets and loosening their suspenders. Women slipped off their heels and longed to take off their nylons.

But the rising temperature and deafening noise did nothing to diminish the delegates' enthusiasm for Stevenson. For a full six minutes, delegates waved "Stevenson for President" signs and "Don't Let Them Take It Away" placards, as the campaign song of the same name began to blare from speakers around the hall.

Adlai wiped his brow and took a sip of water, then waved and laughed and waved some more. The ovation went on. He cleared his throat, tapped on the mike, and raised his hands signaling the crowd to quiet down, but he was ignored.

"I thought . . ." he shouted into the mike. "I thought . . ." and the room began to settle. "I thought I came to welcome *you,* not you *me,*" and he smiled as the delegates laughed and cheering erupted again.

Adlai turned serious, looking down at the podium and not moving, and the delegates took the signal to quiet down.

"Here, my friends, on the prairies of Illinois and of the Middle West," Adlai intoned, "we can see a long way in all directions. . . . Here there are no barriers . . . to ideas and to aspirations . . . no shackles on the mind or spirit . . . no iron conformity." The applause and cheering rushed through the room, again forcing Adlai to pause for a moment, and then he continued, reviewing the triumphs of FDR and the New Deal, and recalling Roosevelt's first nomination for president twenty years before in the same city. Again, applause halted his address.

Sure of his purpose and his audience, Adlai's long face broke into a roguish grin. "Our Republican friends," he went on, "have said the New Deal was all a miserable failure. To them, two decades of progress by Democratic administrations were the misbegotten spawn of bungling, of corruption, of socialism, of waste, and of worse. They captured, they tied, and they dragged that ragged idea into this hall and they furiously beat it to death for a solid week. First the Republicans slaughtered each other, then they went after us. Perhaps the proximity of the stockyards accounts for the carnage." The crowd roared, and Adlai laughed along with them.

After congratulating the delegates on the work they were about to do, Adlai let his smile fade, and looked around the room before finishing his speech. "As the great Justice Oliver Wendell Holmes once said, 'We must sail sometimes with the wind, sometimes against it; but we must sail and not drift or lie at anchor.'"

The crowd rose as if following a conductor's baton, and again shouting and applauding filled the hall. James Reston had been making hash marks in his notebook. Stevenson had been stopped by the crowd's frenzied approval twenty-seven times. Reston scribbled a note that made it into his story in the *New York Times* the next morning: "Stevenson's been trying to talk himself out of the Democratic presidential nomination for the last five months, but he talked himself right into the leading candidate's role this morning."

"What the hell did that Holmes line mean, Adlai?" asked his close aide, Bill Blair, after Stevenson left the stage. "I mean, I'm glad you're taking a nice sail," Blair didn't try to hide his sarcasm, "but which goddamned way are you going?"

"I don't know, Bill," Adlai said wearily. "The presidency . . . I don't feel worthy, that's the truth. And being governor of Illinois should not be treated as a consolation prize, besides . . ."

"I'm sorry," Blair broke in, his voice tight with frustration, "the good people of our state will not walk around full of insulted indignation because you ran for president, for God's sake. Did you hear that crowd out there? They love you. They want you. What more do you want?"

"Keep your voice down, Bill," Adlai said, looking around nervously. "I wish I had the certitude of my friends, believe me. I can hardly sleep. My boys want me to stay in Illinois; their mother is off every night partying . . ." Adlai's voice trailed off with a bitter tinge as he referred to his ex-wife. He put his hand on Blair's arm. "Come on, Bill, stay by me. I need my friends. Let's see what unfolds. Who knows what the Almighty has in store for any of us."

"Well, I think the Almighty would be mighty happy to see you as president. That's what I think. But if you're waiting for a message from on high, so be it. Maybe you're right. Maybe that's exactly what it will take." He put his hand on Adlai's arm. "You know I'm with you. Whatever happens, I'll be there. That's a promise."

CHAPTER 9

Doubt

Eleanor arrived in Chicago the afternoon before her speech, which was scheduled for the last day of the convention. David had been there all week, and caught her up on the convention news as they had dinner in her suite at the Blackstone Hotel. She had sensed something distant in his manner from the moment she arrived, but tried to dismiss it. He hadn't made his usual jokes about a quick dinner to leave more time for other things, or surprised her, as he had done the day they saw the Taj Mahal, asking her to model a lovely new piece of lingerie he had spread seductively on the bed. Some nagging doubt tempered her keen interest in the backroom dealings that seemed to be moving the nomination toward her favorite, Governor Stevenson.

"So, Adlai's speech, you watched it, didn't you?" David said, as he cut a slice of prime rib. Eleanor nodded.

"That pushed him ahead of the pack. But Rayburn had a hell of a problem, especially with those television cameras making everyone want to grab the limelight. The southern delegations were just chomping at the bit, looking for an excuse to stage a walkout like in '48, but this time they would have the whole country watching."

David finished off his wine and pulled the bottle out of the silver cooler that stood next to the table. He gestured with the bottle as if to pour Eleanor some, but she put her hand over the glass. He filled his glass to the top and went on.

"The Harriman people forced a convention rule saying that all state delegations had to pledge their support of the party's nominees. It was aimed at the southerners, of course. So Virginia, South Carolina, and Louisiana refused the loyalty oath and just sat glued to their chairs, daring Rayburn to throw them out. Were you able to follow that on the television?"

"Not very well," Eleanor said, picking at her salad.

"Well, Rayburn knew that if the southern states walked out, Kefauver would take the nomination. Truman was livid."

"Yes, he called me," Eleanor said. "You know how he calls Kefauver 'Cowfever'? He said, 'We can't let Cowfever get it. You've got to do something about Adlai. He's our only hope.' I tried Adlai, but I couldn't reach him."

"Well, Rayburn stalled, and he got a breather with 'women's day,' when all the women spoke, except you, of course. You get the special spot." David patted her hand. "India put on quite a show, too. This time, she had baby carriages and blackboards floating on balloons over the delegates, and every pregnant delegate and guest came up onstage to hold a banner that said, 'Democrats Put Children First.'"

Eleanor nodded and smiled, more to herself than at David.

"Anyway, Stevenson cut a deal with the moderate southerners and got a watered-down version of the loyalty oath passed, which was a setback for Kefauver and Harriman. Then, after Russell, Kefauver, and Kerr were nominated, the clerk called Indiana, and Governor Schricker jumps up and says," David stood up and threw his shoulders back, deepening his voice and looking serious, "'Ninety-two years ago, the nation called from the prairies of Illinois the greatest of Illinois citizens, Abraham Lincoln. Lincoln too was reluctant. But there are times when a man is not permitted to say no. I place before you the man we cannot permit to say no, Adlai E. Stevenson of Illinois.' Or something pretty close to that, and the auditorium just went crazy."

"I did see that on television," Eleanor said. "It seemed like the cheering must have been deafening."

"Oh it was, it was, and the banners and signs went up like fireworks. Then we heard that the Missouri delegation had polled their members, and Truman's alternate had voted for Stevenson. Well, that was the sign the whole convention had been waiting for. If Truman was backing Stevenson, Adlai would just have to accept a draft."

"The president knew he would," Eleanor said.

"How do you know that?"

"Harry called me at Val-Kill. He had just hung up on Adlai."

"Hung up on him?"

"Yes, apparently Adlai called from Bill Blair's house and said to Harry, 'Mr. President, would you be embarrassed if I withdrew my objection to my name being put in nomination at the convention?'"

"He didn't!"

Eleanor couldn't help but laugh. "I know. After all Harry had done to try to get him to run, it was a silly thing to say, but I suspect Adlai was a bit embarrassed and didn't know how to put it."

"So, what did the president say?" David asked, leaning forward with a delighted look on his face.

Eleanor put on her best Missouri accent. "He said, 'Adlai, that's about the most damned foolish question I've been asked this year. I have been trying since January to get you to say that. Why would it embarrass me? What the hell took you so long? Just get out there and win this thing,' and then Harry just hung up."

They both laughed, and Eleanor hoped that she had only imagined any problem between them.

"So," David went on, "Rayburn kept the Dixiecrats on the floor, and he allowed in all twenty Louisiana votes, even though only two delegates had taken the pledge."

"That gave Adlai the momentum," Eleanor said.

"Yes, he's going to be nominated in the morning, right after your amazing speech, which I am quite sure *will* be amazing." David stood up, taking Eleanor's hand as he did and pulling her into his arms.

The next morning, Eleanor was putting on her powder, bending slightly to see her whole face in the bedroom mirror. She caught David's reflection as he sat in bed, reading the paper and taking sips from the china coffee cup that sat on the bed tray.

"By the way, I didn't expect to see you having a drink with Martha last night," Eleanor said as casually as she could.

"Martha Gellhorn?" David asked without looking up from the paper.

"Was there another Martha you had a drink with last night?"

David put the paper down. "We're still friends, dear. I was just a tiny fish on her after-Hemingway string. And that was a year ago. You know Martha. The men are falling at her feet as she runs toward covering the next story. Anyway, she's your friend too. I didn't expect you to arrive so early or I would have been waiting at the door of the suite with bouquets and convention news in my arms." He smiled and picked the paper up again.

"She is my friend." Eleanor wanted to let go, but couldn't. "Or at least I thought so. I was just surprised, with all the other people around, that just the two of you were having a drink, and . . ."

"Eleanor." David pushed himself up against the headrest, folding the paper and laying it on the bedside table. "Is there some problem you have with me talking to Martha? If there is, I promise, I won't even look at her again. I don't want to hurt you in any way. If she walks by, I'll close my eyes. I'll never see her again. I'll . . ."

"Oh, David, stop. I'm sorry." Eleanor turned away, busying herself with checking her handbag, but David's words had made the memory of that April day in 1945 erupt in her mind.

It was spring and she was at a charity luncheon when her driver came in with a White House trooper and whispered in her ear. "Mrs. Roosevelt, please come with us," was all he said, but she feared the worst, and the worst had come. Franklin was dead. It was a cerebral hemorrhage, swift and silent while he was trying to recuperate from the stresses of the war at the Little White House in Warm Springs, Georgia.

"Father is gone. Carry on as he would have you do," she wired the boys, thinking of them in uniform overseas trying not to weep when they read her words. She had told Harry the terrible news, then rushed south.

She remembered how the garden seemed filled with promise as the car pulled up the driveway to the cottage. The roses, trained up against the south front corner, were just in bud. Birds whistled and chirruped their high spirits, already building nests at the top of the white pillars on the front porch. She thought she heard the high-pitched "cheep-cheep" of babies calling for food from one of the tangled, woven bunches of twigs and garden debris. Honeysuckle was heavy as mist in the air. Its smell would never cheer her again.

Inside, only cousins Daisy and Laura were waiting. "Please tell me about Franklin's last moments," she had asked so innocently, so unaware, as she motioned for them to sit by her.

"He seemed tired, but in fine spirits, Eleanor," Daisy had spoken first. "He was signing some papers. It was very sudden; he said he had a pain in his head and he put his hand to his temple like this and then . . ." She couldn't speak through her sobs and Eleanor put her arm around her and looked at Laura.

"Oh, Daisy's told you most of it, but . . ." Laura hesitated and Eleanor looked quizzical.

"Eleanor, I think you should know. I mean, Franklin was having his portrait painted by Elizabeth Shoumatoff. She was painting him at the desk while he was working, and . . ." she stopped again, looking over at the window seat and biting her lip. Daisy looked at her in horror, shaking her head and making soft sobbing sounds.

"And, Elizabeth came because . . ." she stopped again, and then went on in a rush, "because Lucy Mercer Rutherford brought her. She was sitting right there," Laura pointed at the window seat, "when he fainted. And, and, she had been seeing him. Your daughter, Anna—Anna had been arranging for them to see each other in Washington. When you were away, of course. Oh, I'm sorry, Eleanor, I'm terribly sorry, but I thought you should know. I thought it would be best if you . . ."

Eleanor remembered that she stood up as if someone had yelled "fire," feeling her leg hit the coffee table with a sharp jab. Her mouth seemed frozen shut, her eyes frozen open. She clenched her hands in front of her and walked into the bedroom, closing the door behind her.

Franklin's body lay on the near side of the double bed, stiff and still on top of the white spring coverlet. His withered legs inside his trousers, useless for so many years, looked like a child's compared to the bulk of his upper body. A small bowl of cherries was on the bedside table nearest him, a few pits, dried to a deep crimson, had been cast randomly on the wood of the nightstand.

She walked to the far side of the bed. The small fringed lamp on the nightstand had been pulled close to the edge, as if someone wanted to throw more light on that side of the bed. A slim book lay closed, its cover the color of the neat pile of cherry pits that sat in the china ashtray next to it. She picked up the book, running her finger along the gold leaf as she read the binding: Robinson's *Tristram*. Her heart jumped. Franklin had given her the first edition the year before he ran for governor in 1928. They had read it together on languid afternoons from Springwood's terrace, the Hudson flowing steady and serene in the distance. Was that the last time she had felt truly close to him? The last time they had shared something beautiful and intimate that spoke of love? She opened to the page holding a thin leather marker that was painted with a bright yellow Carolina jasmine. In a whisper, she read the passage marked by a tiny star, and as she did, the tears began to stream down her face as if drawn to the pages she held,

> *He saw dark laughter sparkling*
> *Out of her eyes, but only until her face*
> *Found his, and on his mouth a moving fire*
> *Told him why there was death, and what lost song*
> *Ulysses heard, and would have given his hands*
> *And friends to follow and to die for. Slowly, at last . . .*

She closed the book softly, unable to read any more.

"I'll never see Lucy again." That's what Franklin had told her so many years before. She had believed, and been deceived again for her believing. She felt weak with longing for what might have been. Standing at the foot of the bed, she held the walnut footboard with both hands for several minutes, waiting for her spirit to calm, her heart to stop racing. Then she gave her husband the last gift she had left to give, her voice steady, as if he could hear every word, "Franklin, I know that I have been only one of those who served your purposes, and I forgive you. 'Now faith, hope and love abide, these three,' Franklin," she paused, swallowing hard, then finished in a whisper, "'but of these the greatest is love.'"

As she fumbled in her handbag, hiding her face from David, she touched her fingers to the verse from Corinthians. She had carried it with her since that April day.

"Eleanor?" David could tell she was lost in thought. "Eleanor, you're not really angry, are you?" He rose as he spoke and put his arms around her from behind, squeezing her body against his.

Eleanor turned in his cocoon and kissed him lightly on the lips.

"I'm quite all right, but I must go. Meet me backstage. I'd like you to be there when I finish my speech, alright?" and she gave him a quick smile.

As Eleanor came out of her suite, a young woman with a notepad stood up quickly from her seat against the hall wall.

"Mrs. Roosevelt." Without waiting for an answer she held out her hand. "I'm Joan Black . . . Ruby Black's daughter and . . ."

Eleanor had looked vaguely annoyed, but now she broke into a warm smile.

"How is your mother?"

"She's quite well. Thank you. She's writing her memoirs." Joan smiled at the genuine interest Eleanor showed. "I'm following in her footsteps, Mrs. Roosevelt. I'm reporting for the AP, trying to get the political beat. I was hoping you might give me an interview."

"Well, we can walk and talk. I must get to the hall, and after my speech, I'm afraid I'll be leaving rather quickly."

"That's fine, thank you," Joan answered.

"What would you like to ask?" Eleanor said, as she started off toward the elevator. Joan, pen in hand, struggled to keep up with Eleanor's long, purposeful strides, the strides that on this day would carry her to the greatest decision of her life.

CHAPTER 10

"Mrs. FDR Stops the Show"

Chicago, Illinois, July 1952

Eleanor stood backstage, shaking hands and casting furtive glances down the long passage she had taken to get to the chaotic scene behind the convention curtains. David should have been here by now, she thought, worried that he might have been stopped by security. Perhaps she should go back and see. No, there wasn't time. She was scheduled to speak any minute.

"Mrs. Roosevelt? Mrs. Roosevelt?" a young man whose pin read "usher" was holding a glass of water and looking nervous.

"Mr. Rayburn said I should see if you would like some water. It will be just a few minutes more," he said. "Do you need anything?"

"Oh, thank you, I'm fine. But would you mind walking down to the stage entrance in back and being sure that a Dr. Gurewitsch is allowed in? Thank you so much."

A moment later, the band began playing the theme from FDR's presidency, "Happy Days Are Here Again," and Eleanor could hear the cheering and chanting from the other side of the grand drape, its royal blue velvet shivering as the cheers grew louder.

"It's time, Mrs. Roosevelt," another usher walked up and took her by the elbow, as if to escort her down the aisle, but as she stepped past the teaser curtain, he stayed behind. The hall seemed to levitate with joy as she walked to the podium. Frank McKinney stood at the microphone, ready to introduce her, but he made no attempt to gavel the crowd into silence. As she reached him, waving and smiling to the crowd that was mostly hidden from her by the intense glare of the lights, he shouted in her ear.

"Let's let this go on a little. It's good for them to feel united again after all we've been through the last few days."

"Of course," Eleanor cupped her hand next to her mouth and shouted back to him. Besides, she thought, it's electrifying television, not like all those awfully boring speeches the Republicans gave. Eleanor beamed and waved, bending over so far when she recognized someone standing near the edge of the stage that the audience could see the top of her round, flowered hat pinned firmly to her hair. She wore a bright red patterned short-sleeve dress, with a giant cream-colored cattleya orchid corsage pinned at her left shoulder. Even in the hall with the mixing smells of smoke and food and more than two thousand people, she could catch the orchid's strong sweet scent when her head bent the right way.

The International Amphitheatre walls might have cracked from the noise, but finally, banging his gavel, McKinney shouted, "Will the delegates please take their seats." Bang! He slammed the gavel down like a giddy child smashing caps. "Please, please, take your seats, my friends. There are several million people waiting to hear the First Lady of the World speak at our convention."

McKinney stepped aside, and Eleanor moved squarely in front

of the jumble of microphones, adjusting the center one slightly as the room hushed.

"This demonstration is not for me," she began. "This demonstration is for the memory of my husband." Her voice, familiar from so many radio programs and years of speeches in every corner of the nation, reminded Democrats of their best days. These were her people and Franklin's. She was their conscience, the reminder of all that had been great in America and the hope of greatness to come.

"Our president has asked me to speak of the United Nations, which as you know, was the great dream of my husband and me. United . . . Nations." She paused between the two words, emphasizing each of them. "There is a small, articulate minority who want the United States to withdraw from the UN, but with the UN, we do not walk alone but instead are traveling in good company with men and women of goodwill in the free countries of the world. The UN is still the chief machinery in existence for the realization of man's hope for peace. Its destructive critics offer nothing in its place. Perhaps the challenge of today is to recognize the historic truth that we can no longer live apart from the rest of the world. . . . We are the leading democratic nation of the world, a nation which all the world watches. . . . We have a difficult job because all of our failures are seen."

She paused, deepening her voice and looking stern. "And, my friends, we may be facing a *great* failure if we continue to tolerate the intolerable tactics of Senator McCarthy. We would condemn ourselves to an endless struggle for survival in a jungle world." At the mention of McCarthy, delegates began jumping to their feet, stamping and clapping at Eleanor's rebuke.

"At the same time," Eleanor went on, "our successes are seen as well. It is because of those successes, that, as chairman of the Human Rights Commission, I was able to find enough good sense and goodwill among the other delegates to draft and pass the Universal Declaration of Human Rights." At the mention of the document that had just been finalized that spring, another spontaneous round of cheering broke out.

"My friends, we have accomplished much since Franklin and I first came to the White House in 1933, but we have much more we can do working together at home and abroad. For that reason, I hope we are going to be strong enough, and imaginative enough, and take the future with enough spirit of adventure so that we will live it with joy," her smile beamed into the cameras as she finished, "yes, live it with joy and never grow hopeless. Thank you."

Eleanor raised both arms high above her head and waved her hands, as the frenzied cheering rose until there was no possibility of any one person being heard. Finally, she walked offstage, where a dense crowd of well-wishers greeted her. But as she looked around, David was nowhere in sight.

"Eleanor, can you stay for the first vote on the nominees?" Rayburn was at her elbow, his face pink from the heat and excitement.

"No, Sam, I'm sorry. I have to get to the airport."

"Could you walk out through the hall then? The delegates can't get enough of you."

Eleanor walked down the stage steps and into the maelstrom of the convention floor, shaking hands, smiling, and trying to push thoughts of David from her mind. Suddenly, Agnes Myer grabbed her arm, forcing her to stop. Myers's husband had owned the *Washington Post* newspaper. Agnes was a political force in the party and a formidable activist who hadn't always been on the Roosevelts' side. "You really saved the day for political women, Eleanor," she said as if making a pronouncement. "You've let the women of the country know that it's possible to be a woman and a lady and thoroughly political. They won't forget."

"Thank you, Agnes. I hope you're right," Eleanor replied.

"I know I'm right, Eleanor. If more women had your political talent, we would have a woman on the ticket."

"India's been mentioned for vice president," Eleanor said over her shoulder as she moved from Agnes's grasp toward the door.

Rayburn had retaken the rostrum and was calling for the first vote on the nominees even before Eleanor had made it out of the auditorium. "I'll get the results once I'm back in New York," she thought. She just wanted to get home. She just wanted to know what had happened to David.

Watching from the gallery, Joan caught glimpses of Eleanor as the delegates pressed around her, and then she scrambled to find a phone to call in her story. She had been the only reporter to interview the former First Lady before she addressed the convention. She would use what she'd gotten to lead into her report of Eleanor's amazing speech. "The greatest ovation of any speaker at either convention," Joan had jotted in her notebook as she watched the frenzied scene on the convention floor. She could just imagine the next day's headline: "Mrs. FDR Stops the Show."

CHAPTER 11

A Touch of Destiny

When the convention reconvened at 7:00 p.m., a letter from Averill Harriman was read saying that he was dropping out of the race and throwing his support to Stevenson. As they stood under the elongated, three-sided sign for the Michigan delegation that stretched ten feet high, Karen and Cate started screaming and hugging each other.

"That's it. That's it," Karen yelled. "With New York's votes, Stevenson's got it!"

Cate started singing, "'You must take the A Train, to go to Sugar Hill way up in Harlem,'" and Karen joined in. The women locked arms and did their best Ella Fitzgerald imitations, as the other delegates clapped, bouncing to the rhythm and singing along.

As Stevenson waited backstage with the president, Rayburn called for the third ballot roll call. After more speeches accompanying the votes cast by each state, the delegates from the tiny state of Utah put Stevenson over the top. As if a conductor had swung his baton, the speakers began blaring Stevenson's campaign song, "Don't Let Them Take It Away." Karen jumped onto a chair, hoisting her "Stevenson for President" sign as high as she could, and singing along.

Behind the stage curtain, Stevenson held a tentative smile, shaking hands all around as the tumult grew on the convention floor.

"Are you ready?" a jubilant Truman asked, pumping Adlai's hand and pointing toward the noise. Adlai nodded as he turned to Bill Blair, who handed him a sheaf of papers and patted him on the back. "I told you I'd be with you," Blair said, smiling with encouragement.

The delegates cheered wildly, pumping their Stevenson signs as Truman strutted to the microphones to introduce the nominee. "You've nominated a winner," he yelled, squinting into the glaring lights, "and I'm going to take off my coat," and with grand histrionics, he pulled off his suit jacket, "and campaign hard for him . . . I give you the next president of the United States . . . Governor Adlai Stevenson of Illinois!"

Adlai's head was down, as if he was in his own world in the midst of the tumult. Blair gave him a light tap and pointed toward the opening in the curtain. As he stepped out, the cheering rose like the fury of a tornado gaining strength. Adlai felt buffeted by the noise, the rising and subsiding waves made his heart race, and he unconsciously reached inside his suit jacket and patted his chest. The hall looked surreal with the haze of cigarette and cigar smoke illuminated by the high, bright lights so that a gray mist seemed to shroud the scene.

Stevenson began to walk with his odd waddling gait onto the runway and toward the podium. Drops of sweat blossomed on his high bald forehead as the sunlike heat of the television lights beat down with merciless intensity. He looked ill at ease, barely managing a smile, and swiped at his head with a handkerchief he pulled from his pants pocket.

"He looks kind of stunned," Karen said, laughing.

"Well, how would you feel?" Cate replied. The Michigan delegation was one of the closest to the stage, but the two women had pushed forward into the crowd that ringed the runway just behind the television cameramen and photographers who hogged the perimeter. Karen held her sign aloft, trying not to bang other delegates in the head.

"Look, look up," Karen said, pulling on Cate's sleeve. Hundreds of wildly dancing red, white, and blue balloons had been released into the air above the crowd. As the women looked back toward the stage, they saw that Stevenson had paused halfway down the long walkway. He looked toward Truman, who stood beaming next to the rostrum, his hand extended toward the nominee.

"Look at his eyes," Cate said, her voice sounding concerned. "He looks sort of glazed over or something."

Stevenson's eyes seemed to grow wider and he looked over Truman's head into the distance.

"What's he looking at?" Karen said, turning her head to look up and beyond the sea of delegates.

Stevenson started to take another step. He held his speech in front of his body with his left hand, and he seemed to try to raise his right, perhaps to wave. But instead, his arm flopped to his side, his mouth opened, perhaps in a gasp, though it was too noisy to hear, his knees buckled, and he crashed forward to the carpeted floor, his head making a dull thud that sent a small vibration through the planking. He lay absolutely still, the handwritten papers of his acceptance speech still clutched in his fist.

"Oh my God, oh my God." Karen grabbed Cate's arm. The two women strained to see Stevenson, who was instantly surrounded as he lay unmoving on the runway's rough blue carpet. Truman reached him first, kneeling by the governor's side and calling for help as he pressed his finger to Stevenson's neck, trying to find a pulse. Bill Blair had sprinted from the main stage, as had two security guards. The television crews and photographers struggled to clamber onto the runway with their equipment, balancing perilously near the edge as they tried to capture the scene.

Throughout the hall, cheers turned to gasps and sobs, coming in odd counterpoint to the campaign tune that still blared from the speakers. Karen and Cate were pinned shoulder to shoulder as the crowd surged forward, dropping placards and stumbling over chairs as they struggled to see what had happened. Pushing their way through the gawkers, police and paramedics formed a squad around Stevenson's unmoving body.

"Can you see anything?" Karen said to Cate in the loud mumble-filled drone that had fallen over the hall once the music stopped. "I can't see a thing."

"Me either, just a bunch of suits. Oh, look back there, there's a stretcher they're trying to bring out. Those people should move out of the way," she said angrily.

"Has he moved at all?" Karen asked.

"I don't think so," Cate said quietly, and her voice caught with a sob. "How could this be happening? I can't believe it."

"Well, maybe it was from the heat or something," Karen said, sounding unconvinced. They stood watching in silence with the rest of the delegates, who seemed frozen in a tableau of shock. High above, hundreds of bright balloons floated unmoored in a now gaudy and forlorn display.

Truman stood up and backed away to make room for the medical crew, but Bill Blair wouldn't budge.

"Adlai, Adlai," he whispered, bending close to the frozen face and ignoring the tears streaking his cheeks. As Stevenson was placed on a stretcher, his ashen face set like stone, Blair thought about the conversation they had had just days before about the *Washington Star* publisher, Alicia Patterson.

"Alicia's been tenacious as a wolverine about my running for president, but I'm not ready to give her an absolute commitment. What do you think of this, Bill?" Blair remembered how Adlai had held up the letter, then noticed an ink smudge on his finger, wiping it off on his shirt before he began reading, " 'If there's a touch of destiny about the draft business, Alicia, then I will not thwart it.' "

"I don't believe in destiny, Adlai. I believe in decisions," Bill remembered saying to his friend. But as he walked alongside the stretcher, pushing people out of the way, he wondered if he had been wrong.

After Stevenson was carried out, the delegates milled around the floor, reluctant to leave and miss any news about his condition. Finally, a Rayburn aide came to the podium.

"Ladies and gentlemen, the chairman will be here in a few minutes to address the delegates," and the young man quickly walked off the stage.

"What does that mean?" Cate said.

"They're probably going to say he needs to rest tonight and he'll address us tomorrow," Karen answered. She had pulled out a compact and was looking at her face.

"My eyes look like I painted them red. So do yours," she said looking at Cate.

"I don't care. I just want the governor to be all right. That's all I want right now."

An hour later, Rayburn stood at the podium, his face somber, and deep lines etched between his eyes.

"My friends, I am the one who must tell you," his voice betrayed the slightest crack, but he tightened his grip on the sides of the podium and went on, "that Governor Adlai Stevenson is gone." He paused as the room shattered with loud sobs and gasps. "He died instantly from a massive heart attack. I know you join me in mourning the passing of this great statesman and our nominee for president. Our tributes will come in due time, but I must ask you to plan to return tomorrow morning as this convention must finish its business. God rest Governor Stevenson's soul and bless us all. Thank you." Rayburn dropped his head and relaxed his hold on the podium, standing in that pose for a moment as camera bulbs flashed. Then he turned and marched off as the delegates began a somber retreat from the amphitheater.

The next morning, Nicholas Georgieff's poignant photo covered newspaper front pages across the country. He had captured a shirtsleeved, stricken Truman kneeling next to the fallen candidate with the faces of shocked delegates in the background, including that of Karen in her Uncle Sam hat with her "America Needs Stevenson" sign still upright in her hand. The image would win Georgieff a Pulitzer Prize and remind Democrats for generations to come of the most tragic moment in convention history.

CHAPTER 12

The Least Bad Choice

Eleanor knew nothing of the terrible turn of events. She had left the Blackstone as quickly as possible after finding a note from David explaining that he had a patient with a medical emergency at Blythedale Children's Hospital and had to fly back to New York. She had been sitting in Midway Airport for three hours because of a delay in her flight, willing herself to believe that David had told her the truth, trying to stop thinking about whether she had seen Martha Gellhorn in the press gallery during her speech, or perhaps afterward. She was sitting at a table in the Cloud Room, Marshall Field's fine-dining restaurant in the airport's new terminal. As Eleanor watched airplanes come and go, a well-dressed woman and a little fair-haired girl of about five years old approached her.

"Mrs. Roosevelt, I'm sorry to disturb you, but I wanted my daughter to meet you."

Eleanor smiled at the woman. "I'm pleased you came over, Mrs. . . ." Eleanor held out her hand.

"Dorothy Rodham. And this is my daughter, Hillary. Say hello to Mrs. Roosevelt, Hillary. She was First Lady of the United States. She was married to the president of the United States, Franklin Roosevelt."

Eleanor held out her hand, and the little girl took it.

"How do you do, Mrs. Roosevelt. Are you a Republican or the other kind?" she asked, looking earnest.

Eleanor's smile broadened. "I'm the other kind, dear."

"Oh." The girl frowned. "My daddy doesn't like the other kind."

Eleanor laughed, and Dorothy Rodham looked slightly embarrassed.

"Mrs. Roosevelt, I just want to thank you for your work at the United Nations, and all you continue to do for our country. I'm sorry to have disturbed you. Come along, Hillary."

"I'm pleased you said hello. Now wait just a minute." As she spoke, Eleanor rummaged in a convention bag she had on the seat next to her.

"Here," Eleanor said, handing Hillary an "Adlai for President" button. "I was bringing these home to my grandchildren, but there's one for you. I'm not sure you should show it to your father, though." Eleanor looked at Mrs. Rodham, and both women shared a conspiratorial laugh.

After another hour, apologetic officials from United Airlines told Eleanor that her flight was indefinitely delayed. They might have a flight later in the evening, or would she like a ride back to her hotel? She decided to go back to the Blackstone and wait for the proceedings to conclude. On the ride back, she heard that the tide was turning for Stevenson. After getting to her suite, she turned to her correspondence and finished her "My Day" column on the convention. She'd been writing the six-day-a-week column, a kind of diary for the nation, since 1935. More than a hundred newspapers carried it. An urgent knocking interrupted her. When she opened the door, she saw McKinney's aide, the young man who had offered her the water backstage at the amphitheater. He looked out of breath, his hair tousled, and his eyes red.

"Why, what is the matter?" Eleanor asked without preliminaries.

"Mrs. Roosevelt." He swallowed hard, struggling to catch his breath. "We just heard you were in the hotel. You must come to the party's suite right away. Something terrible happened to Governor Stevenson." He paused, putting his arm on the doorjamb and dropping his head.

"What happened?" Eleanor asked sharply.

"He collapsed. On the stage. They took him in an ambulance . . . I . . . I . . . we don't know . . ."

Eleanor had heard enough. Grabbing her key from the desk, she headed for the elevator.

Party leaders had gathered in the headquarters' suite at the Hilton, its air stale despite an air conditioner laboring loudly in the window. The room, crowded with chairs, placards, and the detritus of late nights spent plotting, eating, and drinking now seemed ghostly. Rayburn had just returned from the convention hall where he had conveyed the terrible news.

"We need a day, we need a day," Paul Dever, the governor of Massachusetts groaned, punching the last word as if he could stretch time if he banged on it hard enough.

"Of course, it's respectful to wait a day, and perhaps we need the time to strategize, but it may not be possible. It's Friday night. We can't hold the delegates until Sunday. Other conventions are already arriving in town," said Rayburn, looking at President Truman.

Rayburn, who had kept good order as convention chairman, was thinking of the hours of speeches from the eleven candidates, the battles over the loyalty pledge, taming the maverick Dixiecrats, and the fractious discontent of Democrats in one big room. His instincts told him they had to move fast and hope for unity out of respect for Adlai.

"One thing's for sure, we can't start over," Rayburn went on. "We couldn't find a compromise with the candidates we had and we won't find one now. We need someone the convention can rally around in this time of sorrow . . . and fast." Rayburn sensed that this could be his moment, but he felt terrible for having such thoughts.

"I agree," Frank McKinney, the party chairman spoke up with force. "All the same arguments apply: Estes Kefauver's too liberal; coonskin cap and Tennessee roots or not, he's made too many enemies. We all love Vice President Barkley, but he hasn't gotten any younger since yesterday."

"The presidency would kill him in three months," Truman cut in. "It takes him five minutes to sign his name," he added sadly.

"Averell Harriman's got New York, but that's it," McKinney continued. "He's a Wall Streeter without political experience."

"Well, Russell's a segregationist and Kerr's from the great state of Oil and Gas, and there's no votes there," Dever shot back. "What about our Speaker? Sam, I know you've had some support growing in the delegations."

"I suppose I have . . ."

Truman cut in. "Doesn't work, Sam. I'm sorry. Who was the last Speaker who became president?" he asked rhetorically. "You've had to cut too many deals, appease the special interests, and you've made too many enemies. It's the nature of the job, Sam. You're a hell of a Speaker. The best we've ever had in my opinion, but it won't work to have you run. I just don't see how we can do that. Just don't see it."

No one spoke for a moment. Sam's head hung, as if he was thinking hard. Finally he said, "I don't disagree, Mr. President. I'm not sure I'd want it this way, anyway."

"Gentlemen," McKinney said wearily, pausing and looking slowly around the room, finally landing his gaze on India Edwards, vice chairman of the party and head of the women's division. "India has a proposal and I'm inclined to agree, although it's a long shot, it may be the only shot."

Edwards had been loyal to Truman, and the linchpin in placing women in top administration jobs, including the first woman ambassador, Eugenie Anderson, in Denmark. Edwards had arranged a campaign school for women at the convention telling reporters, "If women are interested in politics, they have a duty to prove it by talking about something besides what their husbands eat for breakfast." On a nod from McKinney, Edwards held up the *Time* magazine that featured Eleanor.

"This is the third time she's been on the cover, gentlemen. She might be more recognizable than Ike, and that's saying a lot. I know you're all aware that there have been attempts to draft Eleanor over the years, but this year there was a lot more noise than you might have realized. She has a great deal of popular support..."

"India, just a minute." Dever's voice was pitched just shy of a shout.

"No, Paul, you wait a minute," India shot back with some heat.

"Paul, let her finish," Truman said quietly.

"Appointing her to the UN was a stroke of genius by our president," India went on. "She is beloved around the world for chairing the commission that passed the Universal Declaration of Human Rights. No one can question her foreign policy experience, and the country wants a diplomat in the White House."

"I'm sorry, Mr. President," Dever said, "I have to speak up here. The Korean war is the hottest issue out there. The public expects action, not talk. Get out, get further in, but do something. Eisenhower's a general, for God's sake. The public will totally trust him on Korea. He'll walk all over her on that issue alone."

"Whatever you can say about Eleanor," Truman replied, "she

won't be walked over," and his mouth turned in a small, knowing smile.

Rayburn had been listening intently. "Paul, you're right about the public wanting a resolution in Korea, but I believe Eleanor can handle that. She's seen war, two great wars, and she can echo FDR as I've heard her do: she hates war. But let's talk winning the election. She takes the family issue away from Ike and Nixon. Let's face it, Adlai's divorce was already starting to play badly. I think women are going to be a big force this time, and Eleanor will pummel the Republicans there. Labor and civil rights groups will go to the mat for her."

"Yes, and the Dixiecrats will have the whole South walk out with them as soon as we put her name in nomination," Dever said glumly.

"A lot of people hate her, Sam," McKinney added, "and some for no other reason than the fact that she's a woman. That's the plain truth."

"It's true people hate her," Sam replied, "and our main job may be keeping her alive. I've seen that woman dodge the Secret Service like the plague, but the ones who hate her would have hated Adlai as well. Hell, I think she might have a better chance than he did, and the truth is . . . we don't have much choice. And we can't change the fact she's a woman."

"Sam's right. We don't have much choice. At least Eleanor will do a great job in carrying the Democratic message. We know that. Can she win? Well, hell, maybe nobody can beat the general," Truman said.

"You're right, Mr. President," Dever said. "I think the only other choice would be to nominate Ike ourselves and throw in the towel."

"That's absurd," India Edwards exploded. "We're Democrats, for God's sake . . ."

Just then, the door opened and Eleanor walked in. Everyone

turned to her, and she could almost feel the beating of the grieving hearts in the room, or perhaps it was just her own. For a moment, the room fell silent, and then Truman spoke.

"Eleanor, all of us loved Adlai, but none more than you. We are so sorry. He was the best of men."

She had suspected the worst; now it was confirmed. Her friend was gone.

Eleanor sat down next to India, clearly struggling to compose herself. After a few silent moments, she spoke.

"It's a tragedy for us all, Harry, a terrible tragedy." Then, calling on the hard-won ability to conquer her emotions, Eleanor said heavily, "We've survived such things before. We have no time for mourning at the moment. We're facing an unprecedented situation. Have you decided anything?"

McKinney shuffled some papers on his lap, and cleared his throat. "Eleanor, we have had a discussion, and we have a proposal that is unanimous." He shot Dever a warning look. "India, could you take it from here?"

India gave a quick nod to McKinney, and raised a letter she had folded in her lap, which she began to read:

"'Dear Mrs. Edwards, I am writing for a group of housewives here on Long Island to tell you that we are ready to start a movement to draft Eleanor Roosevelt for president. We think she is the only Democrat who could surely defeat General Eisenhower.'" Shaking her head from side to side, Eleanor interrupted, "India, we've been over this. I told you that I won't run. I didn't think there was any chance for a woman yet, and I still don't."

But Edwards charged ahead, a woman on a mission.

"Eleanor, this isn't the only letter. There are hundreds, from all over the country, even the South. Everyone knows you supported Adlai. You'll be carrying his torch, and Franklin's. You're the most admired woman in the world, look at the Gallup polls. You can match Eisenhower's fame and stature. And it will give you a chance to really fight McCarthy." Edwards's appeal was calculated. She had heard Eleanor say more than once that McCarthy was the greatest threat to democracy of their time. Edwards stopped for breath, and Truman spoke up.

"Eleanor, it's a risk, but I believe it's one we have to take. We can't refight this nomination. We don't have the heart or the will after this horrible tragedy. The delegates will support you; you heard them yesterday. They know how close you and Adlai were. . . ." He paused and looked down. The room filled with the stiff silence of people who seemed to be holding their breath. Then the president looked straight at Eleanor with that give-'em-hell-Harry look. "You know Franklin would want this, Eleanor. You know darn well . . . if he were here, he would tell you to run."

Eleanor's eyes were on the president as he invoked her husband's name, but in her mind's eye she had a vision of Louis Howe.

It was 1920, and she was on a cross-country barnstorming train with Franklin. He had been chosen as the vice presidential candidate to run with James Cox against Warren Harding and the Republicans' cold-fish vice presidential choice, Calvin Coolidge. Louis Howe, Franklin's political adviser, was the one who had the idea to bring Eleanor along. Women had won the right to vote in August. He said she was bound to be a help, but she couldn't see how.

Eleanor had finally agreed, but she hated the drinking and card playing that went on late into the night, and the way women seemed to play up to Franklin. She had been in a two-year depression since discovering his affair with Lucy Mercer. As the campaign train sped west of the Allegheny Mountains in the fall of 1920, her emotions were still raw. She spent most of her time alone, reading and knitting. Then, one night, Louis came to speak to her.

She thought of how annoyed she'd felt when she saw him. She found Louis unsavory. He had a sickly look, with his gaunt face and clothes that hung on his body like they had been tossed onto him. His fingers were tinted with nicotine and his clothes reeked from his ever-present cigarette. Eleanor also knew that he accounted for a good part of the depletion of Franklin's liquor stock. But he had been Franklin's political strategist since 1911, a political journalist turned campaign genius whose dogged loyalty to Franklin was unquestionable.

As he stood in her doorway, Louis's frail body seemed tossed like a stick balanced on its end every time the train lurched from one side to another. "Hello, Eleanor, may I sit down?"

"Of course, Louis. I'm just finishing a sweater." Louis struggled against the lurching motion as he took the seat across from Eleanor. He tapped a cigarette out of his pack like he was beating a fast light rhythm on a timpani drum. Striking the match with a sharp snap, he inhaled deeply and leaned forward.

"Let me get right to the point, Eleanor. I need your help."

"Louis, I don't think I can offer much . . ."

"Please, let me finish. We need the women's vote and you're the best person on this train to help with that. Would you mind looking at this speech for tomorrow and let me know if it hits the right points, in your opinion?" Without waiting for her answer, he placed the paper on the seat next to her and said good night.

After that, he had other requests. "Eleanor, Franklin goes on entirely too long in his speeches, don't you think?" She did. "Could you stand next to him and give his coat a tug to stop him? He won't mind if you do it."

Soon, her knitting lay untouched as Louis kept her busy.

"Eleanor, do you think you could make a record of campaign events? Eleanor, could you monitor Franklin's press coverage? I can see how you're making friends with some of those women reporters. Eleanor, could you help me draft talking points?"

Yes, Louis had led her to see that she enjoyed hashing over issues, and that she knew more than she realized and had strong opinions. He had also helped her find a new connection with Franklin. Perhaps he didn't love her as she wished he did, but he respected her opinions and welcomed her involvement. If they shared no other passion, at least they shared a passion for social justice.

After the election and after Franklin contracted polio the following year, when he was in danger of fading from political view, Louis and Eleanor plotted together.

"Eleanor," Louis said, shutting the door to her study at Springwood, "have you heard what your mother-in-law is saying to Franklin?"

"Yes, she wants him to be a gentleman farmer here in Hyde Park. I think that would just kill him, Louis."

"I agree and I have a plan." He put his thin hands on her shoulders and smiled. "You'll keep the Roosevelt name alive in New York while he gets well. You already know so many women Democrats. They'll welcome you."

"But Louis, we don't know how long Franklin may be rehabilitating his legs. We don't know how he'll feel. . . ."

"That's right," Louis said, "we don't know, so we have to do what we can and hope. Just hope, Eleanor."

He had been right, of course, and within two years, Eleanor was the most active and visible woman Democrat in New York, editing the *Women's Democratic News,* traveling the state from one end to the other, exhorting women to use their newly won right to vote, and prodding them to get involved in politics. She gave speech after speech, despite shaking from fear and sounding horribly high-pitched.

"Just say what you have to say and sit down," Louis would growl at her after a bad performance. He had coached her, and comforted her, and built her confidence, and as he predicted, Franklin came back. He still couldn't walk of course, but he ran for governor in

1928 anyway. When he won, Eleanor remembered the conspiratorial smile she shared with Louis as Franklin took the oath. They both knew that it was the Democratic women of the state who put Franklin into office.

"You're a natural at this, Eleanor," Louis said one day after they were in the White House, cigarette smoke swirling past the glint in his eye. "I think your Uncle Teddy's looking down from the White House in the sky and grinning."

"Maybe it's in the Roosevelt blood then," she replied, and they both laughed. A year later, at the start of Franklin's second term, Louis was dead. He seemed to know the end was coming when one night he put on his most serious face and asked her to sit by him. She pictured him, coughing and ill, peering at her intently the way Truman and the others were now, as they waited for her answer.

"Why don't you think about running for president in 1940 instead of Franklin?" he had asked. "There's a lot of resistance to the idea of his having a third term, and I believe you could win."

If only Louis were here now, she thought, if only he were here.

"I want you all to understand something very clearly," Eleanor began as she turned to look around the room. "I never wanted to run and I don't want to now," and she paused, standing up and walking over toward the tall windows.

She felt as if a noose had tightened around her neck. Few people realized how sharp her political intellect had become after years with her husband, the political master. She understood how fraught the situation had become. A floor fight was completely out of the question, but absolutely assured if they tried to nominate any of the candidates who had tried but failed in Stevenson's wake. They were turning to her, not because they believed she could beat Eisenhower, but because they hoped she could help them leave Chicago with dignity. Many people thought Stevenson was nothing more than a sacrificial lamb on the altar of Eisenhower's popularity. Stevenson himself thought that. Eleanor knew that other than India, the men sitting around her would see her as nothing more than a sacrifice in a skirt. She would help them keep the New Deal torch aloft, lose with honor, and perhaps after four years, the Democrats would have a decent chance to come back. They were backed into a cave, and she offered the only poor passage out.

"This is the most extraordinary turn of events that anyone could imagine," Eleanor said, as she turned back toward the group. "You know I believe that there are principles critically important to the welfare of this country that must be protected." A vision of Joseph McCarthy flashed through her mind, and the pitch of her voice rose. "I would never do this for myself. Never . . . but for my party . . . certainly for Adlai and his great legacy . . . absolutely for Franklin and what we tried to achieve," and here her voice caught and she paused for a second, "and for the people of our country . . . I *will* do it."

Edwards quickly wiped the tears that sprang into her eyes, and Rayburn's face flushed, but Truman kept his eyes on Eleanor, as if he knew there was more. Returning his gaze, Eleanor spoke again, her voice strong and steady.

"I will do it . . . but understand this—I will do it my way. I am too old to be curtailed in any way in the expression of my own thinking."

"You are saving this party, Eleanor," Truman said, getting up and walking toward her, his hand extended, "and with John Sparkman at your side . . ."

"Sparkman is out of the question, Mr. President. I heard you were putting him up for vice president, and I understand appeasing the South, but not with Sparkman. He's opposed all federal civil rights legislation, and vehemently opposed your integration of the armed forces. He hasn't backed one inch off his support for poll taxes. Do you imagine I could run alongside a man who wants to keep our Negro citizens from voting?"

"He didn't side with the Dixiecrats. He's been a moderate for us, Eleanor. He made an alliance with Russell and with Adlai." Truman tried not to sound angry.

"It's not up for discussion."

Truman felt the sting of her words. Had he been as decisive when FDR died? He knew he hadn't. Who the hell was she to be on a high horse already? His face grew red, and he suddenly wished he hadn't stepped aside. But he was trapped. They all were trapped. As Truman struggled to calm down, he realized it didn't matter; there wasn't a chance in hell she'd win.

"All right, Eleanor, who did you have in mind?" Truman said, trying to sound unconcerned.

"I'm not quite sure. I want a bit of time to think. In the meantime, I'd like to go over the protocol with Sam, since he'll be in the chair, and I would ask that the rest of you strategize about talking to the state delegations." Eleanor motioned for Rayburn to follow her into a small side meeting room.

As Eleanor shut the door, Rayburn said, "I think we have to start with a eulogy, of course . . ."

"Sam, I didn't call you in here for that," Eleanor interrupted. "I wanted a private conversation. Please sit down."

Rayburn sat across from Eleanor on one of the hard metal chairs that had been set up and shuffled around the room all week. He passed his hand with a heavy stroke over his bald head, wondering what Eleanor had in mind now.

"I cannot have a racist like Sparkman one step away from the presidency, not at my age. But I need someone the South respects, someone even the Dixiecrats tolerate and someone who brings a strong electoral delegation. . . . That's you, Sam."

Rayburn's eyes had narrowed in concentration, but they grew wide as Eleanor finished. He sat staring at her, and the gears that made up the political trap of his brain could almost be heard turning.

He saw the brilliance of her scheme at once. She was right. He had just maneuvered, through strong-arming and some chicanery, to give the South a voice at the convention despite their recalcitrance on the loyalty pledge. Long, Battle, and Kennon had all come up to shake his hand. They loved seeing Humphrey and his liberal cohorts having a fit. With him, despite her outspoken support for civil rights, they would keep the South seated through the nomination, however shakily. Together they could guarantee wins in her home state of New York and his of Texas, two big electoral purses. But a woman as president? He doubted it could be done. Women had their place, after all. But he had to admit, Eleanor seemed to stand on top of the idea of womanhood in some way he couldn't quite define. But there was something he didn't understand.

"Eleanor, I'm a segregationist, too. You know that. In fact, John Sparkman's a close friend." Rayburn didn't mention that Sparkman had helped with the plans to position Rayburn to be drafted in case of a deadlock.

"Yes, Sam. But you've pledged to follow the law. I also know you've been pushing your attorney general and the state legislature to get rid of Texas's poll tax. We've worked closely together, Sam. Franklin trusted you, and so do I. I won't ask you to campaign for it, but I will ask you to support civil rights changes. We both know it's coming. I believe deeply that the health of our democracy depends on equal rights."

"It's coming because we've been so hidebound in the South," he said, looking down and shaking his head. "I can't quite get my mind around equal rights, but we can't be terrorizing our own citizens. I agree we have to do better."

"I want your pledge that, if I am president, you will stand with me, and not oppose me, on civil rights. That's all I ask," Eleanor said. "I believe you're more an American than you are a segregationist, Sam."

"I understand Eleanor. . . . Yes, as vice president, I believe I would be obligated to do that. I could give you my word on that," he said thoughtfully. Rayburn looked out the window, and in the silence, they could hear the excited talk from the next room. He wondered how Sparkman would react if he agreed to take the man's place. He knew Sparkman thought Eleanor a meddlesome, trouble-making fool when it came to civil rights. Would he cause trouble in the South for her, or could Rayburn keep him in line? He didn't know the answer, but he knew, whether he joined her or not, the South would be on fire over her candidacy.

"Do you realize how much they hate you in the South, Eleanor?"

"Racists hate me, Sam," she replied. "Remember what Franklin said in '36 when he was announcing the second New Deal? He was railing against the monopolists and speculators—the war profi-teers. 'Government by organized money,' he called it. Then he said, 'they are unanimous in their hate for me, and I welcome their ha-tred.' Well, Sam, the racists hate me, and I welcome their hatred. You know, Franklin's death has done nothing to alter the attacks on me. But, in the long run, I believe the mass of people will form a truthful estimate of people in public life, don't you?"

Rayburn had seen the steel in her eyes before, but it seemed stronger now. "I hope you're right, but you'd better welcome the hatred of the commie hunters too, because that will be coming as well," and Rayburn gave her a wry smile.

"Oh yes, I've been looking forward to confronting Senator Mc-Carthy. I had planned to do it on behalf of Adlai, and, in a way, I will be. And now we have Nixon as well. After what he did to Helen . . ."

"I always thought Richard Nixon had the most hateful face of the five thousand people I've served with in the House," Rayburn said.

Rayburn turned to look out the window again. When he turned back to Eleanor, he had his Speaker face on, the one that said nothing would stand in his way. "Eleanor, I am honored beyond words that you would ask me to run with you. . . . And I am honored to say I will."

"Roosevelt-Rayburn." Eleanor stood and put her hand on his shoulder, looking down at him with a sad but resolute smile. "We'll give the general a race he never dreamed of, Sam. And . . . we are going to be in it to win it."

CHAPTER 13

A Landslide

Byers Peak Ranch, Colorado, July 25, 1952

Ike took a long draw on the thin, sharp air as he cocked his arm
for another cast into the rippling waters of St. Louis Creek. It was
late evening, and he was enjoying a place he loved, the Byers Peak
Ranch, 8,750 feet up in the Rockies. He had a group of close friends
called, "the Gang," and the ranch owners were members. As soon
as the Republican Convention ended, he had flown to Colorado
along with his campaign aides for a mixture of planning and relax-
ation. Reporters had been allowed only fleeting opportunities to
photograph Ike on his daily fly-fishing excursions, where he often
brought along a young man who was new to the campaign.

In the fading light, Ike drew in his line with the Red Quill fly at
the end and turned to Jonathon Chamberlain.

"This one's my favorite. I can use it spring and summer. It looks like a March Brown and a Late March Brown, and those can have a late season hatch. Trout love these mayflies . . . especially when they collapse, which is a real challenge, 'cause they're darned hard to see." Ike finished with a satisfied grin, and looked expectantly at the young man by his side.

Jonathon Chamberlain wasn't used to being dumbstruck. Three years out of Bowdoin College in Maine, where he had been class president and valedictorian, his father's connections had landed him at a top advertising agency in Manhattan. Jonathon didn't shy away from putting out his ideas at staff meetings. He knew they were good. That's how Sherman Adams, Ike's wiry, intense campaign manager, heard about him—that and his family connections. Adams had recommended Jonathon, and he rarely recommended anyone.

"The boy's a Chamberlain, Ike. Can trace his family right back to Joshua Lawrence Chamberlain. I'm not sentimental, you know that, but there's something about him that I'm betting we'll need."

Adams and Eisenhower shared a love of Civil War history, and Joshua Chamberlain was a Union hero with one of the most compelling stories in a time filled with high drama. A professor at Bowdoin College when the war broke out, with a theological background and no military training, Chamberlain volunteered for military service. He quickly rose to lieutenant colonel of the 20th Maine Volunteers. He suffered six wounds in twenty-four battles and had six horses shot from under him before being chosen by Grant to receive the formal surrender of weapons and colors at Appomattox Court House. Ike saw him as the ultimate citizen-soldier.

"I'm glad to have the boy, Sherman. Bring him out to Colorado so I can get to know him better."

Now, Jonathon was standing in hip-high waders in rushing water with the most revered man in the world, trying to find low spots so his six-foot-two frame wouldn't tower over Eisenhower's five feet, ten inches, and he didn't know a thing about the tiny hook covered with spiky, orangish fur and tail that Ike held in his hand.

Jonathon thought about the Democratic Convention that was winding up that night in Chicago. They would be finishing the balloting about now, or maybe they had finished. When he and Ike had come down to the river, it was clear that Stevenson would win, but Jonathon had wanted to listen to the final tally and hear the acceptance speech. Ike, however, grew restless. Stevenson's welcoming speech had made the general nervous. It was too good—moving and polished and convincing. Ike told his crew, "I'd rather read his acceptance speech later," and asked Jonathon to come with him for a fly-fishing lesson. The young man took the invitation as an order.

Jonathon put on the smile that had charmed his teachers and made him a favorite with the prettiest girls, slightly off-kilter but showing fine teeth. He thought of it as his personality offensive: first the smile, then a comic and clever riposte. Then, look long and deeply into their eyes. He had yet to find the girl who could resist. But he wasn't facing a girl.

Jonathon looked at Eisenhower, straightened his stance, and spoke in the broad accent of his roots, where the letter r had dropped from the spoken word. "General, I know I should know this sport, being from Maine and all, but I just always loved to hunt. The most fishing I did was pulling in the pots, um, you know, lobster pots, but I am thrilled to be taught by such an enthusiast," and with his sky blue eyes twinkling, Jonathon picked up another fly with his left hand, and gave a salute with his right that let Ike know he'd never been in the military.

Ike started laughing, and Jonathon was treated to the facewide grin that Eisenhower inherited from his mother and shared with his four brothers. "Glad to see you're honest . . . but I guess I won't ask what you thought of that fried cornmeal mush with chicken giblet gravy and sausages I made for breakfast. Not sure I need that much honesty." Jonathon smiled and kept his mouth shut.

Jonathon knew this trip was a test of sorts. Ike and the others would be seeing if a politically unseasoned young adman could fill the gap that had them all troubled: how to handle the first televised campaign in history. The convention had only been the start. Campaign commercials were being talked about, and increased news coverage, maybe a televised debate. Jonathon was part of the communications team, reporting to Jim Hagerty, but he was expected to focus on TV.

"Someone told me that you have some ideas about television," Ike said to Jonathon as they waded out of the creek to get a drink.

"Yes, sir. I hope you won't take this the wrong way, but I believe we have to think like advertisers, not like politicians." Jonathon spoke cautiously, worried that his ideas might not seem dignified enough to Eisenhower.

"I'm listening," Ike said, squinting as he looked out over the bright water and the mountains beyond.

"We're starting to see what works in advertising. Catchy songs, repetition, slogans people can remember. Like Lucky Strike cigarettes, 'Be Happy, Go Lucky,' or those Old Gold ads with the dancing cigarette packs where you just see the girls' legs and white boots, and they say 'made by tobacco men, not doctors.'"

"So, you want to sell me like a cigarette?" Ike asked, with an edge in his voice that made Jonathon flinch.

"Well, sir, I think we should start with what we know works with the public . . . and go from there." Ike gave him a dubious look.

"Think about it, General," Jonathon plunged ahead, "Betty Furness had an amazing impact selling Westinghouse refrigerators in the TV commercials they ran during our convention. 'You can be *sure* if it's Westinghouse' . . . it was a great line, and now everybody remembers it, just from her standing there with that open fridge and talking to the camera like a real person." Jonathon's voice rose with excitement. "We can do that for you. Not some boring, half-hour talk to the camera. We do something simple, straightforward, a catchy line, maybe a tune . . ."

"Just so we don't forget we're talking about the presidency, not laundry detergent or Silly Putty." Ike stood up abruptly, taking his rod and walking back into deep water.

Jonathon followed, wondering if he had said too much. Ike eyed the water, picking his spot, and Jonathon watched him closely to see how to swing his arm for a good cast. Suddenly, Ike caught sight of Adams rushing down the trail to the river. Ike hadn't expected any interruptions, but he was more surprised to see the square-jawed Yankee walking at such a fast clip, and waving for his attention. The two fishermen could see Adams's look of intense excitement from the middle of the river. Ike waded out with long strides, telling Jonathon to keep working on catching his first trout.

"Sherman, is everything all right?"

"General, we've had some news from Chicago. I'm afraid Adlai Stevenson may be dead. He just collapsed on the stage. He seems to have had a massive heart attack." Adams pulled out a handkerchief and wiped the sweat off his high forehead without taking his eyes off Eisenhower.

"That's terrible, Sherman. My God. I'm terribly saddened to hear that. . . . He's a fine man. Are you sure?" Ike looked down, the lines around his eyes and forehead deepening.

"It wasn't officially announced, but I heard from some people I know. It doesn't look good for him. We should return to headquarters in New York as soon as possible," Adams continued. "It won't look right for you to be vacationing after this, and you'll need to issue a statement, of course. I can't imagine what the Democrats will do if he is gone."

Back at the house, Ike and his team were glued to the radio when they learned that Stevenson had died. Adams made frantic calls to get some intelligence on the Democrats' intentions. At around midnight, he came into the great room of the lodge and asked to talk to Ike privately.

"There's a rumor out there. The Democratic leadership has started to talk to the state delegations about a new ticket," Adams told Ike.

"What kind of rumor?" Ike said, his eyes narrowing.

"Well, at first, Barkley's people were insistent that they should have it, but they caved quickly. Kefauver made a try, too, but I guess he came around to the idea that they needed a ticket that wouldn't rehash the fighting they had all week."

"And?" Ike said with impatience.

"They're saying it's Eleanor Roosevelt and Sam Rayburn," Adams said, watching carefully for Ike's reaction.

"Sam Rayburn's a strong man, and that means they get Texas, of course. But a woman for vice president? I'm not sure even Eleanor can pull that off. The country's not ready. You should hear Mamie talk about these political women . . ."

"General, they're putting Eleanor up for president," Adams interrupted.

Eisenhower stared at Adams as if he'd just been told that the trout had abandoned the river in favor of high ground. He was too stunned to speak.

Finally, he sputtered, "Eleanor! Sherman, that's crazy, that's, that's . . . Are they? Have they? . . . I don't know what to think." Ike stopped short, then he seemed to recover.

"Well, what do you think that means for us?" he finally asked Adams.

"Well, General," Adams could barely suppress his excitement, "I know we've been wary about overconfidence, but between you and me, this can mean only one thing—we're going to win in a landslide."

CHAPTER 14

Far-Off Goals

Chicago, Illinois, July 1952

Franklin Jr. stood at the podium of the Democratic Convention in Chicago, a subdued sea of delegates filling the seats before him. "My friends," he said, "on this tragic day we have eulogized a fallen hero and recognized that we must also move ahead with our party's purpose, as the governor would have wished us to do. I give you Senator Russell Long, from the great state of Louisiana."

Long had brokered the deals that held the South in place for Stevenson's nomination. He had been the standard bearer for the southern bloc, both the Dixiecrats and the more progressive faction of which he was a member. Son of the populist governor and later senator Huey Long, who was assassinated in 1935, Long thought his father was smiling down on him as he took the microphone.

"Mr. Chairman, in light of the tragic turn of events that have taken one of our greatest leaders and our presidential nominee from us, I move that this convention vote immediately to nominate the woman from the great state of New York, who is known as the First Lady of the World. I place in nomination the name of the greatest First Lady this country has ever had, a humanitarian, diplomat, leader, and patriot who with her husband brought America to triumph after its darkest days, who has served with distinction in the United Nations, giving us the Magna Carta of our time, the Universal Declaration of Human Rights . . . our next president . . . Mrs. Franklin Delano Roosevelt!"

The crowd rose, delegates alternating between cheers and sobs, overwhelmed by the historic moment and by the high drama of recent events. Eleanor stood by her seat in the front of the hall and faced the delegates, waving solemnly. She was reminded of the funeral cortege for Franklin, and the stricken faces that lined the street. Tears streamed down the faces of men and women as Rayburn's somber voice asked, "Do I hear any other nominations?"

The delegates grew silent, with muffled words punctuating the air: "Thank you, Eleanor," "We miss you, Adlai," "God give us strength," "It's what Adlai would want," "Franklin's watching over us."

"Hearing no other nominations," Rayburn went on, "I ask that the roll of states be called."

Tradition was being followed, but in a way that no one had seen before. Each state spoke of its grief at Adlai's passing, and gave its assent to the historic moment that seemed almost lost in the shadow of tragedy—the Democrats were nominating a woman for president.

"The great state of North Carolina, in shock and mourning for the great Governor Stevenson, casts all ten votes for Eleanor Roosevelt." So it went, and when Illinois was called, her delegates' sobs reverberated through the hall, and like a contagion, blanketed the great room in grief once again. "Our governor . . ." the head of the Illinois delegation began, and he gasped, heedless of the tears rolling down his face. Charlie Redmont had been Stevenson's aide and confidant, and he couldn't go on. Another delegate stepped up and gently took the paper from Redmont's hands, reading slowly the paean to Illinois' fallen son.

Louisiana, Alabama, Mississippi, and Georgia abstained from voting. The South Carolina delegation held, although Thurmond walked out and several delegates followed. Eleanor's calculation had been right. Rayburn had worked through the night for the limited unity they had achieved that morning.

As Eleanor waited for the roll to end, she thought about what she had done in the last few hours. First she had called David, reaching him at his apartment in Manhattan and telling him the news without preliminaries. There had been a long silence from his end of the call. Finally, he spoke.

"Eleanor, I think this is a terrible idea. I think it is dangerous. Very dangerous. Maureen has told me about the FBI warnings to you. Do you have any idea how this will inflame those maniacs in the KKK?" He didn't wait for her answer, but went on, his voice rising as he got more strident.

"And what about us? We will never get to see each other. You know what a candidate's life is like. How will you stand it? The pressure and attacks and travel?"

"David, please, calm down, don't yell at me. There are points in life where you have no choice."

"That is not true, and you know it. You had a choice. You chose to run. Don't act like your arm was twisted."

"But it was. In a very real way, it was twisted, David. You must understand. We all have certain obligations, certain . . ."

"I'm sorry, Eleanor. I don't understand. And I must go. I'm late to see a patient. Please take care. I suppose I will see you when you get to New York," and he hung up.

She hadn't cried. Instead, she felt numb. Was he using this as an excuse to end their affair? Even if he wasn't, how much could he love her if he wouldn't support her? She thought about the last time they had been together. He had lingered over dinner, then spent an overly long time in the bathroom. When he came out, she had joked about the length of his ritual ablutions, but had he really been avoiding their bed?

With an enormous force of will, she pushed David from her thoughts. She knew she had to call her children before they heard the news some other way. James had been for Kefauver, but he fully supported the turn of events. He had long thought his mother should run for president. Franklin Jr., a New York congressman, and her daughter, Anna, had been happy as well. But Elliott and John had come out for Eisenhower in a *New York Herald Tribune* story only days before.

"I'm sure you'll do what you feel is right," Eleanor had told them, knowing that her youngest son, John, was stubborn and rebellious, and Elliott was unpredictable. Eleanor moved on to her most important calls. She had ideas for the campaign team she wanted, and she needed them to come together quickly.

Molly Dewson had been Eleanor's political ally and friend since plotting Franklin's victory as governor of New York in 1928. Ten years older than Eleanor, Dewson was planning to retire with her lifetime partner, Mary Porter, to a property they owned in Maine. Molly had come to Chicago, seeing it as her last convention. But Eleanor knew it wouldn't be hard to convince Dewson that she still had one more campaign in her.

Eleanor's next call was to Esther Lape. She could think of no one better suited to be her issues adviser. She had also sent word to Joan Black to come to her suite, which was already littered with coffee cups, Coke bottles, and papers in tumbled heaps on almost every surface. When Joan arrived, Eleanor motioned for her to sit next to her on a small settee.

"Mrs. Roosevelt, let me tell you how sorry I am that you lost your friend, and the country lost a great man."

"Thank you. I wish we all had the luxury to mourn. In due time. Have you filed your story for today?"

"No, I'm not filing. Ray Stanerd is covering the convention overall . . ." Joan hesitated. "I have asked to cover you. I'm waiting to get approval."

"I see. Well, I have another proposal for you, and I don't expect you to answer right away. I know how important being a journalist is to you. It's in your blood, after all." Eleanor smiled. "But I feel I need someone young to handle my communications, someone smart and eager and talented. I believe that's you, Joan."

"You want me to join your campaign?" Joan asked in astonishment.

"I want you to consider it, but I must warn you. One of my dearest friends is a journalist I met when I came to the White House. Perhaps you've heard of her—Lorena Hickok?"

Joan had not only heard of Lorena Hickok, she had met her. She had also heard the rumors of a romantic relationship between Eleanor and Hickok, one that the reporters would never write about, but which was much discussed nevertheless.

Eleanor went on. "When Hick and I became friends," Eleanor paused and let out a sigh, "when she came too closely into the circle of White House influence, she felt her craft was compromised. She gave up journalism forever, and she was one of the great ones. You must consider that if you take my offer, that could happen to you."

Joan hesitated. She did love newspaper work; it was in her blood. But I can go back, she thought, I'm not like Hick.

Joan also knew Eleanor wasn't giving her the whole story. Hickok had stayed at the White House because she was so in love with Eleanor she couldn't leave, even after Eleanor broke off the love affair.

"I'll take my chances, Mrs. Roosevelt," Joan said, sitting up in the chair and straightening her plaid peplum. "I would be so honored to be part of your campaign. I'm ready to start right now."

Eleanor's final call had been a total surprise to the man who picked up the phone. Larry O'Brien, a thirty-five-year-old political strategist from Massachusetts, was running the Senate campaign for an up-and-coming congressman named John F. Kennedy. O'Brien's Democratic roots were deep. His father was a bulwark of the Democratic Party in western Massachusetts, who had little Larry working in Al Smith's campaign for president when the boy was eleven years old. He had gone on to law school, but came home to run the family business, O'Brien's Bar and Grill, where regulars came to toss back whiskey, toss around political gossip, and enjoy his mother's cooking.

O'Brien had come to the convention with Kennedy, sitting in on some of the behind-the-scenes meetings. At one gathering, Kennedy had asked O'Brien to share his innovative campaign plan with the group. He had spent the last three congressional cycles before the convention overseeing congressional campaigns in the state of Massachusetts, and it was this experience that led him to a bold idea.

"Go ahead, Larry," Kennedy had said with his broad New England accent. "Whoever pulls out this nomination is going to need a new approach. Tell them what you've been telling me."

"Thank you, Congressman," O'Brien said, as he looked nervously at the group of party leaders sitting around the room.

"In looking at the races in my state, and studying other races around the country, I've been struck by the power of one vote." O'Brien hesitated, thinking this might sound simplistic, and then continued hurriedly, "I mean that literally. I can show you many races that would have been decided by the difference of one vote per precinct, and if that small number of votes is the margin of victory, why would a candidate fail?" Now he was warming up and went on more confidently.

"We lose close elections because we don't get every voter to the polls. I mean phone calls, I mean transportation, I mean more calls, and the only way to get that labor-intensive work done is organization and volunteers." O'Brien noticed India Edwards lean forward slightly with an intent look.

"We need to create state-level organizations of party leaders who we are constantly communicating with. We have to create deeper, stronger statewide organizations that can turn out volunteers. Volunteer workers are the backbone of every political organization, yet campaigns never include a plan for volunteers. Well, I've built a model campaign plan with that idea at its center."

O'Brien recalled his presentation as he listened to Eleanor on the other end of the line.

"Larry, I know you're committed to Kennedy's campaign, but I want you to make an adjustment. I'm sure John will understand." Her voice was stiff as she spoke the last line. She didn't approve of the young Kennedy boys. She'd heard of their carousing with Joe McCarthy in Washington. She felt they should denounce him, and she had told their father just that.

"Larry, I'm offering you the chance to run a presidential campaign. India Edwards talked to me about your plan for campaign volunteers and involving people in elections. I couldn't agree with you more. Ordinary citizens working on campaigns isn't just good campaign strategy, it's good for the democracy, good for the country. I do hope you'll agree to be on my team. I believe we think quite the same way, and I need your help."

O'Brien's mind flooded with so many thoughts at once, he could hardly form a sentence. He grabbed his heavy black-framed glasses off his face and ran his forearm over his brow. He had fair skin that flushed easily, and suddenly he'd begun sweating.

He knew instantly what his father would tell him to do, what any political strategist worth their salt would do. The chance to run a presidential campaign was the ultimate prize. Still . . . a woman? He'd seen Eleanor's name floated in previous elections, but he couldn't recall any poll numbers, other than that she was the most admired woman in the world. But did that translate to votes? How much bounce could she get off her association with FDR? What about Korea? Would Americans buy a woman to end a war? Was her gender an impossible obstacle? O'Brien had to smile at himself. He was already moving into campaign thinking.

Before O'Brien could answer, Eleanor went on, "I want to be frank with you. I have a number of women who will have key positions. Combined with the novelty of a woman as the nominee, I'm afraid it might raise unnecessary criticism. I'd like a man to be head of the campaign so I can balance things out a bit. I'm sure I don't have to point out to you, Larry, that you'll be part of making history. Very fine history, indeed," and he could hear the smile in her voice.

O'Brien thought about his own mother, Mary Catherine. She had sailed from Ireland in 1912 with a brogue as heavy as the freighter that brought her across the ocean. She'd scrubbed floors in the rich houses of Boston and come home at night with raw hands that he could still feel stroking his face. When his father made a little more money and told her she could stop working, she ignored him. She took a job in a shop downtown, and at night she helped her husband organize the neighborhood for the Democratic machine. Little Larry had seen her staff every precinct for an election and get every elderly, lame, and blind Democrat to the polls. She'd pressed leaflets into his hands more times than he could remember. "Take them to every house, son, and don't be missing any. Remember, this is part of your education as much as reading about Columbus or such."

Mary Catherine even pigeonholed parishioners after church, despite the priest's disapproving stares. Like Eleanor, she didn't like the Kennedys, but they were Catholics, and that made up for a myriad of sins. O'Brien suspected his father realized that Mary

Catherine was the better politician, but the old man would never admit it.

"Mrs. Roosevelt, I am far more honored than I can express," O'Brien began. "I'm sure, as you say, that the congressman will understand," he went on, and Eleanor could tell that he wasn't sure at all. "Of course," O'Brien said, "I accept. I only hope your faith in me is well placed."

When he hung up the phone, O'Brien was too stunned to pour a drink, but he knew he would need one before he called Kennedy.

Eleanor's thoughts were pulled back to the convention floor as, after three hours of speeches mixed with anguish and hope, Rayburn's somber voice announced: "The 1952 Democratic Convention has nominated Eleanor Roosevelt as its candidate for president of the United States." He looked toward Eleanor, who had begun to make her way toward the stage: "Fellow Democrats, I give you our nominee for president, Mrs. Franklin Delano Roosevelt."

Eleanor had asked the band to play "America," its strains coming slow and poignant over the subdued cheering and clapping. Walter White, executive secretary of the NAACP understood the choice. As he stood in the gallery looking down at Eleanor, he thought about that day in April 1939, when Marian Anderson, the great contralto, had been banned from singing in the Daughters of the American Revolution hall because she was black. Eleanor had helped arrange for Anderson to sing on the steps of the Lincoln Memorial. He had stood with the seventy-five thousand people who gathered on the National Mall that Easter Sunday to hear her. A hush had fallen over the vast audience as Anderson stepped to the microphone, raising her head high and closing her eyes. She began by singing "America," but she subtly altered the words. "My country 'tis of thee," she sang as the vast crowd seemed to hold its breath. "Sweet land of liberty," and her voice rose and enunciated each word, "*to* thee I sing."

As the convention hall filled with the familiar notes, he sang the words to A. Philip Randolph, who was standing next to him, "'*To thee I sing...*' Do you remember? Eleanor's sending a message. She is surely sending a message, and our people will hear her."

With a grave smile, and her familiar wave, Eleanor stood at the podium, once again looking out at the people who had come together for their country's sake. This time there were no banners, no signs, no balloons.

"My friends," she began, and the hall fell instantly silent. "This is not my moment, nor is it yours," Eleanor went on. "Surely, it is God's hand that has guided us in this fateful time, and we must trust His wisdom in taking our friend, Adlai Stevenson. And so, I will not give a traditional acceptance speech today, or speak of what we can do together as we run this campaign touched by fate. That will have to wait until we have said our formal good-byes to Governor Stevenson. But I have here in my purse a prayer that I carry and often read. Please let me share this with you."

Eleanor took a paper from the handbag she had placed on the podium. She read slowly, and everyone could hear the heaviness in her heart as she began. But as Eleanor went on, standing tall and steady before them, they could hear the lifting of her spirit, and their own, as the words carried and soared through the amphitheater.

> "*Our Father, who has set a restlessness in our hearts, and
>   made us all seekers after that which we can never
>   truly find,
> Draw us away from base content, and set our eyes on
>   far-off goals.
> Keep us at tasks too hard for us that we may be driven to
>   Thee for strength.
> Deliver us from fretfulness and self-pitying; make us sure
>   of the good we cannot see and of the hidden good
>   in the world.*

Open our eyes to simple beauty all around us, and our
          hearts to the loveliness men hide from us because
          we do not try to understand them.
Save us from ourselves,
And show us a vision of a world made new.
Amen."

Throughout the hall, the echo of Eleanor's last word passed through the delegates like a sigh of resignation, and like the breath of acceptance. Now they must move on, it seemed to say. Now the great work of their democracy must begin.

PART II

CHAPTER 15

The General and the Grandmother

Sherman Adams looked glum as he walked into Ike's suite at the Commodore Hotel in Manhattan the afternoon after Eleanor's historic nomination. He dropped a stack of newspapers as thick as two cinder blocks on the coffee table and fell onto the plush couch, throwing his head back against the cushion for a second before he spoke.

"Have you seen any of these?" Adams asked, picking the *New York Times* off the top of the pile and not waiting for an answer. "All the main headlines are about the same, 'Eleanor to Run,' etcetera, etcetera, in screaming big typeface—but these side stories." He jabbed his finger at the page. " 'Democrats Nominate a Woman, Historic First!' 'Eleanor to Truman: I'm Running with Rayburn,' 'Former First Lady as Independent as Ever,' and here's the *Chicago Trib*, for God's sake, 'Eleanor Roosevelt Gives Nation Historic Moment' and 'Roosevelt Dumps Sparkman.' At least you got top bill-ing in the main headline." Adams turned the paper around so Ike could see the headline that read "It's Eleanor Against Ike!"

"The *Trib* will never endorse her. And that Sparkman move has to hurt in the South, don't you think? What are you so worried about?" Ike asked. "Come on, I'm having a late lunch." He pointed to a room service tray set up with white linen and placed on a side table by the window.

"Look, we were ready to treat Stevenson like a dinghy with a thousand-pound anchor named Truman, remember? 'Time for a change,' and all that?" Adams said. "Stevenson was Truman's stalking horse, and that was perfect for us. Just perfect. And, yes, Alabama will be enraged over their man, Sparkman, but putting Rayburn on the ticket will take care of the rest of the South, I'm guessing. I swear, you get an electric shock down there if you try pulling the Republican lever. Except for the anti-Catholic outpouring in '28 against Al Smith, they've voted Democratic in every presidential election since 1876. Does that tell you something, General?" Adams's face had gotten red and he seemed to be talking to himself as much as to Ike.

"Calm down, Sherman. Really, she's still a woman, after all. She can't change that. And there are plenty of men in this country who will hear that screeching voice of hers and be reminded of their wives' worst moments." Ike laughed. "Know what I mean?"

Adams returned a wan smile.

"Oh, you know, I did call Mrs. Roosevelt . . ." Ike said taking a sip of his Coke.

"Ike!" Adams suddenly bleated as he held open the *New York Times*. "What's this? You agreed to a *joint* statement?"

"What's the problem, Sherman? You told me to call Eleanor, and she suggested it. She said she wanted to be sure that there wouldn't be any misinterpretation of either of our statements about Adlai. You know, that we should make sure it wouldn't seem like either of us was trying to get some political advantage from his death. Seemed reasonable to me." Ike took a bite of his roast beef sandwich.

"We could issue our own damn statement without her help. As if you would exploit the situation." Adams was pacing and fuming with equal vigor.

"I thought you weren't worried about Eleanor. 'Landslide,' remember? Those were your words. Here, give me that." Ike pushed his chair back with some force, grabbed the paper from Adams, and began reading, "'As the presidential nominees of our respective parties, we want the country to know that we share a deep respect for Adlai Stevenson, and mourn the passing of this honorable man and patriot. In deference to his memory, neither of us will be campaigning or issuing campaign-related statements until the conclusion of the memorial service we will be attending, to be held on Tuesday, July 29. May his soul rest in peace and God bless our country.' I don't see a problem with that, Sherman."

"Well, I do. She's trying to immediately have herself seen as your equal. Also, she wanted to buy some time to get her campaign going without saying that's what she's doing. So she gets you to cover for her. Don't you get it? A *joint* statement," Adams shot out.

Eisenhower smiled. "That's awfully cynical, Sherm. And my *equal*? Come on. For someone so confident of winning, you seem to be getting a little nervous. I think you're reading this wrong. I'm no fan of Eleanor's. Perle Mesta told me that she was passing stories about Mamie having a drinking problem," Eisenhower's eyes flashed with anger, "but this seemed to make sense."

"Look, I don't believe this country will put a woman in the White House any more than I believe that those unidentified flying objects over Salem last week were aliens, but that doesn't mean we don't run a campaign as if we were facing FDR himself," Adams shot back. "Have you heard the stories about what Eleanor did in the '20s to her own cousin when he ran as a Republican for governor against Al Smith? She tied him to the Teapot Dome scandal when he had nothing to do with it, and drove around in a car with a big teapot on top. Why, I'm already hearing rumors that they're going to harp on the Harding scandals to offset the Truman mess."

"I never heard that story about her," Ike said.

"Trust me, Ike. She's not just a sweet grandma with a famous name, and this ploy to control our statement says to me that we have to stay sharp." Adams grabbed the newspaper back from Ike. "We are going to beat her, general, but we'll have to change our strategy. The truth is, if she were a man, she'd be a formidable opponent. She has critics, but she also has a lot of popular support and goodwill, like you." Adams started ticking off his points on his fingers. "She has a lot of experience in government, even if it isn't formal, but of course, she has no military experience. She's met every foreign leader and won tremendous praise for her work at the UN." Ike had stopped eating and was looking at Adams, a frown etched on his face.

"And she was married to the most revered president since Lincoln and is a constant reminder of the things he did that Americans want to keep."

"That all doesn't sound too good, Sherman. Not for me, anyway."

"Remember, Ike, I said she'd be a problem if she were a man. But she's not. And we just have to keep reminding voters of that. Subtly, of course." Adams looked thoughtful.

"Yeah, Ike, I think that's it. We run a very pro-women campaign. Pro-women *in the home,* that is. We talk about the critical role women play in helping their husbands, taking care of their children, and how we're going to help them do that. We call Eleanor the 'former First Lady,' and 'grandmother' as often as possible. We get Mamie out there as the wonderful, supportive spouse." Adams was getting excited now; he'd even started to smile. "And we play you up as the great general, which you are, and which we were going to do anyway. The public will get the point."

"I hope so, Sherman. I certainly can't imagine they would think a woman, any woman, could run this country, especially with a war going on," Ike said, as he turned back to his lunch.

CHAPTER 16

Eleanor Everywhere

Appalachia, August 1952

The whistle of the "Eleanor Everywhere Express" carried like a freedom song as it chugged into the West Virginia hollows for a series of campaign stops. Larry O'Brien had suggested naming the train after one of the joking criticisms of Eleanor from her White House years.

"Didn't they call you 'Eleanor Everywhere'?" he said to his candidate one day as they were talking over strategy.

Eleanor laughed. "Yes, that and a lot more."

"Right," Larry answered, starting to chuckle. "A man named his clock after you because it never stopped running. I heard that one. And Admiral Byrd at the South Pole had an extra place setting at dinner in case you stopped by."

Eleanor smiled. "You're too young to remember those jokes, Larry."

"Oh, I do my research, Madam Candidate. And I think we should build on the perception that you've been everywhere, met people everywhere, seen how they live, what they deal with. We'll name the train the 'Eleanor Everywhere Express' and we'll tie it into the campaign plan. We're going to organize at the county, district, and state levels, and Sam has agreed to focus heavily on the South, just to remind those yellow-dogs that there's only one Democrat in the race, and that's you.

"Our goal is to contact every voter in every state at least three times." O'Brien held up his index finger. "First, they get a Roosevelt tabloid or some other campaign literature delivered or mailed. Second, they get a call from a volunteer, and third," he held up three fingers, "a poll worker greets them at the poll. And maybe four, in targeted areas, of course" O'Brien thrust four fingers in front of him, "they see Eleanor live and in person . . . on the 'Eleanor Everywhere Express.'" He finished triumphantly, but Eleanor had become distracted.

How many miles had she wandered in those years when she had been called Franklin's "eyes and ears"? Of course, it was so difficult for him to travel, to go where she had gone—into coal mines, through the rutted fields that yielded ripe strawberries and pickers rotted by the backbreaking work. She had gone everywhere to see for herself, to understand, to help Franklin, but also for a reason she never confessed.

She had felt far less lonely in a dust-bowl town in Kansas, eating fatback gravy and bread with a family whose crops had died of thirst and whose cattle had died of hunger, than in the graceful abundance of the White House.

Soon after she and Franklin had moved in, they had been sitting in the Rose Parlor, the windows thrown open to the springlike balm that had overtaken Washington early that year. Franklin was in a lighthearted mood, assuming the joking tone of a general as he directed her to try the furniture she had brought from the Val-Kill factory in different positions around the room. She had finally collapsed, panting and laughing in a chair next to him, and he had reached over and taken her hand.

"Eleanor," he said, his face turning grave, "I've missed you."

"But, Franklin, we've been together far more than usual." She smiled and gave his hand a slight squeeze.

"I know," he said, and she could see in the set of his mouth and the softness that had come into his eyes that his mood had dramatically shifted. "Eleanor, being together so much more has made me realize how much I've missed you these past years. I think you know what I mean, Eleanor. Isn't it time? Can't you find it in your heart to love me again? You must believe me about this—I have never stopped loving you." He leaned toward her, pulling her closer and wrapping his arm around hers, but she could feel her body stiffen. She blinked hard, but the tears came anyway, and she dropped her head, unable to meet Franklin's eyes.

She didn't move. She didn't yield. She didn't answer. A minute ticked by. Finally, she heard Franklin let out a guttural sigh. He pulled his arm back slowly and wheeled himself from the room. That day, she made plans for her first trip as First Lady, the beginning of so many trips, of meeting so many people, of running from her loneliness but not healing it. Never healing it.

"Eleanor?" Larry said, wondering if she was upset about his plans. "Do you want to add something on the campaign organizing?"

"No, Larry, no. I have absolute faith in you," and Eleanor stared out the window as her train entered a clearing and the tiny station came into view.

The local people had answered the train's whistle in a devoted chorus as it pulled into Newburg, West Virginia. Folks in Masonville, Bretz, Reedsville, and Kingwood were waiting by the playhouse-sized station. They washed down the gnats and greasy smelling dust with a bottled Coke, putting a prayer in the rusted, tilting soda machine along with their nickel.

Had anyone stayed behind in Arthurdale? Hattie Johnson didn't think so. She had been a young mother nearly two decades before, with two babies to watch and a jobless husband to worry over when Mrs. Roosevelt had first come by. One of those babies had babies now, Hattie's husband was gone, and she had ridden along in a caravan of neighbors for the chance to see Mrs. Roosevelt again.

Hattie was sure the great lady wouldn't remember her. It was November 1933 when a man had knocked on the door of her tar paper shack and asked if it would be all right for Mrs. Roosevelt to pay a visit later that afternoon. "Mrs. Eleanor Roosevelt, the First Lady?" Hattie had gulped. The man nodded. "I . . . well I, I mean, my Baby Charlie has the cough . . ." The man just looked at her. She didn't know what her husband, Charlie, would think. He'd gotten tired of the sittin' and spittin' and gone to Pittsburgh to look for day work. "I suppose it's all right," she told the man, still unsure. She'd heard about Mrs. Roosevelt going all over. Going to those slum houses in Detroit and hugging those little Negro babies. Even going down into the coal mines, where women weren't supposed to. But coming to Scott's Run? What would Hattie say to her, what could she offer her, and which of the few wood chairs would be most comfortable for the president's wife?

Eleanor knocked on Hattie's door around three o'clock that afternoon. From the window, Hattie could see a few people waiting in the car against the damp chill. On the side of the car, it said, "American Friends Service Committee." She'd seen those people before and knew they were Quakers who wanted to help.

Hattie looked up as she opened the door, remembering the photos, yet still surprised at how tall the lady was and how kind her eyes. "Please come in." Hattie wanted to smile, but nerves froze her face and she spoke to the floor.

"Thank you," Eleanor said, tipping her head slightly as she passed the door frame. She held a small purse in both hands.

"I'm pleased to meet you," Hattie had practiced the line in her mind, trying different variations, settling on the familiar. She held her hand out, limp and damp even in the chill. Eleanor took it in her own and held it as she spoke, "You're good to have me, Mrs. Beauchamp."

"Oh, we pronounce that beech-uhm, but please call me Hattie."

"Thank you, Hattie. Mr. Carson said your boy is sick?"

"Yes, ma'am, he's got the cough. Would you sit down here?" Hattie pointed to a wood plank table with two small ladder-back chairs next to it. "Can I offer you some tea? It's my own kind, from the goldenrod that grows all over here." Just then, a hacking cough came from a cradle across the room. Eleanor was startled by the harsh, sharp sound coming from what looked like a small baby. Hattie rushed over and picked him up. His face was scarlet; the coughing built on itself as Hattie tried to soothe him. A light drizzle had started outside, and Eleanor noticed that the window by the crib had no glass, just some newspaper hanging limply over the opening. It threatened to collapse as the rain grew stronger and beat against it.

Hattie followed Eleanor's eyes. "We can't afford the glass yet, but my husband says soon. It's hard on the little ones."

"How old is he?" Eleanor asked gently.

"Not quite six months, but he's a strong one. He'll get over this." Eleanor heard the defiance in Hattie's voice, and the fear.

As she stood by the tracks waiting for Eleanor's train, Hattie could almost feel Baby Charlie in her arms again. She blinked hard, squeezing her eyes to keep the tears in. Baby Charlie was strong, but not strong enough. Hattie had written Mrs. Roosevelt. She believed the lady would want to know about her Charlie. She carried the letter Eleanor sent back from the White House in her purse. It was the first time she had taken it from her bedside table in eighteen years.

The crowd massed around the rear platform as the train shuddered to a stop. Hattie had squeezed forward, a couple of the bigger men letting her move in front of them so she could see. Some people held homemade signs: "We Need You," "President Eleanor," "Put a Roosevelt Back in the White House." Someone started a chant, "We want Eleanor . . . We want Eleanor," and soon everyone had joined. They clapped in rhythm, getting louder so that Hattie could feel her heart pounding from the swell of excitement.

Eleanor appeared with a crush of aides behind her. She held her large hands high and awkward over her head, twisting her whole arm to wave. The loose flesh of her upper arm swung slightly under her cap sleeves. The teeth that filled her smile made Hattie think of the Chiclets gum her grandson liked so much. I'm sure she won't get to speak, Hattie thought, because no one is going to stop hollering. Hattie was clapping too, and stamping and shouting so hard she was sure she'd have no voice left. Eleanor kept waving and clapping, looking around at the crowd. Suddenly, she seemed to do a double take as she looked toward the center of the throng, and then, as if she had heard an alarm, she headed down the platform steps. People held out their hands to help her with the last high step to the ground. "Excuse me, thank you, excuse me," she said as she moved people aside, looking for the face she had seen from the platform.

Hattie couldn't see what was going on as Eleanor came off the side of the train. Then the crowd seemed to part and there was Eleanor, arms out. She pulled Hattie to her, and as the two women hugged, Hattie's tears for Baby Charlie broke through like an ancient flood. Eleanor knew, knew better than most, and she had remembered, remembered Hattie and remembered Baby Charlie. Hattie understood why; the reason was folded in her purse.

"Dear Hattie," the long-ago letter read, "I was grief-stricken at the news that your baby succumbed to the cough that had gripped him when I visited you. I never speak of this, but I feel I must tell you that I lost a baby too, the first Franklin Jr. He was my third baby and always seemed delicate. He was seven months and nine days when his little heart gave way. We buried him in St. James churchyard on April 10, 1908. I pray that God will sustain you as he did me. Know that we will see our little ones again someday. With fondness and much sympathy, Eleanor Roosevelt."

As the train pulled out of Newburg, Eleanor thought about seeing Hattie again and about Arthurdale. Eleanor had bullied and bludgeoned government agencies to build a town with decent houses and jobs in the heart of a heartbroken countryside. If the government couldn't do that, couldn't give people a chance to pull themselves up out of poverty in the midst of the Depression, what could it do? A phalanx of Republicans had cried "Socialism!" and "A conspiracy for revolution!"

In the end, no industry came to Arthurdale, and the critics were quick to pronounce the experiment a colossal failure. Eleanor knew that Arthurdale would be used by her enemies in the campaign. But deep in the shadows of the passing woods and under the glint of sun off a tin roof in the distance, she believed there were people like Hattie who would be totally on her side. But, as her train raced into the Deep South, Eleanor wondered, were there enough Hatties? Could there possibly be enough?

Eleanor awoke the next morning in Montgomery, Alabama, and went to services at the Dexter Avenue Baptist Church. After the service, Pastor Vernon Johns introduced his niece, Barbara Rose, to Eleanor. The three stood under a catalpa tree in the churchyard hoping for the slightest breeze, the air choked with the overripe smells of late summer flowers. Barbara Rose was eighteen, and had just graduated from the all-black high school in Montgomery. She had transferred there after leading a strike at Moton High, her old school in Farmville, Virginia, the previous year. Her Uncle Vernon had whisked her down to Montgomery because her parents feared for her life.

"So, you're the young lady who stirred up some trouble in Farmville," Eleanor said, shaking Barbara Rose's hand and smiling at the slim girl with thick shoulder-length hair, a heart-shaped face, and fire in her pitch-black eyes. "Please, tell me about that school you had to attend."

Barbara Rose never held back and the words poured out of her.

"In the white school they had *good* books, not torn-up, scratched-over, raggedy ones like we had. They had a lunchroom and really good teachers, and they didn't sit on the floor, or need an umbrella."

"Umbrella?" Eleanor asked.

"Yes. One day, I remember, Thelma Jefferson was sitting in our old tar paper shack, because we needed an extra classroom, and the rain just poured in on her head, and she'd just gotten her hair all done up." Barbara Rose laughed. "It was kind of funny, but it made me mad, too."

"I can understand that," Eleanor said. "But how did you get all the students to follow you out of the school?"

"Well, I called the principal," Barbara Rose started talking faster, "and told him he'd better get down to the bus station fast because two students were under arrest. Then, when he left, I wrote a note like it was from him to all the teachers calling for an all-school assembly. Then, when they got there, I said, 'This is a special *student* meeting to talk about how awful this school is.' And we told the teachers to leave, and when they did, I said to the other students, 'if you want a better school, we've got to do something ourselves.' And then we walked out." She smiled and looked at Eleanor with triumph written on her face.

"That was very brave," Eleanor said.

"And very dangerous," Vernon Johns interrupted, giving Barbara Rose a stern look. "They stayed out for two weeks, and this girl," he put his hands on her shoulders, "she got some NAACP lawyers from Richmond to come over, and now there's a lawsuit to desegregate that school."

"Yes, I know of other cases like that. It's very promising," Eleanor said. "And you're a very promising organizer. We need people like you in my campaign, you know."

"But then the KKK burned a cross in her daddy's front yard," Uncle Vernon went on before Barbara Rose could answer. "And they cut off her family's credit at the bank. We were worried about night riders and lynching, so we brought her down here." Uncle Vernon stroked Barbara Rose's hair.

"I've been doing voter education all summer, Mrs. Roosevelt," Barbara Rose said. "You know, the Constitution says," the girl paused and cleared her throat, then lifted her chin and spoke very clearly, "The right of citizens of the United States to vote shall not be denied or abridged by the United States or by any state on account of race, color, or previous condition of servitude."

"It's impressive that you know that so well," Eleanor said.

"Well, Uncle Vernon made us memorize that amendment."

Pastor Johns laughed. "Didn't do you any harm."

"I'll do anything I can to help you become president, Mrs. Roosevelt." Barbara Rose stuck out her hand and Eleanor took it, holding it in both of hers for a moment, as she held the young woman's eyes.

"I'm going to think of you as a friend, Barbara Rose. If you would, meet me at our campaign headquarters this evening, and we'll see what you can be used for. Is that all right, Pastor Johns?"

"Well, I'll be coming with her, Mrs. Roosevelt. She has a way of getting in trouble. Anyway, we both want to help. In fact, I think every Negro in the South wants to help you."

Eleanor turned to Barbara Rose and took her face in her hands.

"If you do work for me, you must promise that you will take care, my dear. There are people who will want to hurt you for helping me."

"I've read where you told people to 'look fear in the face,'" the girl said earnestly. "I'm ready to do that for you, Mrs. Roosevelt. I'm ready to look fear in the face."

CHAPTER 17

A Proper Order to Man

Meridian, Mississippi, August 1952

Hot air hung over the town of Meridian like a wet shroud, and the morning sun rose in a hazy yellow blur. Edgar Ray Killen had gotten up early, taking his Bible and fresh paper onto the porch, although the air outside was as stifling as it was inside.

At twenty-seven years old, Killen already owned the local saw mill and had also become a Baptist minister. He was working hard to build a congregation, and he still had work to do on Sunday's sermon. He had been getting a pretty good crowd at his church, especially since he started talking more about getting some order in the county. Their sheriff was just too damned soft, and Killen had started making reference to the things he knew his people cared about. The way they thanked him after services had gotten him thinking—maybe he should run for sheriff. He began to read over what he'd written.

"God has ordained a proper order to man, and it's a racist order. The Bible itself is racist in context. God is a racist, being that He created everything after its own kind and never sanctioned crossbreeding or mongrelization. Read it yourself in Genesis, my friends. It says, 'This is the book of the generations of Adam' . . . and Adam was a white man."

Killen imagined himself shouting out the last phrase, his lean body standing straight and hard as a plank from the mill, his long arms stretched high. "These niggers ain't people and everyone knows it. Between them and the commies, the whites are gonna lose everything." He was talking to himself, but it was a rehearsal for what he'd tell the boys at the mill later on.

Since Sam Bowers had appointed him "kleagle," or klavern recruiter and organizer for the Neshoba and Lauderdale counties Ku Klux Klan, Killen had gotten a lot more attention and respect from people. The job gave him a chance to travel around the area, recruit for the Klan, and talk about his church. "It's a good church for whites that care about God and children," he'd say. "Come over and hear a sermon like you haven't heard before," and he'd shake their hands so they could feel the calluses on his own.

This sermon's really gonna shake people up on Sunday, he thought, as he started gathering his papers, then I'm havin' some private talks about gettin' a white man's sheriff for this county. He realized he had taken more time with the sermon than he'd planned. He had to get to the mill.

Killen scribbled a quick note as he stood by the table hurrying to leave: "civil rights crap!" He wanted to remind himself to add something to the sermon about the latest outrage. A new branch of the National Association for the Advancement of Colored People had been started up over in Oxford. He needed to talk to the boys about that, too.

Killen's wife, Madie, walked out to the porch, the screen door slamming behind her.

"I wondered where you were. Do you want some breakfast?" she asked.

"Gotta get to the mill, Madie, you know that," and as he pushed past her, Killen heard the radio news report coming from the kitchen. "The recent nomination of Eleanor Roosevelt at the Democratic Convention . . ." Killen thought about his disgust with the Democrats. He'd voted for Strom in '48, of course. Then, at this year's convention, that prissy-looking commie Stevenson that they picked to run for president had dropped dead.

"God's working his ways on the Democrats," he had commented to his wife. Now he listened as the report continued.

"Mrs. Franklin Delano Roosevelt's historic run has already started as her train is traveling to towns . . ."

Killen looked at his wife with the kind of stare that gave her a sick twist in her stomach. Killen had been in his father's house when Eleanor was First Lady, and he remembered the fury every time her name came up.

His daddy had loved to tell stories about the KKK in the 1920s, when they were four million strong and had political control in Tennessee, Oklahoma, Colorado, Oregon, and especially Indiana.

"Son," he'd say as he clicked off the radio in disgust after hearing Mrs. Roosevelt's voice, "you oughtta know, Ol' Edward Jackson got elected governor of Indiana in 1924, and he made sure the whole state government was full of his brothers from the Klan."

And every time Daddy Killen saw Mrs. Roosevelt in a picture with another one of "her niggers," as he called them, he'd talk about the "Klanbake Convention."

"You didn't see none of that crap in 1924, son. The KKK, we backed William McAdoo against that New Yorker Al Smith, that Catholic." Ed remembered how his father said Catholic with the same intonation he reserved for "nigger."

"Yep, Eddie, it took 103 ballots, but we kept Smith off, even if we didn't get ol' McAdoo. And we kept them commies from passing the anti-Klan plank, and when it was all over," here Ed remembered his father pausing, his eyes bright, "we went to that New Jersey field on Jew-lie fourth and burned a great big cross and one of them effigies of Al Smith. That was before we had the Jews-e-velts in Washington."

Daddy Killen said the Klan stood for something in the 1920s—for order and morality. Even white people that stepped out of line were punished. Once he told Ed about a white woman who'd been divorced, and the boys had stripped her to the waist, tied her to a tree, and beat her real bad. Ed thought about that as he looked at his wife.

"We wouldn't have that bitch running," Killen said bitterly to Madie, "if David Stephenson hadn't been so stupid."

Grand Dragon David Stephenson, a state Klan leader in Indiana, had been a powerful Republican politician when he kidnapped a schoolteacher named Madge Oberholtzer. He put her in a private train car, forced her to drink liquor, and mutilated her so badly one of her nipples was bitten off. She lived long enough to tell police, "David Stephenson did this to me, and he says he's above the law." But he wasn't. Stephenson got a life sentence, and the Klan's best days were over.

Madie had heard the Stephenson story many times, because Ed liked to tell her how he was going to be part of the great Klan revival, how more than twenty years had passed since Stephenson's stupid mistake, and the Klan was needed now more than ever. Sometimes, though, she thought he just liked to tell the grisly details of that poor girl's death so he could see the tears come to Madie's eyes.

"Did you hear that?" Killen asked, looking at his wife and pointing toward the radio. "The Democrats put that nigger-loving bitch up for president and now we're going to have to hear about her all the time." Killen spit the words like his mouth was filled with dirt.

He started pacing around the porch. "She's the one got them

nigger pilots sent to fight during the war, and got them jobs that white men should'a had, too. I remember that. I saw the pictures of them niggers going into them defense plants up North." He pulled the screen door open with a hard jerk. "I gotta get going. I promised the boys we'd do some planning," and he stomped into the house, grabbed the keys to his truck, and sped off to the mill.

The boys were gathered in the parking lot when Killen got there. Mountains of logs lay piled behind them, and some men held their cant hooks, ready to get to work. The smell of fresh-cut logs seasoned the heavy air.

"Hey, Ed, where you been?" Jim Barrow yelled before Killen could even get out of the truck.

"I know, I know. Eleenoor was on the radio and I just had to listen." He gave an ugly laugh. Killen approached the crew with the hint of swagger that their presence seemed to demand. "I got something to say," Killen said loud enough to get the attention of some stragglers who were having smokes and milling around. The circle of about a dozen men grew larger and tighter.

"Boys, this thing with Eleenoor Rosenvelt," and the group laughed, "well, we're not goin' to put up with it. But I can tell you one thing, it's gonna build the Klan, 'cause the woman is an out-and-out nigger-lovin' bitch!"

Over the grunts of agreement and echoing comments, Jim Barrow's sharp voice cut in, "We need to do something now, right now, tonight!"

"Yeah, Jim, I been thinking on that. Over in Lafayette County, that N-A-A-C-P sprung up 'nother chapter at the Second Baptist Church over there. I say we drive over there tonight and give the boy that started that trouble, this Nathan Hodges feller, we give that boy a little surprise package." He winked at Barrow, and the group talked about the plan as they headed into work.

Late that night, a bomb flew through the window of Nathan Hodges's house, and as he dove to the floor, he could hear several cars racing away into the darkness. Killen drove away last, hoping someone might run out. They had brought bats just in case. "That was a good one," he said with satisfaction. "One of you boys got a cigarette?"

"Here ya' go." Barrow handed Killen a lit cigarette. "That *was* a good one; it sent a message that ugly bitch Rosenvelt should hear."

"Oh, we'll make her hear, don't worry," Killen said.

"What you got in mind, Ed?" Barrow could always tell when Killen had a plan.

"You boys know that the KKK put out that $25,000 reward offer for killing that woman." He took a long draw, and let it out slowly. "Well, I just think I might figure out a way to collect on that." And he pressed his foot hard on the pedal as they sped through the cloud-covered Mississippi night.

CHAPTER 18

America's Deal

Philadelphia, Labor Day 1952

Joan and Maureen watched the crowd gather for more than two hours. They squinted into the bright blue sky, nervously watching the clock tower on Independence Hall as its hands crept closer toward five o'clock. The solid red brick building with its white cupola-topped tower had been restored two years earlier to its 1776 appearance, looking oddly out of time with the scene unfolding on its broad grassy plaza.

A massive parking lot had formed around the edges of the plaza. Powder blue Mercury coupes with white walls and white hoods pulled up next to Chevrolet Styleline sedans, but the most popular car seemed to be the Ford Country Squire station wagon. Families poured out of their cars loaded down with blankets and baskets of food for picnics on the lawn, its perimeter fence covered with red, white, and blue bunting. Men wore caps that declared allegiance to their unions—steel and electrical workers, carpenters, and miners. They smoked Camels from packs rolled into T-shirt sleeves and shared beer while their children ran in antic games of tag and dodged the adults. A little boy, scooped up to his father's shoulders, rubbed his hand over his daddy's hair, sniffed his fingers, and made a face as he smelled the Vaseline Cream hair tonic that kept each strand slick and shiny. As if by unwritten agreement, the crowd divided black from white, although no color line was drawn. Some people held copies of the *Philadelphia Inquirer* with Eleanor's "My Day" column, hoping they might get an autograph.

"Did you check the microphones?" Joan asked Maureen.

"Yes, for the third time since *you* checked them," Maureen laughed, "and yes, Eleanor knows where the press will be waiting, and yes, I know this is the most important speech of the campaign. Trust me, Joan, she'll be wonderful."

"I know, I know. I'm a worrywart. If I hadn't just done my nails, I'd have bitten them to the bone. Okay." Joan glanced at the clock tower and checked her watch. "Time for the marching band," and she strode off.

Children began to scream and point as the State Normal School at Cheyney marching band strutted down the lane that had been kept clear in the center of the plaza. Cheerleading girls in matching short flounced skirts handspringed and cartwheeled into view, leading a legion of baton-twirling majorettes followed by the bandleader in his tall, royal blue headdress topped by a red plume that doubled its height. He marched with an impossibly high step, the brass and percussion players behind him pounding out a heart-arresting rhythm as the crowd began to clap and cheer.

Several members of the press held their pens above their waiting pads as if they were in shock, but Scotty Reston was writing with glee.

"Negro marching band—most had never seen—never at white candidate's event . . ."

As the band lined up next to the stage, the raised platform began to fill with state Democratic Party officials. Maurice Splain Jr., Democratic Party chairman, stood at the microphone, looking around with a satisfied smile and waving at people in the crowd.

"Tell me again why we picked a state where the governor and both senators are Republicans," Joan was saying to Larry O'Brien.

"Because it's a must win."

Joan looked skeptical.

"Look at the union members here, Joan. Look at the Negroes. They can carry us over the top in this state, but we have to rally them. After she gives this speech, believe me—we're going to need them."

"I take it Mrs. R. didn't listen to you."

Larry gave a grim laugh. "No, but what did we expect? I think this is probably political suicide. More fodder for McCarthy and the others, as if they needed any. But you know what, Joan?" He put his hand on her shoulder and looked her in the eye.

"You and I aren't running for president—she is. And a big part of me thinks, maybe she ought to just say what she believes, not what we political strategy smart alecks think will win her votes."

"I'm writing that down, Larry, because I have a feeling you won't believe you said that two months from now."

Several weeks before, Eleanor had met with her close friend, Mary McCloud Bethune. The fifteenth of seventeen children born to illiterate sharecroppers in Mayesville, South Carolina, Bethune's parents had been slaves. She was the first in her family to be educated, and had been part of what came to be called the Black Cabinet during the 1930s, advising Franklin and Eleanor on civil rights reforms. Eleanor counted Mary among her closest friends.

As Eleanor headed across the Midwest on a late summer campaign swing, she asked Mary to meet her in Cleveland. They sat to-

gether on two folding chairs in a small storage room in the "Eleanor for President" headquarters in town. Mary was seventy-seven
years old, and Eleanor saw with concern that she moved her large
body with slow care, overfilling the flimsy chair as she lowered herself to it. Mary is so elegant, Eleanor thought, looking fondly at her
older friend's full head of white hair under a smart black hat, and
the three-strand pearl necklace, like the one Eleanor favored. Mary
pulled a small notebook out of her oversized handbag.

"You said this was about the civil rights part of the program
you're going to announce, so I brought you this." Mary handed
Eleanor the book.

"Reconstruction Era Civil Rights Laws," Eleanor read from the
binding.

"That's right," Mary spoke with firm authority. "If you're president, you have the right—no, you have the *duty*," Mary paused and
gave Eleanor a meaningful stare over the top of her glasses, "the
duty to see that these laws are understood and enforced."

"You're talking about executive orders," Eleanor said.

"If necessary, yes. If your Congress won't pass what we need,
well, you need to tell them that another Congress already did."

"But they can overturn an executive order . . ."

"Let them try. You'll veto it. Eleanor, I don't have to tell you
that Truman not only couldn't get the Fair Employment Practices
Commission made permanent, he couldn't pass antipoll tax or
even antilynching legislation. These boys need to be reminded that
they're not the only game in town, and executive orders will be the
way to prove it, if need be."

"And the Supreme Court . . ."

"Let *them* try. Besides, we want them to revisit separate but
equal, don't we?"

"Of course."

"I know it's radical, Eleanor, but you're the only one who might
be able to make a strategy like this work. And making it part of

your program will galvanize the Negro community well beyond the fact of your candidacy. Talk to Spotswood Robinson about it," Mary said, referring to the NAACP attorney who was working on school desegregation cases.

When Eleanor told Larry about her discussion with Mary, his reaction was predictable. "You could lose every southern state with an antagonistic approach like this."

"That's what Sam's doing down there, isn't it?" Eleanor asked. "Assuring them that he'll be a moderating influence? I'll be sure he knows what I'm planning to say."

As Larry stood in front of Independence Hall, waiting for Eleanor to present her plan, he folded his arms over his chest and tried not to look grim.

Suddenly the band stopped in the midst of John Philip Sousa's "Anchor and Star," and struck up "Happy Days Are Here Again." Eleanor had walked out the door of Independence Hall waving her arms high over her head. She was laughing and smiling so that her cheeks puffed out, her eyes crinkled nearly shut, and her teeth, like a row of spanking new domino blanks, lit up her face. She wore a matching rose-colored skirt and jacket and her trademark three-strand pearl necklace. As she neared the stage, the woodwinds fell silent as the brass and percussion players switched songs, standing up and bouncing to the beat as they belted out the hit song "Rocket 88."

"Ooohhhh." Maureen had walked up behind Joan and grabbed her shoulder, moving her back and forth to the irresistible rhythm. "I love this song; what a great choice for her campaign song!"

Joan was laughing. "I agree. Look at the crowd. The plaza looks like a giant dance floor."

Maureen yelled over the music and clapping, "Did you know that Oldsmobile wants to give her a red Rocket 88 convertible for the campaign?"

"You mean, they want to give it to her for all the good publicity they're getting," Joan replied.

Larry had suggested the song. It had a new kind of sound, a subtle departure from rhythm and blues that some people called rock and roll.

"It represents change," he had told Eleanor. "Guys like it because they love that Olds. It's a young people's song, not a gray-haired grandma kind of song, if you see what I mean."

"Larry, I love it. I absolutely love it," Eleanor said. "My grandson played it for me last year, and I couldn't stay in my seat. You know I love to dance . . . and I love to drive." They shared a laugh, both aware that Eleanor, who learned to drive late in life, was unsteady behind the wheel. Just a few years before, she'd crashed into two other cars. Along with her other injuries, the bottom half of Eleanor's two protruding front teeth had broken off as they cracked against the steering wheel. She had porcelain caps put on, asking with shy hesitation if the teeth might be straightened a bit. When the dentist had finished, Eleanor's overbite had disappeared. She had gazed in shock at her new smile—straight, white, and perfect. As she walked onto the stage, her smile beaming at the ecstatic crowd, some people noticed a subtle difference in her familiar face that they couldn't pinpoint.

Chairman Splain was motioning wildly to the bandleader, drawing his index finger across his throat over and over again until the band, with a blaring, syncopated flourish, finally stopped playing. Groans and shouts of "more, more," were heard in the crowd, but Splain had his mouth close to the main microphone as he called for quiet, and the loudspeakers gradually overtook the crowd's protests.

"Thank you, thank you, everyone for that great response to the State Normal School at Cheyney marching band! One of the greatest colleges in this great state. Let's here it for them again!"

The band members stood up and raised their instruments toward the crowd, then, with a coordinated ba-ba-ba-boom, they sat down as one. When the crowd quieted, Splain began again.

"Ladies and gentlemen, today I have the greatest honor that has ever fallen to me. That of introducing my party's nominee for president, but more than that, of introducing a person who I admire, in fact revere because I remember . . ."

"Uh-oh," Joan poked Maureen in the rib, "we've got a talker." The women exchanged wry grins as Splain began to sound like he would recount the entire history of Eleanor's twelve years in the White House followed by her feats in the UN. But the crowd got restless when he started to name and explain New Deal programs. A small contingent of steelworkers stood up and began chanting, "Eleanor, Eleanor," and waving "Steelworkers for Eleanor" signs. Splain looked annoyed, then embarrassed as the chanting grew louder. Finally, he relented.

"Well, I can see it's not me you want to hear." He tried to laugh over the shouts of "you got that right."

"So let me introduce the next president of the United States, Eleanor Roosevelt."

Another short round of "Rocket 88" accompanied Eleanor as she walked to the bank of microphones. The crowd had leapt to its feet, and TV cameras and photographers whirled around to catch the explosive sight of banners and signs thrusting into the air, some carried by children held aloft by their parents.

"Thank you, my friends," Eleanor began as the crowd sat down again. "This is a happy day when we can be with our families, celebrate the lives of working people and remember the freedoms and rights that have taken us to this point in our history. It is those freedoms and rights that I want to speak of today, which is why I have chosen this hallowed spot, where the greatest document in the history of democracy was conceived and executed, our United States Constitution.

"Many of you here are in unions, and while you do not yet represent all of labor, I hope someday you will," Eleanor tried to continue, but the crowd had risen again, and its shouts were drowning her out.

"See what I mean? Those are people who will really work for her and who will definitely vote," Larry said to Joan, looking satisfied. Eleanor raised her arms to settle the crowd, and went on.

"I believe that it is through strength, through the fact that people who know what people need are working to make this country a better place for all people, that we will help the world to accept our leadership and understand that, under our form of government and through our way of life, we have something to offer them. That is why I am proposing a plan that will guide my campaign, a plan drawn from your letters to me, from your conversations with me, from my many years of traveling this country and seeing both what is good and what we can, together, make better."

"Did we ever get a count on the letters?" Joan asked, turning to Maureen.

"After that column she wrote last month asking for people's help and ideas?" asked Maureen, and Joan nodded.

"Two hundred fifty thousand and counting." Joan's mouth dropped open. "And remember she told Larry she wouldn't ask for money? Well, it came in anyway—checks, dollar bills, even coins." Maureen shook her head. "I told her, 'Mrs. R., don't even try to tell me to send this money back.' Oh, listen." Maureen pointed to the stage.

"I am calling this plan America's Deal," Eleanor was saying, "because it is both a promise of what my administration will do for our citizens as well as a challenge to you, *as citizens,* to take part in the changes we all believe are right and are needed.

"First shall be equality of rights for all Americans. Unless we grant four fundamental rights, we are agreeing on a course that will lead to fascism. These four rights are the litmus tests of our democracy: the right to an education according to ability; the right to earn a living according to ability; the right to equal justice before the law; and the right to participate in government through the ballot.

"I vow as your president to honor and enforce both the Fourteenth and Fifteenth Amendments to the United States Constitution. In the last century, many laws were passed to uphold these amendments—laws that have not been enforced. Instead, we have allowed states to violate all concepts of justice and decency without interference by the federal government.

"President Truman made some progress through executive orders integrating the military and the federal workforce, but his other attempts at civil rights reform through legislation were thwarted by Congress. I vow today that if Congress will not recognize its duty to democracy, then I will look back to those laws passed, no doubt in the belief, that seventy-five years after their enactment the rights they sought to restore would be secure.

"Deep-rooted prejudice—the stubborn ignorance of large groups of citizens, which has led to injustice, inequality, and, sometimes, brutality—is a disease. As president, I will end the ugliness and degradation of discrimination so that we are a true beacon of democracy that the world will respect and follow."

The crowd had risen again, and, as if by some unspoken signal, the band began playing "The Battle Hymn of the Republic." As the drawn-out cadences floated over the plaza, men and women began to sing, some with tears in their eyes. In the background, a solemn rhythmic chant began like a Greek chorus, "El-e-nor, El-e-nor."

Eleanor waited, singing softly along with the crowd. When the music faded, she went on.

"The second goal of America's Deal is my guarantee to protect your civil liberties. In this state, two thousand state employees were led by the Republican governor in a loyalty oath after he had banned communism in Pennsylvania." Boos and hisses could be heard throughout the crowd.

"Let us remember that William Penn, who founded this state, was a Quaker who refused to swear any oaths. Today, Quakers are being fired for doing the same. Some are teachers, some doctors and nurses. I will fight against Senator McCarthy and those who follow his tactics of using fear to control thought. Is Senator McCarthy such a coward that he fears open debate with Communists or their sympathizers? Perhaps he is, but I am not." Eleanor's face looked fierce, and the crowd began chanting, "McCarthy's a coward, McCarthy's a coward," so that she had to pause before she could be heard.

"More than most Americans," Eleanor went on, "I know the dangers of communism because I have sat with the Soviets in the UN. I despise the control they hold over men's minds. And that is why I despise what Senator McCarthy has done, for he would use the same methods of fear as the Soviets use to control all thought that is not according to his own pattern, but he does this in our free country! America's Deal is my promise to protect our most sacred freedoms—freedom of speech, freedom of the press, freedom of assembly."

As Eleanor outlined the last goals of her plan, to provide universal health care, government-funded housing assistance, and improved educational assistance, Joan walked into Independence Hall to check on the room for the press conference. As she entered the cool dark entrance hall, she saw Larry talking to a woman who she guessed was not much older than her. He motioned for Joan to join them.

"Joan, meet Alice Lake. She used to work for George Gallup."

"Used to?"

Alice gave her a broad, open smile and Joan thought how much the woman's eyes reminded her of the sky outside. She was a few inches taller than Joan, and thin enough to look like a model in her fitted sheath dress with the mandarin collar. It had that Venetian harlequin pattern that Joan just loved.

"I've left Mr. Gallup because I want to work for Mrs. Roosevelt as her pollster. I've been telling Mr. O'Brien some ideas I have for a new way of polling that can help shape what Mrs. Roosevelt says to people."

"Uh, stop right there." Joan held her hand up like a traffic cop. "Larry, you've heard what Mrs. R. says about these new ideas in polling. She won't allow some poll to dictate what she says. Anyway, I thought these polls were just for the horse race, to say who's going to win or not."

"They have been," Alice seemed totally undeterred by Joan's comments, "but I have a way we can do something far more useful. For instance, Larry told me about America's Deal. It's radical, and the newspapers, not to mention the Republicans, are going to say it's outrageous and worse. But what if we can show it's popular?"

"What if you can't?" Joan shot back.

"Nothing lost. But if we can, we have a powerful scientific tool to use against the naysayers, and to reassure voters."

"It wasn't so scientific in '48, when you said Dewey had it won," Joan said.

"I've come up with methods that will keep that from happening, I'm certain."

"Well, what does Mrs. R. think?" Joan asked.

"That's just it, Joan," Larry said, putting his hand on her shoulder. "We're not going to tell her just yet. That's why I need you to be Alice's contact."

"But, Larry, I think . . ."

"Trust me on this, Joan. I have a hunch it will be just what we need down the road, and if it isn't, well then, it won't matter."

"Okay, Larry, if you say so. I gotta go to the press room. Alice," Joan held out her hand and Alice gave it a firm shake, "welcome to a very crazy ride."

"Nothing I like better," she answered with a wink.

Reporters were already crowded into the meeting room reserved for the press conference, jostling for position up front. As soon as Eleanor walked in, looking flushed and jubilant, questions shot out at her like verbal rockets.

"Mrs. Roosevelt, isn't America's Deal socialism by another name?"

"Are you proposing separate but equal schools or integrated schools?"

"Why are your sons, Elliott and James, still supporting General Eisenhower?"

"Eleanor, would you use federal troops to enforce voting rights?"

"Truman couldn't get universal health care, what makes you think you can?"

"Please, everyone, please." Eleanor laughed as she adjusted the single microphone on the lectern. "I promise to answer all of your questions. Don't worry, I'm happy to stay as long as you like, just let me get a drink of water." She looked expectantly over toward Joan, who was elbowing her way through the throng carrying a glass. The reporters had quieted, some flipping their notebooks as they held their hands in the air hoping to be recognized.

"All right," Eleanor said. "How about you, Ed?" She pointed to the reporter from United Press International.

"Aren't you afraid of losing the entire South with these proposals?" the man spoke up quickly, a touch of aggression in his voice.

"I'm glad you brought that up. Let me read you something I just received from a young campaign worker in Alabama who is registering Negroes to vote. Her name is Barbara Rose Johns." Eleanor opened her purse and unfolded a letter written on lined paper that looked like it had been torn from a notebook.

"'There is lots of excitement here,'" Eleanor read, "'but people are afraid to talk to us sometimes because of being threatened. But we won't give up, don't worry. I carry the Constitution like a Bible, which it is in a way, and I show them where they have the *right* to vote.'" Eleanor folded the letter and put it back in her purse. "If young people like Barbara Rose can show such bravery in support of our democracy, surely I needn't fear the loss of some votes, wouldn't you agree?" Eleanor turned a probing look on the reporter who had asked the question. "We should all pray for the safety of Barbara Rose and others like her, as they are the true heroes of this campaign."

CHAPTER 19

Rough-and-Tumble Politics

Jonathon Chamberlain's problem started at the Hotel Commodore, which served as Citizens for Ike headquarters, or "CFI," as everyone called it. Chester Turnbull, Sherman Adams's top aide, came by Jonathon's desk to ask if he wanted to go for a drink. Kingston Brand, Dewey's liaison to the campaign, was already waiting at the elevator.

Maybe I'll get a chance to talk some substance tonight, Jonathon thought, as the three took a corner booth behind some of the thick-fringed plants that gave the Palm Room its name. As they slid into the booth, Jonathon had the fleeting thought that Turnbull would get wedged between the booth and the table. Something about the man put Jonathon on edge, but he had enough political instinct to know that who you knew often counted more than what you knew. He needed these men to think well of him, especially Turnbull, if he wanted to get more responsibility in the campaign.

Brand loved the Yankees, and he was anxious to moan about the previous night's game. Chicago White Sox pitcher Lou Kretlow had thrown his second consecutive two-hitter, and the Sox beat New York, 7–0.

"Do you believe that hurler Kretlow?" Brand asked as soon as the men were settled. He looked disgusted. "Well, they did have to play in Comiskey Park, I suppose."

Turnbull replied, "Kretlow's a journeyman. The Yankees won't be down for long. Anyway, I want to talk about the campaign. I've got some new ideas I want to discuss with you two."

Jonathon caught the word "two" like a soft pitch right to his glove and settled more comfortably into the booth. Maybe he'd read this guy wrong. He had overheard Turnbull discussing the campaign message at the headquarters. He basically agreed with the man's argument that the campaign should play up Ike the war hero and Nixon the commie hunter to best contrast with Mrs. Roosevelt. "We'll appeal to the security concerns of the lay-dees," Turnbull had said. Taking a quick gulp of his martini, he launched into this latest campaign theory.

"It's taken the females of this country thirty years to realize they got the right to vote, but by God, this election they're going to vote in droves. I'm sure of it. And the most important thing to remember is they don't see Mrs. R. as a female like them. They do not. She's another animal entirely. In fact, I'm betting they don't like the idea that a woman is running at all, former First Lady or not. So we've got to get ready to reel them in and make full use of them." He punctuated the last four words as if his impatient index finger was punching hard on a stubborn elevator button just in front of his face.

"We need to make them feel comfortable and confident that Ike's going to do the job the way they want it done." Turnbull's fleshy face went a ripe red, and his thin lips disappeared in a broad grin. Holding his glass up, he said, "And I've got the slogan they're going to love: 'General Eisenhower, the only man for the job.'" He laughed, so that Jonathon couldn't tell if he was serious or not.

"The ladies want a man to save them from the Communists 'cause they're scared for their babies, and they should be. Son," he said looking straight at Jonathon, "do you realize that it was in this very hotel that Nixon trapped that pinko high-brow Hiss? Right here, goddamn it, he got Hiss. Right here's where they had the hearing. That's the kind of stuff you've got to know, son. Hiss tried to weasel his way around the fact that he knew that Chambers guy, but Nixon got him. Got him right here. Did you know that?"

But Brand interrupted before Jonathon could answer, overeager to back up Turnbull. "Our polls are showing that women are more concerned about getting out of Korea than men. And I don't think they're going to believe a grandmother has the answers."

Jonathon decided to ignore Turnbull's question. Just when I'm starting to trust him, he thought, the guy starts treating me like I'm an idiot. Everyone knew about the Hiss hearing at the Commodore.

"I agree on Korea," Jonathon offered. "Women today are homemakers first and foremost. I think they'll respond to messages appealing to security for their family and male leadership to do that. But I'm afraid there's a problem there, too. I mean, with Stevenson's divorce, we had a great contrast to Ike and Mamie and Dick and Pat. They're two great couples, terrific families, all that. But now we're running against the country's most famous grandmother, I mean all those stories with her kids and grandkids. It all reminds everyone of her marriage to FDR. We don't want voters seeing her as a surrogate continuing her husband's . . ."

Jonathon's words trailed off as he saw the smirk on Turnbull's face.

"Not a problem, son. Not a problem. It's not a problem now, is it Kingston?" The two men exchanged a conspiratorial grin. "Do you want to tell him how much it's not a problem, or should I?" Turnbull asked.

"Go ahead. You're the one who saw the proof." Brand waved for the waitress to bring more drinks.

Turnbull swigged the last of his martini and looked at Jonathon. "I'm going to put it to you bluntly, son. But remember, it's real explosive stuff and we've got to handle it very carefully." Turnbull's eyes were oddly large in an otherwise porcine face, but they narrowed as he spoke to Jonathon. He'd been wondering about this clean-cut kid who hadn't loosened his well-knotted tie and whose shoe leather was overpolished and underworn. Probably just here because his daddy has a lot of dough behind Ike, so his pretty-faced kid gets to ride the campaign train. Well, let's see how prep-school boy handles the real shit. If I can get him to run home to mama, I could get the governor of Wisconsin off my back and bring in his kid.

Turnbull took a dramatic pause, pretending to move his glass to an invisible mark on the white tablecloth, and then he looked at Jonathon.

"She's a dyke, pure and simple and no doubt about it," Turnbull said. "There've been rumors, maybe you heard about them?" Turnbull leaned forward as if waiting for an answer, although he was certain Jonathon wasn't privy to political gossip. "Anyway, there have been rumors, but so what, right? Well, so what is that we just saw a letter, and it's proof positive. No 'so what' anymore. Proof just as pure as twelve-year-old scotch, if you know what I mean."

Jonathon's face had flushed well before Turnbull finished, and he sat back in his chair as if he'd been shoved hard. "You're telling me Eleanor Roosevelt is a queer?"

"That's right, son. And it's a vice. Not to mention, it's a mental illness. Not to mention, mind you, that it's just plain disgusting," Turnbull answered.

Jonathon was nodding slowly as he regained his composure. "What kind of letter?" he asked carefully. "And, how did you see it?"

"That shouldn't concern you, but it's from Mrs. R. to one particular former AP reporter named Lorena Hickok."

Turnbull would be damned before he'd tell this kid the source, although anybody who knew Washington could have guessed pretty easily. Turnbull had gotten the call from Hoover two days before.

"I want you to get a message to your boss, Adams," Hoover had said without preliminaries. "I had Mrs. Roosevelt in for the meeting."

Turnbull understood. The FBI director made it a practice to invite potential political foes, even presidential candidates, to his office for a chat where he would reveal embarrassing information he'd dug up on them. Duly warned, few people had the courage to cross him. He'd run the agency since 1924, and he intended to be there for a lot longer. That's why Hoover had asked Mrs. Roosevelt if she would see him in his office shortly after she got the nomination.

"Mrs. Roosevelt." Hoover had sprung up from behind his desk to greet her, holding the chair for her to sit down, then circling back to his own perch where papers were spread out before him.

Eleanor had never liked the man. She had talked to Franklin many times about firing him, but he said Hoover had too much political power. She couldn't see why. He had the look of a bulldog past its prime—sagged, slow, and growly. Franklin wouldn't even take action after Hoover came to him with a phony tape recording of a supposed sexual interlude between Eleanor and her friend, Joe Lash. Eleanor had been furious, but Franklin was oddly passive, and Hoover stayed.

Eleanor gave Hoover's hand the briefest touch as she sat down. The room felt close and smelled of wood soaked in cigar smoke.

"You know I'm always quite interested in the work of this agency, Mr. Hoover. Please tell me what I can do for you."

"Oh, Mrs. Roosevelt. I want to help you, you see." Hoover shuffled some papers with portentous motions, finally pulling one out and handing it to Eleanor. She recognized her stationery, saw the date of February 1934, and recognized her own letter to Lorena Hickok. She didn't have to read it, she had done so many times before sending it, and even this many years later she knew it spoke explicitly of her longing and love. Eleanor laid the letter on the desk in front of her and looked Hoover in the eyes. He was repressing a smirk, and she fought the urge to walk out and let him think he'd won.

"I had been told that your agents were in the Hyde Park Post Office opening and reading people's mail," Eleanor began, speaking with slow deliberation. "But at that point in my life, I was too naïve to believe that any government official would so subvert the Constitutional freedoms of American citizens. I have since become much wiser, Mr. Hoover." Eleanor stood up and leaned over the desk toward the FBI director, who didn't move from his chair. "You are abetting the worst elements in this country in their zeal to label anyone they disagree with a Communist. That little people have become frightened, that we find ourselves living in the atmosphere of a police state, where people close doors before they state what they think, that can be laid at the doorstep of this agency and this office." Eleanor walked to the door, turning just before she opened it.

"Do what you will, Mr. Hoover. Your time is short."

Eleanor felt herself shaking as she walked out of the office, at the same time wondering what Hoover had brought to Franklin to keep her husband in line.

Hoover had turned bright red and grabbed the telephone as soon as the door shut behind Eleanor. That's when he'd gotten Turnbull on the phone, arranged to show him the letter, and told him it was available to get into play in the campaign.

Turnbull was happy to take the job, and he was relishing the discomfort on Jonathon's face as he pressed the salacious news.

"This Hickok lady and the *First* Lady, they got close after FDR's first election in '33. *Very* close." Turnbull gulped his drink and wiped the back of his hand across his mouth. "And Hickok didn't really bother to hide the fact that she played for the other team. For a while she even moved into the White House. She and Mrs. Roosevelt had some nice trips together. For a couple of years, they were *always* together. Of course, Hickok's friends in the press kept it quiet, but, like I said, there were rumors."

Jonathon still looked skeptical. "What did the letter say?"

"Oh, I can remember the high points, something like 'I want to put my arms around you . . . can't wait to hold you close . . . I look at your ring and know you love me' . . . that kind of thing. Really sickening stuff, I'm telling you, just sickening, sickening stuff." Turnbull folded his arms and sat back with a satisfied look on his face.

Jonathon's astonishment had faded. Instead, he looked worried. Waiting for the waitress to leave their drinks and walk away, he spoke slowly to the other two men.

"Assuming it is true, what do you expect to do with it?"

"Come on, son." Suddenly, Turnbull's familiarity felt grating to Jonathon.

"It's the nail in her coffin, but we put a real thick cloth over the hammer. Know what I mean? Everyone already thinks she's an odd kind of woman. Why else would she run for president? It's a man's job, plain and simple. And the rumors about her woman friend have been out there for a while." Turnbull's voice took on a slight tone of exasperation as Jonathon's expression turned stonier. "We just let some key people know that we can show them *proof,* that's all. Someone like Cholly Knickerbocker over at Hearst. He loves this shit."

"Yeah, or what about Hedda Hopper at the *LA Times*?" Brand offered eagerly.

"Right," Turnbull agreed. "Just tarnish her image enough to help the voters. Let them know that she's not the kind of person they want running the country. See what I mean?"

Jonathon felt his stomach begin to churn. Ever since he was a child, his emotions seemed to settle in his gut, and he recognized the familiar tightening, as if someone were reaching in and squeezing his intestines. He wondered if the general knew about this, but he decided not to ask. He excused himself as soon as possible, saying he had an early meeting. As he walked out, Turnbull raised his glass to Brand. "There's a kid I'm betting we won't be seeing again."

Jonathon's mind was feeling as heavy as his legs as he trudged up five flights to his tiny apartment in Greenwich Village. He tried to remember that he was lucky to have a place of his own. The tide of returning vets was straining all of the city's resources, but especially housing. Jonathon's ties to the Eisenhower political apparatus was pull enough to get him his airless space in an old tenement building, but every newspaper story about a vet left him feeling a mix of guilt and envy. He'd missed going to war by one year. Jonathon hoped he could make up for that by helping the war's great general become president.

As he got ready for bed, taking a cold shower to wash away the sweaty grime, Jonathon thought about the cool evenings of Maine in summer. By contrast, Manhattan nights gathered the thick daytime soup of sun-boiled air and served it black. He fell into bed like a man drunk beyond consciousness. At 7:00 a.m., the alarm clock exhausted its ring to no avail. Jonathon woke and panicked more than an hour later. The morning campaign meeting started at 9:00 a.m. sharp.

As Jonathon hung from a strap on the screeching, careening subway car, he tried to shut out the mass of people pressing against him and the fact that some of them were already rank with sweat. He wanted to focus on the problem that still roiled his mind. He tried to convince himself that, as Turnbull put it, they were just playing the "rough-and-tumble game of politics," but Jonathon couldn't reconcile himself to the rules. He didn't want to seem naïve, or worse yet, weak. He felt sure he could play with the "big boys," the old political pros, because he had an unshakable confidence that they needed new ideas. But this lesbian thing, it wasn't about ideas, it wasn't even about politics. As far as Jonathon was concerned, it was about winning at any cost, even if that meant savaging the reputation of the most admired woman in the world. Did he believe the end justified the means? He didn't think so, but this was politics, and maybe he had to change his thinking.

"What if she is a homophile?" Jonathon thought. "What if it is true?" As he jogged toward the Commodore, he alternated between worrying about Turnbull's revelation and whether or not he'd look like a sweat-soaked mess by the time he reached the office.

CHAPTER 20

Lorena

Eleanor had decided not to tell anyone on the campaign about the real substance of her meeting with J. Edgar Hoover. After the Labor Day press conference, the campaign had been besieged with questions about America's Deal. Joan felt like she was bringing Eleanor bad news day after day.

"Another bunch of editorials, Mrs. R.," Joan said glumly, carrying a stack of newspapers into her regular afternoon meeting in Eleanor's campaign office. They sat on the oak chairs that had been made years before in the Val-Kill furniture factory. Joan had grown used to the stacks of papers that seemed to mushroom in the room every day. But, despite the chaos, Maureen could locate a document in an instant, and she was never far from Eleanor's side. Joan wondered at how Maureen had stepped so seamlessly into the legendary Tommy's place. She liked Maureen's frankness and sense of humor, and admired her efficiency, but her devotion to Eleanor reminded Joan of an apostle. Joan admired Eleanor and basked in her compassionate charisma, but the younger woman didn't believe there were any saints left in the world. She wasn't sure Maureen would agree.

Joan lit a Fatima king-size. Alice, "the secret-poll weapon," as Joan thought of her, had recommended the cigarette, and Joan liked that it seemed sort of exotic.

"That has an odd aroma," Eleanor remarked, as Joan leafed through the newspapers.

"It's Turkish." Joan tilted her head back as she imagined Ann Blyth would do and slowly blew out a thin plume. She was dying to see Blyth in *The World in His Arms,* with Gregory Peck, but she was sure it would be gone from the theaters before she got a chance. Joan looked down at her stack. "Okay, the *Cleveland Plain Dealer* says universal health care is a socialist plot, um, let's see; the *Pittsburgh Sun Telegraph* says FDR is turning over in his grave and would never have endorsed such radical proposals; the *Rocky Mountain News* says America's Deal is dangerous government overreaching. You know how those westerners love the federal government. I won't even bother to go over the southern papers. 'Nigger lover' is one of the nicer things they call you."

"Aren't there any that have something good to say?" Eleanor asked.

"Actually, yes." Joan waved a newspaper over her head.

"Hooray for the *Baltimore Afro-American.* They're fully in support of America's Deal, and they endorsed you."

"Don't make light of that, Joan. That paper reaches beyond Baltimore, into Philadelphia, D.C., Delaware . . ."

"I know, Mrs. R. I just meant it wasn't much of a surprise."

"No, that is not a surprise," Eleanor said, thinking about the surprise and shock of her staff if they saw the letter that Hoover held. She just hoped he wouldn't use it. After all, she was doing so poorly, he wouldn't have to. She was sure he would rather not risk exposing his tactics of reading people's mail. There would be a backlash if that was found out. Perhaps even a congressional investigation. No, she decided it was better to say nothing to anyone at this point and assume it would never come out. But ever since he showed her the letter, she had been struggling to suppress her memories.

As an Associated Press reporter, Lorena had been assigned to cover Eleanor in the '32 campaign. At first, Eleanor ignored the way their eyes seemed to catch for a moment too long, but soon she realized it was no accident. She remembered the way Lorena began to seek her out at odd moments when she was alone, the way their talk about campaign strategy and women's rights soon turned to more.

She remembered being in her sitting room in the White House just after the inauguration in 1933. They sat on the sandstone-colored button sofa with gold fringe that Eleanor had brought from Val-Kill. She loved it because it was deep enough for her to pull her long legs nearly under her as she nestled in the corner. Lorena piled pillows behind her back. Short and thick-bodied, her feet barely reached the floor. The tall southern windows let the low-slung winter sun stream through. It seemed to bleach the white bear's fur rug at their feet. Newspapers were scattered on the back of the couch and the floor, but she and Lorena had drifted from talk of FDR's election and Eleanor's new role to more self-indulgent chatter.

Eleanor remembered the exact moment when their friendship became something more, like a film clip that she could turn on in her mind. She had teased Lorena about cutting her dark wavy hair so short, and then leaned over to tousle it. Instead of dodging her hand, Lorena leaned forward as well, reaching her hand behind Eleanor's head and gently pulling her forward. As their lips touched, hesitantly at first then with insistence, Eleanor forgot her surprise. Later she thought, could anything have been more natural, anything more joyful than making love with Lorena?

After that moment, they had been together as much as possible. She told Lorena secrets she had never shared. On the day of Franklin's first inaugural, she had asked Lorena to come with her to what she thought of as her "secret place."

"We need to get a cab. I want to take you to Rock Creek Cemetery."

"Uh-oh." Lorena gave a doubtful laugh. "Sounds deadly." But Eleanor hadn't smiled, and when they walked past graves that dated back to the early 1700s and behind a grove of holly trees, Eleanor had motioned for Lorena to sit next to her on a stone bench. In front of them was a seated figure in bronze, more than twice life-size, cloaked from head to foot.

"You can't tell if it's a man or a woman, can you?" Eleanor asked. "When I discovered in 1918 that Franklin was having an affair with my social secretary, I would come here and sit for hours by myself. You see, Henry Adams's wife had committed suicide because he had an affair, and he had Saint-Gaudens make this statue for her graveside. Mark Twain called it 'Grief.'"

They sat quietly for a few minutes looking at the enigmatic figure before Eleanor went on. "I used to think about death, too. There were times when following Clover Adams seemed easier than living." Eleanor turned toward Lorena and took her hand.

"But now I have found you, and I have found happiness, and I am glad to be alive."

It's no one's business, Eleanor thought as she looked at Joan, who had taken the papers to a large conference table where she stood clipping and sorting her "stinky news clips," as she called them. She knew Joan's mother, Ruby, and other reporters in the '30s had an idea of what was going on in her private life. But they didn't speak of it, at least not to her. And they certainly didn't write about it.

Of course, the same rules didn't apply anymore, Eleanor thought bitterly. Jack Anderson, that shill for McCarthy, delighted in exposing and passing innuendos about homosexuals in his "Washington Merry-Go-Round" column. Yes, Eleanor thought, that's probably who Hoover would go to first.

Suddenly, she longed to be in the holly grove again, sitting by Clover's statue, hidden from the world, alone with her memories. Running for president felt like a terrible, grotesque mistake. She was going to lose in the worst way, by being slandered and ridiculed. And all her friends and staff, all the people she loved would be dragged down with her, sullied by their association with her, their reputations ruined. How could she have been so terribly, stupidly wrong? Watching Joan, Eleanor felt her throat tighten, and she struggled to breathe.

CHAPTER 21

Bugs and Co-Hogs

Citizens for Ike campaign headquarters at the Hotel Commodore took up the entire tenth floor. The room doors were propped open from one end of the long corridor to the other. Lower-level operatives scurried between bedrooms-turned-offices carrying mimeographed sheets and handwritten messages to those in command.

Jonathon loved the action. The tenth floor was less of a place to him than an organism that pulsed with political drama. At the end of the morning meeting, Sherman Adams took him aside to say that he'd be working with the branding genius Rosser Reeves on the television ads for Ike. Jonathon felt as if he'd won a prize. He'd be doing real work, maybe the most important work in the campaign. Jonathon believed that the rapidly growing reach of television had the power to shape thinking. No one had proven that better than Reeves. Now he'd be the man's aide, hopefully his protégé.

"Hey, Walter," Jonathon said, grabbing the arm of another young man who had rolled up his shirtsleeves, but whose tie was still snug. "How about grabbing some lunch with me? I found a great little spot the other day."

As they stood in line at Maxine's sandwich shop on 45th near Madison Avenue, Jonathon filled Walter Jackson in on his new assignment. Maxine's was a linoleum-and-mirrors kind of place, tucked under the protective grandeur of the Equitable Trust Building. No place within a mile served roast beef as rare, piled as high, for so little money. The two young men took a two-top, with barely enough room for Walter to slide between the adjacent tables to the plastic-covered chair that abutted the wall. The proximity to other diners made Maxine's an impolitic choice for political types who were throwing around the latest gossip and rumors. But there was a certain security in the clatter of plates, the rude cries of the servers announcing that an order was ready, and the cacophonous crescendos of the hungry lunch-hour horde.

Jonathon took quick note of the two women at the table next to him, who looked around his age. He couldn't help but notice the one sitting opposite to him with her back against the wall. Her high-glossed nails matched her red lipstick, and complemented her thick, reddish-brown hair. He hadn't had time for dating in the last two years, much less a relationship. Mary Hancock had wanted to get married, but that was a college fling. He was far from ready at the time. No one since had made him think of much more than a night of pleasure and release.

"I'm telling you, Walter, Reeves's ads will make General Eisenhower a television star." Jonathon had picked up the conversation as soon as the two sat down. "They'll cement his lead, for sure . . ." Both men's heads turned simultaneously as the woman with the painted nails made a short, distinct snorting noise, looked at her companion, and broke into a laugh. She had obviously been listening.

"Did something we say amuse you?" Jonathon asked without

smiling. He placed his sandwich down with exaggerated care and looked her full in the face. She had almond-shaped eyes that couldn't hide her amusement. One hand cupped her mouth, the bright fingers pointed upward. She was struggling to swallow.

"I . . . I'm sorry . . . just a sec . . ." She coughed loudly and took a long sip of soda. "Went down the wrong pipe."

"I think your pipes are fine, it's your manners that went wrong," Jonathon said, turning back to his sandwich and looking at Walter as if they were alone. Walter's lips had parted slightly, as if he had something to say but it had escaped his mind.

"Well, better my manners than my thinking," she shot back as if speaking to her companion. "And, am I mistaken, Molly, or is there an 'r' in manners?" she went on, laughing at Jonathon's accent.

"However you say it, lady, it means the same thing. If your conversation is so boring you have to listen to ours, why don't you just ask—politely, if possible—to join in?"

Joan Black took her first good look at her antagonist. He seemed familiar somehow, but she didn't remember meeting him. Even if I had, she thought, the part in his hair was too neat for her taste. Definitely not the panty raid type, she thought. And definitely not New York. Somewhere in Hicksville, she decided, like New Hampshire or Vermont, or maybe Maine.

"Well, if you insist," Joan said, placing her hands flat on the table, as if she might launch herself into Jonathon's face. "First of all, if you think General Eisenhower could be good on television, you must not have seen him on the air yet. He looks pasty and old. And those glasses! He needs to get rid of those, but then of course he wouldn't be able to read, now would he? And that would be a problem since he doesn't have a clue about running this country. Commanding the army and having a command of the Constitution and presidential authority are quite different. The American people are starting to see that, that's for sure. I'm sure you will, too, if you ever read a real newspaper like the *New York Times,* or is that unavailable where you come from?" Joan asked with mock charm.

"Where I come from, women's minds aren't shut as tight as co-hogs and ladies don't snap like bugs."

"Bugs and co-hogs? Do you dig that, Molly, or have we traveled to another universe?"

"I would think someone as erudite as you seem to think you are would know what Mainer's call clams and lobsters. But I guess you wouldn't find that in the *New York Times*." Jonathon's hands were clenching under the table. What was so infuriating about this girl?

"Probably not," Joan answered in a rising tone. "But you *will* find all the reasons why an informed person wouldn't vote for Eisenhower. You think he's going to get us out of Korea? Fine, but he's going to start another world war, going around saying he'll help arm the rebels in Communist-held countries and refusing to negotiate with the Soviets. But so what, right, Mr. Hip Man from Maine? Because you're probably the type who would vote for the general just because he's not a *woman*." People at the back of the lunch line, which had pressed close to the seated diners, turned their heads as Joan finished with a near shout.

"And you'd probably vote for Mrs. Roosevelt just because she *is* a woman," Jonathon said, the rising hubbub of the crowd being enough of an excuse to pitch his answer just below a yell. "Is that somehow okay? Or maybe because she was FDR's wife? Those are really intelligent reasons to vote for someone with absolutely no experience running anything, much less the invasion of Europe."

"Yes, yes I would," Joan's fury animated her face, "because she is a woman who knows and hates war, and can get us to peace. Because she's a woman who cares about people being treated equally and about fair jobs and wages and about health care. And because it's about time a woman was president of this country. What's wrong with that?" Joan stood up and started to squeeze between the tables to leave. This guy was impossible—a typical Republican dimwit.

"Well, I'm not sure *woman* is the word I'd use for her, unless you want to call her a *woman's* woman," Jonathon said, the sarcasm thick in his reply. As soon as he spoke, he regretted it. The quizzical looks from Walter, Joan, and Molly made him sure of his mistake. He jumped up from his seat, trying to leave ahead of this annoying girl. But Maxine's was like the subway at rush hour, and Jonathon found himself shoulder to shoulder with Joan as they edged their way out.

By the time they reached the sidewalk, Jonathon had cooled down. What could he expect working in the Democratic haven of New York? This was Roosevelt country, after all. "Look," he said touching Joan's arm lightly before she could rush off, "I'm sorry I rattled your cage, Miss . . ."

"Joan Black, and don't feel you have to apologize, but feel free to come to Roosevelt for President headquarters and I'll give you some literature. Maybe you can broaden your thinking." For a moment, Jonathon was stunned, frantically trying to remember if he had said anything that the other camp shouldn't have heard.

"You . . . you work for Mrs. Roosevelt?" he finally managed.

Joan nodded and smiled.

"Well, Miss Black," he said, recovering, "my name's Jonathon Chamberlain." He held out his hand. "And if *you* want to broaden your thinking about Ike, you can find me at his headquarters."

Suddenly, Joan remembered the picture in the newspaper during the convention. This was the guy who caught her eye. Jonathon was surprised to see her laugh without irony.

"I might just take you up on that offer, Mr. Chamberlain," Joan said, as she motioned to Molly. "Come on, we'll be late getting back."

CHAPTER 22

The Truth About Kay

Eleanor's campaign headquarters were just up the block in the Roosevelt Hotel. Whitney Warren and Charles Wetmore, who had designed Grand Central Station, surrounded their cavernous train depot with some of the city's more elegant buildings. Both the Commodore and the Roosevelt hotels were part of this "Terminal City" vision, linked by their architecture if not their warring campaign headquarters.

Joan loved the Roosevelt's neoclassical spectacle. A fitting place to be named for Eleanor's Uncle Teddy, but more fitting, she thought, as the place for his niece to aim for the highest office in the land.

Larry caught her as soon as she walked in the door.

"There you are!" he began, as if she'd been AWOL. "I just got a call from Lou Cowan. He's picked up a rumor on Madison Avenue that Ike is putting together some short TV commercials that they plan to put on right before election day in key areas. They're buying a *lot* of time."

"I picked up something like that, too," Joan answered, not wanting to say more.

"Well, I want you to be sure we have all the tapes from the stations we've let come in and film Mrs. R. here, at Val-Kill, on the train, everything. Lou offered to use it to make some spots for us."

"Where will we target?" Joan asked.

"Hard to tell, but put some calls in to stations in Pennsylvania, Illinois, Texas, and Michigan, oh yeah, and Massachusetts."

"Massachusetts? Don't you have that sewn up, Larry?" Joan asked in a teasing tone.

"I don't like to take chances," he said as he walked away.

Joan sat down at her folding table that served as a desk in the middle of a meeting room that was the campaign bull pen. Newspaper clippings covered the rickety table, along with phone messages and notes to herself. Her habit of taping notes on top of notes taped to the table left little flip-pads of information clinging to the rough surface. She looked at the chaos without seeing it. She couldn't get that Chamberlain guy's comment out of her mind. "A *woman's* woman." Why did he say it like that? What did that sarcastic tone mean? All of her journalist's instincts were kicking in. It reminded her of the answer to a question she had asked just a few days before.

Joan had been looking through press clippings of Eisenhower in Europe, trying to anticipate how his campaign would play up the war-hero angle, when something caught her eye. In picture after picture there appeared a pretty dark-haired woman in some kind of British army uniform. She looked about Joan's age, trim, straight-shouldered, and alert. There she was, her two-button, tricorner hat at a rakish angle, her hair swept off a high forehead, in midsentence with Ike. There she was again, in a broad-knotted tie and shirtsleeves, laughing as she tried out an army motorcycle in the North African desert while Ike watched. In another shot, the two of them in civilian clothes sat astride handsome horses with a caption, "General Eisenhower out for his daily ride at Telegraph Cottage, London." In another, she was sitting in the back of a jeep next to Ike as they visited Hitler's retreat at Berchtesgaden in 1945. And there she was again, standing behind Ike as he triumphantly held up the pens that the Germans used to sign the surrender. As Joan looked at the girl's joyous and relieved smile, she felt tears sting her eyes. They had all been through so much during the war, but this girl had survived the maelstrom, and it showed.

"Hey, Molly." Joan stopped Molly Dewson as she swept by in her perpetual hurry. "Can you take a sec and tell me who this girl is?" Joan held up one of the newspaper photos.

"Well, I guess you were too young to be up on the rumors during the war. It was common knowledge in Washington and New York, if not the country, that Ike's driver, her name was Kay Summersby." Molly pointed to the girl in the picture. "She was doing more than driving, shall we say." Molly walked away without more explanation.

As Joan recalled Molly's words, she remembered the tone of sexual innuendo, the same tone Jonathon had used about Mrs. R. Was he suggesting she had a lover? There wasn't much news there. Dr. Gurewitsch was a perfectly proper companion, and they were both single people. They always took separate hotel rooms, anyway, although everyone knew it was for show. That couldn't be what Jonathon had been hinting at. But the incident reminded Joan that she had wanted to find out more about Kay Summersby. The story intrigued her—so illicit, so romantic. She imagined Ingrid Bergman saying good-bye to Bogey in *Casablanca*. Joan wondered how easily Kay Summersby had let her general go. She taped another note to her desk, "DDE—when returned from Europe?/and what happened to Summersby?" A family friend had served on General Marshall's staff at the Pentagon during the war. She decided to give him a call.

"Henry, it's Joan calling from New York with a gossipy little question."

"What would I expect from Ruby's daughter?" he answered with a laugh that Joan returned.

"I just looked at a bunch of newspaper photos of Ike in Europe during the war, and this Kay Summersby woman is in an awful lot of them. When he came back, did she come, too, by any chance? She looked like she was a top assistant." Joan tried to sound as casual as possible.

"You're too young to know the stories, aren't you?" Henry asked. "No, she didn't come back, but Ike would have liked her to, and that's all I'm saying."

"Hennnnrrrry! You can't do that to me. I'll have to come to that little country house of yours down in Virginia and twist your arm if you don't tell me the whole story."

"Well, at least I'd see you then. I'll tell you this much—there was a letter."

"A letter? To who? What kind of letter? From Ike? What did it say . . . ?"

"Joan, that's it. I mean it. I was working for the army chief of staff. It was a privilege to serve under George Marshall, and I've said enough. Now tell me when you're coming for dinner. I want a date certain."

Joan couldn't sit still the rest of the afternoon. She paced to the windows looking over Madison Avenue then back to her desk, then over to the coffeepot, then down the hall to Molly's cubbyhole to bum a cigarette. A letter . . . did Marshall write Ike and tell him to knock it off with Kay because of the rumors? No, he would have had a lot more to worry about than that. Ike must have written Marshall. How else would Henry know about the letter? But what did he say? Why would he have written Marshall about Kay? She taped down a new note and checked her schedule to see how soon she could get to the Pentagon.

CHAPTER 23

The Secret Fund

September 18 had started out as a good day for the Republican vice presidential candidate. He'd had breakfast in Los Angeles with two big donors who promised five thousand dollars each to the campaign. But as Nixon walked to the waiting campaign train to begin a swing through his home state, an aide told him that the *New York Post* had followed up on the vexing story that had already run in a couple of other papers.

"The *Post*'s a liberal rag. What do you expect?" Nixon tossed off, as he stepped up off the platform and half-turned for a parting wave to the small crowd that had gathered.

"Tell us about the $16,000!" The shout came from a young man, tall enough to be seen over the crowd. "Come on, Tricky Dick, tell us about the $16,000!" he yelled louder, cupping his hands around his mouth.

"Hold the train, hold the train!" Nixon stood a few steps off the ground at the entrance to his car.

"You asked, mister, so I'll answer. You folks know the work I did investigating Communists for the United States," he said, the heat rising in his voice. "Well the Communists and the left-wingers," and here he stared at his heckler, "they're fighting me with every smear that they can find. I've said this would happen, right from the time I got the nomination, I said they would smear me, they would go after me, I said . . ." An aide gave his arm an urgent tug, and with a curt wave, Nixon disappeared.

"Dick, we have to get going, we can talk about it on the trip," Murray Chotiner said as a red-faced Nixon entered the train. Chotiner managed the campaign, but his hardest work was managing Nixon. The candidate could explode like a grenade with a faulty pin, or fall to weeping like a widow in mourning. Chotiner saw his job as keeping the man steady.

By that evening, a copy of the *Post* had landed in Nixon's hands. "Secret Nixon Fund!" the headline screamed. "Secret Rich Men's Trust Fund Keeps Nixon in Style Far beyond His Salary," ran the banner on the next page. According to newsman Leo Katcher, Nixon had a millionaire's club behind him, devoted to helping him enjoy a most comfortable life. The next morning, the *New York Herald*, a Republican outlet, ran a headline calling on Nixon to explain. In California, the tax board announced an investigation of the fund, and the Democratic National Committee sent newspaper editors a courteous reminder that members of Congress are not supposed to engage in bribery and graft.

On board Ike's campaign train, the "Look Ahead Neighbor Special," Sherman Adams found the general in his campaign car working on a sketch of himself. He didn't look up, but took his pencil and began pressing deep horizontal lines across his work before tossing the sketch pad onto the seat.

"Tough to draw on the train," Adams said.

"I thought it might clear my mind. Damn it, Sherman, I should have picked someone I knew better," Ike said, lighting a cigarette with a deep draw.

"Ike, we don't know much yet. I've got Paul Hoffman doing a major investigation, fifty lawyers at least, accountants, all that stuff. It's going to be 'round the clock until this thing is audited, just like you wanted. But I've also sent word quietly to Senator Knowland, just in case we need to replace Dick."

"Did you check with Summerfield?" Eisenhower was referring to the chairman of the Republican Party. Adams sat down heavily.

"Yes, and we'd have to raise a lot more money—a whole lot more. The printing alone for that kind of change would be out of this world."

Ike focused on the pattern of grime that outlined the train window and let out a short, deep cough. Miles rolled by before he spoke. "Get rid of him, Sherman. We'll get the damn money."

Adams looked at the shiny black tip of his shoes and shook his head. Finally, he said, "The reporters are still begging for a comment. You need to talk to them more, Ike."

"Not my favorite thing, but fine, I'll go back there." He coughed again and stubbed out the cigarette. Adams gave him a worried look.

"I'm fine." Ike didn't hide the impatience in his voice. "You just figure out how to get him off the ticket," and he headed for the press car.

"Hello boys," Eisenhower said in a way that made some of the press think they were supposed to salute. "This is off the record, now."

Frustrated at waiting for a chance to question Eisenhower, the reporters' questions poured out in a deluge.

"General, is the Nixon matter closed?"

"Are you satisfied he's an honest man?"

"Doesn't this raise questions of corruption like the ones you've been raising in the campaign against the Democrats?"

"Taft and Hoover approve of the fund. They said they're sure Nixon's an honest man. Isn't that good enough for you?"

Ike walked over to the beer fridge and took out a Budweiser. Snapping off the top, he said, "By no means. Remember, I've only met my running mate a couple of times. I need facts and figures, names and dates. Although, I'm sure he's an honest man."

"Sounds like you might want him off the ticket. Is that right?" asked another reporter.

"Not decided," came Ike's clipped response.

"Was this a millionaires' club? Who were these donors?"

Ike looked impatient. "Senator Nixon has Dana Smith, the fund trustee, preparing a report."

"But General, a report from the man running the fund? Isn't that . . ."

Ike put his beer down with a loud clack. "Listen here," he said, hitting his right fist into the palm of his other hand. "What's the use of campaigning against this business of what has been going on in Washington if we ourselves aren't as clean as a houndstooth?" and the general walked out of the car with the shouts of reporters' questions trailing after him.

The tabloid *New York Mirror* ran a banner headline the next day, "EXPLAIN OR QUIT: IKE TO NIXON." Word reached Nixon quickly, and he told Chotiner he had to speak to Eisenhower right away. He waited for the call to come through to his Portland, Oregon, hotel room, sitting in a hard chair that matched the small Chippendale desk with the telephone he willed to ring. He'd neglected his fingernails in the maelstrom of the last few days. He looked with annoyance at the dirt under their ragged edges. He knew his beard must be a shadow now, it grew so fast. Was his hair unkempt too? He wouldn't move to look at it. His feet were carefully aligned and stuck as if by glue to the thick carpet. Finally, the phone rang.

"Hello, Dick. Is it rainy in Portland?" Eisenhower began.

"Yes, but they say it's passing." Nixon tried to sound cheerful.

"How're Pat and the girls?"

"Oh, just as excited as can be by the whole parade, although it's been a bit of a strain lately—mostly on Pat."

"Of course. Mamie feels the strain too, sometimes. Give Pat my regards."

"Certainly, certainly I will. That's kind of you. Very kind. I just want you to know, General, I'm at your disposal."

"I appreciate that, Dick."

"If you reach a conclusion either now or any time later that I should get off the ticket, you can be sure that I will immediately respect your judgment and do so." There, he'd said it. Nixon pressed the receiver to his ear, his head unmoving.

"I don't believe that's my decision," Eisenhower replied evenly.

"You have to understand, General, I *hope* you understand that I am being smeared for something I didn't do. I never saw a penny personally. This fund was for expenses only. We have the paper to prove it. It's completely aboveboard, completely. But, nevertheless, I will sacrifice my candidacy if you call on me to do so."

"I think we have to see how things unfold," Eisenhower said.

Nixon was growing impatient. He should be getting a word, just a word of support, a bit of encouragement from this man.

"General, you should know that the National Committees have raised $75,000 for me to make my case in a thirty-minute nationwide hookup on radio and television. I've agreed to go on after the Milton Berle show in two days. I believe the country will support me once I've explained and told them the whole story. I have nothing to hide. Absolutely nothing to hide." For a second, Nixon thought the connection had been lost, then Eisenhower spoke.

"That's fine, Dick. Good idea. Send me your remarks so I know what's coming."

Nixon dodged the request. He had no written remarks. He had no idea what he would say.

"Once I've done the broadcast, General, will I have your decision?" Again the line hummed for what seemed like minutes.

"I think we should take three or four days to see how it goes," Eisenhower replied.

"We've really got to get it decided because otherwise it's going to be ballooned bigger than it even is at the present time." Nixon's words were racing past his thoughts. Eisenhower didn't want him. That was clear. But the man was too chicken to say it.

"You know, General," the words shot out, "there comes a time you either have to shit or get off the pot." Nixon's face flamed as his mind caught up with the words that he had just shouted at a five-star general. No one would talk to Ike that way. What an idiot I am, Nixon thought, a complete idiot.

"We'll talk in a few days, Dick," Eisenhower replied stiffly, and the line went dead.

CHAPTER 24

Needing David

Eleanor arrived at the Roosevelt Hotel the day before Nixon's broadcast. David had written, begging her to meet him for one evening.

"We've been apart so long, my love. You have so little time. We have so little time. I can hardly bear it. . . ." Eleanor read the note over as she waited in her suite. She had read it many times. They had been apart, not because she couldn't make time for David, but because she was afraid to. She still wondered if he had continued a dalliance with Martha Gellhorn, or perhaps someone else—someone younger, someone more available. She felt like she was losing all control over her emotions, and she couldn't stand that. Better not to see David at all than to see him when she was filled with doubts and fear, when she felt ashamed that somehow she wasn't as good as other women, as loving, as compliant. But his note had been so heartfelt, so tender, she had finally relented.

She ordered a cold dinner so they wouldn't be disturbed. A bottle of Gruaud-Larose was ready. David liked to tease her, calling the Bordeaux "firm and masculine," as he arched one brow in that way that reminded her of Robert Mitchum in *His Kind of Woman*. She didn't like him to drink. She never liked anyone to drink, but it relaxed him. She could see that, and it made him more playful, even more loving.

Maureen waited at the door to let the doctor in quickly when he knocked. She liked David, and she could see how happy he made Eleanor, but she worried about their liaisons. They were both single, of course, but their age difference would raise eyebrows. So far, the press had been discreet. Occasionally, Maureen was asked if Eleanor was sick, and if not, why was the doctor visiting? She had a standard answer, "Doctor Gurewitsch is a longtime friend and trusted adviser." That was all. She never said more.

David locked the door behind Maureen, then turned to Eleanor. She wore the Elizabeth Arden lace robe that he had bought her in Paris. She thought the large puffed sleeves made her look grand. The robe fell to the floor in an A-line of ivory rose vines embroidered over sheer silk. David threw his suit jacket over a chair as he walked to her. He stood for a moment looking at her hair, her eyes, her lips, then with both hands on either side of her face, he swept her hair back and tilted her face toward his.

"How I've missed you," he spoke softly, kissing her gently at first, then with more urgency. It seemed only moments before they were lying in each other's arms, entwined so that every part of his body touched a part of hers. She wondered at how she could forget the feel of him, the smell of him, the soft smooth skin below his armpit that felt almost like a woman's, the hair on his chest that she pressed with her hand as he made her body rise to his touch. She wondered that her pleasure could be so exquisite. She'd been taught that women her age were sexless. Another lie from a Victorian age of lies, she thought.

"We're like the two halves of the coin, aren't we, David? You feel that way don't you?"

"Yes, darling, I do. We shouldn't be apart, shouldn't separate the coin. I so wish you hadn't done this campaign. And I am afraid for you, afraid for your safety, and these relentless attacks . . ." Frustration began to tinge his voice.

Eleanor kissed him and placed her fingers over his lips. "Please, let's not talk about it again. Please . . . this is our evening. Just ours."

"Eleanor," David sat up and moved away so he could turn to look at her, "Tommy called me. I know Maureen has taken over as your secretary, but she still goes to Tommy on many things. Maureen told her about the latest letters, and Tommy told me."

Tommy's cancer had spread and she was confined to her apartment. Everyone knew the inevitable outcome, but Tommy refused to act as if she was on anything more than temporary leave. She insisted that Maureen call every day and keep her up on every aspect of Eleanor's life.

Tommy had fielded many threats over the years. She knew Eleanor's candidacy would bring out the vilest people intent on hurting her boss and friend. No matter how much Maureen tried, she couldn't avoid Tommy's relentless questioning. "Tell me about the letters today, Maureen. All of the letters," she would say.

Most of the letters had a similar quality. They were garden-variety threats and ranting, but recently Tommy had grown concerned by a particular spate of letters written in the same hand.

"To the Most Admired Bitch in the World," the first letter began. "If God had wanted you to live, He would not have let you run for president. It is His plan that by striking down Adlai Stevenson He has placed you in line for His wrath. We will act by His inviting because in His wisdom we know He does not want a woman to lead America, and not a nigger-lover woman. This we know."

The next three letters said only, "By His plan, the time is coming," but they had an odd signature: "KKK" with the last "K" twice as big as the other two. There was no way for Eleanor or the FBI to know that it was a signature Edgar Ray Killen had adopted in recent years.

Tommy had instructed Maureen to give the letters to the FBI, but she had also called David.

"David, I've gotten so many threats over the years. The FBI is looking into it. . . ." Eleanor said.

"The FBI? Eleanor, Hoover would as likely see you gone as the nut who's writing these," David said, jumping out of bed to pace across the room.

Eleanor laughed. "Well, if that were true, I suppose Hoover could have gotten rid of me by now."

"Don't pull this brave-face thing on me. This is *serious*. Tommy's right. These letters are different," David shot back.

"Well, what do you want? Do you honestly think I would drop out over this?" Eleanor grabbed her robe and stood to face him.

"How dare you ask me to back down out of fear. David, you should know me better than that." Then Eleanor's voice softened. "I don't fear these people. If I did, if I ever had, I couldn't have lived the life I've had." She stepped close to him. "I only fear losing you."

"And I you," David said as they embraced. Eleanor tried to believe him. If he left me, she thought as he held her close, I don't know how I would bear it.

CHAPTER 25

An On-Air Defense

September 23, 1952

"It's impressive, Mrs. R.," Joan reported the next morning over breakfast. "The Republicans have sixty-four NBC TV stations, 194 CBS radio stations, and the whole Mutual Radio Network. They're betting the country's going to listen, and I think they're right."

"Do we have any idea what he's going to say?" Eleanor asked, and Rayburn, who had joined her for breakfast, looked expectantly at Joan.

"No. Word is even Ike doesn't know. My friends on Ike's press detail tell me that most of the general's staff want Nixon gone, and probably the general, too. I can't imagine what he could say to save himself." Joan poured more coffee and drained the cup. "I have to run, unless you need me."

"Where are you off to?" Eleanor asked.

"Just gathering some background on Ike from the Pentagon." Joan tried to sound casual, but Eleanor caught a tone of evasion.

"The Pentagon?" Sam asked sharply before Eleanor could. "What's going on?"

Just then, Larry O'Brien walked in holding the headline from the *New York Times* out in front of him for all to see.

"Nixon's on the ropes and about to be knocked out. Talk about 'hoisted by your own petard,' this takes the cake, doesn't it? He is creamed! Pass me the coffee, will ya?" and he took a seat as Joan excused herself and quickly left the room.

Both campaigns were in the same posture at 9:00 p.m. eastern standard time on September 23. Ike, Eleanor, and their key staff members were seated in their respective hotel suites watching the end of the Milton Berle show. That night Berle, the host of the Texaco Star Theater, was dressed in drag, a red wig askew on his head after an evening of slapstick shenanigans. Berle began to sing "Near You," his signature sign-off, and all over the country Americans waited for the political drama that would follow. They weren't going to miss the chance to watch a public political execution, and by the dead man's own hand at that.

At the El Capitan Theatre in Hollywood, Nixon sat onstage in a small wooden chair behind a writing desk that had been pushed up against a narrow bookcase, giving the effect of a homey library. Just before he had left the Ambassador Hotel, Dewey had called, using the code name "Mr. Chapman," so that even Chotiner didn't know who was on the line.

"Listen, Dick, Ike's top advisers just met. I'm sorry to tell you this, but they want you to resign at the end of your statement. I don't necessarily agree, but I said I would tell you."

"His advisers? What about Ike? What does he want?" Nixon asked.

"I didn't speak to him, Dick."

"Well, listen here, it's a little late for this. I'm walking out the door. And you tell them, you tell them I've been around politics a little bit myself, so they'll just have to wait and see what I do," and Nixon slammed down the receiver.

But the conversation echoed in his mind as he waited for the producer to signal him to begin. If only those bastards around Ike knew—he gave a short, sardonic laugh—that all he had were some notes he'd made on those United Airlines seat-back post-cards as he flew to Los Angeles. He hadn't made up his mind what to say, but damn them. Damn all of them. He wasn't a quitter. He was a fighter. How dare they try to give him an order like that?

"One minute, Senator Nixon."

He wiped his brow and looked at Pat, who was seated in a floral easy chair just off camera, her smile already frozen in place. She didn't move, and they didn't speak. The ladies will like her, Nixon thought, as he folded his hands with care and stared at the camera, waiting for his cue.

"Three . . . two . . . one . . . you're on, Senator."

The camera closed in tight, showing Nixon from the waist up. He looked straight into the camera and spoke as if he'd been re-hearsing all day.

"My fellow Americans, I come before you tonight as a candidate for the vice presidency and as a man whose honesty and integrity have been questioned. . . ."

Nixon labeled the charges a smear and assured the American people that he would give them the facts. Had he taken $18,000 from a group of supporters? Yes, but did he take any of that for personal use, or handle it secretly? Absolutely not, came the fer-vent reply.

"Every penny of it was used to pay for political expenses that I did not think should be charged to the taxpayers of the United States. . . .

"Do you think that when I or any other senator makes a politi-cal speech and has it printed, that the printing of that speech and the mailing of that speech should be charged to the taxpayers?" he asked. "Do you think, for example, when I or any other senator makes a trip to his home state to make a purely political speech that the cost of that trip should be charged to the taxpayers?"

No, of course not. He knew his audience would agree that they shouldn't have to pay for politics. Then how could a man of modest means get by? He could put his wife on the payroll, but that would be wrong, Nixon said, even though Pat was a wonderful stenographer. He turned toward her, and the camera followed his eyes. Pat Nixon sat in profile, watching her husband, a slight smile on her lips, her high cheekbones rouged and every muscle in her body frozen.

As the camera panned back to Nixon, he held up a sheet of paper and began to read a list of their assets and debts: a small inheritance from Pat's father and one from his grandfather, the $80 rent on their first apartment, the house in Washington that cost $41,000 and had a $20,000 mortgage, his $4,000 in life insurance, and no stocks or bonds.

"Well, that's about it. That's what we have and that's what we owe. It isn't very much, but Pat and I have the satisfaction that every dime we've got is honestly ours." Then, in an unsubtle reminder of the Truman administration's mink coat scandal, he said, "Pat doesn't have a mink coat, but she does have a respectable Republican cloth coat. And I always tell her that she'd look good in anything.

"One other thing I probably should tell you. . . . A man down in Texas heard Pat on the radio mention the fact that our two youngsters would like to have a dog. And, believe it or not, the day before we left on this campaign trip, we got a message from Union Station in Baltimore saying they had a package for us. . . . It was a little cocker spaniel dog in a crate that he'd sent all the way from Texas. Black and white spotted. And our little girl, Tricia, the six-year-old, named it Checkers. And you know, the kids, like all kids, love the dog, and I just want to say this right now, that regardless of what they say about it, we're gonna keep it."

Eleanor smacked her hand on the arm of her chair, startling her aides. What had angered her in the puppy story? They sensed her fury as they listened to Nixon's closing exhortation. The country needed saving, he said, rising from his chair and shaking a fist at the camera, and Ike was the man to do it. He would not resign, he told the audience. He would leave it up to the people listening to decide if he should do that. He said that they should let the Republican Committee know their feelings, and then the broadcast came to an abrupt end.

Nixon stormed off the set, sure that his talk was a disaster.

"I didn't see the producer's signal, goddamn it!" He flung his notes to the floor. "I looked like a goddamn fool!"

"Dick, it's all right." Pat touched his shoulder as she followed behind him. He swung his hand out and back without turning, and she stopped short, jerking her head back with a practiced motion to avoid the blow. Chotiner arrived in the dressing room with the small group of supporters who had been watching in the studio. "Dick," Chotiner said with genuine glee, "that was a masterpiece. Daryl Zanuck already called. No kidding, it was . . ."

"It was a flop. I didn't stop in time. I didn't give them the address of the committee. How will anyone be able to write?" Nixon's jaw trembled, and then he began to sob.

Sitting with her aides at the Roosevelt Hotel, Eleanor scribbled some notes on a pad and whispered something to Maureen as she stood up and grabbed her purse.

"Eleanor, what did you think?" O'Brien asked, wondering why she seemed so agitated.

"Grand political theater, Larry, but it won't work, not if I have anything to do with it. How dare he use Fala!"

"Fala?" O'Brien was mystified. Nixon hadn't mentioned the Scottie dog that never left FDR's side. But Rayburn smiled and nodded.

"I'll explain it to you, Larry, don't worry," Rayburn said.

"Yes, Sam, do explain," Eleanor agreed. "This phony Checkers business! Nixon knew exactly what he was doing. He's sly, but he won't get away with it. Come along. We're going to Hyde Park. Joan, get out a press release tonight. Tell them I'm holding a press conference at Franklin's graveside tomorrow at 4:00 p.m. to respond to Senator Nixon's remarks. Be sure to let Murrow know. He'll want a television camera crew there."

CHAPTER 26

Checkers and Fala

A bright blue sky reflected the brilliant colors of the trees surrounding Springwood in Hyde Park. Franklin had been born at the redbrick estate on the Hudson River, and he lay buried in sight of the great house, in a rose garden that still held some blooms. The previous April, another small grave had been added inside the simple iron fence. Fala, the pert black Scottie that America adored, had died and was buried by his master. As the reporters gathered round, Eleanor stood just in front of Fala's grave.

"Thank you for coming," Eleanor began. "I know that thousands of people have already responded favorably to Senator Nixon's request that they tell the Republican National Committee whether he should stay on the ticket.

"Americans are fair people, and the senator rightfully pointed out that the burden on public servants of modest means to conduct their political life is unfair. But the answer to this unfairness is not to take money from sources that, no matter how respectable, may bring undue influence to bear.

"These rich friends of Senator Nixon might expect some return for their gifts at a given point. We all know the weakness of human nature, and the senator made clear his great need for this money. Can we really be assured that he would vote his conscience against the interests of these moneyed men? I would not raise this question of the senator's rectitude, but he raised it himself by telling the story about his dog, Checkers."

The reporters exchanged quizzical glances. Only Rayburn and O'Brien, standing just outside the press crowd, arms folded over their chests, had any idea what Eleanor would say.

"Like all of us, Senator Nixon remembers the Fala speech, as it has come to be called. In September 1944, my husband spoke before the Teamsters Union. He had been falsely accused by the Republican Party of spending millions in taxpayers' money to send a destroyer to get Fala off an Aleutian Island where Franklin had supposedly forgotten his dog. Yes, I see some of you nodding. You remember, of course," and Eleanor smiled with satisfaction.

"Franklin said Fala's Scottish soul was furious over the charge, and that he had not been the same dog since the Republicans' attack." Eleanor paused and shared the reporters' chuckles as they scribbled furiously on their pads.

"That is why I have come to Fala's graveside. We only lost him a few months ago, and his tough little soul still lingers here. And I can tell you, he is quite furious again. He does not appreciate Senator Nixon using his poor puppy, Checkers, to distract from the senator's misdeeds, although he understands such behavior. After all, Fala's full name was Murray, the Outlaw of Falahill." More guffaws came from the press.

"If Senator Nixon's use of this fund has truly been divorced from any influence over his Senate actions, he should have given us an accounting of his legislative record, and the interests of the men who built his fund. Instead, he tried to distract the American people with a dog story, hoping he could triumph as Franklin did. Well, Senator," Eleanor shook her finger like an angry schoolmarm, "Fala has this to say to Checkers, 'My master never tried to change the subject. He was always honest with the American people. And he was no man's pawn. My advice would be to find another home.'"

As the laughter died down, Rayburn turned to O'Brien. "Nixon may be 'creamed,' as you like to say, after all."

Eleanor knew that television reporter Edward R. Murrow would cover the Fala speech. Murrow had made his name as a hugely popular commentator on radio who examined the issues of the day with tough, insightful zeal. He had started a groundbreaking television show, *See It Now*, in late 1951. Audiences eager for their first chance to watch politics unfold on television had learned that Murrow was the man to watch. Next to the *Milton Berle Show* and *I Love Lucy*, he had the biggest audience on TV.

At 6:30 p.m., two hours after she left Hyde Park, Murrow led his broadcast with Eleanor's press conference. He added his own stinging commentary, which took up Eleanor's cry that Nixon had evaded the real question: had his donors influenced his actions in Congress? The next morning, the headline of the *Chicago Tribune* was echoed across the country: "Fala to Checkers: Run Away!" Every vote that Nixon had taken as a congressman and senator was being scrutinized, and the names and corporate affiliations of his donors were popping up in stories that raised uncomfortable questions.

Nixon went into lockdown, refusing to talk to the press or anyone but Chotiner.

"I'm telling you, Dick, he can't afford to lose you, no matter what." Chotiner tried to reassure him. His source inside Ike's campaign had told him the night before that, although Eisenhower was holding his nose, he knew he couldn't afford either the campaign money or the political damage within the party that dropping Nixon would cost. Taft and the Old Guard wouldn't tolerate letting him go. Better to appear loyal to his running mate, show the country a united front, and hope the whole thing would blow over. When the telephone finally rang, Nixon started to reach for it, but Chotiner grabbed it first.

"Certainly, Sherman. He's right here, just working on some papers. Just a minute." He handed the receiver to Nixon and made a fist with his other hand, mouthing the words, "be strong."

"Hold on for the general, Senator," Adams said. Chotiner could see the tremble in Nixon's hand.

"Dick, I have to be quick," Ike said, sounding like he was reading off a cue card. "We can't let Eleanor Roosevelt and the Democrats push us off our game. I'm sure this whole thing will blow over. We'll talk in a few days." The line went dead, and Nixon slammed the phone down as his whole body started to shake.

CHAPTER 27

A Pentagon Paper

Arlington, Virginia, September 20, 1952

Joan Black stood in front of a dark walnut desk, its matching inbox empty, its outbox full of straightened papers. Other than a freestanding nameplate with "Mrs. M. C. Casperson" etched in block letters, which Joan guessed could be seen from twenty yards away, there were no adornments. A standing fan droned in the corner; its spinning face recirculated the musty gasps of file drawers infrequently opened and stuffed with decades of moldering papers. There was no other movement in the room.

"Can I help you?" a trim woman appeared from the endless rows of gray file cabinets that stood sentry behind the desk. Her brown fitted suit had the creaseless look of military wear. She stayed standing behind the desk, looking at Joan through thick-rimmed black glasses, her hands folded and held at her waist. She looks like she's either going to conduct a funeral service or pull out a ruler and rap my knuckles, Joan thought.

"Mrs. Casperson? I'm Joan Black, and, ummm, have I found the Office of Archival, Personnel and Departmental Records . . . ummm, for the army? I already went to the wrong one," Joan gave a nervous laugh, "and I think I've been on a hundred different stairways here. . . ."

"Then you have thirty-one to go. And yes, I am Mrs. Casperson, and yes, as it says on the door, this is the office you want. Now, what do you want from this office?"

Joan had the awful feeling that this was not going to go well. Damn it, she thought. Couldn't I get some nice, helpful, friendly young clerk? This had to work. She would just have to make it work.

"Well, I guess this may be a bit irregular, but I need a record from a file . . ."

"We have forms that you will need to fill out," Casperson opened one of her desk drawers as she talked, "for archival records."

"Well, it's probably a record in the personnel part. I mean, I'm sure it is, and . . ."

"Those are not available except to the person for whom the file is kept, their immediate supervisors, and certain persons with appropriate clearances." Casperson had closed her drawer with enough force for Joan to be sure that it was now joined in perfect harmony with the face of the desk.

"Yes. Yes, of course. That makes perfect sense, but . . ."

"There are no 'buts' in the matter of personnel files."

"Maybe I should start over," Joan said, noticing that Casperson's hands were again folded, her look inscrutable.

"This has to do with Mrs. Eleanor Roosevelt." Joan thought she caught a slight widening of Casperson's eyes. "I *work* for her." Joan placed a card on the desk in front of the unmoving woman.

"She's the former First Lady. Of course, you know that. Sorry, I just meant that *when* she was First Lady, Mrs. Roosevelt had some correspondence with General Eisenhower during the war. And then after her husband died," Joan paused as Casperson licked her lips with the tip of her tongue and bobbed her head with a slight motion, "when Mrs. Roosevelt was going through her papers, she sent back to many well-known people the letters they had sent her. So, she sent General Eisenhower several letters like that, that he had written her, for his historical file, of course. And well, now you know, of course, she's running against him for president, and she thought she remembered that he had written her a letter about her husband's death," Joan began embellishing on the story she had planned to give, "a letter that was really very kind, and she felt that it would contribute to the bipartisan spirit she's trying to foster if she could quote from that letter, so," she started talking faster, "Mrs. Roosevelt asked me to see if I could just *look* in the file and see if I found the letter and could just copy what the kind thing was the general wrote." Joan's heart pounded as she finished. The slow tick-tick of the plain black wall clock's giant minute hand sounded like the prelude to a bomb.

Casperson unfolded her hands. She pulled out her chair with studied care and lowered herself into it. Then, lips tight, she motioned for Joan to sit down. Casperson looked at her lap for a moment, smoothing her skirt. She pulled Joan's card toward her and studied it.

"I met Mrs. Roosevelt," she said, without looking up. "It was April 20, 1945, not long before VE Day. My husband was at Walter Reed Hospital. He had only just gotten there. His wounds were so . . ." she paused and smoothed her skirt again. "He was wounded in the Apennine Mountains near Florence, in Italy. Mrs. Roosevelt came to his bedside, even though her husband had been buried only days before. She sat on his bed and she spoke to Thomas. He just lit up so." Joan could see her eyes had misted. "She stayed a long time. She'd been to Escanaba, you see. That's where we're . . . we were, from, in

Michigan. I didn't say much, but Thomas, he talked to her quite a while. And it was so hard for him to speak. But she was patient, so patient and kind. You would have thought she had the whole day to be with him, as if he were her own son." She stopped and tucked her chin down as she swallowed hard. "Thomas died the next day. That's how I remember the date so well, you see." She took a deep breath, and Joan could hear the puff of exhalation, as if some part of the shrapnel-sharp memory had been released.

"Miss Black, is it? Follow me." Casperson stood up with a quick turn, and Joan hurried behind. They wound through the maze of shelves and file cabinets to a small, windowless room with a table and one chair. Joan waited, glad to have an ashtray. Thirty minutes later, Casperson returned, showing the effort as she pulled two large boxes on a trolley behind her.

"These are nonclassified correspondences between General Eisenhower, high-ranking military personnel, and government officials during the war years only. You have exactly twenty minutes, Miss Black, that's all I can give you. Do not remove anything. I will check."

Joan struggled to get the first box on the table, and stood up to see inside. From what Henry had said, it must have been a letter to Marshall, but when? She figured it would have been toward the end of the war, since Henry said Ike wanted Kay Summersby to come back to the States. The files were chronological. She knew Ike had returned to the States in November, so she started with October 1945. Nothing. September 1945. Nothing, and the clock had ticked off more than half her time. She knew Casperson would return to the minute.

Joan picked up the folder for August and noticed that there was an unmarked sleeve file next to it that looked like a placeholder. She assumed it was empty, but it seemed out of place, so she pulled it out anyway. It was so thin that she had to slide her nail along the opening to see inside. There were just two letters, written on the personal stationery supplied by the military and placed in the exact middle of the file, their corners aligned. She blew inside so the file popped open and gently pulled the papers out.

The first was dated August 20, 1945, from General Eisenhower to General Marshall:

Dear George,

   I am writing about a matter of great personal importance to me. I do this with reluctance and regret. I hope and trust you will understand that I have agonized over writing to you in this way.

   I am asking that I be allowed to return to the United States as quickly as possible and be relieved of duty. I am planning to divorce Mamie so that I can marry that Englishwoman you met, Kay Summersby. Understand that I would never do anything to dishonor you or the army we serve. This is strictly my decision, and I intend to proceed with the utmost discretion.

                                                      Sincerely,
                                                      Ike

The second was dated a week later, in reply:

Ike,

   Your request is denied. You will return to the United States when needed and ordered to do so. Further, if you even come close to instigating divorce proceedings, I will bust you out of the army and see to it that you will not draw a peaceful breath for the rest of your life. Do not mention such a thing like this to me again or I will make your life a living hell.

                                                      George

By the time Casperson returned, Joan had copied the letters on a page in the middle of her notebook. On a page at the front, she made up a couple of lines that might have come from the letter she was supposedly looking for. But Casperson never checked; she returned looking agitated and took Joan to a back stairway to leave. An officer from the army chief of staff's office was on his way, and she didn't want any questions to be asked.

Just as she seated herself and put Joan's card in her drawer, the man appeared. "Mrs. Casperson," the hurried-looking major said as he handed her a letter. "As you can see, this request is from the president himself."

She saw the eagle-emblazoned seal first. That was shock enough. But President Truman was requesting two letters from the wartime nonclassified files of General Eisenhower. She read the instructions, tensing from the strain of hiding the tremors that shot through her. Mrs. Casperson did not believe in coincidences.

"This may take a few minutes, Major. Please feel free to sit down."

She wasn't surprised to find the letters in an unmarked file envelope. She was even less surprised at how easily it opened and how hurriedly the letters seemed to have been replaced. She scanned them to be sure they were the right ones, and then willed herself to forget what she had read, along with the young woman who had lied to her. Mrs. Casperson was a professional and a patriot, but she was also a woman who lost all the love in her life to a terrible war. The president had asked for two letters, and she would supply them.

CHAPTER 28

Joan's Mission

New York City, September 21, 1952

Joan found O'Brien as soon as she arrived at campaign headquarters in the morning, and asked if they could talk in private. He had turned a hotel bedroom into a personal office and meeting room, but when he and Joan walked in, a gaggle of staff members were folding and stuffing envelopes at a long aluminum table.

"Come on, we'll get the back booth downstairs and have some breakfast," Larry said. The hotel coffee shop had become a favored alternative spot for small staff meetings. As Joan waited for her favorite, blueberry pancakes, she told Larry about Eisenhower's letter and Marshall's reply.

"Don't go far," O'Brien told Joan. "We'll meet as soon as Eleanor can free up some time."

Joan sat in nervous anticipation in the suite reserved for top-level meetings. Rayburn walked in, looking grim and speaking in low tones to Eleanor. O'Brien followed with his usual legal pad of notes, and closed the door behind him.

"Well, Joan, why don't you explain about the letter." When he thought she had finished, O'Brien started to go on, but Joan interrupted.

"I'm sorry, Mr. O'Brien. Um, there's one more thing." She couldn't bring herself to look at Mrs. Roosevelt, so she stared at the tip of her brand-new navy stiletto heels.

"It may be nothing, but . . ." She told them about her conversation with Jonathon, but, as she fumbled to describe what she thought his innuendo meant, Eleanor interrupted her.

"Joan, I appreciate your reporter's nose for the story behind the story. Let me stop you there." Eleanor took a breath, and then she told her team about Hoover and her love letter.

"That goddamn slimy piece of crap . . ." O'Brien was fuming and looked like he was ready to rush out of the room and find a baseball bat to cave in Hoover's head. But Rayburn acted like he'd just heard that Eleanor had been caught wearing last year's fashion.

"That settles it," the Speaker began. "Hoover went to Ike's people so he wouldn't be tarred with this. So we need to let them know that we have a bomb, too—that we know about the Marshall letter."

"But it's locked up in the Pentagon. We can't prove . . ." Larry began.

"No, Larry," Rayburn interrupted. "Truman has the Marshall letter. He called me last night. He'd heard some rumors that the Taft people were trying to get their hands on it to have something over Ike. He was heading them off."

O'Brien smiled at Eleanor, and she managed a slight smile in return.

"Leave it to Harry," Eleanor said. She thought of Lucy's letters that she had found so long ago. Did Mamie know about Ike's affair? Eleanor had had suspicions about Lucy. Did Mamie live in a world of doubt and fear as she had, reading every look and comment as a sign? How odd that she and her opponent's wife would share the cancer of betrayal. Mamie seemed to lack affectations, a spritely, smiling woman in tune with her times, happy to support her man. Or so it seemed. Somehow, Ike's letter gave Eleanor a different kind of determination about winning. Maybe Mamie would thank her if she did.

"What's the president going to do with the letter?" O'Brien asked. "He's not thinking of using it, is he?"

"I'm sure not," Eleanor replied, "but I'll call Harry." She paused, looking thoughtful. "Ike just announced a swing through Missouri. Why doesn't Harry invite him to the house as a show of bipartisanship and goodwill? Ike will be hard-pressed to say 'no' to the president."

"I like it," O'Brien said, also thinking out loud. "They have a few minutes alone. Truman shows him the letter, assures him of discretion, and tells Ike he expects the same."

"All right," Rayburn cut in. "But we have to be sure Ike's team really has been contacted by Hoover. Maybe this young man of Joan's meant something else, or was referring to an old rumor."

"Joan, can you have a talk with him? Use all those good reporter skills you have and find out if your hunch is right? And do it right away."

"Okay, I think I can do that," Joan said, nodding and wishing she hadn't been such a smart aleck with Jonathon Chamberlain.

Jonathon agreed to meet Joan in Bryant Park, far enough from their respective headquarters that they could have privacy. Still, Joan picked a bench in a corner far from the sidewalk and sheltered by the low-hanging branches of a large pin oak. Indian summer had settled over the city, with warm moist air brushing against cheeks like invisible tufts of cotton, muting car horns, and turning harried businessmen into strollers on the crowded sidewalks.

Joan had arrived early, telling herself that she wanted to get settled and feel prepared, while trying to deny that she was at all anxious to see the smug Mr. Chamberlain. Bolstering her courage the night before, she had made an emergency visit to Lord & Taylor on Fifth Avenue. Three hours and countless dresses later, she had settled on a sleeveless black rayon jersey dress by Claire McCardell. The V-neck had a vaguely Roman look, with the narrow folds of the bodice crisscrossed at the waist by thin cloth cords that tied in the front. In a sop to modesty that Joan had spent a long time debating, the V-neck also had cords that could tie it closed at the top.

"Don't worry," the saleswoman had said, seeing Joan frown as the bodice pulled closed. "You can loosen these top strings and show as much as you want," and she had given a meaningful glance at Joan's cleavage.

"Thank goodness for another warm day," Joan thought as she walked up, stopping short as she saw Jonathon pacing near the bench they had chosen. She quickly put on her best "working the room" face and gave her hair one more pat, wishing she could check her lipstick, too.

"Nice to see you again," Joan said, extending her hand as she marched toward Jonathon. He had on a very starched-looking bright white shirt with a blue paisley tie. At least he left his jacket in the office, Joan noticed, thinking he didn't look as stuffy as she remembered.

"Nice to see you," Jonathon said, waving a hand toward the bench with a mock flourish and a smile. "After you."

Joan sat at one end and turned slightly with her legs crossed, feeling prim. She lit a Fatima hoping her hand didn't look like it was shaking. Jonathon sat facing her, although he brought one knee up onto the bench and threw his arm over the back as if he were ready to talk about baseball scores.

"First off, I want to apologize, Mr. . . . ."

"I told you on the phone, please call me Jon. I really would prefer it."

"Okay, well then, call me Joan, of course." Joan gave a stiff smile, trying not to think about how his eyes reminded her of her grandmother's blue willow china. "I am sorry, anyway, for coming on so strong when we met. I think people can respectfully disagree, and obviously we do, I mean with our choice of candidates." She stopped short, not sure where she was heading or how to get to the main reason for their meeting.

"Look, I was pretty unpleasant too. Let's call it even." There was that smile again. What was it, Joan wondered—something like a little boy, but not cute, more like endearing and vulnerable. She looked down and pretended to tighten the tie on her dress.

"Hey, what did you do before you made the mistake of working for Mrs. Roosevelt?" Jon asked with a teasing laugh.

Joan laughed, too, and they chatted for a while about their backgrounds until Joan realized she had forgotten why she was there.

"So how do you like campaign work?" Joan asked, trying to pivot to her main purpose.

"I like it a lot. I've gotten to do some amazing things. More than I expected."

"Yeah? That's great. Campaigns aren't always fun. Sometimes some really nasty stuff goes on." She watched his face, but he didn't react.

"I mean, I have to read all these columns all the time, like Jack Anderson and Drew Pearson, to keep track of what's being said about Mrs. R., because my mom told me people used to leak things, even untrue things, just to get stuff in these gossipy columns and try to ruin a campaign." She could see Jonathon's face redden slightly.

"I suppose that happens," he mumbled, tilting his head up and reaching his hand out as if distracted by a falling leaf.

"I just think that kind of thing is so wrong, don't you?" Joan asked. "I know Mrs. Roosevelt would never allow that kind of thing in her campaign. Of course, I can't imagine the general would either," she added quickly.

Jonathon's eyes narrowed, and he looked at her as if examining her face. "No," he spoke slowly, "I can't imagine the general doing anything like that either."

"I mean, I'll tell you truthfully, Jon, there've been rumors around our office about the general, and I can tell you, Mrs. R. made it clear we couldn't even talk about that stuff in front of her." Joan sat up straighter and lifted her chin a bit.

"What kind of rumors?"

"Really, Jon. I wouldn't even dignify them by repeating them. Why, you've probably heard some too, I'm guessing, about Mrs. Roosevelt. I mean, anyone who's on the inside in a campaign, like you seem to be . . ." He didn't answer. "You have heard something about her haven't you? Come on," Joan tapped her fingernail on his knee and put on a conspiratorial smile, "haven't you?"

"Maybe."

Joan arched one brow and blew a trail of smoke over Jonathon's head. "Maybe? That sounds like a 'yes' to me," she said with a soft laugh.

"Okay, sure, of course, but I'm sure it was untrue, and frankly, between you and me, it was disgusting. I am absolutely certain the general would throw someone out on their ear if he knew they talked about it. But, yeah, there was a rumor about your candidate, too."

"That's good to hear about the general. That he's so ethical, I mean. After the Nixon thing, I think people had some concerns." Jonathon frowned and started to say something.

"Sorry, sorry," Joan said quickly. "Jon, really, I want you to know I respect General Eisenhower a great deal. Are you traveling much?" She decided it was time to change the subject.

"Oh yeah, quite a bit. All over the Midwest, a western swing, and then down to Texas a couple weeks before election day."

"Really? Well, let's keep in touch. I think we're going down to Texas toward the end, too. That's Rayburn country, you know?" She smiled.

"Maybe," Jonathon said amiably, "but the Interstate Theaters' poll shows Ike leading by better than 30 percent in Texas."

"Check out the Burden Survey. It has the race a lot closer than that down there."

"Ike has the ranchers, don't forget."

"Uh-huh, but Mrs. R. has labor, Negroes, and the small farmers." They both laughed.

"Okay," Jonathon stood up and offered Joan his hand. As she took it and balanced onto her five-inch stiletto heels, he said, "Let's agree, if we're in Texas at the same time, we'll finish this debate over steaks and Manhattans."

"Martinis, but otherwise I agree," Joan said, thinking she finally had a reason to look forward to going to Texas.

CHAPTER 29

Leave It to Harry

When Joan found Eleanor back at headquarters, the candidate was on a call, but motioned Joan to sit down.

"Barbara Rose," Eleanor's tone was stern, "that doesn't sound like an accident. I don't want you traveling alone. Please. I must go now. Take care, dear."

"What happened?" Joan asked, knowing that Eleanor frequently spoke with the young woman who was registering Negro voters in the South.

"Her car was sideswiped, but she insists it was an accident, even though the other driver didn't stop. She wouldn't have even told me if her uncle, Vernon Johns, hadn't called. He's worried she's taking too many risks, and I'm afraid I agree. But the girl is filled with such fire." Eleanor shook her head.

"I kind of hate to give you my news," Joan said. "You have so much on your mind. . . ."

"You've found something out." Eleanor didn't pose it as a question.

"Yes, I'm quite sure. Ike's camp has the letter. I'm sorry." Joan made a show of getting out a cigarette.

"I'll call the president right now, and Joan." Eleanor waited until Joan met her eyes.

"You must know how much I appreciate all you've done."

When Eleanor got Truman on the line, she wasted little time.

"Mr. President, I wonder if you have a minute to talk about the campaign."

"Of course, Eleanor. I hope you're going to tell me you've changed your mind about tying me down to Missouri for the campaign. You know, I'm ready to 'give 'em hell' across the country. I'm chomping at the bit, here, Eleanor. That statement by McCarthy after you announced America's Deal? Calling it the work of the Communist Party in your campaign. Then suggesting Maureen Corr's a Communist because she emigrated from Ireland! Saying he might call her to testify. It makes my blood boil. He's the lowest form of . . ."

"Maureen's tough as can be, Mr. President, but I'm furious about that too. He's obviously afraid to call me, so he's picking on her."

"I've got to believe voters can see through that kind of filthy smear. But the things Ike and especially Nixon are saying about my administration, I just wish I could answer them myself. . . . Why, I'm ready to . . ."

"I understand, Harry, but you agreed with Sam about this when we discussed it, as do I. The more you barnstorm the more reason they have to attack you. It just gives the local papers an excuse to talk about the past, and we must be talking about the future. If you can deliver Missouri, and I know you can, that's most important. That could make the difference, you know. And that would be the best answer to them . . . for us to win."

Truman rolled his eyes at the other end of the phone, but he didn't tell Eleanor what he'd been saying to close friends, that he didn't think she had a chance in hell.

"I do understand, Eleanor. I just don't like it, although I must say, Bess enjoys being home. Anyway, I hope you're not letting the press get you down. They didn't think I could win either, though you're a different kind of underdog." Truman laughed. "The kind they've never seen before."

"Well, Larry and I both see what you did in '48 as the key. We've been everywhere and we're not stopping, but Harry, I need your help with something else." Truman caught the more serious tone in her voice.

"Whatever you need, Eleanor. You know that."

Eleanor explained about the two letters, touching as lightly as possible on the nature of her letter to Lorena. Truman didn't probe. He quickly agreed to invite Ike to visit him that weekend back home in Independence.

Reporters and cameramen were already in place when General Eisenhower drove up to the "Summer White House," as Truman's quaint whitewashed Victorian had been called since he assumed the presidency. Bess's grandfather had built the gingerbread fancy with its gables and fretwork spandrels just after the Civil War. The Trumans had lived there since their marriage in 1919.

Truman met Ike at the door wearing casual clothes. The president smiled and gave an enthusiastic wave to the press. He ushered Eisenhower in with an arm on his back, as if he were welcoming a long lost brother back home.

"Come into the library, Ike. Bess took off to see Margaret, but she sends her regards."

"So does Mamie," said Ike, taking off his suit jacket and laying it across a chair. He sat down across from Truman, a small coffee table between them, and lit a cigarette. "I appreciate your asking to see me, Mr. President. I think it's good for the country," Ike said, unsure what was really on Harry's mind.

"As do I, but I have to be blunt, General. This is a bigger good-will invite than you might have guessed." Truman opened a folder on the table and handed Ike the letter he had written to Marshall at the end of the war.

Ike's face lost its color, then the blood rushed back so that he looked like he'd been wandering unprotected in the desert for days. He put the paper down carefully, and then stubbed out his cigarette, avoiding Truman's eyes.

"I want you to know why I took this from the file, Ike," Truman said carefully. "I got word that Taft was nosing around for it. In politics, Ike, everybody wants to have something over somebody else. This letter would be like money in the bank for Taft." Truman picked up the letter and pulled a lighter out of his pocket. As Ike watched, he held the flame to the bottom of the paper, and then dropped it into the ashtray as it disintegrated into a blackened heap. Ike's shoulders slumped slightly as if someone had called out "at ease."

"Mr. President . . . I . . . I don't know what to . . ."

Truman held up his hand. "I was going to do that in any event, Ike, but in the meantime, something's come up—something involving Mrs. Roosevelt and people in your campaign. Oddly enough, it concerns a letter. And I'm guessing you don't know about it, so I'm going to tell you and I'm asking you to take care of it. . . ."

Twenty minutes after he arrived, General Eisenhower came out smiling. An equally jovial Truman escorted him onto the broad porch, where they posed for pictures.

"What did you discuss, Mr. President?" the reporters called out.

"Oh, boys, I told the general I agree with his call for a bipartisan approach to ending the war. We may disagree on the reason we got into Korea . . ." Truman laughed and gave Ike a pat on the back, "but we are in total agreement that we need to win the peace."

"That's right, gentlemen," Ike said. "Even though this man is from Independence," the reporters chuckled, "we still share a desire to bring our boys home and keep our country safe. And I might add"—Eisenhower turned to Truman and looked him in the eye—"our president may be the most honorable man I know."

CHAPTER 30

A Strong Majority

Pittsburgh, Pennsylvania, September 25, 1952

Joan hugged Alice Lake as she walked into the "Eleanor for President" campaign headquarters in the Union Labor Temple, where many of the local labor unions had their headquarters. Volunteers from several carpenters' locals were hammering signs together and loading them into cars and trucks parked in the alley, cigarettes dangling from their mouths as they worked. As Alice and Joan walked through the large, bustling room, Alice thought there must be fifty phones going with people swinging their hands to dial as fast as possible, repeating set phrases when they got an answer, and making notes on index cards. Coke bottles sat next to Clark candy bar wrappers, and paper containers for french fries next to oversize bottles of Heinz ketchup.

A long folding table had been set up for meetings in a cramped room that had a small window facing the alley. Alice and Joan sat down without interrupting their chatter about campaign gossip and the problems they'd encountered being women in arenas dominated by men.

"Excuse me, ladies." A tall burly man came into the room holding a tray of sandwiches.

"Can I offer you ladies the spesh-e-ality of Steeltown? A Primanti sandwich?"

"Is that coleslaw and french fries in between the bread?" Joan asked pointing to a sandwich, which was several inches thick.

"You got it. This one's kolbassi and cheese with fries, slaw, and tomato, and this one's tuna and cheese with . . ."

"I know," Alice said wrinkling her nose, "fries, slaw, and tomato."

"Yeah." He smiled.

"Thanks anyway," Joan said, looking at Alice and smiling. The man left looking disappointed, and a moment later, Eleanor came into the room. Alice jumped out of her chair, stubbing out her cigarette, flushing slightly, and looking unsure whether to curtsy, salute, or step forward to shake hands.

"Eleanor, please meet Alice Lake," said Larry, who was in town for meetings with some of the labor leaders. "She's done some research for us."

Eleanor walked up smiling with her hand extended. "What kind of research, Miss Lake?"

"I, well I have . . ." the young woman seemed stunned into silence for a moment. "Mrs. Roosevelt, I just want to say how absolutely honored and humbled I am to meet you. I can't tell you how much I admire all you've done as First Lady and . . ."

"Please, my dear. That's very kind. Let's sit down, and why don't you tell me what this is all about."

"Of course. I'm sorry."

Joan hid a smile. She and Alice had formed a great friendship debating campaign strategy and issues for Alice's poll, as well as whether Balenciaga's dresses were more elegant than Chanel's. They also shared an unrestrained adoration of their candidate. As Joan watched Alice, she felt like she was reliving her first meeting with Mrs. R. in the hallway at the Blackstone Hotel during the convention. That moment seemed like it happened ages ago, she thought.

Alice sat down and pulled out several thick packets of mimeographed paper from a large briefcase. Then she rummaged some more, and looked up, slightly embarrassed.

"Before we start, Mrs. Roosevelt, could I ask you to sign these for me?" She held out two copies of Eleanor's book, *It's Up to the Women*.

"They're for my associates who helped me with this research. If you could sign it to them." Alice held out a pen, and Eleanor took it with a look of surprise.

"I can't imagine how you found these after all these years. I can see why you're a researcher," Eleanor said.

"We were determined." Alice looked pleased. "Um, you could just sign one to Tresa and one to Anita. Oh, thank you so much. Now, let me get to this." Alice pointed at the packet of paper.

"Mrs. Roosevelt, I've been conducting a poll using questions based on America's Deal and on your viability as a candidate."

"Larry?" Eleanor looked at her campaign manager. "I don't remember discussing this."

"Can't trouble the candidate with everything, can we? Alice, go on," he said hurriedly.

"Just a minute, Miss Lake. I must tell you, I'm very skeptical of polling methods, especially since the last presidential election."

"I understand. Please let me tell you what we've done differently." Alice was feeling confident now, and pulled out a one-page chart. "Here you can see the differences between then and now." She pointed to two columns, one labeled "1948" and the other "1952."

"We still sent interviewers to three hundred locations, as you can see here. Well, actually to about 275 because of costs." She flipped a page. "But they used to be sent only to shopping centers or movie theaters where they would interview anyone who fit their quota for age and sex. This time, I sent them to specific streets and gave them detailed instructions on the people to interview. They couldn't just question the person who answered the door, for instance. I'm sure this greatly improves the poll's reliability." Alice paused and looked up from her notes, thinking there might be a question.

"Go on," Eleanor said, clearly interested.

"If you look in your package there, you'll see the questions and responses. But here's a summary." Alice handed her another small packet of papers.

"First of all, there's a lot of interest in this race. Sixty-four percent of voters have already given it a lot of thought. Not surprising, I guess. Neither is the finding that voters don't like the direction the country is going in, but this will be of great interest: in order of priority, voters are most concerned about the Korean War, health care, communism, and to a lesser degree, race issues and agricultural issues."

"Health care as a top priority certainly seems right considering what people around the country have said to me," Eleanor said as she studied the numbers. She turned a page. "Ah, well, this seems to confirm all those awful newspaper reports. Eisenhower is twenty-seven points ahead of me?"

"Yes, and there's a good deal of intensity on both sides," Alice said, "but, look further," she said hurriedly. "We've got you within ten points after we tried out messages for and against you and Eisenhower."

"Striking distance," Larry said, smacking the table.

"Hopefully," Alice said. "Here are some of the main points. Voters do want a male leader in time of war, *but* they prefer a diplomatic solution in Korea. Mrs. Roosevelt is a more polarizing figure than Eisenhower, *but* voters truly admire her work for the UN.

Fifty-eight percent approve of her job performance as First Lady, and they're more impressed with her campaign than with Eisenhower's. Still, 82 percent approve of his job as general in World War II, with only 7 percent disapproving."

"Wow," Joan said letting out a loud breath.

"Voters don't like Truman's job performance, and they just plain don't like Nixon. He's a liability to Eisenhower, while Rayburn is a net plus for you."

"Won't Sam be happy to hear that," Eleanor said, laughing.

"Bottom line, voters see you as sharing their values and as compassionate. They believe you'll fight to protect New Deal programs, but you have to be careful to keep your distance from Truman's policies. When asked if you were strong enough to lead in times of war, 30 percent agreed."

"Men take care of war, what can I say?" Larry looked at Eleanor and shook his head. "Even though less than half the people on this survey," Larry pointed to his paper, "think Ike shares their values, damn if they'll just forget that so he can lead the troops again."

Well, they also see him as strong against communism," Alice said, "while Mrs. Roosevelt is seen as soft on communism."

"What about race relations?" Eleanor asked.

"There's lots of intensity there, but the majority supports segregation; then again, two-thirds want universal health care." Alice tried to sound upbeat.

Eleanor smiled ruefully. "This is very impressive, Alice, and I want to study it further, but how would you sum up the bottom line?" Eleanor asked.

The young woman didn't hesitate. "Talk about health care, working people, and human rights, like you do in America's Deal. Emphasize your work on the Marshall Plan and your approach to foreign policy as balancing diplomacy and strength. Emphasize Eisenhower's inexperience as an executive and the Nixon corruption problems. General Eisenhower definitely has an edge among those voters whose biggest concern is the war in Korea, but if there's some way you could say he'd be part of a solution . . ."

"I see," Eleanor said, looking thoughtful. "Anything else?"

"Well," Alice looked down for a minute, as if gathering her thoughts, and took a deep breath, "this may sound kind of crazy, but you've got to somehow convince voters they're voting for you, Eleanor Roosevelt, as a leader and, well, not for a woman."

"Alice?" Joan interrupted with a giggle. "I think the fact that our candidate is a woman is a little hard to hide."

"Okay, I know. But, these numbers are pretty clear—a strong majority of Americans just won't vote for a woman as president."

CHAPTER 31

The Bravest by Far

Crossing the Indiana/Illinois Border, October 2, 1952

"Not again," Jim Hagerty whispered to Jonathon Chamberlain. "I'm not going to be able to bear this singing all the way to Milwaukee."

"The sons of the Prophet are many and bold . . . and quite unaccustomed to fear." Ike tried to project the song over the train's rumble, and Jonathon couldn't help but think of a largemouth bass gasping on the shore. Ike sang and walked through the train car sweeping his arms straight out through the air in time to his rhythm, nearly whacking some of his aides in the head. "Come on, come on," he urged between stanzas.

"But the bravest by far in the ranks of the Shah . . . was Abdul Abulbul Amir."

Hagerty mumbled the words.

"Come on Jim . . . don't you know the words? 'If you wanted a man to encourage the van . . . Or harass the foe from the rear.' " Ike looked expectant, and Hagerty managed to raise his voice a bit.

Ike laughed and sang even louder. "Storm fort or redoubt . . . you had only to shout for Abdul Abulbul Amir." It was a soldier's song, and he insisted on singing all twenty verses. "At least he's in a good mood," Hagerty said to Jonathon, "at least until I show him this." Hagerty held up the *New York Herald Tribune* and pointed to a piece by John Crosby, the television critic: "Eleanor Roosevelt is a television personality the likes of which has not been seen ever before. She's setting a pace that will not only be almost impossible for succeeding candidates to follow, but one that will be pretty hard for her to maintain, I suspect."

"I read it," Jonathon said. "I'm sure it's why O'Brien's still calling for a debate every chance he gets."

"A debate!" Hagerty said. "That's all we need. Put Ike under those white hot lights for an hour? He'll look like butter melting. Not to mention, that woman is a debater. You should hear Dulles talk about her performance at the first UN meeting. Evidently, she creamed the star prosecutor of the Soviet Union—without notes. No sir, no debate—not as long as I'm running communications."

Hagerty pulled a handkerchief from his pocket, took off his glasses, and began cleaning each lens with care.

"By the way, she's on *Meet the Press* tonight," Jonathon offered, looking like he was worried he might get blamed for her appearance.

Hagerty glared and said, "Well, I think this speech that Ike's going to give praising Marshall, with McCarthy on the dais will get the attention of the press."

Eisenhower owed General George Catlett Marshall his career. The man who many called the greatest general since George Washington, the man who had engineered the postwar European reconstruction that bore his name, had plucked Eisenhower from the ranks after Pearl Harbor and set him on the road to military greatness. When McCarthy called Marshall a "front man for traitors" and "the man who had aided the Communist drive for world domination," the press begged Ike for a response.

"What do you have to say to Senator McCarthy's accusations against General Marshall?" reporters kept hectoring Ike. But political caution caught Ike's tongue. Wisconsin was a key electoral state, and McCarthy owned it. No one, Sherman Adams kept reminding Ike, could judge McCarthy's impact on the national vote.

"I feel dirty from the touch of that man," Ike told Adams. "Marshall resigned as secretary of state because of McCarthy's smears. You realize that, don't you?"

Adams nodded, waiting for what he could tell was an order in the making.

"I'm sick of handling these phony patriots with kid gloves. I think it's time to take on McCarthy in his backyard. I want to pay a personal tribute to Marshall right on that stage. Do you understand? A tribute." Adams had told Hagerty to make it happen.

Hagerty pulled Ike's speech out of a pile of papers and handed it to Jonathon.

"That paragraph Ike wanted on Marshall is in there. It's going to set McCarthy's teeth on edge. Listen to this." Hagerty grabbed the speech out of Jonathon's hand. " 'General Marshall is a man and a soldier,' " he read, " 'dedicated with a singular selflessness and the profoundest patriotism to the service of America. Calling him disloyal, or in any way un-American is the way freedom must *not* defend itself. Promoting unfounded attacks and scurrilous rumors which threaten people's reputations and livelihoods is despicable.'

"Get copies of this speech out to the *New York Times,* maybe a couple of others in advance," Hagerty told Jonathon, handing back the paper. "Ike taking on McCarthy should trump Mrs. Roosevelt's yammering on *Meet the Press.* Maybe even get the press off of the Nixon mess."

As the train chugged out of Evansville toward Carbondale, Jonathon walked through the cars with the Milwaukee speech, giving it to selected reporters. Turnbull, who Jonathon found more distasteful than ever, was sitting in the press car, shooting the breeze with Cal Thompson of the *Chicago Tribune*. He tried to act nonchalant when Jonathon came by and handed Thompson the speech.

Turnbull didn't know if Jonathon had heard. Adams had taken Turnbull into his private car to tell him that his services would no longer be needed after this trip. Adams had mumbled something about needing to conserve campaign funds, but Turnbull suspected there was another reason having to do with his pressing the campaign to use the scurrilous information he'd gotten on Eleanor, and he was fuming. As Thompson leafed through the speech, Turnbull read over his shoulder.

"Looks like the standard speech on corruption and all that . . . hey, take a look at this." Thompson handed Turnbull the speech, pointing to the section praising Marshall and implicitly criticizing McCarthy.

"Did you know he was going to do that?" Thompson asked.

"Of course," Turnbull bluffed. "Yeah, of course I did," Turnbull hesitated, "but you know, there was another line we talked about including. Excuse me a minute, will you? I'd better go tell Hagerty." Turnbull hoisted himself off the well-worn leather seat as the train slowed to a crawl for a whistle-stop in Harrisburg. He lumbered to the door and lowered his bulk to the platform as soon as the shuddering sigh of the engine assured him it was safe. He pulled a black leather-bound book out of his vest pocket as he walked, and got Walter Kohler, Wisconsin's governor, on the phone on his first try.

"Can't talk long Walt, but you're about to have a big, very big problem. That speech Ike's giving in Milwaukee? He's going to screw McCarthy to the wall. Just remember, you didn't hear it from me. Not from me, understand?"

CHAPTER 32

"An Undeniable Act
of Political Cowardice"

Milwaukee, Wisconsin, October 4, 1952

The press corps looked eager as the train pulled into Milwaukee. Some reporters had already composed headlines: "Ike to McCarthy: Marshall's the Patriot," "McCarthy's Milwaukee Spanking," "General Eisenhower Takes McCarthy to the Woodshed."

Eisenhower's motorcade wound from the rail yard along the Menomenee River east of Hawley Street, past Lake Michigan and into the city center, where crowds broke through the police line and forced the six black Cadillac stretch limousines to a sharp stop. Senator McCarthy, relegated to the last car, took the opportunity to hop out and shoulder his way into the car behind Eisenhower's. The crowd enveloped the motorcade, grabbing and waving the

American flags that flapped on the dual flagpoles installed standard on the front fenders.

"Let's hope your Milwaukeeans keep this up in the stadium," Adams said to Governor Kohler. Ike had been having more luck attracting cheering crowds in the streets than interested ones at his speeches. That spring, the Milwaukee Braves had gotten a new baseball stadium that could hold twenty thousand fans. In a city of half a million, Adams hoped to pack the place, but he was disappointed again. As they walked through the tunnel and out to the bunting-covered platform, he guessed two thousand people were in the bleachers. He also guessed that he was being optimistic.

After the presentation of the colors, the singing of the "Star-Spangled Banner," and the Pledge of Allegiance, a German band played. A dancing flock of girls, some as young as five, with hair plaited like milkmaids and boys in lederhosen held toothsome smiles and stared at the empty nosebleed seats despite their missteps. Next came the presentation of a bathtub-sized basket reeking with Polish sausage. Finally, a crate wrapped in an enormous blue ribbon was carried in on the shoulders of four beefy, mustachioed men, their hair parted in the middle and pasted to their heads. Inside was Milwaukee's pride—Pabst Blue Ribbon beer.

"That'll fill the beer fridge for the next month." Ike laughed, as McCarthy got up to introduce him to roars of "Joe, Joe, Joe."

"Thank you, thank you. Please, I'm here for one job only—to introduce our next speaker. He is a great American who'll make a great president." Applause echoed in great waves across the ball field, but it intensified as McCarthy added, "But I want to tell you that I will continue to call them as I see them, regardless of who happens to be president."

Ike got up, his arms raised in full wave, and walked to the microphone without a glance at McCarthy. Word had spread within the media that the speech would be a sensation. The array of radio and television microphones bent toward Ike on snaking necks like cobras with engorged black, brass, and silver heads. ABC's mike was wrapped in the latest innovation—a wire hood that served as a windscreen, although the air was calm.

Ike laid his speech on the podium and pulled out his glasses. Two rows behind him, McCarthy leaned back in his chair, arms folded. Kohler sat next to him, looking nervous.

The two men had surprised Ike in his campaign car two nights before, telling him that if he criticized McCarthy in Milwaukee, he could kiss off any chance of winning Wisconsin on election day. Then McCarthy met with Ike in private, coming out of the compartment with a set and angry look on his face. Kohler figured the meeting hadn't gone well, and he was expecting an ugly scene onstage.

Ike moved past the standard greetings to local officials and quickly began laying into the Truman administration.

"This administration is honeycombed with Communists. This we know. We lost China, and we surrendered whole nations in Eastern Europe to the Communists because of the Reds in Washington."

He paused and gave a fierce look toward the stands. "A government rotten at the core means—in its most ugly triumph—treason itself. In every proven case, we have the right—we have the duty—to call a Red a Red. I will apply the strictest test of loyalty and patriotism to federal employees."

The crowd's cheers forced Ike to pause, and McCarthy beamed, straightening his elephant-spotted tie and refolding his arms like a proud father.

"Communism has insinuated itself into our schools," Ike went on, "our public forums, some of our news channels, some of our labor unions, and most terrifyingly, into government itself. This penetration has meant treason itself."

Ike had moved on to other issues, although, after the Nixon fiasco, the corruption theme had been dropped. "Taxes must be cut overall by 55 percent; we will reduce inflation and bring down high prices," Ike promised. "And I will be sure we win the peace in Korea by ending the drift and makeshift, make-believe policies of the past." As the crowd started to cheer, Ike raised his arms, begging for another moment to finish.

"Senator McCarthy and I have our differences, but we both want to rid the government of the incompetents, the dishonest, and the subversive and disloyal. If you agree with me, you must not only send me to Washington, you must elect every Republican on the ticket so that I will have the means to succeed."

As Ike finished, the crowd jumped to its feet. From the stadium speakers, the "I like Ike" campaign song bubbled and bounced its simple rhythm over the crowd, and many people sang along. Photographers raced to the edge of the stage or jumped to the platform, and flashes sparkled like mini-fireworks as a grinning McCarthy stretched his arm across a row of chairs and gripped the hand Ike seemed to be extending as far from his body as possible. Kohler was caught by the cameras standing behind the men's moment of contact, looking on with jovial approval. With one quick shake, Ike pulled away.

The press corps, sitting in a cordoned area to the side of the stage, raced to find telephones. Scotty Reston couldn't get the words out fast enough as he talked to his editor.

"That's right, not a word about Marshall. Not a word about McCarthy or his tactics. No, it was more than that; he made a point of *praising* McCarthy. Okay, here's the lead: 'If the government of our country is the real hope of any moral basis for political action in the world, then today, on a stage in Milwaukee, General Eisenhower did much to damage his right to sit in the White House. Having trumpeted this as the day when Senator Joseph McCarthy's reckless accusations would be challenged on his home soil, the man who commanded all Allied forces in Europe could not keep command of his own good intentions. Instead, Eisenhower deleted from his speech, which had been handed to reporters yesterday, a critical paragraph defending the patriotism of his mentor, General George C. Marshall.'"

The *Times* story was echoed in papers across the country. The *Milwaukee Journal Sentinel* ended an enraged editorial with an endorsement of Eleanor Roosevelt. "Eisenhower," they wrote, "had committed a wholly unexpected, but undeniable act of political cowardice."

When the story broke, Eleanor was in Detroit having breakfast with her friend Walter Reuther, head of the United Auto Workers' union. They sat at a table in the grimy Capitol Coffee Shop. In Detroit, Reuther was nearly as recognizable as the former First Lady, but most of the patrons were rushing off to work and gave the two a quick nod. A couple of men with union pins on their jackets stopped to say, "We're with you, Mrs. Roosevelt. We'll turn out the vote, don't worry."

"I like to come here, Eleanor," Reuther said. "It's close to the plant. We cited this place for not hiring Negroes two years ago as part of the Antidiscrimination Department's activity, and now look." Reuther pointed over the counter to the pass-through window from the kitchen. Two Negro men were wearing white aprons, busily cracking eggs and flipping pancakes.

"We need more *action* like that Walter, and less *talk* about ending discrimination," Eleanor said.

"Excuse me, Mrs. R.," Maureen sounded short of breath as she hurried up to the table. She had been traveling with Eleanor more and more, at Tommy's insistence. "I just checked in with headquarters and Mr. O'Brien said he needs you to call right away. There's a big story about Ike on the front pages today."

At three o'clock that afternoon, Joan jockeyed reporters into the Wayne Room at the Statler Hotel on Washington Street in Detroit. Eleanor stood in front of a single microphone, as Joan urged the reporters to find seats and looked nervously at the two-story vaulted ceiling. It was never a good idea to have Eleanor speak where her "turkey gobble," as she called it, would bounce back like a tin Ping-Pong ball off the ceiling.

"Ladies and gentlemen of the press," Eleanor began. "I take no delight in this moment, for it is a low moment in this campaign. I cannot tell you I am anything other than profoundly disappointed, and frankly astonished, at General Eisenhower's actions in Milwaukee, which have been well detailed by you.

"This kind of political backsliding and calculation only serves to further obscure the general's true positions, and reinforce the most cynical view of political campaigning. Where *does* the general stand on the assault of McCarthy and his ilk on our democratic principles? Where *does* he stand on the role his mentor, George Marshall, might play as we move forward with critical foreign policy decisions? Was this unfortunate display of capitulation a sign that he agrees with the isolationist sentiment of McCarthy? If so, what of Korea? As candidates, we owe the American people a full, honest, and searching discussion of these and other issues."

Eleanor paused, so conscious of the moment that she could feel her heart begin to pound. How proud Franklin and Louis would be that she had seized the opening. O'Brien had nearly jumped through the telephone as they talked, and when she reached Rayburn in Missouri, she appreciated his knowing chuckle. "I guess their nationally advertised product of a general didn't live up to his packaging."

"As you all are well aware," Eleanor went on, "I have asked many times for the general to agree to a historic event for this election—a televised debate. Two major networks, NBC and CBS, have offered us free airtime for this event. We all saw the American people's interest in the nationally televised party conventions. I believe that that innovation helped strengthen our democracy. It allowed people, young and old, to see their democracy at work. We have a chance to do even more with the frank, open, and respectful give-and-take of a formal debate.

"I do not know why the general has refused this idea. But I do know this; he cannot expect the American people to elect him president if they do not know where he stands on the crucial issues of the day, and one of those issues is the true danger posed by Senator McCarthy and his cronies.

"I call on the general to have that discussion with me. I stand ready at any time and any place. If he was irresolute yesterday, unable to stay firm in his position, he has a chance to stand up today and show purpose by agreeing to this proposal. If his reputation for courage abandoned him yesterday, let him put his courage on display once more by answering the questions of his fellow citizens through a fair and full debate with me."

Hagerty's head dropped into his hands as he listened to Eleanor's words come from the radio. The debacle that Ike's staff was calling the blackest day of the race had just gotten blacker.

CHAPTER 33

Prep

Washington, D.C., October 15, 1952

The capital city was in the thrall of an early October Indian summer day, its moist warm glow scented by the first fallen leaves. Workers in federal office buildings cranked and tugged at windows that had been shut against the coming chill. They stole extra minutes at lunch. The women pulled pleated skirts up from midcalf and took off their buttoned-up suit jackets, especially where a prim white blouse had a colorful tie at the neck. Men shook the legs on loose-fitting trousers and hoped the autumn glory would last through a weekend game of football.

At the Mayflower Hotel, the doorman looked away for a moment, and Eleanor appeared, pulling the heavy gold-plated door open on her own and breaking for the outside. She turned left with purpose and complete inattention to the man rushing behind her.

"Eleanor, please, just a minute." Larry O'Brien tried not to shout as he twisted and sidestepped to dodge the people walking down Connecticut Avenue. Some of the pedestrians did a double take. That tall gray-haired woman with the lace-up, block-heeled black shoes looked familiar. Those who had been in Washington during the Roosevelt years weren't surprised. Eleanor had taken daily walks and horseback rides through Rock Creek Park when she lived at the White House, often eluding her security detail. There were smiles, nods, and whispers as O'Brien finally caught up with her.

"Ah, Larry, it's a lovely day, and one must get one's exercise. You seem out of breath." Eleanor reached over to give his stomach a pat as she kept walking. "You know, Larry, you must watch what you're eating and exercise more. It's quite important for good health. When I worked for the Office of Civil Defense during the war . . ."

"Eleanor, all right. Fine." O'Brien was buttoning his suit jacket with some difficulty. "I'm not letting you change the subject here. You can't just walk out. We have to do this debate preparation. No candidate goes into a debate without . . ."

"Larry, do you really think I am some kind of witless school-girl?" Eleanor paused for a moment and turned toward O'Brien, then marched off again, still talking. "Do you think the UN was an international social club?" Eleanor stopped by the light at K Street, and looked straight ahead as if she was intensely interested in the park across the street. As the light changed, she went on, "I've spent more time arguing my positions over the years than Eisenhower has giving orders. He's a successful general with no political conviction and arrogance born of giving command . . . not answering questions. Those are not good qualifications for a debater. Come, let's sit here in the sun."

They had reached the crisscrossing pathways of Farragut Square Park, and Eleanor picked a bench near a ginkgo tree. The fan-shaped leaves had turned a bright yellow gold and the darker seed balls, like small apricots, were just beginning to litter the ground and give off their distinctive rancid odor.

"What is that smell?" O'Brien asked, wrinkling his nose.

"The ginkgo tree? They're quite wonderful," Eleanor said, pointing to the tree on the lawn next to them. "In China I saw one that was fifteen hundred years old. They're very tenacious. After the bombing of Hiroshima, they were among the few living things that survived. The Chinese think the seeds contain an aphrodisiac and other special medical properties. That tree's very unique, very special, but it's often rejected just because the female's seeds have that rather unusual odor. Some cities are actually uprooting them and tossing them out. They simply make people too uncomfortable." Eleanor paused. "I'm afraid I'm a bit of a ginkgo, Larry. We are hoping that I'm not so offensive to so many people that I get tossed aside, aren't we?" Eleanor said, giving O'Brien a sharp look.

"As a woman, you mean," O'Brien said, rather than asked.

"Not only that," Eleanor replied, "although that's a lot of it. I think Ike's camp is *depending* on women being offended by my running. He may be right. Have you seen those "Moms for Mamie"?

"Oh, yes. I think they've been at every campaign stop with that ridiculous short fringe of hair on their foreheads."

"Those are called 'bangs,'" Eleanor offered.

"Bangs, fine. I even heard some women were using little nail scissors like Mamie said she did to cut hers the first time. Silly. But I believe they're a minority."

"Not if *Woman's Home Companion* has anything to do with it," Eleanor said. "Did you read that article? Mamie is 'no bluestocking feminist.' Now, who do you think they were really talking about? And *Ladies' Home Journal* saying Mamie's 'not trying to be an intellectual.' I do take that personally." Eleanor gave a short laugh.

"Well, even if she did try, she'd fail," Larry said. "I've been carrying this quote around just to remind me what we're up against, as if

I need it." He began to read in as high-pitched and simpering a voice as he could manage: "'Our lives revolve around our men, and that is the way it should be. What real satisfaction is there without them? Being a wife is the best career that life has to offer a woman.' Thank you, Mrs. Eisenhower, for that bit of wisdom."

Eleanor didn't laugh. "There are a lot of women who believe that," she said. "For them, there's only one version of womanhood, and I'm not it. But I do think the reaction to my being a woman isn't as bad as the outrage over America's Deal. Some people would rather inhale those ginkgo seeds whole than see that passed."

"No, Eleanor. Some people would rather kill you than see that passed. You have to stop trotting around unprotected. Like today. I know you're still getting those threatening letters." O'Brien sounded exasperated, but Eleanor changed the subject.

"I'm done with having Franklin Jr. interrogating me. He makes a poor Walter Cronkite. And making poor Molly be a stand-in for Ike is a bit ludicrous."

"It was your suggestion, Eleanor. Remember? And Franklin's just asking you questions we all worked on. This is the first and only nationally televised debate. Cronkite knows he's setting a standard. He'll be thorough and tough, I'm sure. You know they're calling him an 'anchor' these days? New term for the guy running the show. There's a reason they didn't call it a 'feather.'"

"My whole life has been a preparation, Larry," Eleanor said, getting up and letting her long strides carry her ahead of her campaign manager.

"What did you say?" Larry was panting as he tried to catch up.

"Never mind. You'd better save your breath. You do need to get more exercise," and she gave him a disapproving look.

CHAPTER 34

The Great Debate

Washington, D.C., October 21, 1952

Constitution Hall, the largest auditorium in Washington, bustled for days before "The Great Debate," as newspapers were already calling the face-off between Eleanor and Ike. The city had an ironic kind of neutrality as the debate venue, since residents didn't have the right to vote for president. Ike's people hoped it would remind voters of Truman's failed administration, particularly corruption in the capital, since Nixon's fund scandal had muted direct talk about it. Then came Ike's visit to Truman's house.

"Whatever possessed you to say that about Truman right on his front porch?" Sherman Adams had asked in frustration the day after Ike's meeting with the president in Independence.

"It's what I believe, Sherman. Let's leave it at that."

"Fine, Ike, but it makes it awfully hard for you to turn around and call the man corrupt after you called him 'one of the most honorable men I know,'" Adams said, biting off his words. "And it makes it pretty hard for the campaign to keep hammering Eleanor for Truman's mistakes." But he could see that Ike wasn't going to say any more on the subject.

Eleanor's staff hoped that holding the debate in Washington would evoke memories of FDR and Eleanor's years as First Lady. But for the week before the event, the press seemed intent on lowering expectations for the general and portraying Eleanor as a desperate candidate. Arriving by train at Union Station the day of the debate, Eleanor agreed to an impromptu press conference.

"Come along, come along," Eleanor said to reporters as she walked under the barrel-vaulted ceiling of the station, its coffered expanse adorned with nearly a hundred pounds of gold leaf. Her voice bounced around the monumental Beaux-Arts space like a flying piccolo. She led the group into the presidential suite in the front corner of the Great Hall, which Joan had hurriedly secured.

"Mrs. Roosevelt, isn't it true that you have the advantage in this debate as the far more experienced debater?" *Time*'s Carl Miller shouted out the first question.

"I have been listening to the general for several months now, Carl. I have no doubt that he is superb at arguing his positions, and I look forward to a vigorous exchange."

"But Mrs. Roosevelt, isn't this debate really a ploy to make you appear on an equal footing with the general and take advantage of his postwar popularity?" This time, the *Chicago Tribune*'s Roy Stout barely hid his contempt. Joan, standing to the side of the room, shook her head in frustration.

"I frankly do not understand," Eleanor said, her voice rising, "the insistent need by some members of the press to analyze every moment of a political campaign in the most cynical light possible. Everything candidates do is not political strategy. Perhaps you should consider that we actually have strong beliefs, values, and opinions. I have one reason, and only one reason for participating in tonight's debate. That reason is to allow the American people the opportunity to judge for themselves between myself and General Eisenhower through an honest and fair discussion of the issues. Yes, Scotty?"

"It is the case, Mrs. Roosevelt," said Scotty Reston from the *New York Times*, "that the national polls all have you losing this race by pretty big margins. Are you counting on some miracle tonight to turn that around?"

Eleanor smiled. "There's always a role for Divine Providence." Some of the reporters chuckled. "But if polls decided elections, the man in the White House today would be President Dewey, wouldn't he? And you may find it interesting to know that I have some polls of my own."

"You have your own pollster?" This time, it was the AP reporter, sounding skeptical. "No candidate has ever done that, have they Mrs. Roosevelt?"

"Some of you may remember Emil Hurja," Eleanor replied, "who helped my husband understand the way New Deal programs were being received by the public. There is a great deal of speculation by the press as to how my America's Deal is viewed by voters. So I have found my own method for judging that, and I am quite satisfied."

"Does your poll tell you who's going to win?" came the next question, with a hint of sarcasm.

"Speaker Rayburn and I are in it to win it, and we shall all know what the *voters'* decision is very soon," Eleanor said.

As Eleanor walked out of the room, Carl Miller from *Time* grabbed Reston's arm. "What do you think, Scotty, is there a chance in hell that she could even come close to pulling this off?"

"She's putting on a bit. She knows enough about politics to know she doesn't have a chance. But the lady's always been a fighter. This polling thing. Another rabbit out of the hat. She won't roll over, I'm sure of that."

The candidates had agreed on a simple format of opening and closing statements, with Cronkite asking questions of each of them and time limits on the answers. Eleanor had proposed that the candidates be allowed to question each other, but that had been swiftly and firmly rejected.

Behind the scenes, the two sides sparred over the size of the audience, how applause and heckling would be controlled, whether to allow signs and even buttons, and how many staff members could be backstage. But the question of the stage itself set off the biggest storm, and Larry O'Brien and Sherman Adams had met at the hall the day of the event to resolve it, along with their media aides, Joan Black and Jonathon Chamberlain.

"We meet again, and we're not even in Texas," Joan said, smiling and shaking Jonathon's hand. They were walking behind their principals who were in deep discussion. Suddenly, Adams marched across the stage, grabbed a chair, and slammed it down next to one of the two standing microphones that were on either side of the desk where Cronkite would be sitting.

"Look, Larry. Cronkite's sitting down. It will look much better for them not to be hovering over him at microphones." He marched back to grab another chair and put it by the other mike, as Larry stood with his hands folded and a slight smile on his face.

"Sherm, just admit it. She's taller than Ike, and you don't like the way that might look. How about this? She'll wear really low heels."

Adams gave him a poisonous look.

"They're going to shake hands anyway, Sherm," Larry went on amiably. "Everyone will see then that she towers over him."

"She does not *tower* over him," Adams shot back. "And he has a war injury. Standing on his leg for an hour could be painful."

"He tripped getting off a plane, didn't he? Should we tell the press that's why they're sitting down?" Larry tried to sound innocent.

Joan and Jonathon caught each other's eye and tried not to laugh.

"I think there's a compromise," Jonathon offered. Both men looked at him.

"Why not have them each get up at a podium mike when they give their opening and closing statements, and sit during questioning?"

"And, of course, shake hands in front of the desk when they come out and at the end," Joan added quickly. "For the photographers. You know they'll want that shot, of course."

"Okay," Adams said, "I could go along with that. But we don't want a high-back wing chair, but we do want a chair with arms."

"Can you grab a few minutes for a drink later?" Jonathon said quietly to Joan, as the two older men continued haggling. "A martini?" He gave Joan that crooked, incorrigible smile, and she realized with a start that she had missed seeing him over the last few weeks.

"Going for drinks with the enemy?" she replied with a smile.

"I'm all for diplomatic solutions to even the most contentious and highly charged situations."

"Uh-huh. Well how do I know you're not just trying to get me drunk and find out Mrs. R.'s plan for ending the war in Korea?"

"That would be futile, since I know she doesn't have one," Jonathon said with the smug tone that reminded Joan of the kind of people she hated, the ones who might be wrong, but who were never in doubt.

"Really? And Ike does?" she responded, feeling her face get hot. " 'Asians should fight Asians'? You call that a plan?"

Jonathon folded his arms and looked down at her, reacting without thinking. "Well, it's not America's *Steal,* that's for sure. Now there's a plan. Double everyone's taxes so the government can give houses away to commies and use the army to fight our countrymen instead of our real enemies."

"That's the stupidest . . . not everyone has sixteen thousand dollars for a house like some rich Yankees from famous military families in Maine." Joan's whisper became a hiss, and without waiting for an answer, she turned and caught up with O'Brien, who had shaken hands with Adams and was leaving the stage. Jonathon nearly shouted after her, but it suddenly occurred to him that she must have done some research. How would she know about his family otherwise? He smiled as her heels clicked away across the wood floor, thinking she was sure to have cooled down by the time they met in Texas.

CHAPTER 35

Kay's Man

Washington, D.C., October 21, 1952

By 7:30 on the evening of the debate, more than three thousand partisans for Eleanor and Ike, who had been given equal numbers of tickets to hand out, filled the seats in Constitution Hall. Signs had been banned, but under the glass ceiling that was just beginning to show the evening stars, excited attendees wore their allegiance on their clothing.

The hall had the look of a confused party convention without the balloons and giant state signs. Donkey and elephant hats and pins competed with pie-sized "Eleanor for President" and "I Like Ike" buttons. Shirts, dresses, and pants had been stenciled and stitched with slogans and the candidates' names. Leaflets had been banned, but cards appeared from pockets and purses declaring the virtues of the nominees. While the stage remained empty, the television cameras for the sponsoring networks, CBS and NBC, panned the room and reporters did random interviews around the floor of the hall, struggling to hear over the rising noise of excited chatter.

Finally, Walter Cronkite walked onstage, and an insistent hushing began to quiet the room as people scrambled to their seats. The thirty-six-year-old Cronkite had only joined CBS two years before. His receding hair, neat mustache, and warm family-man looks were familiar thanks to his coverage of both party conventions. He was a new breed of broadcaster, with his reassuring manner and penchant for capturing the drama of the moment.

As stagehands held up giant hand-stenciled "Quiet" signs, the cameras began to roll. Across the country, more than seventy million Americans were settling into sofas and shushing children as they watched the grainy black-and-white picture that filled the small oval of their television sets.

Cronkite sat at a large walnut desk and looked straight into the camera. A neat stack of papers and a microphone were on the desk in front of him. Two mahogany Regency Carver chairs had been placed on either side of the desk, with small matching tripod tables that each held a pitcher of water and a glass. Microphones had been placed next to each chair at seat height. A few feet to the side of the chairs were podiums for opening and closing statements, and behind the set a single American flag on a standing pole was set off to one side of the stage.

As the camera slowly panned in to frame Cronkite, he began to speak in his slightly singsong sonorous voice. "Good evening, ladies and gentlemen, and thank you for joining us on this historic night when you will see the first-ever televised presidential debate. We are inside beautiful DAR Constitution Hall, only blocks from the White House in our nation's capital. Exactly two weeks from now, the American people will decide which of the nominees in our debate tonight will sit in the Oval Office as president of these United States."

Cronkite continued with his introduction, thanking Westing-house for its sponsorship, and plugging both sponsoring networks before he called for the candidates' to join him onstage. From either side of the proscenium arch, General Dwight D. Eisenhower and Eleanor Roosevelt walked out, turning as they approached each other to wave and smile at the crowd. Cameras panned across the seats as pandemonium broke out with clapping, cheering, and wild waving of arms and hats. Although the audience had been warned to stay seated, people jumped up with spontaneous enthu-siasm that was quickly squelched by the small army of D.C. police and plainclothes FBI agents positioned around the hall.

They were reacting to several letters that threatened to blow up Constitution Hall during the event. Edgar Ray Killen had sent them, hoping to disrupt the event. He turned on his television just long enough to satisfy himself that he'd at least caused a stir, and smiled when he heard the commentators talking about the extreme security measures. Then he switched the set off quickly, having no desire to listen to the woman he intended to kill.

Eleanor wore a light-tan suit, the slightly flared skirt falling mid-calf above her heavy-heeled black walking shoes that raised her height to just over six feet. Her simple five-button hip-length jacket had a broad lapel and modest neckline that showed her trademark pearls. Her hair was swept back in soft waves and pinned in a simple chignon. She looked relaxed and happy as she extended her hand and approached Eisenhower as if they were long-lost friends.

The general wore a dark gray suit, bright white shirt, and navy tie. He walked toward Eleanor, struggling to maintain his smile as he worried that he might sneeze. He was in the midst of yet another cold, and he had two handkerchiefs ready, although he hoped he could avoid using either one. Adams had counseled him to make the handshake as brief as possible, but as they met, Eleanor put both her hands around Ike's and seemed in no hurry to let go.

"General, thank you for agreeing to this debate. It is a great moment for the country."

"Thank you, Mrs. Roosevelt," Ike replied, the thought flashing through his mind that he'd had no choice but to agree after the McCarthy/Marshall debacle.

The crowd was cheering and calling out their names, and the cameras zoomed in on the wonderful vignette of the candidates' first campaign embrace.

"I want to wish you good luck, Ike. I am looking forward to a robust and fruitful exchange."

"As am I." Ike tried not to seem abrupt as he turned and pulled away from Eleanor, walking quickly to his seat.

Both candidates used their five-minute opening statements to reiterate their plans for the country. Since he won the coin toss, Eisenhower went first, and when they both had finished, Cronkite began the questioning.

"General Eisenhower, I'll start with you, and you know you have three minutes to respond. The American people are greatly concerned by the war in Korea. There seems to be no plan for the peace. What will you do as president about Korea?"

"Mr. Cronkite," Ike began, looking toward the desk and glancing down at some note cards he held in his hand, "a small country, Korea has been, for more than two years, the battleground for the costliest foreign war our nation has fought, excepting the two world wars. It has been a symbol of the failed foreign policy of our nation. There is a Korean war because our leadership failed to check and to turn back Communist ambition before it savagely attacked us. The record of failure dates back with red-letter folly to September 1947. It was then that General Albert Wedemeyer, returned from a presidential mission to the Far East, submitted to the president this warning."

Ike paused to read off the large lettering on one of the cards he held, "'The withdrawal of American military forces from Korea would result in the occupation of South Korea by either Soviet troops or, as seems more likely, by the Korean military units trained under Soviet auspices in North Korea.'"

As Ike talked, Sherman Adams raced from one side of the stage to the other behind the curtains. When Ike looked up from his reading, Adams frantically tried to get his attention from a spot in the wings, punching his index finger toward the audience and mouthing, as if speaking to a small child, "look that way." But Ike didn't notice, and continued his answer as if only he and Cronkite were in the hall.

"That warning to the president was disregarded and suppressed by the administration," Ike continued. "Our troops were withdrawn, and we only heard silence—stubborn, sullen silence from the administration." Ike paused, shuffling through his note cards again.

"When the enemy struck, on that June day of 1950, what did America do? It did what it always has done in all its times of peril. It appealed to the heroism of its youth. The answer to that appeal has been what any American knew it would be. It has been sheer valor—valor on all the Korean mountainsides that, each day, bear fresh scars of new graves. But, where do we go from here? When comes the end? Is there an end?" Ike's head seemed to bob up and down as he checked his notes. He went on, his head in profile on camera.

"My answer is this: The first task of a new administration will be to review and reexamine every course of action open to us with one goal in view—to bring the Korean War to an early and honorable end. This is my pledge to the American people. The job of ending the Korean War means a personal trip to Korea. I shall make that trip. Only in that way could I learn how best to serve the American people in the cause of peace. I shall go to Korea." Eisenhower's face looked stern and determined as he went on.

"A foreign policy is the face and voice of a whole people. It is all that the world sees and hears and understands about a single nation." Ike raised his voice slightly, and spoke as if he were exhorting his troops.

"We know that victory can come only with the gift of God's help. In this spirit, humble servants of a proud ideal, we do soberly say: the cause of peace is our crusade."

As people began to applaud, Cronkite interrupted. "Please, ladies and gentlemen. We will hold all applause until after closing statements. Thank you, General." He turned toward Eleanor, who was leaning forward slightly in her chair, her hands folded on her empty lap. "Mrs. Roosevelt, would you like to respond?"

"Yes, thank you, Mr. Cronkite," she said looking at him, then turning and speaking directly to the audience. "I am very impressed with what the general has just said, and I believe that he shares the desire of the whole country to end the war in Korea. But I must correct one point. When the administration was warned in 1947 of the possibility of Communist aggression in Korea, General Eisenhower was chairman of the Joint Chiefs of Staff and closely involved with all administration decisions involving the Russians and the Chinese. I say this only to make clear that finger-pointing by either political party or candidate with regard to Korea is rather pointless, after all, and we must instead move forward with a plan for winning the peace." Eleanor's tone was measured. She seemed to be saying, what could be more reasonable than what I'm proposing?

"I do not believe that our Korean plan should be partisan. Both parties, indeed all Americans, share the goal of maintaining and ensuring our continued freedom and safety from foreign enemies while we extricate ourselves from this tragic war. As we look to solutions, we must consider wise diplomacy and imaginative nonmilitary use of our economic resources, especially through the United Nations. We must be cautious that by answering communism with force of arms we do not inadvertently encourage its spread, for military bastions tend to increase local burdens and contribute in impoverished countries to the desperation on which communism feeds. I agree, the next president must go to Korea, assess the situation personally, and firmly sue for peace."

Joan Black, sitting in the balcony with Maureen, started to applaud.

"Whoops," Joan sat on her hands. "I think she got the better of that one, don't you?" she asked Maureen.

"I'm not sure. He would do better to look at the audience, but he does sound very . . . well, very military and in charge. Voters like that, I think."

"But he looks so pasty," Joan said, "and he must be sweating because his head's started to shine like a flesh-colored bulb." She giggled.

"Well, if the candidate with the most hair was guaranteed victory, we'd be made in the shade." Maureen laughed.

Cronkite moved on to domestic issues, touching on taxes, job creation, civil rights, and the question of loyalty oaths. Then he asked the question Eleanor's team had hoped to avoid.

"Mrs. Roosevelt, we have come to the last question in this debate, and it is one that comes up often in your historic run for president. Many newspapers have editorialized about it and Americans seem to have strong opinions about it, but do *you* think the country is ready to accept a woman as president?"

Eleanor gave a quick smile, and spoke first to Cronkite before turning to the audience. "As you know, Mr. Cronkite, I have stated publicly in the past that I did not think the country was ready for a woman president. Tonight, I would like to say that I was mistaken. I say that because of the extraordinary response I have gotten to my candidacy from all parts of this country that has showed me what people truly care about."

As Eleanor spoke, Ike shuffled through his cards. He and his advisers had spent a long time framing an answer to the question they hoped Cronkite would ask, and now he had. Ike glanced at the card, a high-minded litany of the virtues of women as home-makers, mothers, helpmates, and the "quiet backbone of a great country," the phrase Ike himself had coined. He looked up, feeling confident and ready, as Eleanor continued.

"Many women have assured me that they look upon politics as a serious matter year in and year out. It is associated with their patriotism and their duty to their country. They may be at home or in factories or offices, but they have the same interest in elect-ing good people to represent them, as do men. And while these women may not themselves want to enter politics, they welcome anyone, man or woman, to represent them to the best possible ef-fect. They have told me this, and I believe them."

Ike looked out to the audience as Eleanor spoke, trying to gauge reactions in the faces of the crowd. Suddenly, under his carefully applied makeup, the color drained from his face. A woman seated next to the center aisle, about ten rows back, ducked her head as he looked her way. He had the distinct impression that she had been staring at him. She wore a simple dark shirtwaist dress open at the neck and notable for having no political paraphernalia on it. Her thick, dark, and wavy hair was swept back off a high forehead. But what caught Ike's eye was the way she held her slim shoulders, drawn back and square, even as she let her head drop with a slight tilt. That movement, the quick touch of her hand to her hair, he recognized it instantly. It was Kay.

Eleanor continued. "I believe we are about to have a collective coming of age! Women have been participants in government for more than thirty years. We have had the first woman member of a president's cabinet, Secretary of Labor Frances Perkins. We have had women in Congress and as governors and state legislators all over the country. This year, both parties talked of women as vice presidential nominees. The influence of women has emerged. It is a regular occurrence for politicians to ask, 'What will the women think about this?' I believe it is thanks to women that there is greater concern in government for the welfare of human beings . . ."

Ike heard Eleanor continue her answer, but she seemed far away. He tried not to stare at Kay. Mamie was right in the front row. His managers had insisted that she be there, knowing it was a good chance to get the two of them on television after the historic event. He didn't want to act strange in any way, yet he knew his emotions were careening dangerously out of control. He thought he could feel his heartbeat, and his hands had grown sweaty. Why had Kay come? Surely, she wouldn't try to speak to him. What if she did? For a moment, he thought he had caught a whiff of her perfume. It took all his will to listen, as Eleanor's cadence seemed to signal that she was coming to the end of her answer.

"And it was not only I, but so many women who showed throughout the Second World War that they could bring compassion to the battlefront, rise to any challenge, show the utmost courage, stand beside men . . ."

"Yes," Ike thought. Kay had shown courage and more. He thought of her driving through London, steady, imperturbable, as bombs dropped around them and buildings crashed to the ground. How she would work alongside him, twelve-, sixteen-, twenty-hour days with good cheer. How stalwart she was when she arrived in North Africa on a lifeboat after her ship, the *Strathallen*, had been sunk by the Germans. He had been frantic with worry, but after that, he realized Kay could do anything.

"So I ask you," Eleanor was saying, "to remember that women will work for a cause, and that is what I am asking on behalf of my campaign, that women *and* men join what I believe is a cause for a better and more progressive country. We are a nation of opportunity and fairness. I trust that every American will judge my campaign as they do General Eisenhower's, by our programs and vision for America. Thank you."

"General Eisenhower?" Cronkite looked expectantly at Eisenhower, who stared back as if he had no intention of speaking.

"General Eisenhower, would you like to respond?"

Ike placed the pack of note cards on the table next to him, and took a sip of water. Still standing in the wings, Sherman Adams looked quizzical. This was the perfect moment to grab the women's vote and bring it home, so to speak. He must just be pausing for effect, Adams thought.

For the first time in the debate, Eisenhower looked at the audience, leaning forward in his chair with his hands on his knees as he began speaking.

"My opponent is right. Women have risen to every challenge our country has faced, including that of war. It would be unpatriotic and morally wrong to vote for any candidate simply because they are male and not female. I do not want anyone to vote for me on that basis alone." Ike sat back and looked at Cronkite. He had nothing more to say.

Sherman Adams thought he would be sick. He could see the headline in the next day's newspapers, "Ike to Country: Don't Vote for Me Because I'm a Man."

But he was wrong. Ike's wife would dominate the press coverage instead.

Mamie had instantly caught the change in her husband's demeanor when he saw Kay, and she turned to follow his gaze. Mamie was just in time to see a slim, dark-haired woman walking quickly up the aisle and out of the auditorium. As reporters besieged the general's wife after the event, she tried to contain the nausea that threatened to overwhelm her.

"Mrs. Eisenhower, what do you think of your husband's statement? Doesn't it matter that Mrs. Roosevelt's a woman?"

Mamie looked stunned, then suddenly fierce.

"As far as I'm concerned, it doesn't matter if people vote for my husband or Mrs. Roosevelt. Just so they vote."

CHAPTER 36

The KKK Votes with Bullets

Dallas, Texas, October 28, 1952

Sam Rayburn was in his glory. He had often told Eleanor that his favorite spot on earth was his hometown of Bonham, Texas. When he suggested they drive there in the morning, before the major speech she had scheduled in Dallas later that day, Eleanor had readily agreed.

Sam picked up Eleanor, David, and Joan at nine o'clock sharp from the Adolphus Hotel in downtown Dallas. He was driving his gleaming black Cadillac with sparkling whitewalls, and he had an ear-to-ear grin on his face. Driving northeast from the city to the northern edge of the Blackland Prairie, Sam regaled his passengers with stories of his boyhood.

"Everybody worked like the devil. There were eleven kids, after all. But most of us went to college. That's what made me determined to try to help the average man get a break," Sam said as he pulled into the drive of his family house, then veered off toward the barn. He had promised to show Eleanor his favorite horse, Pansy.

David marveled at how relaxed Eleanor seemed to be. Perhaps she's happy this will all be over soon, he thought. She can go back to living at Val-Kill and globe-trotting for good causes. He was relieved that she had stopped talking about the ridiculous fantasy of winning. There wasn't a serious commentator in the country who gave her a chance. Well, she'd done her part, and he was just relieved she'd lived through it.

"You look happy, darling," David said, "and like you have something up your sleeve." He ran his hand up her arm and under the cap sleeve of her lilac dress, as he sat next to her in the car.

"I do," Eleanor said, laughing like a girl, "but you won't find it there."

"What's the big secret in this speech today?" David asked. "Do you know, Joan?"

"Nope, I'm just a messenger. But I wish I did." Joan cast a rueful eye at Eleanor from her post in the passenger seat next to Sam.

"Now, now. Sam and I have conferred on this, and I think it's better if it stays between us until my speech," Eleanor said.

"I agree," Sam added. "It's just a commonsense idea, that's all. And if you have common sense, you have all the sense you need."

"So why the secrecy?" David pressed.

"Well, Sam's right," Eleanor replied, "but sometimes common sense can get people very upset. Don't worry. You'll know soon enough." They had gotten out of the car and gone into the barn. "She's a beauty, Sam," Eleanor said, stroking the white marking on Pansy's face. "I wish we had time for a ride."

"So do I," Sam said, "but we've got a tight schedule. We've got to leave here in two hours to get back to Dallas in time."

"You mean the mayor of Bonham's going to keep his remarks short?" Eleanor said, laughing.

"He'll do what I told him to do," Sam said. "Don't you worry about that."

In town, the citizens of Bonham, along with spectators who had driven from surrounding rural areas and farms, lined the streets ten deep to see "Mr. Sam" and his famous guest. Two visitors had driven five hundred miles through the night, due west from the eastern border of Mississippi. They kept the windows rolled down in the pickup's cab, smoking endless cigarettes and plotting as they rode across the top of Louisiana's boot then turned north along the outskirts of Dallas, getting to Bonham as the speakers' platform was being hammered together in the center of Main Street.

"Where ya' going to keep the gun?" Jim Barrow asked as Edgar Ray Killen parked the dusty black truck at the edge of a grassy lot where a few cars were just starting to pull in.

Killen held the pistol low on his lap, turning it over as if he was studying it for the first time.

"Wouldn't my Daddy be proud?" Killen cradled his father's World War II service revolver, a Remington Rand .45 caliber automatic. He read the words stamped along the barrel, "United States Property," and ran his finger over the rough grip. Then he reached over and put the weapon in the glove compartment.

"Come on. Let's go see what the setup is like and figure out where you should wait," Killen said to Barrow, and the two men, blending in with their roughened jeans and white cotton T-shirts, walked toward the place where Eleanor would soon be welcomed as the guest of honor.

Jonathon Chamberlain was also in Bonham. The television commercials for Ike that he had been working on with Rosser Reeves were done. The "I Like Ike" ads had just started playing in key districts and were getting an enthusiastic response, with their parade of cartoon animals and people marching along with Ike banners and signs to the beat of the catchy tune.

Jonathon had been reassigned to follow Eleanor for the last days of the campaign and report anything that might need a quick response by Ike. He didn't mind the assignment at all, knowing he was sure to run into Joan at some point.

Jonathon positioned himself by the bunting-covered speakers' platform with its huge "Bonham, Texas" banner printed in Old West lettering. He jostled his way to the front row of spectators, craning his neck to see if Joan was anywhere in sight. The mayor and some local officials were already pacing on the raised platform in front of an American flag and Texas's lone-star flag, both flapping gently. Someone tested the microphone, competing to raise the noise level with the local high school band that was tuning up. The whole thing reminded Jonathon of a county fair. Some people rode horses into town, and behind the buildings a battalion of pickup trucks were parked at crazy angles. Jonathon smelled barbecued pork and cotton candy, remembering with a pang in his stomach that he hadn't had a chance to eat.

Suddenly, cheers could be heard echoing from the far end of town. The Bonham Fire Company's bright red engine came into view, its siren intermittently cutting the air with an earsplitting shriek. The police chief came next, then Sam and Eleanor waving from a black Cadillac convertible. Two police cruisers took up the rear, and the crowd closed in behind the slow-moving motorcade, cheering as they filled Main Street and moved toward the speakers' platform. The band had struck up, "Texas, Our Texas," and some people in the crowd began to sing the state song.

Jonathon heard a sharp and familiar voice cutting through the noise saying, "Please move back, please don't push on the rope." He turned to see Joan trying to adjust the ropes that cordoned a lane from the street to the stairs of the platform. He pushed his way closer and tapped her arm.

"Glad to see you made it," he said. "Want some help?"

Joan looked flustered. "No, I don't need any help, and I can't talk now. Please," she said, turning sharply and tapping a woman's arm, "could you step back so Mrs. Roosevelt and Mr. Rayburn will have room to walk to the stage?"

Jonathon decided to wait for a better time to propose a martini. He looked down the street and saw that all but the car with Eleanor and Sam had peeled off a block before the stage.

Their car stopped just a few feet from the lane that Joan was struggling to keep open, and Sam stepped out. He was only five feet, six inches tall, and the top of his head, as bald as the claypan near the Red River, was the only glimpse of him that most of the crowd could see. He held his hand out for Eleanor, and then walked ahead as they both slowly moved along the rope line, shaking hands and chatting. Looking up, Eleanor could see Joan and David waiting near the stage steps. She gave them a delighted smile, as if she hadn't seen them in months. David had the rueful thought that she often looked happier on the campaign trail than anywhere else.

Jonathon had maneuvered to a spot just opposite the stage stairs, standing behind a woman whose head he could easily see over. Sam and Eleanor seemed to be having conversations with everyone along the line, but as they slowly moved closer to Jonathon, he felt the crowd press up against his back and sides. People were cheering and reaching their hands over the shoulders of people in front of them.

Jonathon looked to his left at a towheaded two-year-old on his father's shoulders who was screaming in fright at the commotion. His mother was shouting for her husband to pass the little boy to her. Just in front of them against the rope, Jonathon noticed a man wearing a hip-length fawn-colored work coat, unnecessary since the temperature was well in the seventies. The man's hands were stuffed into the coat's deep front pockets, and compared to the rest of the crowd, he seemed frozen, staring through the pandemonium in the direction of the approaching candidates. *There's a crank in every crowd,* Jonathon thought, looking back toward Eleanor, and wondering how often hecklers disturbed her speeches.

Sam stopped just before Jonathon's spot along the rope line and turned toward the stairs. With a few more handshakes, Eleanor did the same. As she stepped up the makeshift wooden stairs, David stood to the side, bending to speak into her ear and lending his hand as a railing. The band had switched to "The Marines' Hymn." Jonathon began singing, "From the hall of Montezuu-uma," in a full-throated tenor that made Joan look his way. She couldn't help but smile when she spotted his face above the crowd, his mouth opened wide in song. He winked at her and stepped to the side, hoping to find a spot to slip under the rope after Eleanor was up onstage.

Suddenly, a small but odd movement caught Jonathon's eye. The strange man in the work coat had pulled his right hand partway out of his pocket, then shoved it back. Jonathon could see by the stretch of the coat's fabric that something hard was in the man's pocket. Reacting without thinking, Jonathon pushed past a middle-aged woman in a flowered shirtwaist who stood to the man's right.

"Young man!" The woman turned and gave him a nasty look, as he jostled her hard enough that she started to stumble.

"I'm sorry," Jonathon said, but as he spoke, he saw the man's arm come up again. This time, he pulled the pistol out all the way, aiming at Eleanor just as she was reaching the top of the stairs. It seemed to Jonathon that the shot came at the same moment that he lunged, a staccato burst like a drummer hitting one cracking beat out of rhythm. Jonathon was only a couple of inches taller, but decidedly heavier than the assailant. Hanging onto the gun, the man tried to push Jonathon off as they stumbled into the frantic crowd that was trying to move away from them. People were screaming and ducking their heads. An older man and what looked like his son, dressed in overalls and baseball caps, rushed over. The younger man grabbed the assassin's gun arm and pushed it up as another wild shot went off harmlessly into the air. Jonathon reached up and wrested the gun from the man's hand, bringing the weapon down with furious force against his face. Edgar Ray Killen fell to the ground, the three men dropping next to him, pinning his arms and legs. Jonathon's ears pounded from the rush of adrenaline, but suddenly he registered the cries of the people around him.

"Oh my God, it's Eleanor."

"Are you sure it was her that got hit? Are you sure?"

"Can you see her? I can't see her."

Jonathon jumped up and nearly threw people out of his way as he fought to get to the stage. He felt a surge of relief as he caught sight of Joan standing not far from her spot near the stairs, tears streaming down her face as she tried to see through a circle of men kneeling on the ground in front of her. Jonathon rushed over and pulled her close. She leaned into him, trying to control the sobs that were welling inside her. Someone had signaled the band to stop playing. The only sounds were occasional shouts and the loud hum of voices as the police moved the crowd away from the scene. Holding each other without speaking, Joan and Jonathon stared at the dusty ground where Eleanor lay. David knelt beside her, frantically trying to stanch the blood that seemed to be everywhere.

CHAPTER 37

David's Choice

Jonathon had made contact with Killen in the split second that he pulled the trigger. Killen aimed for Eleanor's head, but Jonathon's attack had forced the shooter's arm down and to the left, sending the bullet into Eleanor's upper arm, where it lodged against her bone. She spun off the stairs from the impact, tumbling backward and over the side. David had just let go of her hand when suddenly he was breaking her fall.

"Eleanor? Eleanor?" David held her head in his hand as he knelt beside her, at first unsure what had sent her careening off the stairs.

"I must have blacked out for a second," Eleanor said softly, as she opened her eyes and David leaned closer. Then he saw the blood and realized with relief that the gash that sent blood oozing over his hand was from her arm.

"Try not to move," David said gently. "Your arm is wounded. We need to stop the bleeding and get you to a hospital."

An hour later, Eleanor sat on the bed in a private room at the Sam Rayburn Memorial VA Center, opened the previous year on the east side of Bonham. David had been rushing in and out after her wound had been cleaned and bandaged, but Joan hadn't left her side.

"How's it feeling, Mrs. R.?" Joan asked, pouring more water into Eleanor's bedside glass.

"The same as ten minutes ago, Joan." Eleanor's irritation was clear. "You do not need to sit here like I'm a sick puppy dog. Has Sam gone on to Dallas as I asked and made sure they understand we're going ahead with my speech? Have you talked to Maureen? I don't want her and Tommy worrying." Tommy's condition had worsened, and Eleanor had insisted that Maureen stay with the woman who had been at Eleanor's side for so many years.

"All taken care of," Joan said, as David bustled into the room.

"David, if I leave now, we should just make it in time for my speech. Remember, I have to go to the Adolphus and get a new dress. What is the holdup? Why am I still in this room?" Eleanor looked around the white-walled hospital room as if it had invited her contempt. She had never been admitted to a hospital in her life.

"I think we should run a few tests," David replied. "I'm concerned about more than the wound. You suffered a trauma, and you fell. I'm not sure if you hit your head. At your age, there are . . ."

"David!" Eleanor swung her legs over the side of the bed, wincing slightly from the motion. Her left forearm was in a sling across her midsection, and her upper arm was heavily bandaged and taped under a hospital gown and robe. Almost any movement of her head was painful. "This is a flesh wound. Now, I am getting dressed this minute, and I will need a car waiting downstairs. Joan, did you find something for me to wear until I can change at the hotel?"

"Yes." Joan hesitated. "One of the nurses had a dress . . ."

"Eleanor," David cut in. "It's not a flesh wound. You're carrying a bullet. I am going to have to insist that you . . ."

"No David." Eleanor's voice was commanding. "I am going to have to insist that you respect my wishes. The country will vote for a president in one week. I don't have time for more *tests*." Eleanor stood up, pushing herself off the bed with her right hand. "Do you mind helping me get dressed, Joan, or shall I call a nurse?"

Joan glanced at David. She could see that he was struggling to control himself.

"A nurse would probably be more helpful. I'll go find one," Joan said as she left the room, pulling the door shut behind her.

For a second the room was silent, and then David exploded. "This goes beyond selfishness, Eleanor. This is madness, absolute madness. You won't let us take out the bullet, you won't be thoroughly checked, and now you just want to leave? No one expects you to give this talk after you've been shot, for God's sake. A man tried to kill you. Don't you realize that?"

Eleanor walked to the small window and pulled up the Venetian blind, looking out without responding.

"He may not be the only one." David's voice was angry and pleading. "They could have a backup plan for the Cotton Bowl. You'll be standing exposed to thousands of people. You can't be protected. We don't know who else . . ."

"David." Eleanor turned to face him. Her hair was uncombed, and the hospital robe barely reached her knees, but David recognized the look of determination in her eyes. "I have been afraid many times in my life. I nearly lost Franklin more than once. An assassin tried to kill him, too. And I have had many, many threats. You know that. And you should know by now that I won't be intimidated by these people." She stopped and walked back to the bed, sitting down and taking a sip of water. Looking toward the window, she said, "David, there are other terrible fears too, aren't there? The fear of failing the ones you love, those who depend on you, the fear of loss and loneliness. My fear of losing you." She looked at him, hoping he would say what she wanted to hear—that he would stand by her no matter what she did.

But David's face hardened. "If you're asking if you've failed me, I think I've made that clear enough ever since you started this absurd adventure. Frankly, if you insist on doing this speech, on being so reckless, I cannot think anything other than that you care more for your presidential ambitions than for me, or for us."

So, he's finally said it, Eleanor thought. He's danced around an ultimatum for months, now he's cast it at my feet. His point was logical, of course. She knew she could cancel the speech without blame. Voters would assume she couldn't, or wouldn't want to go ahead with it, but that wasn't what mattered. What mattered was what she felt she must do.

She had fooled herself into thinking that David understood how she had survived in her life, but now she saw that he did not. She didn't blame him. He had never known the fear and isolation of a child whose mother scorns her for her looks, despite that child's desperate efforts to please. How could he understand the terror of a six-year-old, left by a drunken father outside a bar, waiting for hours, unsure of what to do or where to go, as strange men looked at her and the night grew darker? What of the horror of being thrown into a lifeboat from a great sinking ship, as she was from the *Britannic* when she was three years old, only to have her parents set sail again a week later, leaving their terrified daughter—certain her parents would never return—in the care of her aunt? And no one had betrayed David as Franklin had betrayed her. He hadn't spent forty years in a marriage where love and fear of loss were one and the same.

No, David didn't understand the years of doubt and shame and guilt. He could never fathom the litany of stories she made up to comfort herself and to explain the terrifying world around her. Without that understanding, he could never grasp how she had learned to survive—how she had finally determined that she had to rely on herself, make herself strong, take responsibility at every turn, or face sinking under the weight of her disappointment in those she trusted and loved.

Now, David wanted her to do the opposite; to give in to fear or lose his love. And he thought her choice had to do with ambition. How foolish he could be at times, Eleanor thought. She hated that word. Ambition was pitiless; it found despicable any merit that it could not use. Was it possible that after all their time together, David knew her so little?

"David, don't you think love is important to me? That you are important to me? But what good am I to you if I'm not true to myself?" For the first time, she was telling him thoughts that had been forming in her mind over months on the campaign trail—why she had agreed to run against his wishes, why she wouldn't give up.

"I must feel useful, David, or I'm not fit to love or be loved. Whatever form being useful may take, it is the price we pay for the air we breathe, the food we eat, and the privilege of being alive. Whether I win or lose, this campaign has made me feel useful. I won't give that up out of fear." She looked at him with imploring eyes, hoping to see understanding in his face.

"Useful?" David said, sounding bitter.

"Yes. Can't you see that?" Eleanor implored him. "It will be easier for the next woman who runs, and more women will be willing to run because I have tried. I truly believe that. And I've been able to speak to so many people about the ideas you and I both care so much about. Isn't that useful?"

"Not to me. Not to us. Why can't you believe I love you as you are? What about happiness, Eleanor? Would it be so hard to be happy together without these demands you put on yourself?"

"For me, being useful is the beginning of happiness, the way I become the person you want to love . . . and self-pity and withdrawal from the battle are the beginning of misery." Eleanor's voice became defiant.

"Do I sound self-pitying, then?" David's eyes flashed with anger. "Dress it up how you want, Eleanor—as usefulness, if that makes you happy. It still looks like ambition to me. You've been caught up in something that has changed you. Perhaps it was about usefulness before this campaign, but now, as far as I can see, it's all about tilting at this windmill of winning the presidency."

David pulled off his stethoscope and stuffed it in the pocket of his doctor's coat. "Do what you must, but don't look for me to be there again when you fall." David's eyes were glassy and he wiped at them with his handkerchief as he threw the door open and left the room.

CHAPTER 38

Teddy's Niece

Maureen couldn't help but pace inside Tommy's cottage, holding the telephone in one hand and the heavy black receiver to her ear with the other. Without realizing it, she squeezed the receiver, her knuckles going white with the effort, as if she could squeeze out some information. Tommy sat under a blanket in her platform rocker, listening to the radio with a look of intense concentration.

"Yes, yes, nurse, yes, I'm holding." Maureen stamped her foot in frustration. "For God's sake, how hard could it be to find Joan or David? I'm sure they're with Mrs. R."

"At least Joan called and we know she's alive," Tommy said. "Those bastards couldn't kill her. If I know her, she'll be giving that speech in an hour."

"That's crazy, Tommy." Maureen looked at the older woman whom she had stayed behind to care for, then she let out a short chuckle. "No, I guess that's not so crazy."

"And here's the latest report from Sam Rayburn VA Hospital. . . ." The radio announcer's tone was as serious as an undertaker.

"We have word that Mrs. Eleanor Roosevelt will be leaving the hospital shortly and traveling to Dallas."

Tommy looked at Maureen with a knowing smile, and Maureen wondered if her eyes were watery from relief or the cancer that was overwhelming her.

"Hello? Hello?" Suddenly, Maureen was shouting into the phone. "David, can you hear me? How is she? We haven't heard from Joan in an hour."

As David updated Maureen on Eleanor's condition, his recalcitrant patient refused the assistance of a wheelchair and walked out of the hospital. Telling the reporters waiting outside that she would speak to them in Dallas, she and Joan sped off alone from Bonham.

Word of the shooting had spread like a brush fire among the fifteen thousand people who had been pouring over the Texas State Fair grounds and into the Cotton Bowl stadium to hear Eleanor and their homegrown legend, Sam Rayburn. Rumors were rampant. Mrs. Roosevelt had been killed, or wounded, or shot in the head, or not hurt at all. Some people said Rayburn was the victim. Others said it was a Communist plot to disrupt the election and Eisenhower would be next. Had anyone heard whether Ike had canceled speeches, changed his schedule, or asked for FBI protection? Hundreds of people left the stadium as soon as they heard the news, assuming the event would be canceled, only to turn around and go back after hearing on the radio that it wasn't.

Kip Johnson from the *Dallas Morning News* had called his editor, Al Trayman, from the stadium when the rumors started flying.

"What's going on, Al? There's a crazy rumor." Johnson was the only reporter assigned to cover the speech. The paper had already endorsed Eisenhower.

"It's not crazy. Roosevelt got shot. I've got Cal going flat out over to Bonham, and Roger's going to her hotel. You stay there in case they announce anything. Probably Rayburn will speak. Other than the reporters from other papers assigned to her campaign, there's no one on the story but us. What a break!"

"How badly was she hurt?" Johnson asked.

"All I know is, she's not dead. But I heard it was a .45. I'm guessing she's done for the campaign. She's no spring chicken."

"It's really strange considering what happened to Teddy Roosevelt," Johnson said.

"What are you talking about?"

"Her uncle Teddy got shot in 1912, when he ran on the Bull Moose ticket, right before he was supposed to give a speech. Shot point blank in the chest with a .32. It went right through the copy of his speech that was in his pocket and lodged against his rib."

"Come on!"

"It's true. No kidding. Not only that, he refused to be treated and gave the speech with the bullet still in him."

Trayman let out a long whistle. "Amazing. Well, TR was a real man and a great president. That's the difference right there. I hate to say it, I don't wish the lady ill, but maybe this incident will get the public to understand that a woman just isn't fit to be president."

"I hear you," Johnson replied, "but I think voters knew that already. Gotta go. I think they're making an announcement."

"Ladies and gentlemen, quiet please." Mr. Sam was standing on the stage that stretched across the center of the grass playing field. "Please stay in the stadium. Mrs. Roosevelt *is* on her way." Some people in the crowd began cheering, and the murmuring of thousands of people grew louder.

"I repeat," Sam shouted into the mike, "Mrs. Roosevelt will be here in about forty-five minutes. She has been injured." People began hushing each other, anxious to hear the news. "But she will not be stopped from speaking to you today. Thank you." The crowd escorted Sam off the stage with shouts and cheers. "I hope she knows what the hell she's doing," Sam said to his aide. "If she can't make it, or collapses once she's here, it'll look worse than if she just called it off. Not sure I'd take the chance." He shook his head, looking up at the vast crowd of his fellow Texans in the stands. With more televisions in people's homes and radio coverage of the campaign, it was getting harder and harder to turn people out for rallies. But this was the only major event planned in Texas. Sam had made it clear to the state's Democratic Party that he didn't want Eleanor to be disappointed in the crowd, and he could tell that the committeemen had worked like hell to get their people out.

A little more than an hour after she was scheduled to begin, Eleanor arrived at the Cotton Bowl. Despite the warmth of the day, she'd chosen a long and loose-sleeved dress, hoping the cloud-filled sky and intermittent breeze would keep her comfortable.

"How's the pain?" Joan asked just before they got out of the car.

"It's tolerable," Eleanor said, but as she turned to get out of the car, Joan could see the effort etched on her face and the painful grimace as she stood up. "Thank goodness for your young man," Eleanor said as they walked in, surrounded by Dallas police. "He saved my life. He's quite the hero."

"Um, well, he's not exactly my young man. He works for Ike and . . ."

Eleanor laughed, and Joan thought with relief that it was the first time she had seen Eleanor smile since the shooting. "Joan, you should see your face when you talk about him. At the hospital? When you told me the story?" Eleanor chuckled and shook her head, following her escorts into the stadium.

The lighter ceremonial parts of the program had been dropped. Matt Price, a twelve-year-old member of the 4-H Club didn't get to parade his prize longhorn. The Cotton Bowl queen, Rebecca Sizelove, and her entourage were sidelined to front seats reserved for dignitaries, and the platter of Dallas's best chicken-fried steak and hot tamales that was going to be presented to Eleanor, was sent to Buckner's Orphan Home.

After the presentation of colors and the pledge, Dallas mayor Jean Baptiste Adoue Jr. thanked the crowd for their patience, breaking down in tears as he talked about the debt of the nation to the Roosevelts and his anger over the heinous attack on Eleanor. Then he introduced Sam Rayburn. Most of the crowd had learned that Rayburn had been only a few feet away from the shooting. They stamped and cheered and took five minutes to be quieted as Rayburn gave a grim smile and sporadic waves of his arm. When he finally could speak, he gave a brief account of the shooting, assuring the audience that they would get more than their fill of the details from the press. Then he launched into a political sidewinder.

"My friends," Sam began, "when the Republicans spew hate and venom, when they rile people up with lies and fear, then we get what we had today, a crazed attack on one of the most beloved leaders in America. They are hypocrites and worse. Eisenhower and Nixon whine and complain about corruption, yet what do they offer? Nixon's secret fund? A bunch of fat cats paying to fly him around to spit out lies? And what did those fat cats get for their money? When I'm in the White House, I promise you, we will find out that answer. And did Eisenhower tell you any more in the debate than that he's against everything the New Deal stands for?"

A loud "No!" echoed across the field.

"That's right. He didn't. They don't have a plan; they just have a big painful need to attack Democrats. Well, a jackass can kick a barn down, but it takes a carpenter to build one."

The crowd roared, and Sam turned to the band and swept both arms up, giving the signal for them to play, then he turned back to the microphone.

"Everyone, please, welcome the next president of the United States along with me as we sing our national anthem."

As the Woodrow Wilson High School band struck up the strains of the "Star-Spangled Banner," the crowd rose to sing. Hands were held over hearts, and many people began to cry as the song rose to its crescendo. As the song finished, the bandleader held his baton high, the last note soaring, as thousands of voices spent their longest breath to keep the word "brave" lingering in the air.

At that moment, Eleanor began her walk across the red carpet that had been laid from the stands to the stage, a cordon of police on either side of her. The crowd, already on its feet, seemed to lose all control. Banners and signs dotted the stands, but she didn't turn to see the outpouring until she reached the podium. When she did, a slight smile played across her face, and she slowly waved her right hand. The cheering and clapping went on for five minutes, then ten, interrupted only by chants of "We Want Eleanor," and simply "El-ee-nor, El-ee-nor." Sam walked up to her several times, urging her to sit down until the crowd settled, but she refused.

Slowly, people settled into their seats, telling others to do the same.

"My friends," Eleanor began, her voice lower and graver than most people had heard it before. "I will ask your indulgence by listening with patience and not interrupting me. I will try my best, but there is a bullet in my arm, and I will confess to you that it is painful. But my concern is for many other things, least of all for my own well-being. Even as I speak, our young men in uniform are being shot and killed in Korea. Far too many of them have been wounded. Far too many have died. I have had a long and good life. But every day, their young lives are being taken. This must end."

Scattered applause broke out in the stands, but people hushed each other and an almost breathless silence seemed to envelope the bowl of the stadium. Eleanor paused, rubbing her right hand gently over the spot on her arm where the bullet had entered, and Sam gave a worried look.

"The tragedy of this war is what has driven me to speak to you today. I believe, as I have said repeatedly, that we must have a bipartisan solution. We must put politics behind us and purpose before us in seeking the best way to peace. During the debate, I felt that General Eisenhower made an excellent and heartfelt declaration of his intentions in this regard should he win this race."

Some booing came from the crowd, and Eleanor held up her hand with a stern look.

"He and I are much in agreement on how to proceed, although I am more on the side of pursuing strong economic measures rather than favoring military solutions. Still, I believe the next president must go to Korea, must reevaluate all options, must work closely with the world community, and must have the strongest possible support at home for doing so." Eleanor paused, straightening her back and giving a glance toward Sam, who gave an encouraging nod.

"I am here today, in the state where General Eisenhower was born, to make a pledge and an offer. Should I win the presidency, I pledge to the American people that my first act as president will be to offer General Eisenhower the position of secretary of defense so that he can work by my side as we bring this war to an end."

Surprised chatter came from scattered spots around the stadium. People turned and looked at one another, asking if they had heard Eleanor correctly.

Eleanor raised her voice slightly, sounding more determined, but otherwise ignoring the reaction.

"My husband trusted and relied on the general during the last war, and that trust was well placed. His is a record of the highest achievement. Now another Roosevelt is calling on this military man to lend his expertise to the nation's most pressing military cause. The question voters must ask is, 'How will the nation be best served?' I say it is by a team that includes both myself and General Eisenhower, and I hope he will pledge to accept this offer should I win next Tuesday. Now I must thank you, my friends, and take care of this meddlesome wound. God bless you all and our great country."

As Eleanor left the stage to the pounding cheers of the crowd, Joan stood speechless at the side of the stage looking at Jonathon. He had begged her to let him stand with her for the talk, worried that something else might happen. She was happy to agree.

"Yeah," Jonathon said, reacting to the look on Joan's face. "She did just say what you think she said." He looked stunned.

"What . . . well, I didn't expect that. I mean what do you think Ike will do?" Joan asked.

"I don't know, but I'd better get to a phone and get myself on a plane." Without thinking, Jonathon put his arms around Joan, bending over to kiss her as if the commotion around them didn't exist. She held onto him, running her hands over the muscles in his back.

"I guess I'll see you sometime after our victory on election day," Joan said, laughing as she looked up at him.

"You bet." He was smiling, too. "But I so hate to think of you being disappointed, and I never got to buy you that steak. Tell you what—I'll get you the biggest steak in New York and a row of martinis. You'll need something to ease your pain after the general's elected."

"The pain? You're kooky, my friend." Joan was starting to think about the reaction the press would have to the shooting and Eleanor's proposal. She looked like a light had come on in her head. "I'm willing to bet that I'll be buying that steak for you, Jonathon," and she patted his chest.

"Really?" he said laughing. "Well, I think I'll just take that bet."

CHAPTER 39

She Is Eleanor

New York City, November 4, 1952

"Here it is, Larry." Joan awkwardly dropped a thick binder from its cradle in her right arm onto Larry O'Brien's desk at campaign headquarters while trying not to spill the coffee in her other hand. "Every article I could get since last Tuesday. And by the way, those publicity chairmen you set up have been great."

"And?"

"Well." Joan fell into a metal chair and lit a Fatima, then quickly stubbed it out. Larry hated the smell. "Sorry, I was up most of the night."

"Spare me, Joan. This is the most important day of your life. Be happy you're here at the crack of dawn. Now what about the coverage?"

Joan gave him a rueful stare and took a sip of coffee. "The first two days were heavy, heavy on the shooting—Killen stories, how Ike's aide had saved Eleanor's life, Eleanor's condition, and comparisons to Teddy's shooting. Did you know about that, by the way?"

"Oh yes. You need to read more history, Joanie. You'll find stranger coincidences than that. But what about the Ike as secretary of defense idea?"

"That got buried until about Saturday. Honestly, I think this article by Richard Rovere in *The New Yorker* is the most important piece. It's been referenced a lot. I think it changed the coverage back to 'hey, can she actually be president?'" Joan handed Larry a copy of *The New Yorker*, folded open to an article titled simply "She is Eleanor" in Rovere's "Letter from Washington" column.

Larry read out loud, "'This week, as the nation was forced to face the virulent southern weed of native-born menace . . . an unlikely thought began to form in the often-static public mind.'" Joan settled back, happy to suck down some caffeine without interruption.

Larry continued. "'As Eisenhower expressed his condolences and moved back to the comfort of arousing voters with powerful sermons on communism and sloth, Roosevelt was transformed without words. Threatened with death, she stood up, bullet in body, and threatened to subvert the great American institution that elevates partisanship over problem solving. She promised to bring General Eisenhower into the fold of her administration, and, for his part of this epic moment, he dodged a reply. She refused to demagogue her appointment with assassination, though her running mate couldn't be restrained in that regard. She insisted that hate must be met with the sword, not of vengeance, but of greater civil rights and liberties. Reminding America that strengthening democracy is all, she brushed aside discussion of her courage and fortitude, but America could not.'

"'Last Tuesday, in the span of a few hours, Roosevelt became something more than a candidate, more than a politician, most firmly she became something more than a woman. She is so unique a product of class and conscience, idealism and rationality, compassion, tough-minded experience, and unabashed courage that she commands her own particular category of humanity. She is Eleanor.'"

Larry put the magazine down with a thoughtful look on his face. "That's powerful stuff," he said.

"Yeah, I agree, and some of the press has started calling her 'Eleanorean,' whatever that means. Sounds better than 'Mrs. Dead in the Water,' but most of them are still predicting an Eisenhower landslide."

"We shall see. Anyway, stay with Eleanor today. She'll be driving up to Hyde Park to vote in a little while. I'll be field-marshaling the poll workers."

"Right. I know, 'checkers' and 'runners.'"

Larry smiled. "I'm proud of you. That's right. Checkers let us know who's voted. Runners get the rest to the polls. Win or lose Joan, I don't think I'll ever work in another campaign with the number of volunteers we've had, or the enthusiasm—labor chairmen, farm chairmen, youth chairmen, veterans' chairmen. I mean, I recommended we have one for each district, but honestly?" he stopped and raised an eyebrow as he looked at Joan. "I never thought we'd get the response we did. Never thought we'd blanket the country— Michigan, Missouri, Pennsylvania, even Tennessee . . . hell, we didn't do too badly in Arizona."

"I'll keep your confession to myself," Joan said, smiling. "That flyer you sent out on how important one vote was, how much just one vote mattered in those past elections you listed? I think that was powerful. It probably got a lot of people to help out."

"Thanks. I'd like to think so, but the truth is it's all about her." He tapped *The New Yorker* on his desk. "Rovere's so right. There's no one like her. Man, woman, whoever. We're lucky to have been a part of this."

"Whatever happens," Joan added.

"Right, whatever happens."

They both turned to see Eleanor walk in. Her arm hung in a sling so that her suit jacket could only be draped over her left shoulder, but instead it hung off her right forearm.

"Joan, could you help me, please," Eleanor said in frustration. "I just can't manage to get this jacket over my shoulder." She bent over and twisted awkwardly, trying to use the force of gravity to get the jacket in place.

"Oh, Mrs. R., don't do that. I'll get it." Joan pulled the jacket around, and Eleanor shrugged her shoulder to try to make it more comfortable.

"Aah." Eleanor let out a sharp breath. "I'm afraid it still hurts to move that arm. Are you ready to go, Joan?"

"Yes, we were just looking at the coverage in the press."

"I won't even ask about the coverage. I've known some wonderful journalists. Your mother, of course," Eleanor said nodding at Joan. "Louis used to say they had the highest ethics of any profession, but they can be a pessimistic lot. What do you two think of General Eisenhower taking off those cartoon ads? You know, that 'I Like Ike' jingly thing?"

"I think he realized they were silly and looked especially ridiculous considering the serious turn of events. After your shooting, it made him look like the empty uniform he is," Larry said.

"I heard Rosser Reeves was frosted about it," Joan said.

"Frosted?" Eleanor asked.

"That means mad, really mad."

"Now who might have told you that?" Eleanor asked in a teasing tone.

Joan's face started to blush, and she walked toward the door, lighting a Fatima as she went.

"We'll be back this afternoon, Larry," Eleanor said. "I heard the weather report across the country is quite good, by the way."

"Yes, I heard that, too. Don't worry, we'll be turning Democrats out at the polls. Lots of 'em."

"Oh, and Larry, Barbara Rose Johns called me last night. She's predicting we'll hold the solid South except for Alabama and Mississippi."

"That's nineteen electoral votes worth of 'except,'" Larry said. "Am I supposed to be happy about that?"

"It would be worse if we hadn't had her, Larry. She's an amazing girl."

"You were right about her, Eleanor. She's been terrific down there," Larry replied, as he turned to answer his phone. "But I still hope she's wrong about Alabama and Mississippi."

When she reached Hyde Park, Eleanor cheerfully posed for the cameras as she went in and after she came out of the curtained booth in her polling place at the Town Hall. Then she drove to Val-Kill for lunch and to finalize arrangements for her children and grandchildren to come to the ballroom at the Roosevelt Hotel.

As she sat at the long table with all five of her children, the smallest grandchildren scurried through the room and the older ones sat with the adults trying to look grown-up. Everyone's mouths watered over the smells of fresh squash soup and newly baked bread.

"I have an announcement," Eleanor said, clicking a glass with her spoon. "No matter what happens," she assured them, "tonight will be a victory celebration and we shall dance to my favorite steel drum music. And remember to thank Mrs. Curnan for this wonderful meal." Just as she finished, the telephone rang.

"Don't get up, dear," Eleanor said to her grandson, Curtis, who had jumped from his chair. "I'll get it."

"Oh, my God!" Eleanor's exclamation could be heard clearly coming from the hall where the phone was kept. After a minute or two of tense silence, her voice took an angry turn. "I am coming down there. No, I will not hear of it. You tell her, I *am* coming."

"Children," Eleanor's face was taut as she came back into the kitchen, and her words came rapidly, "something terrible has happened. Barbara Rose Johns, a wonderful young Negro organizer for me, has been attacked in Alabama. She's in the hospital. I must go there. Where's Maureen?"

"I'm here, Mrs. R.," Maureen had just come in to join the others for lunch.

How quickly can we get down to Montgomery, Alabama?"

"I'm sorry? When do you . . . ?"

"Right now, Maureen. Please make arrangements right now." Eleanor left the room without saying any more. She was too heartsick to answer the questions in everyone's eyes. She couldn't bear telling them the horror of what had happened to the girl.

Eleanor thought back to that visit she made to Vernon Johns's church the day she met Barbara Rose. Some members of the congregation were alarmed by the sign their pastor had posted to advertise that week's sermon: "It's Safe to Murder Negroes in Montgomery." Eleanor remembered the remnants of a cross that had been burned in front of the church the night before she arrived, and the smell of charred wood lingering in the air. Yet she had encouraged Barbara Rose to work in her campaign. No, it was more than that. She had asked for the girl's help. Eleanor felt naïve and selfish. She should have insisted Barbara Rose come north if she wanted to help, or told her she was too young to take such risks. But the girl had reminded her of herself at the same age, when she had been forced to leave her beloved headmistress, Mademoiselle Souvestre, at Allenswood Academy in England and return to New York for her formal presentation to high society.

She thought about how she hated the boring, simpering culture of debutantes, with their endless rounds of teas and dances and flirting with eligible men. Her only bright spot was the escape she had found in volunteering for a new organization, the Junior League. They had sent her, and other privileged girls, into the worst slums in New York to teach the children calisthenics and dance. She had seen the children's tired, sad eyes from endless hours of grinding work in factories where they were often in danger of losing a limb or their life. She had ventured into their tenements and been too shocked to speak, fighting to hold back her tears—five, seven, ten, or more people in an airless room that stank from the smells of too many bodies and failed sanitation.

Her family had railed against her going to the Bowery, claiming she would catch some dreaded disease or be assaulted by the drunks and thieves that lived there, but she had gone anyway. When she met Barbara Rose, she saw her own youthful defiance in the girl's face. Eleanor knew that was why she had encouraged her, but the realization didn't assuage her guilt.

Vernon Johns was the one who called. He said Barbara Rose had begged him not to, but he knew Eleanor would want to be told what happened. Eleanor could hear the rage in his voice as he told her, without sparing the horror, of his niece's ordeal.

The previous evening, after Barbara Rose had finished her call to Eleanor to give her report, she had worked until after midnight, and then left the headquarters in Montgomery to drive to the Johnses' house. Uncle Vernon had begged her to call him if she stayed so late and was leaving alone. She had assured him earlier in the day that she would let him know if she needed him, but she had the invulnerable spirit of youth, and decided not to bother him.

On a stretch of road that ran like a dark tunnel through cypress trees hung with thick moss and vines, her car had been forced off the road by two others. The men had jumped out so quickly she didn't have time to lock the doors, but it wouldn't have mattered. They were determined to teach her a lesson and had made sure that no one would interfere.

There were seven or eight men, she couldn't remember for sure. They wore Klan hoods, but no robes, so she could see their jeans and work shirts in the few moments before she was blindfolded.

They dragged her into the woods, putting a noose around her neck as she stumbled along. They didn't speak, and when she screamed, they slapped her hard across the face. She was thrown on her back, her skirt and panties torn off, and her arms pinned down. One after another they pushed inside her, grunting and smelling of tobacco and sweat and evil. When they were done, they threw the noose over the tree and Barbara Rose began whispering the Lord's Prayer, tears streaming down her face, but they only pulled the noose far enough so that she coughed and gagged while they beat her with whips. When they finally left her curled on the ground, whimpering and shivering with shock, one man spoke, "Tell that bitch who you work for that this was for her."

CHAPTER 40

The Miracle in Montgomery

Within an hour, the wire services had spread the news that Eleanor Roosevelt was on her way to Alabama. Television and radio stations cut into their regular programming to explain why Eleanor had rushed to the blacks-only wing of Jackson Hospital in Montgomery. In the CBS studio in New York City, Walter Cronkite was reviewing the plans for election night with his boss, Sig Mickelson.

"Okay, we're starting at eight tonight and we'll be ready to go all night," Mickelson, who led the CBS news team, was saying to Cronkite. They stood near workers banging together the walls of boards with numbers that moved by thumbwheels, and the scaffolding that employees would climb to turn the wheels each time new precinct numbers came in.

"Remember, Truman had to wait until the results came in from Ohio at 8:30 the next morning," Mickelson said.

"Well, it's hard to believe the predictions are so wrong this time. I'm guessing she'll have to concede by midnight, maybe a little after," Cronkite replied. "But who knows? We have our new electric brain. Maybe it will tell us something we don't know."

He laughed and pointed at a false panel covered with small lights, a teletype, and mysterious dials. The Remington Rand Corporation had convinced Mickelson that UNIVAC, the first general-service computer, could predict the election based on an algorithm that would compute early returns. But the machine, weighing sixteen thousand pounds, was too large to move to the studio from its home in Philadelphia, so CBS dummied up a machine for Cronkite to hover over while results from the real machine were relayed by telephone.

"Come on, Walter, you have to admit, it *looks* impressive," said Mickelson.

"Yes, but you don't really think they can predict the election with a computer, do you?"

"Who knows? Probably baloney. But viewers like this kind of science-fiction stuff, and they've never seen one of these machines."

"Sig, they're not seeing one now," Cronkite laughed. Suddenly, a production assistant rushed up.

"Mr. Mickelson, Mr. Cronkite, you'd better come to the newsroom. Something's happened, and Mrs. Roosevelt is leaving New York."

When Mickelson heard the story, his reaction was immediate. "Walter, get your makeup on. We're starting the coverage right now."

Eleanor's friend, the financier Bernard Baruch, had offered her his private plane, and she reached Montgomery at six that evening. As she, Joan, and Maureen came down the small plane's steps, three Secret Service agents approached them.

"Mrs. Roosevelt, the president has asked us to accompany you."

"That's not necessary," Eleanor replied.

"I'm sorry ma'am, but we have a direct order from the president, and I must inform you that there is a crowd-control problem developing by the hospital."

"What do you mean?"

"Ma'am, we have people driving into Montgomery from all over. Negroes and whites, ma'am. They seem to want to be here for you and the girl."

"I see."

"The city is very tense, ma'am. The local police, well, they are not very happy about this, but they are aware that the president has asked for calm. He made a public statement while you were in the air. The 101st Airborne is here as well, a couple hundred of them."

"Federal troops?"

"As I said, ma'am, it's very tense."

"Very well, I understand. Thank you for explaining," Eleanor said, as she followed the agent to a waiting car.

"What the hell have we stepped into?" Joan whispered to Maureen.

"We're going to take you in through the emergency entrance at the back," the Secret Service agent explained to Eleanor, as the hospital came into sight. "The local police have kept that clear for ambulances and critical deliveries."

As they crept through the line of cars that was winding its way toward the hospital, Eleanor realized that there were vehicles as far as she could see in any direction. Finally, they reached a small roadway blocked by tall cones and surrounded by police. The agent waved his badge from the car window and the cones were moved aside. In the twilight, Eleanor could just make out the hostile stares of the police officers as she drove by them to the hospital entrance.

When Eleanor reached Barbara Rose's room, the girl was standing by the window, wearing a white terry cloth bathrobe that must
have come from home. She had combed her hair and tried to cover
her bruises with makeup. The small, stark room smelled of an-
tiseptic, starched linens, and a bag of fried chicken that Barbara
Rose's mother had brought an hour before. Eleanor's eyes filled as
she looked at the girl, and neither could speak, as Eleanor took her
in her arms, holding her gently as they both wept.

"Mrs. Roosevelt," Barbara Rose said, trying to steady her voice.
"Have you looked out front?"

"No, dear, I haven't." Eleanor walked to the window. The hospital
was opposite Oak Park. From the front entrance, across the broad
street, and over the forty acres of the park, people stood shoulder
to shoulder, Negroes and whites, as far as she could see. Some held
candles that flickered more brightly as the night darkened. Many
held radios. The window was open, but there was little noise, just
a muted drone, as if everyone was speaking in a low voice. Some
people held signs, but Eleanor couldn't make out the words.

"What do their signs say, do you know?" Eleanor asked Barbara
Rose.

"Uncle Vernon said they say things like 'We love you, Barbara
Rose.'" she looked down, clearly embarrassed. "Some say 'We need
Eleanor' and things like that. I think they would want to see you,
Mrs. Roosevelt."

Joan was listening from the doorway. "Mrs. R., I think I could
get a loudspeaker hooked up pretty quickly. But I'm afraid the Secret Service won't want you exposing yourself. . . ."

"That is a wonderful idea, Joan. Please get it done as quickly as
you can."

It took nearly two hours, but at a few minutes after eight in the
evening, Eleanor stood on the front steps of the hospital. The Secret
Service, after finding their protests ignored, insisted that she stand

behind a podium and allow them to flank her on either side. Joan had been besieged by radio and television reporters as soon as she walked out of the hospital. They wanted to broadcast Eleanor as she addressed the crowd, so their wires and microphones were hastily attached to the podium.

Cronkite had been reporting all afternoon and through the early evening as the crowd swelled in Montgomery, taking quick breaks from the set only during commercials.

"We're back, ladies and gentlemen, and the 'miracle in Montgomery,' goes on. I call it that because in the heart of the segregated South something is happening that has never been seen before. Negroes and sympathetic whites are standing, not separated by race, but side by side as they flow into Montgomery to show their support for Barbara Rose Johns, the young woman who was brutally assaulted for her role in attempting to assure voting rights for Negroes. And, presumably, the crowd also wants to show their support for Eleanor Roosevelt's candidacy for president. Just a minute, please." There was a brief pause, and those watching on television could see Cronkite cocking his head as he listened to someone on his earpiece, then he went on. "Our reporter on the scene, himself a southerner from Louisiana, Howard K. Smith, has a live report—Howard?"

"Thank you, Walter." Smith's words came through with a slight crackle. "I have just finished walking part of the perimeter of this vast throng. Police estimate ten thousand people have descended on this city and more are pouring in, not only from surrounding states but also from Pennsylvania, Missouri, and Illinois. The majority is here in sympathy, but incidents of violence along some of the roads leading to Montgomery have been reported, including rock throwing and shots fired at cars. But in front of Jackson Hospital, the soldiers of the 101st Airborne, sent by President Truman, are quelling potential rioting as it flares up in spots at the edges of this otherwise respectful mass of people. I witnessed one group of young troublemakers, bats in hand, approaching from the west side, but they were halted by soldiers in riot gear and quickly shuttled away. Hold on, Walter. I believe Mrs. Roosevelt is about to speak."

As soon as Eleanor was spotted coming out of the hospital's front doors, the crowd began to slowly chant her name, then someone began singing, and the solemn cadence of "Amazing Grace" spread through the throng. Joan and Maureen stood with their arms around each other, singing and swaying slowly as they stood near the hospital doors.

"My mother used to sing this to me," Maureen said, her eyes shiny and her brogue thick. The song went on, growing in fullness as those who knew all six verses carried the others along.

"But God, who call'd me here below, Will be forever mine." Joan sang out the last words in a sweet, high tenor that blended into the swell of song that enveloped them, and she hugged Maureen tighter.

As the last voices faded away, Eleanor raised her right hand. "My friends, thank you for bringing your courage and compassion to Montgomery. You have given a brave young woman hope that her ordeal was not in vain, and you have given me strength for whatever may lie ahead. Polls are closing here, in the East, and in a few hours, all across our great country. To those beyond this great gathering, I ask only that you honor the sacrifice and courage of Barbara Rose Johns by casting your vote, whomever you may choose to cast it for. The right to vote, the sanctity of our Constitution, and the civil rights and liberties of every citizen are far more important than any one person or any candidate. I want you to know that General Eisenhower has called to express his sympathy and his anger over this terrible assault. I would hope that every American is outraged that in this country such violent attempts to intimidate any person would go on. I do not feel this is the time for a political speech, but we are going to leave this apparatus in place so that I may speak to you again once the election has been decided. I only ask that if you choose to stay, you remain peaceful and respectful of one another. Thank you."

There was scattered applause as Eleanor walked back into the hospital, and she could hear the sound of competing hymns, as if many church choirs were singing at once.

CHAPTER 41

The People's Choice

As Eleanor disappeared inside the hospital, Cronkite picked up his report.

"Well, we have heard extraordinary words from an extraordinary woman. And we are getting our first precinct reports in now."

The camera switched to the large board, where numbers had been flipped for New York, Maryland, and Connecticut.

"As I said earlier, all of these numbers are being fed into UNI-VAC," Cronkite had gotten up and walked over to the mock-up of the computer. A man sat behind the machine, as if he were manipulating the various dials and buttons.

"Soon," Cronkite said, "reports will come out on this teletype machine," and he pointed to what looked like an oversized type-writer. "Oh wait, here's something coming in right now. We'll report the findings after this commercial break."

Mickelson came rushing out. "We just heard from Eckert. He, Mauchly, and Woodbury have a prediction from UNIVAC, and they all agree it's got to be right. They say the early returns show a dead heat, way too close to call."

"That can't be right," Cronkite said, clearly irritated. "Every poll we had showed Eisenhower with a huge lead. I knew this contraption was a gimmick."

"Could be, but they sounded very certain."

"They wrote the algorithm, what else would they say?" Cronkite replied. "I'm not comfortable reporting their prediction on the air. Not yet, anyway. Tell them to run their numbers again."

Half an hour later, Woodbury called back with a new report that Cronkite used on the air.

"We have just been told that UNIVAC has a prediction. General Eisenhower is the heavy favorite to win by more than one hundred electoral votes." As soon as he went to commercial break, Woodbury called in again, greatly agitated and talking quickly. "I made a mistake. I put in the wrong number for New York. The original prediction was right. This race is a dead heat, I'm absolutely certain."

But Cronkite and Mickelson were still wary of the untested computer and decided against another announcement.

In Montgomery, Joan and Maureen paced the hospital's halls with a small transistor radio. They had just heard Cronkite's prediction that an Eisenhower landslide was coming, but refused to believe it. They decided not to interrupt Eleanor, who sat in Barbara Rose's room, chatting with the girl's parents and Vernon Johns.

Later, after Barbara Rose fell asleep, Eleanor sat in the hall and dictated her next "My Day" column to Maureen. Despite the campaign, she had continued to write it six days a week. Some newspapers had refused to carry the column, saying it gave her an unfair advantage in the campaign, but many others continued running it, arguing that her unvarnished reports of life as a candidate were a valuable civics lesson for their readers.

"Mrs. R., we didn't want to bother you, but there was a report an hour ago or so." Maureen looked down at her pad.

"Now, now, Maureen. They don't have all the results yet, do they?"

"No, but they have a prediction that's pretty bad."

"Never mind predictions." Eleanor waved her hand dismissively. "Come, let's get this done." She began dictating. "By the time you read this, the election will be decided. Whatever the outcome, I hope everyone will remember that they are blessed to live in a nation that is a democracy, and that while we are not perfect, we are striving toward our most cherished goals of life, liberty, and the pursuit of happiness." When Eleanor finished, she told Maureen to get some rest. "What about you?" Maureen asked.

"I'll fall asleep in the chair in Barbara Rose's room, don't worry." Eleanor wasn't sure how much time had passed when she woke with a start to Joan's urgent whisper.

"Mrs. R., wake up. Come out here. Listen to this!" Joan was holding the radio in front of her as she stood in the doorway trying not to wake Barbara Rose. Cronkite's familiar baritone came through the small speaker.

Eleanor got up quickly and walked into the hall. Joan held the radio next to both of their ears.

"It is now 3:00 a.m., and I must tell you that hours ago the UNI-VAC predicted that this would be a close election. We did not believe that that could be true, and so we decided to stick with our prediction that Eisenhower had a substantial lead. But this machine," he patted the top of the phony UNIVAC, "has proven us wrong. The following states have gone for Dwight D. Eisenhower: Connecticut, Delaware, Florida, Indiana, Iowa, Kansas, Maine, Minnesota, Mississippi, Nebraska, New Hampshire, New Jersey, Ohio, Oklahoma, Vermont, Virginia, Senator McCarthy's state of

Wisconsin, and the state where Ike's rival now sits, Alabama, giving Eisenhower a total of 173 electoral votes." Cronkite paused and shuffled some papers, then the camera switched back to the large board with the list of states.

"As expected, Mrs. Roosevelt has won the electoral votes of six of the states known as part of the 'solid South': Arkansas, Georgia, Kentucky, Louisiana, North Carolina, and South Carolina. Thanks, no doubt, to the organizing efforts of her able campaign manager, Larry O'Brien, she has also won Massachusetts, where he is from, and her home state of New York. Surprisingly, however, and probably thanks to labor and the Negro vote, she has also won Michigan and Pennsylvania, and, no doubt thanks to New Deal programs including the Tennessee Valley Authority and rural assistance programs like Arthurdale, she has won Tennessee and West Virginia. Ladies and gentlemen, that gives Mrs. Roosevelt 194 electoral votes, putting her in the lead by twenty-five electoral votes.

"This is, of course, an absolutely astonishing development, perhaps explained by our exit polls, which showed an unexpectedly strong vote by women for Mrs. Roosevelt. Oh, wait just a moment." Cronkite pressed his earpiece against his head for a moment, as the men on the scaffolding scrambled to change the number wheels.

"This just in, California and Colorado have gone for Ike, bringing his electoral total to 211, putting him now in the lead."

"Well, our lead didn't last long, did it?" Eleanor said, smiling. "I should go call Larry . . ."

"Wait, there's more." Joan was bouncing with excitement. "Maybe it'll change back. . . ."

"We now have all the western states. Idaho, Montana, North Dakota and South Dakota, New Mexico, Nevada, Oregon and Washington, Utah and Wyoming have all gone for Ike. And Texas, Illinois, and Missouri can be added to Mrs. Roosevelt's totals. And the new totals are." Cronkite paused for a moment. "Two hundred fifty-six electoral votes for Dwight D. Eisenhower and Mrs. Roo-

sevelt has 258 electoral votes. Folks, this is as close a race as anyone could imagine. And it all comes down to tiny Rhode Island
with its four electoral votes, Arizona, also with four, and the state
of Maryland with nine electoral votes. Election officials in Rhode
Island and Maryland report problems with voting machines, and
they cannot tell us when they will release their final tally, so stay
tuned."

Eleanor looked stunned. Maureen and Joan were grinning, but
neither could think of what to say. Finally, Joan trotted off, calling
over her shoulder, "I'll get Larry on the phone."

Eleanor followed Joan to the phone booth that had become
their main link to campaign headquarters.

"I take it you heard CBS's report?" Larry said, his voice high
with excitement.

"I did, but I can't quite believe it," Eleanor responded. "Rhode
Island, Arizona, and Maryland?"

"Eleanor, Rhode Island's been Democratic for more than a decade, and we have Pastore running for Senate there, and the whole
state's *Italian*." Larry practically yelled into the phone. "I just talked
to the state chairman in Maryland, E. Brooke Lee," Larry went on,
talking quickly. "They had record registration there and he thinks
we'll pull it out, maybe by fifty thousand votes. That would put us
over the top *without* Rhode Island."

At that moment, Eleanor could hear Cronkite's voice in the
background as Larry turned up the radio.

"Larry? Larry, are you there?" For a minute there was silence,
then Larry came back on the line, sounding subdued. "They just
declared Maryland for Ike. He's at 265. We have to take Rhode Island *and* Arizona. That would get us to 266."

"Well, what about Arizona?" Eleanor asked.

"Very hard to say." Eleanor knew by Larry's tone that he wasn't
hopeful. "I've talked to a lot of people and no one's willing to predict. Republicans are definitely stronger there than when Truman

carried it in '48. This Barry Goldwater who's running against Mc-
Farland for Senate has hammered the Dems hard there. McFar-
land's pretty worried."

"Why is their count so slow?" Eleanor asked.

"I'm not sure," Larry replied. "I heard Goldwater's workers made
a lot of ballot challenges. Call me as soon as anything changes. And
Sam wants to talk to you, but he's catching some sleep. Call back by
seven if there isn't any news before that."

When Eleanor returned to the phone booth, the sun was just
coming up in Montgomery. Rayburn's familiar drawl came over
the line. "Eleanor, how are you holding up?"

"I'm fine, Sam. A little stunned."

"I hope you have an acceptance speech ready," Rayburn laughed.
"That day at the convention when you said we could win? I have
to be honest, I thought you'd come right off the spool. But there's
nothing like politics for surprises, is there? I sure wish Franklin
could be here now."

"Yes, Sam. I do as well."

In her mind, Eleanor could hear Franklin's familiar voice, his
patrician intonation pitched at a tenor, saying, "What you have
done, Eleanor, it is fine. It is very fine, indeed." Tears stung her eyes.
They had been the best of friends, the best of political partners.
If he strayed in love, he never strayed from his faith in her. She
wished she could take his hand now, hold it to her cheek, and tell
him she understood that they had had a special love that no one
else would ever understand.

She touched her hand to her collar where, that morning, she had
carefully placed a gold fleur-de-lis pin inset with pearls. Franklin
had given it to her on their honeymoon in 1905. They were in
Florence, looking out at the quilt of terra-cotta rooftops from the
top of Giotto's Bell Tower at Il Duomo. It was near sunset, and the
famous dome rose like a giant ginger-colored Faberge egg against
the royal blue sky. Eleanor told Franklin she could imagine it en-

crusted with jewels. She was wearing the white, broad-brimmed, lace-covered hat she had just bought in Paris. Franklin tipped up the front of it and brought his lips to hers in a lingering, tender kiss. Then he asked, "Will this jewel do?" and pulled the little box with the pin out of his pocket and handed it to her. At that instant, she felt absolutely safe and loved.

How had she gone from that moment to this one? From the girl who longed only for love and security to the woman who was waiting to hear if she would be elected president?

"I truly think, Sam, that we shape our lives and we shape ourselves."

"I do, too, Eleanor. And I've always admired that about you—the way you take personal responsibility. Now we may have more responsibility than we bargained for." He gave a short laugh, then said urgently, "Hold on, just hold on, Eleanor."

She could barely hear Cronkite in the background over the telephone line. As she tried to make out his words, she saw Maureen running down the hall, her heels clacking loudly on the checked tiles of the floor.

"We are waiting ... go to ... and we have just had ..." Cronkite's voice faded in and out as Eleanor strained to hear. As Maureen got closer, Eleanor could see that tears were streaming down her face. Joan ran behind her, her flimsy stiletto heels slowing her down. In frustration, she stopped long enough to tear them off and fling them against the wall.

Eleanor let the phone drop and shoved open the door of the phone booth, hurrying into the hall. Maureen's face looked so contorted and strained, Eleanor was sure something terrible had happened—perhaps to Tommy.

"Mrs. R." Maureen threw her arms around Eleanor's waist and pressed her head against her chest like a child, too overcome to speak. Eleanor could feel her heart begin to race.

"Maureen, is it Tommy?"

Before Maureen could answer, Joan ran up panting, desperately trying to gasp out her words.

"Rhode Island *and* Arizona." Joan took a gulp of air. Then she began yelling and crying at the same time. "You've won! You've won, Mrs. Roosevelt! You've won by one vote. One electoral vote. Oh, my God. Oh, my God." She looked up into Eleanor's face, her voice awestruck. "They've elected you *president of the United States.*"

Epilogue

Washington, D.C., January 20, 1953

The leaden winter sky gave way to the sun's first weak rays, slowly at first, then growing bolder as they lightened the fallow fields of Maryland's eastern shore, skimmed over the Chesapeake Bay, and brought the east front of the U.S. Capitol into relief against the expanse of the Mall that lay beyond. Workers had swarmed over the East Portico of the Capitol for a week, constructing and adorning the grand podium for the presidential inauguration that was about to take place.

Despite the freezing temperature, thousands of people had arrived before sunrise to find a spot on the grounds around and under the grandstand, which stood on enormous stiltlike wooden legs facing the marble stage where the ceremony would be held. More than a million people were expected to watch Eleanor Roosevelt take the oath of office and cheer her along the parade route. Washington strained to accommodate the massive onslaught, housing eight thousand people in Pullman cars at Union Station the night before, and turning hotel storage rooms into sleeping space.

Across First Street, in the office of Fred Vinson, chief justice of the Supreme Court, the oldest inaugural Bible, printed in Dutch in 1686, lay in a wooden box ready for transport. Franklin Roosevelt had used this book for all four of his presidential inaugurations.

At twelve noon, the chief justice would stand in his formal robes with the president-elect beside him, her family, dignitaries, and friends surrounding them. As her husband had done before her, Eleanor would place her hand on the page that held I Corinthians 13, its words of love so familiar to her. Then the chief justice would ask her to repeat after him. In the 164 years since George Washington was inaugurated, thirty-three men had spoken the words that Eleanor would say: "I do solemnly swear that I will faithfully execute the office of president of the United States, and will to the best of my ability, preserve, protect and defend the Constitution of the United States."

Tens of millions of Americans would watch the historic moment on television; millions more would listen to her on radio around the world. And high atop the Capitol's massive dome, sturdy as the nation that placed her there, the Statue of Freedom in her flowing robes, one hand on a sheathed sword, the other grasping the laurel wreath of victory, would bear witness.

A⁺
AUTHOR
INSIGHTS,
EXTRAS, &
MORE...

FROM

**ROBIN
GERBER**

AND

AVON A

A Note from the Author

Although this book is a work of fiction, it is rooted in fact. As much as possible, I used the actual words of historical figures, especially Eleanor and Ike. Eleanor's speech to the Indian parliament in chapter 3 is an example, as is Nixon's "Checkers Speech" in chapter 25 and Eisenhower's statements at the debate in chapter 34.

In part 1, Eleanor did discover her husband's marital betrayal as depicted in chapter 1, and she did travel east at Truman's request with David Gurewitsch, who was likely her lover. Her book about that trip is called *India and the Awakening East,* and her still-insightful statement about Islam in chapter 3 is taken from that book. There was a movement to draft Eleanor to run for president, starting as early as 1940, and the letters to the editor in chapter 3 are real, as is the photo of her with Truman referred to in chapter 2. Similarly, the visit to Eisenhower by Jacquelin Cochran did happen, and his affair with Kay Summersby (later Morgan) is based on facts, including those in Kay's moving memoir, *Past Forgetting: My Love Affair with Dwight D. Eisenhower*. The machinations at both political conventions are taken from real events, other than Adlai Stevenson's death and Eleanor's nomination. Stevenson did die suddenly from a heart attack in 1965. And, as far as I know, Hillary did not meet Eleanor.

In part 2, Larry O'Brien's campaign strategy is taken from the 1960 Kennedy Campaign Manual. Barbara Rose Johns was the courageous teenager who led a walkout at Moton High School that helped spur the group of cases that led to the landmark *Brown vs. Board of Education* decision by the Supreme Court.

Edgar Ray Killen is currently in jail for the murder of three civil rights workers in 1964, but there is no evidence that he ever tried to kill Eleanor Roosevelt. The Eleanor letter to Lorena did exist, although J. Edgar Hoover did not purloin it. President Truman did claim to have taken and destroyed the Eisenhower letter to Marshall requesting a divorce from Mamie and Marshall's reply. Nixon's secret fund and televised explanation are taken from history. And while he did get the idea of using Checkers in his speech from FDR's "Fala Speech," Eleanor's press conference is fictional. Eisenhower's retracted rebuke of McCarthy causing a political firestorm did occur, although no debate followed. The networks offered free time for a debate, but Stevenson declined and it never occurred. Cronkite's coverage of election night, and the appearance of UNIVAC, is based on real events.

I wrote this book because Eleanor Roosevelt has been a great inspiration in my life, but also because I believe she made one huge mistake. She should have run for president. If she had, at worst she would have opened the door for other women, at best she could have won. I think she *would* have won.

Contents

A Discussion with Robin Gerber

Robin Gerber, a political columnist and commentator, spent more than a decade working on Capitol Hill, both as a congressional staff member and as a government affairs director for two major national organizations. Robin combined her love and knowledge of history and politics to write *Eleanor vs. Ike*. The following interview provides a window into the inspiration behind this book.

What made you want to write *Eleanor vs. Ike*?

After I published the advice book *Leadership the Eleanor Roosevelt Way,* I began giving keynote talks about the leadership lessons that grow from the story of Eleanor's life. At one such talk, an audience member said, "You make Eleanor sound so perfect. Didn't she ever do anything wrong?" No one had ever asked me that before, yet the answer seemed to pop immediately into my head. "Yes," I answered. "She should have run for president." I knew that Eleanor had been encouraged to run, and after that audience encounter, I began to look more deeply into why she had not. The more I investigated, the more convinced I became that she had made a mistake, or miscalculation. Her reasons, which I include in various places in the book, were unconvincing, even, I believe, to herself. If she had it to do again, I thought to myself, I bet she'd take the plunge. Then, one day in 2006, as I read yet another story about Hillary Rodham Clinton's possible candidacy, I realized Eleanor could run after all—at least as a construct of my imagination. I got really excited when I realized that 1952 was the most logical year for her to run, and there were huge parallels between then and 2008. I think I always had in mind that the story could have a parable quality, because I was quite certain that Hillary would run.

Did you enjoy writing the book?

I *loved* writing this book. It's my first fiction, so I had no idea what I was in for. I had a huge learning curve. But even at the hardest moments, when I was terrified that my plot lines wouldn't work out or felt completely at sea on how to stage a scene, I felt exhilarated. I was born in 1952, so learning so much about that year, from music, television, and movies to cars, clothes, and slang terms, was fascinating in a very personal way. As a history lover, I enjoyed going back to episodes I thought I knew well, like the Nixon secret fund, or the Alger Hiss case, and learning the details I never knew or had forgotten. It was often hard not to get off on historical tangents, just because they were so astonishing, weird, or serendipitous. Some of the "outtakes" that I've put on my Web site are hard cuts I made because, although the history was amazing, it didn't advance the story.

What do you think *Eleanor vs. Ike* can teach women today?

My complete answer to this question is in my book, *Leadership the Eleanor Roosevelt Way*. The short answer is encapsulated in the revelation Eleanor has at the end of the novel, when she reflects on how she went from a scared, loveless, insecure young woman to a candidate for president. "We shape our lives and we shape ourselves," she said, capturing one of the most important values in her life—that everyone must take personal responsibility.

Eleanor believed in action. "It's as easy to plan as it is to dream," she said. Whatever our pursuits, women today must take responsibility for discovering and pursuing their passion with fearless energy, because Eleanor also said, "You must do the thing you think you cannot do."

If Eleanor Roosevelt were running for president today, what do you think would happen?

She would win in a landslide! There is a deep hunger in our country for a leader of conviction, integrity, demonstrated compassion, and authentic humanity. These were the hallmarks of Eleanor's leadership and her life, and people were deeply drawn to her because of it. I've lost count of the people who have said to me, "if only Eleanor were here today."

The Facts Behind the Fiction:
A Timeline of the Key Dates of
Eleanor Roosevelt's Life

While much of *Eleanor vs. Ike* is fiction, much of it is drawn from the actual events and people that helped shape Eleanor Roosevelt's life. The timeline below provides an overview of the key dates in Eleanor Roosevelt's seventy-eight magnificent years.

October 11, 1884: Elliot and Anna Roosevelt have their first child, Anna Eleanor.

1892: Eleanor's mother dies of diphtheria. Eleanor and her brothers, Elliot Jr. and Hall, go to live with Anna's mother.

1893: Eleanor's brother, Elliot Jr., dies at the age of four.

1894: Eleanor's father dies of the effects of alcoholism and addiction.

1899: Eleanor goes to study with Marie Souvestre at Allenswood, a girls' school outside of London.

1902: Eleanor leaves Allenswood and returns to New York to make her debut in society.

1905: Eleanor marries Franklin Delano Roosevelt.

1906: Eleanor has her first child and only girl, Anna.

1907: Eleanor has her second child, James.

1909: Eleanor has her third child, Franklin Jr., who dies in infancy.

1910: Eleanor has her fourth child, Elliott. Franklin is elected to state office and the family moves to Albany, New York.

1913: Franklin becomes assistant secretary of the navy and the family moves to Washington, D.C.

1914: Eleanor has her fifth child, Franklin Jr.

1916: Eleanor has her last child, John, a year before the United States enters World War I.

1918: Eleanor discovers Franklin's affair with Lucy Mercer.

1920: Eleanor accompanies Franklin on his losing vice presidential campaign.

1921: Franklin contracts polio.

1922–1928: Eleanor becomes increasingly active in Democratic politics; Franklin is elected governor of New York in 1928.

1932: Franklin is elected president of the United States.

1933: Eleanor holds her first women-only press conference, begins writing for publication as First Lady and traveling extensively.

1936: Franklin is reelected.

1940: Eleanor speaks on Franklin's behalf at the Democratic Convention. He wins an unprecedented third term.

1941: Japanese bomb Pearl Harbor and the United States enters World War II.

1943: Eleanor visits U.S. troops in the South Pacific.

1945: Eleanor joins NAACP Board of Directors after years of work to secure greater civil rights for African Americans. In April, Franklin dies. In September, World War II ends with the surrender of the Japanese.

1946: Eleanor begins drafting the Universal Declaration of Human Rights as head of the United Nations Human Rights Commission.

1948: Human Rights Declaration is passed by the United Nations.

1950: Eleanor begins work on television and radio with NBC studios.

1952: Eleanor supports Adlai Stevenson for president, but he loses to Eisenhower.

1960: Eleanor gives John F. Kennedy her support for the presidency.

November 7, 1962: Eleanor dies at the age of seventy-eight.

What If? A Fascinating Poll That Explores How the Public Would Have Responded if Eleanor Roosevelt Had Run for President.

Although it's very common today for candidates to use pollsters to shape campaign strategies and messages, this was not being done in 1952. Eleanor would have been ahead of her time, as was the fictional pollster Alice Lake, in doing a poll of this kind. That's why Lake Research Partners, who wrote and designed this poll, made it historically accurate. They made sure that the methodology and terminology used in the poll was consistent with other polls, like the national Gallup polls, that were being used in 1952. Below is the poll summary that Alice used to brief Eleanor in chapter 30.

ROOSEVELT VS. EISENHOWER
Nationwide–September 1952
Poll Summary

Context

- A solid majority of voters (64 percent) has already given much thought to the upcoming election. Thirty-four percent say they have given it little thought, while only 2 percent have given it no thought at all. This is higher than we usually see at this point in an election year. The circumstances surrounding this campaign have certainly increased the amount of attention people are paying.

- Voters are not optimistic about the direction of the country, with about half (51 percent) saying things are going in the wrong direction.

- Voters are most concerned about the Korean War (19 percent), but health care (15 percent) and communism (13 percent) are also top issues. Race issues (10 percent) and agricultural concerns (10 percent) complete the list of top-tier issues. These problems will most interest voters in this campaign.

The Presidential Ballot

- Looking at the initial ballot question, Eleanor Roosevelt is currently 27 points behind Dwight Eisenhower (59 percent to 32 percent), and support for each candidate is remarkably intense. Two months out from the election, only 7 percent of voters are undecided.

- This will be an uphill battle. We will see later, however, that there is surprising movement after the messages, even though the race appears quite polarized. While Eisenhower has a majority, it is not an overwhelming one. Nonetheless, Roosevelt will need to do more than just win undecided voters to take this election. She will need to erode Eisenhower's support significantly.

- After messaging (messages for and against Roosevelt and messages against Eisenhower), there is strong movement in the ballot, though Eisenhower maintains his majority.

- Eisenhower's lead shrinks to only ten points (53 percent to 43 percent), though his overall support is only down 6 points from the initial ballot at the beginning of the survey. Meanwhile, Roosevelt's support has solidified and increased measurably.

This movement is a good indication that, by focusing on the most important issues and using the right messages, Roosevelt can move voters into her column. Roosevelt's gains come primarily from Democrats and women.

The Vice Presidential Ballot

- In order to get a sense of the general effect of the vice president on the overall ticket, we asked which vice president the voters would prefer. On the vice presidential ballot, Sam Rayburn leads Richard Nixon by +13 points, 48 percent to 35 percent. Thirteen percent of voters are undecided on the vice presidential ballot.

- There is also greater intensity among those who support Rayburn than there is among those who support Nixon. Thirty-one percent of voters choose Rayburn outright (as opposed to merely leaning toward Rayburn), compared to just 19 percent who choose Nixon outright.

Attitudes on the Campaign and Job Approval

- *Even though Eleanor Roosevelt got off to a late start, voters are impressed with her campaign.* Voters are positive on Roosevelt's job performance as First Lady, with 58 percent approving and 34 percent disapproving. Additionally, they have a favorable view of her job performance as UN ambassador, with 52 percent approving and 28 percent disapproving. Still, they are less familiar with her role as UN ambassador, as one in five voters (20 percent) had no opinion of her performance in that role, compared to fewer than one in ten (8 percent) who had no opinion on her role as First Lady.

- Voters are also far more impressed with Roosevelt's campaign than with Eisenhower's. Not only do 59 percent of voters rate Roosevelt's campaign as good/fair (38 percent good, 21 percent fair), but fewer than one in four rate her campaign as disappointing, for a net of +35 points. In contrast, Eisenhower's campaign is only net +1 (24 percent good, 21 percent fair, 44 percent disappointing).

- Eisenhower gets high marks for his job as general in World War II. Eighty-two percent approve, while less than one in ten (7 percent) disapprove. Success in World War II is, without a doubt, among Eisenhower's greatest strengths.

- Not surprisingly, voters disapprove of Truman's job performance by a wide margin. Just over one in four voters (26 percent) approve of his performance, while nearly two in three (65 percent) disapprove.

- When voters are asked which of the past four presidents had the best ideas on how to run the country, former president Roosevelt receives a plurality of the votes, with 46 percent. Coolidge (30 percent), Hoover (14 percent), and Truman (6 percent) trail fairly significantly. While this roughly represents the partisan split of the country, the fact that former president Roosevelt receives nearly half of all votes when there are four options is particularly impressive.

Leadership, the War, and Gender

- Voters disapprove of Truman's decision to relieve General MacArthur from his role as commander of UN forces by wide margins (–32 points). Fifty-nine percent disapprove of this action. Voters split, however, on the question of whether or not to expand the war from a limited war in Korea to a general war against China, with 42 percent approving and 39 percent disapproving of this proposal.

- When asked to choose between two statements, one asserting we need a male leader during a time of war and uncertain economy and the other asserting we need a new type of leader, specifically a woman, voters overwhelmingly agree with the first statement by a margin of +67 (81 percent male statement, 14 percent female statement).

- However, when Eleanor Roosevelt's name replaces the generic woman in the second question, the margin shrinks dramatically to +28 (63 percent male statement, 35 percent Eleanor Roosevelt statement).

- *While voters still prefer male leadership in times of war, they are far more likely to consider Eleanor Roosevelt as a national leader than a generic female candidate, indicating that they are more ready to accept her leadership on such matters than they would be for other women.* Yet, despite Roosevelt's advantage over a generic female candidate, there is still an uphill climb to have majority acceptance.

Attitudes on Public Figures

- Eisenhower and Roosevelt are the two most popular figures tested in the survey, followed by the Republican and Democratic Parties, respectively. Voters prove to have the most negative impression of Nixon, with more than half rating the vice presidential candidate between –1 and –5.

- Three-quarters of Americans have a positive impression of Eisenhower, with four in ten giving him a rating of +5 (+1 to +5: 74 percent; +5: 41 percent). Moreover, less than 20 percent give him a negative rating (18 percent).

- While Roosevelt also receives positive marks, with 63 percent having a positive impression of the former First Lady, voters are almost two times more likely to have a negative impression of her than of Eisenhower (35 percent compared to 18 percent). Roosevelt is a more polarizing figure than Eisenhower, limiting the terrain on which to gain votes.

- Voters nationwide are more likely to have an opinion of Roosevelt than other female figures tested, and they are also two times more likely to have a positive impression of her than these other figures (Zero/DK/No opinion: Eleanor Roosevelt—2 percent; Frances Perkins—44 percent; Margaret Chase Smith—45 percent).

- Six in ten voters have a positive impression of the Democratic Party, though less than a majority give President Harry Truman a positive rating (44 percent). Voters are net negative in their impression of Truman, with 49 percent giving the president a negative rating. (His job performance numbers are even lower.) Just more than one-third rate the Democratic Party between –1 and –5 (35 percent).

- The Republican Party fares similarly to the Democratic Party, with 62 percent having a positive rating. Voters tend to be less likely to give the Republicans a negative rating than they are to give the Democrats a rating of –1 to –5 (Republican Party: 31 percent; Democratic Party: 35 percent).

- Joseph McCarthy has a net positive rating among voters, and one-third say they would rate him a zero or have no opinion of him (+1 to +5: 40 percent; –1 to –5: 27 percent).

- Although voters split in their assessment of the New Deal (+1 to +5: 49 percent; −1 to −5: 48 percent), they prove more favorable toward the United Nations. More than half of voters have a positive rating for this organization overall (58 percent), and 37 percent rate it a +5. Given the strong marks for the United Nations, it is critical for Roosevelt to emphasize her role at the UN and her support for its founding.

- Voters split in their rating of Sam Rayburn (+1 to +5: 30 percent; −1 to −5: 30 percent). However, they are more likely to rate the Democratic vice presidential candidate a zero or say they have no opinion of him than they are to give him a positive or negative rating. For the remainder of the campaign, Rayburn should work on increasing his visibility in targeted states and delivering his home state of Texas.

- In addition to their low marks for Nixon, voters are net negative in their impression of Douglas MacArthur. Forty-one percent rate the former general of Allied forces in the Far East negatively, while just more than one-quarter (27 percent) give the general a positive rating.

Traits—Eleanor Roosevelt

- Roosevelt has a robust image. A majority feels that she shares their values (53 percent) and even more see her as compassionate (70 percent).

- In terms of experience, one-third agree that she is inexperienced, while nearly half (48 percent) feel this does not describe Roosevelt well. However, phrased differently, just one-quarter feel that she has the right experience, versus 50 percent who say that this does not describe her well. One-quarter is unsure. It will be important to frame Roosevelt's experience in terms of a broader choice on direction in Korea.

- Looking at policy, 85 percent believe that she will fight to protect New Deal programs, with one-third saying this describes her very well. This is a mixed bag, however, and it is stronger to talk about continuing the legacy of the Roosevelt administration than the politics of the New Deal. Nearly half (47 percent) also believe that Roosevelt will continue Truman's failed policies, though 42 percent disagree with this notion.

- In terms of leadership, 57 percent report that "weak" is *not* a word that describes her well; only nearly one-quarter (24 percent) do see her in this light. Only one-third (35 percent) agree that she is able to lead in times of war, though this drops slightly when phrased "strong enough to lead in times of war" (30 percent). Voters tend to think that Roosevelt is *not* too emotional to be president, by a margin of +7.

- Two-thirds of voters see Roosevelt as too controversial (66 percent), while a majority feels she is too liberal (54 percent). More than one-third (38 percent) see her as soft on communism, while 44 percent hold the opposite view. Despite the attacks from McCarthy, only her strongest opponents buy this assertion.

Traits—Dwight Eisenhower

- More than two-thirds of voters see Eisenhower as honest and trustworthy, with 38 percent saying this describes him very well. However, less than half (46 percent) believe that he shares their values. An additional 40 percent perceive him as being out of touch with the needs of most Americans, though a majority (54 percent) does not believe this to be true.

- Half of voters (51 percent) see Eisenhower as talking down to people, though 35 percent disagree with this sentiment. Even more so, voters see Eisenhower as talking down to women, with nearly two-thirds (63 percent) agreeing, and 39 percent in strong agreement.

- A strong majority (78 percent) say that Eisenhower has the right experience, with just 17 percent disagreeing. However, more than one-half (54 percent) report that he does not have enough government experience.

- In terms of policy, voters are slightly more likely to think that Eisenhower will undermine New Deal programs, with 49 percent disagreeing and 42 percent agreeing. Voters tend to think, however, that he will bring about change (66 percent).

- Voters overwhelmingly consider Eisenhower a strong opponent to communism, with nearly one-half (47 percent) saying this describes him very well.

Presidential Traits

- Top traits that voters would like to see in their next president include experience, a strong leader, and a man. At least seven in ten rate each of these characteristics at the highest position, and roughly nine in ten rate each positively.

- A second tier of traits includes: shares your values (66 percent top position), a strong military leader (64 percent), is independent (62 percent), and has governing experience (61 percent).

- Voters give higher marks to a president who seeks a diplomatic solution to the conflict in Korea (53 percent top position) than to a leader who supports a military solution (32 percent). There is also greater intensity of opposition to taking the military route (35 percent lower position).

- Race is an issue that divides the electorate. A majority (55 percent) give positive marks to a president who supports segregation, though 30 percent rank this trait at the very bottom of the scale. More than one-third (36 percent) favor a president who supports civil rights, while 60 percent would be opposed to a candidate with this trait (46 percent strongly). Though the majority falls on the side of segregation, there is intensity around this issue on both sides.

- Nearly two-thirds (65 percent) give a positive mark to a president who supports universal health care, while just 21 percent mark it negatively. Fourteen percent are unsure or have no opinion on this issue. There is greater ambivalence around the continuation of the programs of the New Deal and Fair Deal, with 42 percent unsure. Roughly one-third (34 percent) see this continuation as a positive trait, while 24 percent view it negatively.

- Three-quarters of voters give negative ratings to the idea of a woman president, with nearly half (48 percent) rating this strongly negative. Fourteen percent see this as a positive trait and 11 percent are unsure.

Critiques of Eisenhower and Roosevelt

- Eisenhower is particularly vulnerable to criticisms that he picked a corrupt running mate who has been bought by special-interest groups. Slightly less than half of voters (46 percent) feel this raises very serious doubts for them (rate 5 on a 5-point scale) about Eisenhower's candidacy.

- Voters also give some credence to claims that Eisenhower is too inexperienced politically (37 percent serious doubts) and that he is an opportunist who was recruited by both parties and waited for the easiest chance to get elected (32 percent serious doubts).

- Key critiques of Roosevelt center on her support for racial integration (41 percent serious doubts) and the fact that women should work in the home and leave the stresses of the presidency to men (41 percent serious doubts).

- With less intensity, roughly one-third of voters (34 percent) report having serious doubts about the statement that Democrats have been running the country for too long, while creating expensive, bureaucratic, and ineffective welfare that runs up the national debt, and that they have let Communists infiltrate the country.

Positive Eleanor Roosevelt Messages

- Roosevelt receives high marks for her work on health care and human rights. A plurality of voters (44 percent say extremely convincing) are strongly persuaded by the message that Roosevelt is a strong advocate for policies to help working people and that she will fight for universal health care coverage so that all Americans will have access to health care services (mean rating of 3.6 on 5-point scale). Voters respond with similar intensity to the statement that she stands up for those who do not have power by campaigning to establish a minimum wage, working to end child labor, standing up for worker safety, and by serving as the first chairman of the United Nations Human Rights Commission (42 percent extremely convincing; mean 3.6).

- Statements on Roosevelt's experience and strength on defense receive more polarized reactions. Roughly three in ten (31 percent) of voters say it is extremely convincing that she has helped to establish a bipartisan organization to respond to the threat of Nazism and worked to implement the Marshall Plan and that she has a well-rounded approach to our place in the world that must rely on diplomacy and a strong military. However, intensity is nearly as much on the other extreme, with 28 percent saying this message is not convincing at all to them (mean rating of 3.0 on 5-point scale). There is a big gender gap on their perceptions, with women giving her more credit.

- Similarly, while 32 percent say it is extremely convincing to them to hear that Roosevelt has more experience in the White House than any candidate for president, given her work while her husband was in office and her work for the United Nations Human Rights Commission, nearly three in ten (29 percent) feel this is not at all convincing to them (mean rating of 3.0).

To see the poll questions, responses, and additional information, go to: http://www.robingerber.com.

A candidate's poll today would have substantial differences in methodology and terminology. To learn more, go to Lake Research Partners: http://www.lakesnellperry.com.

Recommended Reading:
Other Books About the Life of Eleanor Roosevelt

If you'd like to learn more about Eleanor Roosevelt's life, Robin Gerber recommends the following books:

Eleanor and Franklin, by Joseph P. Lash
No Ordinary Time, by Doris Kearns Goodwin
Eleanor Roosevelt Vols. I and II, by Blanche Wiesen Cook
Leadership the Eleanor Roosevelt Way, by Robin Gerber
Courage in a Dangerous World, by Allida Black
The Three Roosevelts, by James MacGregor Burns and Susan
  Dunn

Discussion Questions:
Make Eleanor a Part of Your Book Club!

If you would like to discuss *Eleanor vs. Ike* in your next reading group, please visit http://www.robingerber.com and http://www.harpercollins.com/Readers/readingGroups.aspx for discussion questions. Robin Gerber would love to phone in to your reading group, so be sure to locate her contact information on her website to set up a time for her to "visit"!

Robin Gerber

ROBIN GERBER is the author of *Leadership the Eleanor Roosevelt Way: Timeless Strategies from the First Lady of Courage* and *Katharine Graham: The Leadership Journey of an American Icon*. A nationally known political commentator on women, leadership, and politics, she has appeared on numerous radio and television shows and as an opinion writer for national newspapers. Robin spent fifteen years on Capitol Hill working for the U.S. Congress and as a lobbyist.